MW01138870

Our First
Book Of Stories
Volume IV

By Ric Bauer
& Ric O'Shay

ISBN-13: 978-1505282986
ISBN-10: 1505282985

First Edition
$16.00 U.S.

I dedicate this book to my Mother and Father.

They showed me the world.

I was amazed.

Ric Bauer

Half of the following stories are fictional.

The other half are made up.

Ric O'Shay

Table of Contents

April May in June

April May was the prettiest girl in our trailer park, and she lived in the prettiest trailer too. Her trailer had real dirt and flowers around it, not gravel and weeds like the others did. All of my friends fell in love with April May. I did too because truth be told, no boy could resist her. April May was the same age as we were but she acted a lot better. She was tall and skinny and her long blonde hair blew in the breeze like those lace nighties that some of the moms hung out to dry. My friends liked to tease April May but I didn't because I loved her more than they did. For me it was true love, not the kind that makes people shoot each other or hit each other with beer bottles and junk like they do on the TV or in our trailer park. And so, because my love for her was true, April May seemed to like me more than she liked my crazy friends. Early on she'd smile at me and wave to me and sometimes even talk to me if I was real lucky.

April May and her mom moved into our trailer park on June 1st 1969. It was the first day of summer vacation. All of my friends were excited to go fishin' and swimmin' that day but when a movin' van pulled into our trailer park and I saw April May step out of it, I forgot all about fishin' and swimmin'. I told my friends to go on along without me because I was sick. It weren't really a lie though because I was heart-sick in love with April May from the very moment I first saw her.

The very next day, April May and her mom dumped bags of dirt along the sides of their trailer and stuck the roots of store-bought flowers in it. April May watered those flowers before the sun got too hot and I watched her do it from my bedroom window. I really wanted to go outside and talk to her but my fear let me down.

The next mornin', April May caught me watchin' her from my bedroom window. Most girls would have yelled, "Mind your own damn self!" but April May didn't. She just smiled and waved at me and then went about waterin' her flowers. Some mornin's, when I'd hear her water can splashin', it made me want to pee somethin' fierce. As hard as it was though, I always managed to hold it in until April May had finished her waterin' and had gone back inside her trailer.

One day in the middle of June, I watched my mom and Aunt Shirley step into April May's trailer with momma's coupon box. It seemed like they were in there forever because by the time they stepped out it was almost suppertime. When momma told me to put a shirt on for supper I had a feelin' that somethin' was up. As I sat down to an empty plate awaitin' stew and biscuits, I watched as April May's mom tapped on the outside of our screen door. When April May's mom stepped into our trailer it was the first up-close look I got of her. April May's mom was as pretty as a movie star. She had pink lips and white teeth and the cleanest skin I'd ever seen. I was starin' so hard at her I didn't even notice that April May had come inside as well and was starin' at me starin' at her mom. April May was patient though and she smiled real pretty at me anyway when I finally did look her way. I smiled back at her wonderin' if she would ever be as pretty as her mom was. I decided if that were to happen, I would love April May even more. That thought worried me though seein' as how my stomach already twisted into knots whenever I saw April May. I couldn't imagine what would happen to me if she got any prettier than she already was.

I stood up from the table before April May and her mom and my mom and Aunt Shirley took their seats.

"What a fine gentleman," April May's pretty mom said in my direction. Then she smiled at me and I stopped breathin'.

"Oh, he can be on occasion," Aunt Shirley announced to the other three who laughed and giggled while my mom teased me by messin' up the hair on the top of my head. Little did I know at the time that strands of my hair were pointin' straight up in the air. I looked like Alfalfa from the Little Rascals that entire supper. I discovered that embarrassin' fact later that night when I looked in the bathroom mirror while brushin' my teeth. If April May had noticed my silly lookin' hair though, she never did mention a word of it to nobody.

I remember eatin' slower than usual that night so as not to spill gravy down the front of my chin like I usually did. I didn't want April May to think that a slob was in love with her. I may have said a few words durin' that supper but to be honest, I don't remember what they were. I spent most of the time listenin' to the women talk about restaurants and beauty parlors and shoppin' stores and whatnot while I kept my napkin at the ready for any wayward gravy. Whenever April May giggled at Aunt Shirley's jokes she'd look over at me. That gave me a warm feelin' inside and I'd laugh right along with her. It was almost like we were alone together sharin' some secret funny things just between the two of us.

As the weeks passed by, me and April May became best friends. Near the end of that summer I kissed my first girl. I sure was glad that girl was April May. Right after we done it she told me that I was the first boy that she had ever kissed. Then she kissed me again so I guess I was the first and second boy. We both liked kissin' each other a lot after that.

Come October, a handsome man in a fancy car began callin' on April May's mom on the weekends. One Saturday night he took the four of us out to the movies. I think he caught me and April May holdin' hands in the dark theatre but he never did say nothin' about it to nobody. I liked him a lot for that. I liked him just fine until he gave April May's mom a big ol' diamond ring at Christmastime.

While April May's mother and her new step-father were on their honeymoon in Las Vegas, April May slept over at our house for three nights in Aunt Shirley's room. I was in heaven the whole time havin' her so close to me. It felt like me and April May was on our very own honeymoon.

Shortly after the happy newlyweds returned from their honeymoon, they emptied their trailer into a U-Haul truck and moved across town to a new house and a new life. As much as I missed April May and holdin' her hand and kissin' her lips, I think I missed watchin' her water her flowers even more. Sometimes when I'd close my eyes, I could still see her doin' it. The following Spring after April May and her mom had moved away, I watered the flowers they'd left behind. They never did come back though.

Big Apple Core

I lived in the lower east side of Manhattan for a while. I had to work two, full-time jobs to afford the rent though. One of my jobs was shoveling fish guts at the fish market - my other job was mopping up human guts from the O.R. floors at Bellevue Hospital. George Washington was only four years old when Bellevue was founded. I think the rock-hard bagels in their cafeteria were baked about the same time. I came home from work exhausted as usual one night and climbed the six flights of ancient, creaking, crooked, splintered wood stairs up to my tiny, dingy, depressing, windowless, over-priced, cramped apartment only to discover rats sitting on my couch drinking my beer. When I complained about it to my landlord he evicted me on the spot for being a trouble maker. Not having the first and last month's rent for a new place, I found myself forced to live in the subway tunnels where sneaky rats would steal my comic books at night while I slept. Those dirty rats didn't even read my comics - they just tore them to shreds for their nests. The nerve of some rats.

Since I had lost my bathroom when I lost my apartment, I was limited to a weekly bathing ritual which I would conduct at my aunt's apartment in the Bronx on Saturday mornings. The subway tunnels where I lived were actually a tad cleaner than my aunt's neighborhood but at least her water wasn't ice cold and dripping out of a rusty iron pipe like it was in the subway. On the contrary, the water in my aunt's apartment was almost lukewarm and dripped out of a rusty shower head and faucet. Although my co-workers at the hospital never did seem to notice, by the middle of the work week, the guys at the fish market would start complaining about the way that I smelled and by Friday, they would avoid me altogether. I finally told the guys that I had over-active musk glands so they stopped complaining and started feeling sorry for me. The folks at the hospital on the other hand, were either too distracted by the constant "hospital smell" around them to notice or were too cranked up on "borrowed" prescription drugs to even care. At times though, I did get a few dirty looks from some of the patients or visitors when they weren't busy dying or worrying about their obscene medical bills. Having to live such a stinky life, I was, needless to say - lonely. I desired female companionship in the worst way but I was too ashamed of my body odor to come within ten feet of any woman to whom I was attracted. I didn't want to risk repulsed rejection should a woman catch an unpleasant whiff of my pungent drift.

One day (I'm not sure which day) I mentioned my body odor and loneliness issues to one of the O.R. surgeons; Dr. Schnoz, who, ironic as it was, performed nose jobs. Dr. Schnoz claimed that he knew the perfect girl for me; a patient of his for whom he had botched a nose-job so severely that she could not then, nor probably ever would again, have the ability to smell. The good doctor took me to his office, pulled out the woman's file, showed me her "before" and "after" photos and then asked me if I would like to meet her.

"I sure would, Doc," I said. "Despite her large, disfigured nose, she is quite beautiful. I'd love to meet her - can you arrange it and put in a good word for me?"

The doctor said that he'd be happy to and would introduce us after her follow-up appointment with him. He was facing the possibility of a malpractice suit from her so he had hoped that anything he could do to take her mind off of it might sway things in his favor.

The next day when I entered Doctor Schnoz's office to meet her, the girl he had spoken of suddenly stopped talking to him. She jumped out of her seat, ran straight up to me and inexplicably, threw her arms around me! It felt incredible to be that close to an actual female person with such nice female body parts pressing themselves against me.

The girl hugged me for what seemed like an eternity before she whispered in my ear, "Where have you been all of my life, handsome?"

So I began explaining to her where I had been for the past thirty-three years. After I'd finished, two hours and twenty minutes later, she agreed to see me again. During the course of our conversation I learned from her that the doctor had claimed that I was a wealthy, Wall Street executive. That lie explained her enthusiastic reaction to meeting me but didn't explain why she hadn't noticed my maintenance man scrubs or the mop in my hand when we met. When she eventually *did* notice, I fibbed in explaining to her that I actually *was* a successful Wall Street investment banker until I lost all of my fortune in the crash of '07. She said that it didn't really matter to her one way or the other after having gotten to know me. We finished our conversation in the hospital cafeteria over coffee and rock-hard bagels. We drank the coffee but tossed the nasty bagels in the trash after one bite.

"Six thousand dollars for a botched nose job - you'd think they could afford fresh bagels!" she said laughing.

I was so happy about my new-found girlfriend that I picked up a brand new comic book that night for the rats. I read it first though on the subway ride home.

Our first date was to be the very next Friday night. I was so excited! In order to prevent the guys at work from overhearing my conversation and making fun of me, I phoned my new girlfriend from the storage shed at the fish market. I called her a half hour before my shift was over to ask her where she'd like to go out that evening. She said that she didn't want to "go out" anywhere but wanted instead, to spend time with me at her apartment. Well, that sounded great to me - a new girlfriend, alone, in her apartment, what could be better? So I said, "Sure, that's sounds perfect."

She said, "Wonderful! I'll cook a nice dinner for you and me and my parents. I've told them all about you and they're both dying to meet you."

Well, I was petrified. My girlfriend couldn't smell and didn't know that I stunk, but surely her parents would be able to. They'd be disgusted and would tell their daughter that I stink.

"Oh, what can I do?" I cried out loud.

I walked out of the storage shed and into the fish market in a daze bumping into everything along the way. The guys knew that something was wrong and asked me what it was. Immediately after I explained it to them they tore off all of my clothes and began spraying me with a high-pressure hose. Three of them got a giant tub of hot soapy water and used brooms to scrub me down from head to toe. After they rinsed me off with the hose, I dried myself with shop rags and then changed into a fresh uniform that somebody had brought me from the storage locker. I walked out of the fish market that night with my head held high to chants of; "You smell great!" and, "Go get her, tiger!" and, "Ask her if she has a sister!"

At first, I couldn't decide which was better that night; the way that my buddies at work had come through for me when

I needed them most, the delicious macaroni and cheese and fish stick dinner that my girlfriend had cooked for the four of us, the fact that her Mom had said that I was almost as handsome as Woody Allen, or her Dad's comment that I seemed like a man who could be trusted with his precious daughter. Later that night though, after her parents had finally left, I decided that the best part of the evening was the sexual intercourse I had with my new girlfriend.

A week after our first date, I moved out of the subway tunnels and into my girlfriend's apartment. The following Monday, while my subway car sat idle at a station two stops from hers, I glanced through the window past the scrambling mob of passengers and into the dark shadows beyond. It was there that I happened to notice a rat holding its nose with one paw while pointing directly at me with its other. The rat was apparently insinuating to the other rats gathered around him; "Hey look... there goes stinky!"

Three other rats held their bellies and laughed while a forth kicked its tiny rat legs in the air as it rolled around laughing on a tattered comic book.

"The nerve of some rats," I mumbled to myself.

But then I smiled nevertheless.

Cheerleaders from Mars

They came from the planet Mars those cheerleaders from Mars did. Due to a guidance system malfunction however, they landed by accident that day in the middle of a hot and barren desert. The cheerleaders were beautiful. They wore tiny titanium tops and puny plutonium panties. They shook fuzzy platinum pom-poms made of real live Pom-poms[1]. Their rapid and windy descent to Earth had messed up their beautiful hair so they brushed it and combed it back to its original neat and tidy appearance. The cheerleaders giggled in Martian as they took a leisurely bath together. Unlike the communal baths of the ancient Greeks or Romans though, the cheerleaders from Mars bathed in a pool of dehydrated water that they had magically drawn out of thin air. As the driver of an oncoming bus noticed the wet and naked cheerleaders up ahead of him, he could hardly believe his eyes. The driver slowed his bus down bringing it to a stop along the side of the desert highway. He opened the bus door and then smiled broadly at the half-naked cheerleaders who were busily re-dressing themselves after their bath.

"My goodness, girls... do you need a lift?" the driver asked them as a rush of hot desert air blew up and into his heavily starched shorts.

"::>> :.'.:.:>>..':.:<<.:<'><'>::>:<>..," a cheerleader replied to the driver as she stood at the foot of the bus' steps.

"Well, come in out of the heat then," the driver offered, to which the cheerleaders did and to which the driver watched as they stepped up and into the bus marching past him, one after another, in their dazzling skimpy outfits.

"Heading to a football game?" the bus driver asked none of the girls in particular.

"<::>> :.:'.:>..>.'.::<<.:<><::'>:>':::>:<>..<", the twelfth, last and tallest cheerleader replied.

Not having understood a single word that she'd said, the driver simply smiled politely and then closed the bus door. He assumed that the girls were foreign exchange students who'd wound up lost in the middle of the desert. He didn't realize at the time though just how foreign they actually were.

The Earthling passengers on board the swaying bus looked up from their seats as the girls bounced about trying to grab a seat for themselves. The cheerleaders had never been on a bus before. It proved to be a much bumpier ride than their ultra-smooth teleportation system was. But they found empty seats and settled in quickly and watched as desert cactus flew past their windows.

About ten miles down the road the cheerleaders ate one of the passengers. She was a little old lady traveling alone. The cheerleaders giggled as they nibbled away on her bones. Not quite believing what they had just witnessed, the other passengers looked on, dazed and confused. They assumed that it must have been the desert heat playing tricks on their minds and so, they settled back in their seats and relaxed. After their meal, the cheerleaders fussed with one another's hair and gossiped about cute Martian boys. A short while later, the tallest cheerleader stood up and called out what was apparently, an order. The rest of the squad immediately jumped to their feet and then filed into the aisle of the bus where they began to practice their cheers in preparation for the big game.

">:.':.:>>.,.':::<<.:<'> <'>::>..::..>< >::::< <':':':'><><>..::...::':>

>.'.::<<.:<> <::'>:> <:.'::.>> >'::<<.:<'><'>:<," the cheerleaders chanted in unison as they jumped into the air and did flips off the backs of their seats. The girls hung suspended in midair as they spun around in circles floating mere inches above the passengers' heads. They zipped through the bus like hummingbirds; front-to-back, up and down, cheering all the while; ">..::..><><':' :'><><>..::..::'< :>><.:>..>.' <<.:<><::'>:>."

The Earthling passengers were astounded as they looked on at the spectacle. They became spellbound by the exotic sounds of the melodic cheers. As the cheers became ethereal, the passengers became mesmerized. Fifty miles later, having worked up an insatiable appetite, the cheerleaders ate the remaining passengers. As they tore their victims to pieces, the cheerleaders fed bits of the passengers to their hungry pet Pom-poms while they passed larger pieces around to one another as one might do at an Earth barbecue. The bus driver, having witnessed portions of the carnage and the subsequent feast in his rearview mirror, became alarmed and then wondered, *How am I going to explain all of the unclaimed luggage?* As he pondered his dilemma, the driver suddenly became concerned that the cheerleaders might eat him as well, and so, he raised his hand and motioned the tallest cheerleader up to the front of the bus. He asked her as politely as he could if they were planning to eat him as well to which she replied, "<::>> <::'>:>'::>:<>..<."

The bus driver wondered, *What the heck does that mean?* He imagined that he'd find out sooner or later but then he thought, *Surely they won't eat me while I'm driving the bus.* And so, the driver planned to keep on driving no matter what because if he were to stop the bus in the middle of the desert then he too would surely become; a kicking and screaming meal for the demonic cheerleaders from hell!

Fifty miles later, the bus stalled in the desert. The gas gage was at midpoint so the driver feared the worst. He tried to radio for help but couldn't get a signal. His cell phone had died as well so he figured that he would be next. The bus sat idle in the heat of the desert while the driver fiddled around in the fuming engine compartment. The cheerleaders became restless and a little bit hungry. They stared at the heavy bus driver through the back window and licked their green lips. Sweat soaked the driver's shirt and shorts; it looked like gravy to the girls. The exhausted and defeated driver reentered the bus and sat down in his seat. He trembled as the cheerleaders surrounded him. The tallest among them bent down toward the driver. Her green lips parted, her jaws snapped open, long sharp fangs dripped on the driver's thick, meaty neck which was about to be ripped wide open when suddenly, a loud piercing sound signaled. The girls came to attention and looked to their leader as she pulled a transponder out of her skin pocket. She held the transponder up to her forehead and listened intently before responding, "'><.:'.:>>.'.:: <<.:<.::.>>."

"What's up?" the bus driver asked nervously.

The lead cheerleader replied, ">.:: << .:<.:':..>'>'.:::<," which is Martian for; "We're on the wrong planet," and then, all of sudden, the cheerleaders vanished. The bus driver let out a huge sigh of relief as he sank heavily in his seat.

A short while later, the driver became startled and sat up suddenly. At first dazed and confused, he then came to his senses and recalled his situation as he tried to restart the bus' engine. The driver held his breath as he turned the key. The bus' engine turned over and roared alive running.

The driver shouted out loud, "Woo Hoo!"

The passengers behind the driver cheered and then rushed up the aisle to take turns patting him on the back. The driver stared blankly through the bus' windshield as the passengers finally returned to their seats. A teenage boy lingered behind and then asked the driver, "Did you have a good nap? Are you okay to drive?"

"Uh, yeah... sure," the driver replied groggily.

"What's that book you're reading?" the boy asked him.

"Book?" the driver asked.

"The book in your lap," the boy pointed out.

The driver then noticed the book that was lying in his lap. He picked the book up, studied it briefly, and then turned the book's cover toward the boy. The teenager read the book's title out loud; "Man-Eating Cheerleaders from Mars. Wow, that's cool!" the boy said and then he turned away to retake his seat.

"Hey, kid..." the driver shouted, "do you want it?" he asked, holding the book aloft as he turned around in his seat toward the back of the empty bus.

1. Pom-pom: An indigenous Martian creature that resembles a cheerleader's pom-pom.

Christmas Present from Christmas Past

I'll be spending Christmas in jail this year, prison actually. Jail sounds pretty good right about now. I can do jail. They let you out of jail. Prison, well that's another story altogether.

I've spent the past ten Christmases in prison and I'll be spending the next five to ten in prison, depending on my behavior, and the mood of the parole board that is. Word in the yard though is that the parole board has been in a bad mood lately and a bad mood is never a good thing so I'm banking on ten more years, ten long years behind these steel bars, ten more Christmases on this back-breaking bunk, ten more Christmases pacing this cold hard floor and each and every one of them without that, oh-so-glorious Christmas spirit that I felt every year when I was a boy, an innocent boy, a bright-eyed, optimistic happy boy who tried hard to be good all year long so that maybe, he'd get something nice from Santa Claus. So I *was* good and I did most of the good things that good boys do but Santa Claus never showed up with my just reward. It was my drunken father who'd show up instead, some years. He'd hand me an un-wrapped trinket and then tell me whiskey-breathed stories about all of the wonderful things that he'd done. I didn't believe any of his stories though, they didn't seem to be the kinds of things that a whiskey-breathed man would do. But I kept quiet. I kept quiet and listened to my father's stories while I listened for Santa's sleigh bells. To this day, I still listen for those bells.

The other night I thought that I'd heard Santa's sleigh bells. I was lying on my bunk with my eyes closed. It was an unusually cold night but the thin, itchy wool blanket that I had pulled up high, just below my nose, almost kept me warm. And way off in the distance... sleigh bells! Faint at first, the bells grew louder and clearer and then louder still but I kept my eyes closed so as not to ward off Santa and miss out on my just reward. As the sound of the sleigh bells became louder and my excitement grew to a point where I could no longer control it, I opened my eyes ever so slightly and peaked out through my eyelashes. I saw a star, a bright star in the black night sky that twinkled through my lashes. And then, I heard a voice, a deep, booming, friendly voice that called out my name. It must be Santa Claus! As I opened my eyes the bare light bulb star shined on a guard. The guard jingled his keys as he unlocked and then opened my cell door. Santa-guard stepped into my cell and handed me a sliced up fruitcake. It was laid open atop brown postal wrapping paper. Good ol' Aunt Shirley had come through again this year.

I offered the guard a slice of my fruitcake and took one for myself. We ate in silence until the guard finished his slice and then mumbled, "Merry Christmas." I lay back down then, alone again on my bunk, the heavy fruitcake resting on my chest. It felt warm to me. It felt as if Aunt Shirley had just slid it out of the oven in her cozy kitchen. That warmth on my chest, that warmth in my heart, kept the rest of me warm as I drifted off to sleep. When I awoke the next morning, Christmas morning, the fruitcake was gone, gone as if it had never been there at all.

Damn the Green Grass!

He took a curious interest in almost everything to some degree and an obsessive interest in other things to extreme degrees. Those character traits however, proved to become both a blessing and a curse. Throughout his life he was constantly engaged in the study and teaching of world history and philosophy and theology. As busy as he was though, he would still find time for any friend, colleague or stranger who felt the need to reach out to him. His vast interests were a blessing. They kept him perpetually curious and left him little time for boredom. His curiosity however, became a curse on his personal self. Due to his extreme preoccupation with external interests, he had taken little if any interest in his own self. That realization left him, now in the twilight of his years, wondering what his own life had truly been about. Why was it that he had spent every waking hour reading, studying, listening, observing, evaluating, concluding, and teaching, if that routine only served to promote even more curiosity? Had he really *learned* anything at all? Did universally accepted *answers* imply metaphysically honest *truths*? If he could know and understand everything, would there be no questions left to ask? He thought not. He felt then, a sudden and desperate compulsion to leave academics behind in order to explore his own, inner psyche. To that end, he found himself in the process of selling most of his earthly possessions. The act of selling his books (in truth, a fairly substantial library) took the greatest toll on his meager sentimentality.

"I've found a buyer for your books, sir."

"Wonderful! Great work and such speed!"

"The buyer is a university library that has decided to invest its federal grant money on your entire collection, sir."

"Money well spent and some of it my very own in the form of federal taxes."

"Ha, right you are, sir."

"I'll be paying for the right to purchase my own property."

"You are most generous, sir."

"Ha, and you, James, are quite the patronizing humorist."

"Kind of you to say so, sir."

"Now stop that will you?"

"I will, sir."

"Good. It was starting to become tedious."

"I am sorry to have subjected you to tedium, sir."

"Out of curiosity, which university bought my books?"

"Franklin Smith, sir."

"My Alma Mater and former employer?"

"No less."

"Incredible, incredible I say!"

"And why would that be, sir?"

"Because I *stole* half of my collection from their archives!"

"You are quite the thief, sir."

"That may very well be, but a learned thief no less."

"No less, sir. Why do you suppose that the university never caught on to you?"

"I suppose it was because, while serving as their dean of academics, I also served as the university's archives auditor. I knew that I would have the opportunity to return any of the books should someone request a volume, so let's just say that the books were in a state of perpetual renewal and just happened to be in my possession."

"Brilliant, sir."

"The brilliance is, the federal government is bequeathing our tax dollars to enable my university to buy their own books back from me."

"My head is spinning, sir."

"As it should be, economics is indeed the devil's art. As I recall, Linda Blair's character Regan in the movie *The Exorcist* was studying economics at the time of her possession."

"Ha! I am sorry, sir, but I cannot patronize you regards *that* claim."

"I was just testing you, James, just making sure that you're paying attention."

"Sorry, what was that, sir...?"

"I said, all things considered, please do offer the university a very *generous* discount."

"Consider it done, sir."

As James turned to leave the professor's study in order to phone the university, he hesitated in anticipation of additional conversation. He was not disappointed.

"Tell me, James, do you find our impending worldwide quest for the meaning of life, enticing?"

"I do, sir."

"Are you certain?"

"I am indeed, sir."

"I feel the need to query you, James, because I can never quite tell what you're thinking."

"Nor I, sir."

"You can never tell what I'm thinking? Why would that be? I *never* shut up or ever hold anything back from you or anyone else in my company. How could you not *know* what I'm thinking?"

"That is not what I meant, sir. I always know what *you're*

thinking, but I can never tell what *I'm* thinking."

"I see... so, you know what I'm thinking, is that it?"

"Yes indeed, sir. That is what you *pay* me to do."

"Oh... right you are, James, right you are, and... what is it that I'm thinking right now?"

"You are thinking, lunch, sir."

"Damn! You're good!"

"And, right *you* are, sir."

James left the room. He phoned the university and then returned with lunch for the two of them which he placed on the professor's enormous, antique mahogany desk the top of which was unusually clear of its usual clutter. Since the sale of the professor's Federal era kitchen table and his Colonial era dining table, they had recently taken to dine in the study. The professor's desk would be the last of the furniture to go, lest they were to commence eating on produce crates. The professor however, would never stoop so low.

"Earlier, James, you said that you can never tell what *you* are thinking."

"I did, sir, pass the Grey Poupon please..."

"Care to explain?"

"I enjoy mustard on my sandwich, sir."

"Seriously, James, what did you mean when you said that you can never tell what *you* are thinking?"

"I'd rather not say, sir. To my knowledge, I've never complained about anything to you and I do not wish to start now. Can we just call it, a passing statement?"

"You know me better than that, my good man."

"And there it is, sir, *your* good man, *your* faithful servant, *your* butler, driver, cook and confidante. I can never tell what I'm thinking because I do not have the luxury of being my own man. I'm much too busy being *your* man."

"But, James... I feel much the same way about my own life! I've given my entire life to academics and feel as if I've never had the opportunity to actually enjoy life itself, to understand its meanings as they apply to me, to actually *live* my life in the pure, true sense of the word."

"But you *have* had opportunities, sir. You've simply chosen not to take them."

"Exactly, James! I realize that now. Do you realize that you *too* have chosen your own path and have forgone your *own* opportunities to do otherwise?"

"I do indeed, sir. It upsets me to consider the possibility that another path may have been more fulfilling and that is why I tend not to think or talk about it. But you've forced my hand, sir. I very much appreciate the opportunity to work for you these past six years. Whether or not another path or opportunity would have resulted in a better life for me is impossible to predict. Maybe I *did* make the best choice for myself when I chose to work for you. Maybe you *did* make the best choice for your life when you devoted it to academics. In my opinion, 'the grass is always greener,' is fair warning that the myth and mirage of so-called, 'true happiness,' can never be realized because no matter which side of the fence we're on, we're *always* on the other side. Who's to say that the grass isn't greener on *our* side of the fence, on the very paths that we've chosen? To suggest that no matter what we do we are bound to regret our decisions and should expect disappointment is to suspend all hope for happiness altogether. *Damn* the green grass, sir, I *am* happy!"

"And it's painfully apparent by the way you shout it to be so. But could you be happier?" the professor asked.

"For the love of God, sir! *Anything* is possible, but far fewer things are probable."

"I'm just asking, James."

James stood up. He turned then and proceeded to walk out of the room announcing, "I need a glass of wine."

"See... I told you, James... you *can* be happier!"

James stopped in his tracks. He turned back toward the professor in apparent disgust but then suddenly burst into laughter. Moments later, while James was in the kitchen, the professor shouted in his direction, "And bring *two* glasses!"

James returned to the study with two, nearly identical crystal goblets of Cabernet Sauvignon representing the last of that very fine bottle. The glasses would have been identical had not one of them contained just a touch more wine. James handed that glass to the professor. As the professor raised his glass James followed suit. The professor toasted, "To greener grass!"

To which James offered, "To the other side!"

"Ah yes, my good man, to the other side indeed; to the other side of the fence, to the other side of town, to the other side of the planet."

"To the other side of midnight and to the dark side of the moon," James added to their toast.

"And to the other side *itself;* be it heaven, be it hell or be it the great unknown, the empty darkness, the quiet void or eternal rest," the professor suggested and then asked, "What say you, James; judgment day or solo journey into oblivion?"

"Only after I do in fact die, sir, will I have an opinion on the matter."

"Surely though, you've considered the possibilities."

"I have considered them, sir, but I still retain my neutrality.

I'll know when I get there I imagine," James imagined.

"But do you have a *preference*? Would you prefer judgment day or something less, something less, less... damn it... something *less* judgmental?"

"May I suggest, sir, that a suitable synonym for something less judgmental might be; something *less profound* or perhaps; something *more arbitrary?*"

"You may if you answer my question."

"I suppose it would depend on the verdict, sir. If I knew that I was destined for heaven, I'd be in favor of judgment. On the other hand, if I knew that I was to burn in hell for all eternity, I'd probably be opposed to it."

"Probably? What possible benefit could you find in eternal damnation?"

"The way I see it, sir, if all the good people end up in heaven and all the sinners in hell, hell may very well be, one *hell* of a party. You know... wine, women and song and all that jazz but without those annoying last-call, closing-time curfews or those inevitable horrendous hangovers the morning after."

"So what you're saying is, throughout human history, clerics have painted hell as eternal damnation in order to frighten their flocks and keep them in line while in truth, hell is a sinner's paradise, a desirable den of iniquity?"

"No, sir, that is what *you* are saying, but as always, I enjoy your reasoning."

"But what then, James, of violent, murderous criminals in hell? Surely they'll end up right alongside the simple drunks and fornicators and common riffraff. Wouldn't the most savage sinners spoil the festivities for the rest?"

"Spoil it in what way, sir, by killing dead people?"

"Ha! And now it is *I* who enjoy *your* reasoning, my good

man. But let's just say that the violent criminals give their fellow hellions a good beating. Could you enjoy wine, women and song while nursing broken ribs or a cracked skull?"

"Not so much, sir. May I opt out of hell for the great unknown instead?" James inquired.

"When purchasing a ticket, James, you must first designate the destination."

"Agreed. However, at what point in time must the ticket be purchased and are the choices of destinations made available at such time? One wouldn't purchase a ticket to Tokyo from a train station in San Francisco."

"So it must follow then; if you *knew* that no route to heaven existed, as does no train service from San Francisco to Tokyo, there would be no reason to metaphorically purchase a ticket to heaven by believing in God, attending church and living a righteous life."

"Agreed, sir, you've made my point."

The professor thought out loud, "When we say, 'purchase a ticket,' we are of course referring to 'earning a right of travel' and that 'travel' is our route to the afterlife. But if we've no faith in God then we must believe that our afterlife destination is un-earned, it just exists out there somewhere waiting for us. There would be no need to purchase a ticket because the right of travel would be cost-free, it would have no preconditions, no requirement to subordinate one's self to a non-existent God. So what would remain then is only the journey which would commence when we die and end upon arrival at whatever destination awaits us. I cannot *know* that heaven exists any more than I can *know* that it does *not* exist. So, I need only purchase a ticket if I *think* there is a God, in other words, if I *believe* God to exist."

"But if passage to heaven requires the purchase of a ticket, wouldn't that make heaven's god a bloody capitalist?" James wondered aloud.

"I suppose it would, at least according to the church. One must *earn* their ticket to an afterlife in heaven by remaining righteous enough in life to be judged worthy after death. Those tickets are then redeemed by God."

"Do all faiths require tickets, sir?"

"That is a question for a student of theology, James."

"And an even *better* question to ask a professor of history, philosophy and theology such as yourself, sir."

"You'll have to excuse the wine, James, what is it that you wish to know?"

"Well, I am obviously familiar with the Christian Biblical belief-in-Jesus path to heaven, sir, but what of the other religions you've studied and taught? What paths to salvation do Jews, Muslims, Hindus, and Buddhists recommend?

"Why, they recommend their own of course!"

"Ha! Very good, sir, but seriously..."

"Did you not study those faiths in school, James?"

"I did study them, sir... but it's been so long ago I would appreciate a refresher."

"And a refresher you will have for the meager sum of one refreshed glass of refreshing wine."

"Right away, sir, but be advised... the '82 is finished."

"Those were the last two glasses?"

"I'm afraid so, sir. Your beloved retirement gift, not unlike your accomplished career, is as they say; history."

"And such a *fine* history it was, James. Well... onto the '84 then!"

"The '84 it is, sir."

James ducked his head upon entering the cool, fragrant depths of the professor's wine cellar. He did so with a touch of sadness knowing that it would soon be stocked by the new owners of the estate. Over the past six years it was James who had handled the bottles with care. Most of the professor's extensive wine collection had recently been sold to private connoisseurs and fine restaurants throughout the area. As a result, the once-full racks were now nearly empty. The '84 was easily located, nestled amongst its last half-dozen companions. James cradled the bottle as he climbed the cellar steps into the pantry where he liberated two glasses of wine from twenty-five years of subterranean limbo. While allowing the wine to breathe and adjust to the light and temperature of the day, James sliced a selection of cheeses to accompany the assortment of crackers he arranged with care on a sterling silver tray. As he did so, his thoughts wandered. The wine cellar reminded James of his own faraway home; a dark and gloomy place, but one that always managed to maintain a comfortable moderate climate. It was a place where James felt comfortably alone, a place that he missed on some days, a place that he missed most nights. James' sense of duty and devotion to the professor however, helped him to temper his longings for home. Having little family of his own and fewer friends with whom to pass the time, James found himself drawn closer to his surroundings than those with families normally would. He held close to his heart the vivid sights and sounds and personalities of the places he called home. He felt an intimacy with certain special places that he'd often discover and explore. Although he devoted himself to his duties toward others, once fulfilled, James would immerse himself in the local history and architecture and parklands of the places in which he lived. His current home in its particular locale, over and above all of the others before it, would remain forever to him; a vivid and cherished memory.

"Refresh my memory, James, what was it that we were discussing?" the professor asked as he took a glass of wine from James with one hand while selecting a bit of cheese from the tray with his other.

"The salvation of Jews, Muslims, Hindus, and Buddhists," James reminded the professor.

"But of course! Let's begin, shall we?"

"As you wish, sir."

"A Hindu is a person who professes any one of a variety of Indian faiths which include among many others, Hinduism, Buddhism and Sikhism. Hinduism itself, James, is actually a conglomerate of views and traditions much of which is based not only on theology, but also on philosophy and mythology."

"Your lucrative specialties, sir."

"They *have* paid a portion of the bills 'tis true, but if not for my dearly departed wife's inheritance of this estate, we'd be moving out of a much smaller house these upcoming days."

"So... we'd have a lot less work to do then."

"Ha-ha, right you are, James! Now then, where were we?"

"Hinduism, sir."

"Hinduism it is, my fine man."

By that point in their conversation, the professor had been enjoying and succumbing to the fruits of the vine at a much quicker pace and with greater effect than he would have in the not-too-distant past. The recent accelerated aging of the professor's psyche had made wine, all the more potent.

"Hinduism is actually a Western term for much of India's

social system, a system that embraces a wide variety of religious beliefs throughout what is an incredibly diverse region of the world. Hinduism itself has no founder. It has no prophets or creed. It does however; emphasize *dharma* which to Hindus represents *the right way to live*. It also recognizes *samsara* as a perpetual cyclical path from here to the afterlife, what we in the West know as *reincarnation.* In Hindu belief, both one's life *and* afterlife occur here on earth. Afterlife is resurrection but in a transformative state."

"Like for example; when a mass-murderer is reincarnated as a butterfly?" James suggested.

"Not quite, my good man. A mass-murderer would more likely be reincarnated as a dung beetle or a maggot."

"That sounds fair," James conceded.

"One's *karma* in life determines their next life; good karma/good afterlife, bad karma/bad afterlife," the professor explained.

"Quite appropriate indeed," James concurred.

"As it should be," the professor said and then continued. "But a Hindu's greatest spiritual goal is to reach *moksha;* the final and permanent release from the cycle of *samsara.*"

"And how is that accomplished?" James wondered.

"By reaching self-realization or *atma-jnana;* a spiritual awakening to one's non-physical, pure form of being or *essence.* It is attainable only by way of deep meditation and through one's total understanding of and devotion to *The Supreme*, a.k.a. *Shiva* or *Vishnu.*"

"How would one know if they had successfully *reached* moksha?" James asked.

"The definition of so-called *knowledge* exists only in the physical world, James. The spiritual state of moksha is beyond knowledge, it is incomprehensible to anyone who has not yet reached it."

"So, I will only know, if and when I get there?"

"Exactly."

"So there is no earth-based proof that moksha or Shiva or Vishnu actually exist?"

"Of course not, James, and that is why they call it *faith*," the professor reminded him.

"As I recall from my studies, Buddhism is similar to and has roots in Hinduism," James recalled.

"And you recall correctly, James. Buddhism was founded by its prophet Prince Gautama Siddhartha who is known as *the enlightened one* or simply *Buddha*. Buddha abandoned his family and all of his earthly possessions in search of truth or *enlightenment*. He spent the remainder of his long life teaching others *The Four Noble Truths*: life is suffering, attachment causes suffering, suffering can be eliminated, and the method by which suffering can be eliminated leads one on a path to self-enlightenment, a spiritual state free from all human suffering. That spiritual state is known as *Nirvana*. To various degrees, the many forms of Buddhism share many doctrines and traditions with the many forms of Hinduism. The variety is exponentially limitless, as is the cosmos itself."

"I imagine I will only know if I've reached Nirvana, if and when I get there?" James concluded.

"You're catching on, James. There is spiritual hope for you yet!" the professor teased.

"And you, sir?" James asked.

"Let's save that for later shall we?"

"As you wish, sir."

"Judaism is the great-grandfather of Christianity. Its central text is the *Tanakh,* the canon of the Hebrew Bible which was pilfered and expanded upon in the Old Testament of the Christian Bible. Some Jews accept Jesus Christ as a historical figure but none consider him God incarnate as do Christians. Jews show reverence for their patriarch Abraham and believe in one God whose name they pronounce; *Yahweh,* who, with Moses leading the way through the desert, delivered the Israelites from bondage in Egypt and chose them to teach God's laws to the world as prescribed in the Torah. Jews believe that when they die, their souls live on for eternity. A good Jew's soul will enjoy everlasting salvation with God because all Jews' souls are already a part of God. However, a bad Jew will not be cast into hell because the Hebrew version of God is not so cruel as to have created a hell."

"So where do bad Jews go?" James asked.

"Miami Beach," the professor claimed.

"Surely you jest, professor?" James laughed.

"I do indeed, James. Jews believe that bad souls can actually redeem themselves by being good after the death of the host's physical body."

"If that were the case, sir, there'd be no incentive to be good while a physical being on earth."

"I suppose not, James, not if you get a second chance at salvation."

"Who could pass that up? And why aren't more people Jewish?"

"Because Jews are the chosen people. They are born as such."

"Sounds exclusive to me," James surmised.

"It is indeed, James, and that is why other faiths were developed; to give Gentiles a shot at salvation. You've said that you're familiar with Christianity so you must know that anyone at all can become a Christian by simply accepting Jesus Christ as their lord, god and savior?"

"I do, and I consider it tempting," James confessed.

"But there are risks," the professor warned.

"Risks?"

"The risk of being cast into the extreme torture of hell for all of eternity if you don't measure up," the professor reminded him.

"That's a bit harsh I'd say," James said, a bit harshly.

"The whole business of faith is harsh, James. It is very serious business and is not to be taken lightly."

"And what of Islam..." James prompted the professor.

"Islam is basically, an Arab knock-off of Christianity with Allah serving as their version of God. According to Muslim belief, as recorded in their holy scripture the Qur'an, the prophet Mohammed served as the last, perfect messenger of God after Jesus and Moses before him gave it their best shot. Along with Judaism and Christianity, Islam shares the common patriarch Abraham who proceeded in lineage, all of the western prophets and supposedly spoke to the one, true, mono-theistic God; Allah. For Muslims, Allah is all-powerful and all-meddling. He controls and influences virtually everything. If you believe in Allah you'd better not step out of line because as do Christians, Muslims believe in hell."

"So when it comes down to choosing a favorite descendent of Abraham; Moses, Jesus or Mohammed, it's like choosing between a favorite Beetle; John, Paul, George or Ringo."

"They are all indeed, choices, James, although I'd imagine that Hindus and Buddhists might opt for Yoko."

"Right you are, professor!" James said laughing and then he

asked the professor, "And as for *you,* sir, may I inquire *now* of your own personal beliefs?"

"Me...? I'm more a fan of the Rolling Stones, you know... a sympathy for the devil type."

"He has been called a fallen angel by some, sir."

"And that's exactly how I feel most of the time, James. We are *all* fallen angels, just trying to get back on our feet. Whether or not there actually is a god remains to be seen. If God decides that he does in fact exist, I imagine he'll decide what to do with me once I've departed for greener pastures. If God decides that he *doesn't* exist, then I imagine he'll have no say in the matter."

"So would you call yourself an agnostic, sir?"

"Somewhat, James, I tend to suspend my belief in God for the selfish sake of my own salvation while I search for more substantial reasons for his existence, as do you apparently."

"So... we're not necessarily non-believers, but are potential believers should we be given good enough reason. Most others lean toward faith I imagine, as an insurance policy against eternal damnation," James suggested.

"And why not? If God *does* exist, that policy may cover them, if they've chosen the right god that is."

"Door number one, two or three, sir?"

"John, Paul, George, Ringo or Yoko... and if God doesn't exist, the faithful have lost nothing, nothing except a lifetime of Sunday mornings, Saturday afternoons or daily prayers."

"Could it be, sir, that the actual truth lies somewhere in between?"

"In what way, James?"

"Let's say that God does in fact exist for those who believe in him, but doesn't exist for those who don't?"

"Anything is possible I suppose but *that* possibility would surprise me the most."

"So it's either/or then?"

"It is in my book, James. There have been countless, so-called *miracles* that the faithful attribute to God, things that the unfaithful attribute to luck, coincidence or happenstance. I don't think that those things can be attributed to both a god and to a world without a god."

"Which argument *against* the existence of god carries the most weight with you, sir?"

"It would be that of the Greek philosopher Epicurus who surmised; *Is God willing to prevent evil, but not able? Then he is not omnipotent. Is he able, but not willing? Then he is malevolent. Is he both able, and willing? Then whence come evil? Is he neither able nor willing? Then why call him God?*"

"He makes excellent points, sir. They push me toward disbelief."

"They push me toward disbelief in an omnipotent god, one who is hands-on and all-powerful. I can't imagine an omnipotent god deciding to kill a quarter million people in the Indian Ocean tsunami of '04, or a quarter million Haitians in the earthquake of 2010, or twenty thousand souls during Japan's 2011 earthquake and tsunami."

"It *would* make heaven quite a bit more crowded, sir."

"Or hell, James."

"Would a crowded hell make it even more unbearable, sir?"

"It certainly wouldn't help, James."

"Would one more glass of the '84 make our current lives more bearable, sir?"

"It certainly would, James."

As they proceeded to make their lives more bearable, the

sun began to set through the bows of the old oaks on the estate's front lawn. As daylight dimmed beyond the study's banks of lead-lined windows, James pulled the chain on the professor's desk lamp. The two of them sat then quietly in the lamp's warm green glow as they finished their wine.

"Let's pick up where we've left off, tomorrow, James," the professor announced, rising slowly and stiffly from his chair. "I must save my most compelling rhetoric for another day."

"I very much look forward to it, sir. Do sleep well," James offered.

"And you, James," the professor replied.

The professor did not rise the next day. He had died quietly in his sleep. James was shocked and shaken at first but he eventually gathered enough strength to make the necessary phone calls and attend to the tasks at hand. With James' assistance, the professor's family made elaborate funeral arrangements. The services were attended by hundreds of mourners: extended family members, close and casual friends, fellow faculty members, former students across several academic decades and anonymous admirers of the professor's numerous written works. During the final graveside benediction, James found himself admiring the cemetery's impeccably manicured, beautiful green grass. He also happened to notice, on the other side of the cemetery's black-iron fence, the unkempt and drought-stricken weeds along the bustling public right-of-way.

"Damn the green grass!" James thought to himself. "I opt for the weeds."

That night at the professor's estate, after the last of the grief-stricken mourners had become merrily drunk and then eventually departed, James found himself alone in the house and alone in his room. He piled his pillows one atop the other, kicked off his shoes and sat up on his bed. James energized his transponder to record the last of his notes; "Human grief can be fickle and fleeting and in some cases appear disingenuous. Some Humans may actually celebrate the death of others having been personally spared its effects themselves. On the other hand, Humans who have had close personal ties with the deceased, appear to be to some degree devastated by the death of their friend or loved-one. In extreme cases, those most affected exhibit emotional trauma resembling physical incapacitation as if they themselves had suffered the actual physiological effects of death."

James transmitted his notes, paused, and then activated his transponder's teleportation function. He held the device tightly to his chest, pressed its flashing button, closed his eyes and then vanished. As his essence was transported light years away to a distant galaxy and to his own eternally eclipsed, bleak and colorless planet, James had fleeting visions of Earth's beautiful green grass.

The professor knocked lightly on James' bedroom door. It was uncharacteristic of James to sleep later than the professor had and so, the professor knocked again, waited, announced his presence and then opened the door. He was greeted by the radiance of brilliant white light. The professor squinted as he felt his way slowly through the doorway. Once past it, he regained his sight. It was a sight that made the professor grin with joy; a beautiful cloudless blue sky and an infinite expanse of shimmering green grass.

Exurbia

Exurbia - Chapter First

Hallo to you. My name Harry. Harry Butz. I live in Exurbia with my wife Keisha and also my son Fuzzy. We are happy family. I cut grass and clean pool and drive car. Keisha cook food and wash clothes and clean house. Fuzzy mostly laugh and pee pants sometimes. Our boss man is capitalist. Capitalist means rich men who make a-lot of money off poor people and spend it on their selfs. Some Capitalists own slave factories in other countries like the sweat shop where me and Keisha used to work and sweat. But now we work in Exurbia and live in tool shed garage and sleep on bags of fertilizer. It much better than sweat shop. Now we are how they say - upward mobile. Our family have cat pet. Cat pet have only one eye but it still catch mouse we share for dinner with bone scraps Keisha bring home from kitchen. Boss have wife and mistress and boss wife have some boyfriend or girlfriend every day sometimes. They are very happy. They always drink and laugh and throw fancy party for rich friends like they are. House is quiet Sunday mornings though when boss and boss wife go to church in sports car with no top. On Sunday mornings Keisha and me and Fuzzy sneak inside big house to take big bath together. We use guest bathtub on third floor boss probably forgot he have. One time we all fall asleep in nice warm bathtub and boss come home Uh-Oh! But boss never find us because we sneak out bathroom window and slide down drainpipe dripping wet and soapy wet and giggling wet and run back to tool shed garage so much fun in Exurbia that day!

Exurbia - Chapter Second

One morning at midnight police-men come. Police take boss man in car. Boss wife cry and cry and cry then call boyfriend. They swim in pool naked. Boyfriend look good - boss wife look like wet sock. Next day boss come back home and find man size wet sock at pool. He say - This man size wet sock not mine! Who man size wet sock this is? Wife say - Oh that belong to Harry (that is me) Boss say - OK. I never tell boss man sock not mine. End of that story.

Exurbia - Chapter Third

Monday I clean pool and find big shiny gold diamond ring stuck in filter. I say - Keisha! Keisha! Lookie here what Harry find Honeycakes! Keisha say - Oh My who you think lost that big shiny gold diamond ring? I say - I do-not know that Keisha should we keep it Honeycakes? Keisha say - Boss lady have twenty rings like that if it her ring she not miss it. So we keep it. Next day I drive boss lady to shop for shoes and panties. When she go in one fancy shop Harry sneak across street to jewelry shop. I ask jewelry man how much big shiny gold diamond ring worth. He look at ring then look at me then look at ring then look at me then he say - $30 dollar. I say - $30 dollar! That all? He say - Yes it fake ring. Later that night Keisha and Fuzzy and me take bus to Frosty Queen shop. We eat chocolate and vanilla and strawberry ice creams with fudge-sauce and chop-nuts and whippy-cream it so good we laugh and sing all the way home on bus. Best part - we still have $15 dollar left over from money jewelry man gave me for big shiny fake ring! Woo Boy Harry love America!

Exurbia - Chapter Fourth

Boss man and boss wife have boy son like my Fuzzy. But boss man son have two pony and my Fuzzy have zero pony. Today boss man son have big birthday party with many more little birthday party boys and little birthday party girls and big funny clown with red nose on face. Keisha work hard at party all day and I shovel pony poop all day. Tonight Fuzzy sleep in big house with birthday party boys and girls. Keisha and me alone tonight so I can kiss her ears and her lips and her other nice things two. She is so beautiful and gentle soft I love her more every time I see her again. I love her first time I see her in our country many years ago long time. I ask her marry me and take my name. She say - Yes Harry I will be Keisha Butz! Harry so happy he kiss his Keisha for one hour. One year later we have baby but baby die. So sad so sad we cry for a year but now we have little Fuzzy Butz so sadness not so strong now. Fuzzy is good boy we love him and tell him so even when he bad boy sometimes. I kiss his ears two but he laugh loud not like my Keisha who close her eyes and smile and then she say - Oh Harry in nice soft voice.

Exurbia - Chapter Fifth

I look and I look and I even look some more but Harry can-not find my pencil nowhere so Harry can-not write chapter fifth. So sad am I. I wrote this sentence and other sentence in front of it with crayon I borrow from Fuzzy but he need it now to draw picture of kitty cats and doggy dogs and ducky ducks to. Fuzzy like ducks back in our country. Maybe I buy him duck on his birthday. He like pony to but pony two much money.

Exurbia - Chapter Sixth

Harry happy find pencil but now paper running low on empty space. That OK Harry go to night school soon - Thank You America! Keisha say if I learn more good things maybe I get better job and more money coming in for Fuzzy future. I do anything for Fuzzy and Keisha to. So I say - OK my Keisha your Harry go to night school and be better man for you. Keisha say - Oh my Harry Dear you already the best man for me. Sometime Harry almost cry when Keisha say sweet thing to me like that. But I hide my tears to be strong man. I just hug and kiss my Keisha instead of cry and then I tickle Fuzzy so he laugh to much and pee pants sometimes.

Exurbia - Chapter Last

Harry very busy now to study in night school so my story is the ending here. Goodbye. End of Exurbia story.

Exurbia - Extra Words I Forgot

Thank you Fuzzy for crayon I borrow.
Thank you Keisha for candle I borrow to write story.
Thank you reader for read my story.

Fleas on the Moon (Luna-Ticks)

It was a dark and stormy night, but Max had to pee so I opened the back porch screen door and watched as he disappeared into the night. I waited for Max on the porch with an old towel ready to dry him off as soon as his sorry butt returned but as lightning crashed and rain poured down I began to worry. Max was usually quick about his business when it was raining. Soon thereafter, my worry turned into fear. Did a flying tree branch clunk him on the head? Did his leg get stuck in a gopher hole? Did he get struck by lightning? "Oh, No!" I howled as I dashed out into the howling storm.

The relentless rain soaked me to the bone as I searched high and low and the middle. There was no sign of Max anywhere though, at least not anywhere that I was looking. I began then to sob in anxious desperation, or maybe it was just rainwater running down my face. Either way, I was really bummed out and worried. After two minutes of searching I finally gave up and dashed back into the house at the very moment that a blinding bolt of lightning exploded in our yard. "Max!" I howled as the house went dark.

I lit a match to find my candle and then I lit the candle to find my flashlight and then I used the flashlight to search for my lantern. Ironically, the lantern was right next to the matches. Under the light of the lantern I pawed through the Yellow Pages in search of the phone number for emergency assistance. There it was; 9-1-1.

Half-way through dialing the number, I heard scratching at the front door. I ran through the house, unlocked the door and then swung it wide open. "Max!" I yelped.

Max jumped up on me and began licking my face with his

tongue. We looked into each other's eyes, relieved and happy as the house lights came back on.

"Why didn't you ring the doorbell, Max?" I asked him.

"I tried to but it didn't work," he explained.

"Oh yeah... the power," I thought out loud.

"The lightning scared me so I ran up front, did my business under the old oak tree and then wound up on the front porch," Max reported.

"Well, you did the right thing," I said as we hugged each other; the both of us smelling like wet dogs.

On the back porch the very next night around midnight, as the midnight moon hung low in the midnight sky, Max was sleeping soundly in his upstairs bedroom while I was busy soaking and scrubbing the dried mud off of his Scooby-Doo slippers that were soiled in the storm the night before. Just as I was about to begin scrubbing my own matching slippers, I felt a tap on my shoulder. I turned around to find my sleepy-eyed Max just standing there.

"Can't sleep?" I asked him.

"Got to pee," he announced.

I watched as Max wagged his tail in anticipation while he searched for a suitable pee-spot in the backyard. The clear skies above promised that there would be no harrowing weather disasters on that fine evening. Since I'm a southpaw, I picked up my scrub brush in my left paw and one of my four dirty slippers in my right paw and then got to work scrubbing the dried mud from Scooby-Doo's stupid, silly grin. All of a sudden, Max began to howl at the moon.

"Like father like son," I said to myself with a laugh and then I bent over to lick my balls.

Happiness is No Laughing Matter

As the day slowly acquiesced to early evening, my bright sunlit window began to glow in dimmer shades of orange and then red and then indigo or some combination thereof I cannot now quite describe. It was a somber glow which most people I imagine would have found comforting after a hectic day at work or a busy day with family or friends. At such times, those people would settle in for the evening after having dined together. Some of them might play cards or board games or watch a movie on television together and share popcorn with one other. Some it is true, might argue with one another or even shout at one another until one or the other ended the confrontation by storming away angry. But as the night would wear on, many of those angry would eventually surrender their senseless battles and rejoin their loved ones. They'd offer a conciliatory hug that would evolve into a comforting affectionate truce. I too had experienced such conflict of emotional affection, during my childhood, so many years ago. At times I could still feel the warm and comforting rèmnants of such human touch and interaction. At times I'd feel it so vividly that not having it in my life made it even more painful for me to be alone. The pain that I felt was often *almost* too much to bear. Despite those desperate feelings I tried hard to ignore the constant pain of loneliness. I'd do so by reading or writing or by dining alone in busy restaurants or by going to the movies alone in theaters filled with happy souls. Nevertheless, the ever-present pain of isolation eventually became too much to bear. The pain was winning. It was beating me down. It was gaining advantage as its persistent, silent presence enveloped me in such a horrible dread that escape from it seemed impossible. As was previously mentioned, I had *attempted* escape and at times I *did* gain temporary relief from the pain, but that pain always managed to find me again. It would find me and push me back into that dark place where I had last felt it. The pain of loneliness haunted me. It was my one and only constant companion. It kept me company.

The glow that came through my window served to remind me that yet another lonely day had come and gone and yet another lonely night was sure to follow. I *could* have gone out and wandered the streets. I *could* have sat in a barroom and pretended that I actually enjoyed drinking. I *could* have potentially met someone and struck up a conversation; that had happened many times before but in the long run, chances were overwhelming that I'd end up right back home alone again where I would curse the loneliness as it hung there, cold and silent, mocking me.

One night, I decided to Google; "I'm Lonely." Apparently, I wasn't the only one to have taken that desperate step because I discovered therein; lengthy life stories of the forlorn and lonely most of which made me even more depressed. The best advice I stumbled upon was so very obvious that it was of no help whatsoever; "Get out of the house and live life." The life outside I'd discovered to that point had been one of a world passing me by. It was preoccupied with itself. It was totally disinterested in me. It wouldn't even consider making me a part of it in any way. Everyone who appeared to be engaged in the actual art of "living" seemed to be doing so within long-established social circles the portals of which, if not totally barred and locked, were at least closed and uninviting. No matter where I found myself I was always the clueless new kid with a tray full of lousy food standing alone in an otherwise crowded cafeteria. There were plenty of empty seats to be had but no open hearts to be found. And so, I ate alone in the din of a hundred conversations as my inner-voice pleaded in vain; *Let me in!*

In their defense, most people were at least polite and could even be considerate on occasion. They'd smile at me, act mildly courteous and might even return a response to a random comment I'd toss their way. But any attempt I made to actually relate to a stranger in order to be accepted in some small way was eventually dismissed. Without fail, those mysterious strangers always seemed to have more important or immediate issues involving those with whom they were most comfortable; their private, tightly-knit circle of friends.

Sleep on the other hand, had always been an easy friend to me. Not wanting to fall victim to drug or alcohol abuse, for the most part, I tended to avoid those unreliable escape mechanisms. I learned instead to transform the physiological necessity of sleep into a comforting crutch upon which I could lean as I ignored the devastating effects of depression. If sleep were ever to lose its ability to temporarily carry me through the depths of depression, the next and last resort I dared imagine was suicide; perpetual sleep, perpetual relief. With my luck though, suicide would prove to be nothing more than eternal damnation at the hands of a vengeful God. And so it was that every night, and many a morning, afternoon and evening, I'd avoid the potential pitfalls of suicide by simply closing my eyes and falling asleep. The relief I'd find in sleeping was well worth the risk of the occasional screaming nightmare I'd wake up to because those bad dreams were more tolerable to me than the actual life I was living.

Over the course of my gloomy existence, I'd found that by merely ignoring loneliness, I could lessen its effects to some extent. But loneliness is tough to ignore when you're alone; especially when you're alone and idle. I noticed that the busier I was, the less time I had left over to feel lonely. Regrettably though, I'd always been much too inherently lazy to stay busy enough during the day to thoroughly ignore my perpetual sadness. My part-time night job didn't help matters much. It didn't keep me preoccupied often enough or long enough to battle the loneliness that would eventually creep back in and resume creeping me out.

At the time that my life took a dramatic turn for the better, I happened to be in an unusually decent state of mind. I was making my way to work that night on the cross-town bus when I experienced a strange sensation that something good was going to happen. A short time later when I arrived at work, I felt that same feeling again while waiting backstage. The comedian ahead of me was bombing badly. The ruthless audience was disappointed and bored. From what I could tell the groans and boos were outnumbering the feeble laughs two-to-one. Hopefully, I'd be able to swing the mood. I was at least, up to the challenge. As he passed by me, I tapped the shoulder of my defeated predecessor in consolation before I myself, faced the firing squad.

(scattered applause)

Thank you, thank you!

(a bit more scattered applause)

Thank you very much! You are either *way* too kind or more likely, *way* too stoned!

(snickers)

Sorry I'm late. I was in traffic court this afternoon and as a result, I had to take a slow, city bus here.

(snickers)

The judge asked me why I was driving fifteen miles an hour in a fifty-five mile an hour zone. I told her that I couldn't help it because, despite the fact that I had passed the breathalyzer test, I was actually pretty darn drunk at the time.

(laughter)

Well, *she* didn't think it was funny. She suspended my driver's license on the spot, impounded my car and then fined me five hundred dollars. I told the judge that I was poor and didn't have five hundred dollars. I suggested to her that since I was only driving fifteen miles an hour, maybe a fifteen dollar fine would be more appropriate.

(snickers)

I was surprised when she actually agreed with me but was immediately bummed-out when she increased my fine to five hundred and fifteen dollars.

(laughter)

As the bailiff ushered me out of the courtroom, I turned back toward the judge and asked her, "Your honor, since you've suspended my driver's license and impounded my car, is there any chance that you can give me a ride home?"

(laughter)

The judge grinned before she cited me for contempt of court and then tacked another five hundred dollars onto my fine.

(laughter)

Well, thanks *a lot* for laughing at my misfortune. With what I earn in this dump it'll take me six months to pay off my fine. And seeing as how you all think it's so funny, I think I'll let *you* do most of my work for me this evening.

At that point, I walked out into the audience and began handing out notecards to random people at each of the thirty or so tables. The cards that I was passing out had my best jokes written on them. I gave the audience instructions to read the cards and then pass them along to the next table. Having handed out all of my cards, I returned to the stage where I sat on a stool and pretended to check my cellphone for messages. As the audience members read their cards aloud to one another they'd laugh amongst themselves and then look up at me. I'd point at them, slap my knee and laugh right along with them as if I knew exactly what they were laughing at. The cards got passed along from table-to-table where they were read by others and so on and so forth. When the audience had finally finished reading and laughing at my jokes, I went back into the audience to collect my cards. Way in the back of the room, a sultry woman in a sexy black dress sitting alone at the bar motioned to me as she held up one of my cards. I hadn't noticed her earlier when I'd handed out the cards. I smiled at her when I tried to take my card back but she teased me by holding onto it tightly. And then, she tugged the card out from my fingertips, flipped it over, wrote something on the back of it and then handed the card back to me. Not wanting to be fooled a second time, I took it from her tentatively. After she'd let me take the card, I read what she had written on it; *May I buy you a drink?*

I looked at her and smiled until I recognized who she was; the very same judge I had stood before earlier that day. My jaw dropped. She smiled at me coyly and winked. Before I had the nerve or the chance to say anything, she turned back to her drink and began engaging the person who was sitting next to her at the bar.

I went back on stage, wrapped up my act, thanked the audience for being such good sports, took a deep bow and then a deeper breath as I returned to the bar where I slipped onto a stool next to the judge.

"I thought you were funny in court today so I thought I'd catch your act," she said before I had the chance to defend or make a fool of myself.

"Wow, I am honored, your honor," I said as a three-piece band settled in on stage and began playing sad, sappy blues.

Later that night at my place, I poured two glasses of wine. I decided against my Boogie Fever disco compilation album and put on some sultry Smoky Robinson instead. We sat on my old threadbare sofa, sipped my cheap wine and talked and laughed as we shared bits and pieces of our life stories. At one point that night, our hands touched accidentally. At another point, our lips touched repeatedly on purpose. Shortly thereafter, I discovered what it was exactly, that the judge had been hiding under her robe earlier that day.

I didn't wake up alone the next morning. There was no need to battle depression that entire day. I surrendered myself willingly and peacefully to whatever might lie ahead. I was totally unaware at the time though, that my life sentence of happiness had just begun.

- Case Dismissed -

Happy Hour and a Half

I'd been thinking lately about smoking cigarettes again. I hadn't done so for fifteen years or more but those good ol' days kept popping into my head; hazy visions of crowded barrooms and pubs and saloons and taverns, laughing with good friends, dancing with bad girls, their skimpy dance floor clothes on the floor marking the end of perfect night out. Those boozed-up crazy times were usually a riot and I had always enjoyed them with a cigarette in my hand.

I walked into a bar the other day for the first time in ten years or so and saw folks there my age who looked as if they'd never left the place; drinks in hand, cigarettes in hand, a wet wad of cash scattered in front of them dusted with ashes and peanut shells and bound for the cash drawer in a never-ending cycle of shit-faced investment. If I had any money to invest, I'd bet it all on the drunks.

At the time of this story, tomorrow was a Friday which meant that a Friday night would soon follow. It had been a long time since I'd partied with drunks on a Friday night so I was thinking about giving it a go for ol' time's sake. But, should I? I wondered. Then again... why not? I thought. What harm could come of it? Live a little for a change! Okay, that's it! I finally decided. I'm gonna do it! I'm gonna buy me a pack of smokes, hit up the ATM for a hundred bucks, head straight to the nearest bar and invest it as fast as I can in one hell of a hangover - Oh won't that be grand? It probably wouldn't be because truth be told, it usually wasn't. Chances were good that I'd be better off staying home and just writing about it instead. We shall see.

About thirty minutes into happy hour I realized that I should slow down because the third, two-dollar rum and Coke sitting in front of me was already half empty. As it stood, we were both half drunk. Over the years, I had understandably lost my youthful athletic edge, but who knew that you could lose your ability to consume massive amounts of alcohol while still acting relatively sober? Not me apparently, so some half-dozen drinks and two or three shots of something else later, I discovered by accident that I had reacquired my ability to abandon all reason.

As too-loud music blared from a worn and tired jukebox saddened by a lifetime of entertaining ungrateful drunks who paid it little attention unless it skipped or fell silent as it did then (some four or five hours after I'd first arrived) the bar's full armament of obnoxious fluorescent lights beamed alive. The heretofore dark and mysterious patrons were suddenly exposed for what they truly were; a pathetic mob of pasty-faced, squinty-eyed alcoholics and future lung cancer patients who appeared either mildly surprised, totally confused or royally pissed-off that their night of binge-drinking had come to an abrupt end.

"You Don't Have To Go Home But You Can't Stay Here!" the bartender bellowed for the umpteenth time of his un-distinguished career as mixologist, best friend, worst enemy and at the time; only sober person in Jack's Bar & Grill.

And so, I took my unwilling place in line and proceeded to stumble behind those in front of me in an orderly manner out the front door and onto the strip-mall's parking lot feeling like an Ellis Island immigrant arriving in a Brave New World filled with opportunity and danger. As I fondled the keys in my pocket and began a search for a car that resembled my own, an attractive, middle-aged, bleached blonde fumbled with her own set of keys. She was attempting to unlock her car door but was having trouble seeing in the dark shadows of the dim, parking lot lights.

"Having trouble?" I asked her.

The blonde froze for a second, looked up a bit startled at first but then said cheerfully, "Oh hi there!" and then asked, "Looking for a good time, sailor?"

She laughed at her own joke with a silly drunken good-natured giggle until she realized that it wasn't actually a joke at all but was in fact; a sincere plea for companionship. She didn't savor the prospect of another lonely night, another empty bed and another morning alone with her faithful lipstick stained coffee cup from which she'd sip while ignoring the kitchen radio's robotic six a.m. weather forecast and traffic report that ushered her off to work most Tuesdays through Saturdays.

"No, seriously," she suggested, "how about some coffee or something?"

To which I replied, "I could use some something."

She laughed again but that time with good reason and soon thereafter with happy shivers and a long deep warm wet kiss of gratitude as I lay exhausted atop her. She was several years older than I was and slept easily and comfortably; her slow, shallow, whiskey breath puffing across my numb face and swirling head.

I awoke early the next morning but resumed sleeping intermittently until midday while my brain punished me with constant painful throbbing against the inside of my skull that denied me any actual rest. I lay there naked in an otherwise empty bed in an otherwise empty bedroom until the door swung open and an incredibly beautiful woman with long strawberry blonde hair entered the room as gracefully as a prima ballerina taking center stage. The audience of me became instantly mesmerized.

"Good morning, handsome. I'm Angelica, Angelica Demón, your lover's roommate. Dianne had to run off to work. She asked me to look after you but judging from the looks of you, I may not be much help at all," she reported after which she tipped a glass to my lips and poured what tasted like cold bitter water down my parched throat.

"I'll be back in a few," she said as she laid an ice cold hand towel across my throbbing forehead.

I was awakened by Angelica's return some twenty minutes later. She had a fluffy white bath towel draped over her arm and a toothbrush in her long slender fingers. She turned the shower valve on in the adjoining bathroom and then said, "Come join me if you're up to it."

I was up to it in an instant as I felt a sudden and miraculous recovery.

"What was it that you gave me to drink," I asked her as I jumped off of the bed and back to life, "some kind of miracle hang-over cure?"

"It was cyanide," she said.

"Cyanide?" I asked, confused and astonished. "Why on earth would you give me cyanide? Isn't that poisonous?"

"You were suffering. I gave you cyanide to relieve your suffering," she explained.

"So, you're trying to kill me?" I asked, not totally processing the implications of my question.

"No, silly boy, I'm not *trying* to kill you!"

I breathed a sigh of relief.

"I already *have* killed you."

"So, you're saying that I'm dead?" I asked her doubtfully with a nervous laugh of mild trepidation.

"Yes, dear, you are no longer alive *and* no longer suffering in case you hadn't noticed. I cannot bear to just stand by and watch people suffer. Besides, living guys are too demanding and tend to be more trouble than they're worth."

And with that, she slipped out of her clothes, grabbed me between the legs and tugged me gently into the shower with her where she wrapped her arms around me and pressed her soft slender legs against mine. I became dripping wet instantly in the steaming hot shower, as did she.

As things began to heat up between us, she pressed her warm wet lips to my ear and then asked me in a whisper, "So... how does it feel to be dead?"

"Not as bad as I thought it would be," I suddenly realized.

Over the years I've made more than my fair share of bad decisions but some of my best decisions were those that I'd made to *not* do something. My recent decision to *not* buy a pack of cigarettes and start smoking again was a good one. My decision to *not* go out to a bar and start drinking again was a good one. My decision to *not* do those things and simply stay at home and *write* about doing those things was a good decision. After all, alcohol and tobacco can kill a man. Besides, my new girlfriend doesn't drink a drop and second-hand smoke makes her gag. I'd really hate to disappoint her or worse yet, get on her bad side.

"So how's your story coming along?" Angelica asked me.

"I'm afraid it's come to dead end, my dear," I confessed.

- Last Call -

Hungry?

I'm a meat-and-potatoes guy, so much so, that one of my nicknames happens to be "meat-and-potatoes guy." I will on occasional though, add a second vegetable to my meat and potatoes if I'm in the mood for some ketchup. But usually, I just stick to the basics. Don't get me wrong, I *do* like *other* vegetables but only if they're raw or lightly stir-fried and still crispy. Nothing tastes worse to me than slimy, mushy, over-cooked vegetables. The smell of them reminds me of that week old pond water in a jar that you'd bring into sixth grade science class to look at under a microscope, or maybe the smell at the bottom of a wet barrel of grass clippings that's sat in the sun too long, or a wet dog with bad breath.

I love cold sliced tomatoes and chopped tomatoes in salsa and I love spaghetti and pizza sauce but I hate, absolutely hate, hot tomatoes of any kind, in or on, or near any of my food. In my opinion, stewed tomatoes are absolutely disgusting. Big chunks of stewed tomatoes in my spaghetti sauce, or sliced hot tomatoes on my pizza; the thought alone makes me want to vomit hot tomato chunks. As I mentioned, I love *cold* sliced tomatoes, especially if they're on a hot or cold sandwich, but if they're on a hot sandwich I have to eat them fast before they themselves become hot and therefore disgusting.

And speaking of pizza, keep it simple for Pete's sake! Sauce and cheese and one or two other toppings is enough already! I've eaten slices of pizza before (but only free ones) that had sauce and cheese and pepperoni and sausage and mushrooms and three different kinds of peppers and two different kinds of onions and ham and pineapple chunks and shredded chicken and anchovies and olives and yes... those disgusting hot tomato slices. Eating a slice of pizza like that is like trying to gag down a hot salad with chunks of meat in it. Who does that and actually enjoys it? Not me. I choose to torture my intestinal tract with hot peppers and hot sauce instead. I'm addicted to the stuff. If I'm not sweating bullets, it's not hot enough. If I don't immediately gasp and grab blindly for a glass of ice water or a cold beer with tears in my eyes, it's not nearly hot enough.

And speaking of beer, although I enjoy drinking beer on occasion, I'm not a fan of micro-brews. To me, they always taste home-made for some reason. I prefer *professional* beer. Micro-brews taste like some amateur brew master threw in way too many ingredients (the same goes for banana splits and Italian soups and of course; deluxe pizzas - enough with the ingredients already!). When I drink a beer I don't want to feel like I'm eating a mouthful of berries or a bowl of oatmeal granola. I don't want to feel like I'm drinking barley-flavored malt or brandy-flavored-hops or strong, wheat-flavored ice coffee. When I drink a beer, I don't want to think about the beer I'm drinking. It should just taste good in a simple way without any unnecessary, extemporaneous ingredients confusing the situation. When I drink a beer, I don't want to question what I'm drinking, become surprised by it, or feel obligated to critique it with my friends...

"My heavens, this beer tastes like lemon-raspberry lavender potpourri on a sunny spring morning in the foothills of the snow-capped Bavarian Alps, but with a nutty flavor!"

"It's really that good?"

"It is I tell you!"

"Let me have a sip, I might order one... Wow, you're right! The flavors are literally dancing on my tongue! My taste buds are having tiny orgasms!"

Even though it wouldn't make much noise, I can almost hear *real* Bavarian brew masters rolling over in their graves. And then there are those Brits, ah yes, the Brits who try to ruin beer altogether by brewing their own dark, thick, disgusting version of it. And to make matters worse, they serve it warm for God's sake! I wouldn't pour that rot-gut Guinness Stout down my toilet for fear that it might ruin my pipes. British beer reminds me of that tobacco juice that squirts out of a squashed grasshopper. Who the hell wants to drink that disgusting swill? Not me.

So, I was out with my friends, we'd finished our appetizers and our ridiculous, tutti-frutti beers (there weren't any normal lagers or pilsners on the café's ridiculous drink menu) when our incredibly annoying waiter asks us for the umpteenth time in the past twenty minutes, "Is everything okay? Can I get you anything else?"

We shook our heads "No" to those very same questions he'd already asked us during every interrupted bite of our food that we'd taken that evening.

So the waiter begins removing dirty dishes and empty glasses from our table. As he's doing so, it seems as if he's expecting us to thank him for doing his job; "Are you finished with this...? I'll get this out of the way for you."

He'll do it *for* us? What does that mean? Are we supposed to do it ourselves but he's such a nice guy he'll do it *for* us?

Gee whiz thanks, waiter! If that dirty dish and empty glass had sat there any longer, I would have died! You saved my life so I'll leave you an even bigger tip now because I won't have to take that dirty dish and empty glass back to the kitchen myself and hand it to the dishwasher where I would have slipped on your disgustingly greasy floor and cracked my skull wide open and died!

On his umpteenth plus one stop at our table, the waiter asked us, "Will you be dining with us tonight, or would you care for a dessert perhaps? We have pomegranate kiwi sorbet with black maple syrup over sweet rice, or pickled caramel truffles topped with cloves and strawberry drizzle."

"Got any apple pie?" I asked him.

"Sorry, no."

"Check please."

So we paid the check and made our way out the door when someone in our party suggested, "Anyone up for a double-minted triple-chocolate mocha with whipped dairy cream?"

Oddly enough, everyone was except me. So I ditched my party and went to the bar in the bowling alley next door.

The bartender there asked me, "What are you drinking?"

"Nothing yet," I said.

He walked away immediately. I think he was jealous of my keen sense of humor so I just sat there and tried to make sense of the inverted labels on the liquor bottles hanging upside down in front of me. After having waited on a few other customers and taking his sweet time about it, the bartender sauntered over to me and asked, "Would you like to order a drink now?"

I said, "How about a Premium Dry Ice Genuine Draft Cold Filtered Ultra Lager Light and a bag of those chips?"

"Bottle or tap?" he asked.

I wondered; draft beer in a *bottle?* Is that like, fresh frozen? I chose tap.

"Barbecue, sour cream and onion, sea salt and vinegar, peppercorn, chipotle, cheddar or regular chips?" he asked.

"Regular," I said, because I like to keep things simple.

Ten minutes later, a wannabe gang of droopy-drawer punks walked into the place. They started shooting pool and playing loud obnoxious rap music on the juke box because the bowling alley wasn't nearly noisy enough already.

So I chugged my beer, threw three dollars on the bar and walked out of the place munching on what was left of my chips. Two blocks later, I ran into my friends/roommates as they were leaving the Extended Pinky Coffee Shop.

"Hungry?" they asked me in silly unison.

"A little," I said, as I brushed potato chip crumbs off my chin with my crumb-covered fingers.

"We were thinking pizza," they said.

"I'm in!" I said, because at three hundred and thirty-five pounds, I always was.

My three friends decided to share a four-slice, disgustingly deluxe personal-size pizza. I ordered a twelve-slice pepperoni pizza for myself and one of Giuseppe's famous 128oz. Pepsis that requires two hands to hold onto and comes with a straw the diameter of a garden hose. After finishing my own pizza, I helped the girls finish theirs by gagging down the last disgustingly deluxe slice. The girls eat like birds and show it. I don't think any of them weigh more than a hundred pounds which is a good thing I guess because if they did, we'd never fit into our queen-size bed. Did I mention that despite the fact that the four of us share a tiny one-bedroom apartment, life for me is pretty darn good? Well, it is and it got even better that night when we went home and shared a little late-night dessert, if you know what I mean.

So we left the pizza joint and found my car right where I had parked it, dog-gone-it! I always leave my keys in the ignition with the hope that somebody might steal my car so I can get a better one with the insurance money. But there it was; right where I'd left it because apparently, nobody else wants it either. If gas weren't so darn expensive I'd leave my car running to sweeten the deal but with my luck it would still be there with an empty gas tank when I returned. For some reason, the girls always complain when they have to push my crappy car home while I steer. To be fair though, it *is* kind of tough for them in high heels. So we jumped in my car and it started up, thank goodness, and then we headed on home. Destiny sat up front with me as usual because she's my best friend and she likes to play with my radio even though it only gets AM stations now (the FM button broke off last week). So we listened to static classic rock and static gospel and static hillbilly music while Gypsy and Bambi giggled in the backseat.

The four of us left Kansas together after graduating high school last year. I told the girls back then that I'd take them to California so they could become movie stars while I started my own dot com empire. I work in sales now during the day, mostly Marvel and DC at the comic book store and I DJ for the girls most nights. They're professional dancers at a gentlemen's club, although after six months working there, we've yet to see any gentlemen in the crowd. But we have fun and get along good and laugh and head to the beach on days off where the girls work on their tans and I work on my sunburnt freckle collection. The girls rub baby lotion on me at night so I don't peel too much. It's slimy but it feels good.

So we made it home that night and the girls jumped in the shower together while I played video games. The girls are always running around our apartment half-naked or totally so trying to distract me, but I'm real good at ignoring them as I score mega points in the Third Realm of Zor and my on-line buddies hate me as usual. My buds hate me even more when they catch a sneak-peek of the girls running around naked in the background of my web-cam. Later that night, when the girls had settled into bed I decided that it was time for some late-night dessert, if you know what I mean. So I got up from the sofa on my third try, stretched, yawned, scratched, and then made my way to the fridge to see if there was any left-over cheesecake.

"Dog-gone-it!" I complained to myself. "I must have finished it all last night."

"I'm heading to 7-11!" I shouted. "You girls want anything?"

Bambi came running out from the bedroom bare-chested in her pink panties and shrieked, "I do... I do... but I don't know what I want. Can I come with you...?"

She's such a pest.

Ivana

He lost his virginity suddenly and unexpectedly and happily during his second week of summer camp in June of 1952. He recalled it quite vividly. At the time, he was familiar with the so-called "birds and bees" but it was mostly nothing more than a mysterious fable to him. Although he understood the schoolbook mechanics of copulation and reproduction, he could not comprehend how it would manifest itself in terms of actual physical sensation. But he had often wondered. He had experienced the way things functioned on his end, but he had no convincing idea of what awaited him in that; oh so mysterious realm of womanhood. His increasing desire for sexual adventure expanded his imagination. His imagination in turn, fueled the flames of his desire. His desire tested the limits of his patience while the actual experience remained a faraway fantasy that was often so temptingly close and yet, so far out of reach. Both he and his epiphany came easily and suddenly in the splendid form of the summer camp's forty-two year old nurse; Miss Ivana Lovue. She, the camp nurse, was a down-to-earth, hard-working yet fun-loving French expatriate who spoke excellent English albeit with a charming and sexy accent. Although she was stunningly statuesque; tall and shapely, strong yet feminine, she was neither glamorous nor particularly beautiful in the traditional sense. But he was nevertheless mesmerized by the enigmatic appeal of her unique and exotic allure. From the moment that he'd first laid eyes on her ten days prior, he had found Miss Lovue to be totally and utterly irresistible. He was left in absolute awe of her. Ivana Lovue was an erotic goddess who had cast him easily under her sensuous spell long before she had casually suggested that he join her in bed. And when she did suggest it, the earth immediately stopped turning beneath his feet; his time had finally come! He could not have imagined another woman lying before him then. He gazed upon Ivana as one would a classically painted figure; with a deep sense of reverence and admiration that transcended superficial earthly lust. In his prejudiced eyes she was a living, breathing masterpiece of exquisite feminine form. At her gracefully seasoned age, Ivana Lovue may have lost her pristine youthfulness, but Lewis found her to be perfectly soft and warm and delicious indeed both inside and out. She was a delectable slice of heaven, a most wonderful and gratifying experience and was in his opinion, oh, so terribly sexy!

"Miss Lovue..."

"Ivana please, Lewis."

"Miss Ivana," Lewis continued, "did I... did I... do okay?"

"You did just fine, Lewis. *Quite* fine I might add," she said as she lay on her back and stared contentedly at the sloping beams of her cabin roof.

"It happened to be my very first time in case you weren't aware," Lewis confessed.

"Well, you performed like a pro, my dear boy," she said and then she rolled onto her side to peck him thankfully on his cheek.

"I assume that it wasn't *your* first time," Lewis queried.

"You assume correctly, Lewis. It was my four thousand nine hundred and ninetieth time."

"Wow, you actually keep count?" Lewis asked astonished as he propped himself up on his elbows.

"It's a rough estimate, Lewis. Let's just say... five thousand times give or take a few hundred," she explained, a sly and mischievous smile curling her lips.

"Wow, five-thousand times! And my very first attempt was, as you say... quite fine?"

"I have no complaints whatsoever, Lewis. In fact, I very much look forward to your second attempt. Do you?" she asked temptingly.

"To be honest, Miss Ivana..."

"Lewis, please, just Ivana, no?"

"Sorry, to be honest, *Ivana*... I really didn't know what to expect. I really didn't know how good having sex would be, how *pleasurable* it would be. But now that I do know I have to say that I'd very much like to make love with you on a regular basis."

"Ha-ha! It's settled then. We will make love again and again until you tire of me."

"I can't imagine that ever happening, Ivana. I mean... I can imagine *making love* to you again... right now, this very instant in fact, but I *can't imagine* ever tiring of you."

"They all do eventually," she claimed.

"They?"

"Men do, men tire of their women and then move on to others."

"And women don't?" he asked.

"Not nearly as often, Lewis. Women are usually more dedicated to their lovers than men are. Women find themselves more emotionally attached whereas men have a tendency to be more physically attracted. Men are genetically programmed slaves to sex and therefore constantly seek to satisfy their unabashed insatiable lust with whoever can best fulfill it. Soon enough, you will find a much younger, sexier,

Ivana

more beautiful woman and forget all about Ivana. You'll see."

"Don't be so sure, Ivana. It took me long enough to find my first, sexy, beautiful lover. I'm in no hurry whatsoever to find another," he said as he slid his arm across her soft bare hips and gazed lovingly into her gorgeous, sparkling green eyes.

"You are quite the Don Juan," she said and then she smiled and blushed while batting her long black eyelashes playfully like a shy and serious schoolgirl would.

Lewis leaned in for a passionate kiss. And then he leaned in further and then even further still for his second encounter.

As it turned out, their second experience was even more incredible for him and even more satisfying to her. The couple became then, physically addicted to one another as their third and fourth encounters followed thereafter late into the night and drove them both into a state of euphoric exhaustion until they lay again, motionless, in the dark cabin.

Ivana switched on her night-table lamp. She lit a cigarette, puffed it lightly and then blew a vertical column of blue smoke up and into the air. It hung suspended momentarily like a pillar of spun wool but was then suddenly turned away as it rushed out of the cabin's screen window toward the starlit night sky. She puffed again lightly and asked Lewis quietly if he would like a puff. When she didn't hear an immediate reply she knew, without looking in his direction, that the poor boy had fallen fast asleep. She was grateful for that. Lewis had worn the old girl out something fierce. He'd given her the thrill-ride of her life and she'd smiled through it all like a wide-eyed schoolgirl at a summer carnival. Ivana slept soundly and deeply for the first time in weeks that night. She dreamt of a long, soothing, sleepy ride home to her childhood farmhouse in the French countryside.

- 64 -

"Ivana," her father whispered as he rocked his daughter gently by her shoulder, "wake up, dear, we are home now."

"Papa?" she asked through trembling pursed lips as her eyes opened slightly to the cool night air.

"Yes, Ivana, it is me, my dear. We are home now."

"Oh, Papa, I'm too sleepy to walk. Can you carry me please?" she asked him and then she closed her eyes and fell back to sleep.

Her aging father slipped his strong muscular arms beneath his daughter and slid her gently off the seat of his farm truck. He gathered her up and held her close to his heart with one hand and closed the truck's door as quietly as he could with his other. He carried her the fifty paces to their farmhouse where he laid her down gently on her soft feather bed. She rolled over subconsciously onto her side facing her father and brought her knees up toward her chest. Anton Lovue draped a warm thick quilt atop his daughter. He tucked her in snugly and kissed her silky soft, six year old cheek.

"Ivana..." Lewis whispered as he brushed her long black hair away from her sleeping eyes, "...it's time to wake up now."

"Papa?" she asked through pursed lips as she opened her eyes ever so slightly to the cool morning air.

"Papa?" Lewis asked gently.

"Louie," she said, opening her eyes wider to the new day, "so sorry, dear, I was dreaming."

"Was it a good dream?" he asked.

"It was indeed," she said and then she sat up and pulled Lewis to her breast, "and it was a wonderful night as well," she whispered in his ear.

Lewis thought then, for a few brief moments, that he too had been dreaming.

Ivana Lovue's private cabin was somewhat isolated from the rest of the camp. It was situated alone amongst a thick stand of maple trees down a short dirt path off the camp's main gravel road. Lewis walked that path back toward the main road, a new man that morning. He felt strong yet relaxed, content and so alive! He breathed in the fresh morning air and savored its sweetness. The birds sang their songs just for him that morning. He winked grateful approval to them all. His footsteps floated inches off the ground as he gazed into the memory of Ivana's beautiful green eyes. He arrived back at his own cabin just as both of his cabin-mates were leaving through the screen door.

"Well, well...! Good morning, Lewis!" Jack greeted his friend with sudden surprise.

"Late night, Lewis?" his cabin-mate Sam inquired.

"Yes it is, Jack, and yes it was, Sam," Lewis replied, smiling.

"Do tell!" Jack urged.

"Yes, do tell!" Sam agreed.

"Later, chums, I've got to freshen up quick. I'll catch up with you at breakfast."

"We'll save you a seat in the mess hall, but only if you tell all," Jack offered.

"It's a bargain then," Lewis agreed as he entered the cabin leaving his younger, fellow camp counselors to continue on their way.

At the time, Lewis was a twenty-four year old professor of English Literature at the local college. He was working his first summer camp counseling job in order to supplement his less-than-generous, junior professor salary. His cabin sat in a row of three others lined up along the camp's main gravel road. The men's open-air communal shower stalls were tucked in behind the men's cabins. As Lewis stood upon the wet, wood plank floor of one of the stalls, he bathed himself in heaps of soap suds. He was singing an old Civil War victory song when Ivana happened to stroll by. She recognized his voice immediately and wandered off the road toward it.

"I didn't know you could sing," she announced suddenly as she peeked over the top of his stall.

"Ivana, good Lord!" Lewis said startled as he washed suds out of his eyes. "You'll get us both fired I say!"

"Nonsense, my boy, everyone's sat down to breakfast by now. We are alone, yet again. May I join you for a quick rinse?"

By the time that Lewis had swung the stall's door open, Ivana had tossed her dress over the top of the adjacent stall and was standing before him dis-robed. She entered the shower stall squeaking like a child at the shock of cold water. She grabbed Lewis tightly in her arms.

"Louie, I'm freezing! Please warm me up," she pleaded to which he willingly complied by rubbing her bare back and legs vigorously with his strong, soapy hands. The couple kissed deeply as they rinsed themselves off; their excited, chilled bodies becoming warmer. Lewis dried Ivana with his towel and then dried himself as she slipped back into her dress. The couple dashed then into his cabin and quickly combed one another's hair without the benefit of a mirror. They both desperately wanted to dive onto Lewis' cot but they decided against it and were on the camp's road in a matter of minutes. The couple hurried along hand-in-hand, but as they approached the mess hall they separated and walked farther apart. So as not to cause a scandal, Ivana entered the mess hall alone while Lewis hesitated outside. He had never been happier in his life. He smiled on the outside while laughing ecstatically on the inside, until that is, when he was suddenly reminded by his growling belly that he was nearly famished.

"Slow down, mate, you'll choke to death," Jack warned his friend as Lewis shoveled massive bites of pancakes into his grateful gullet.

"I skipped... dinner... last night... I'm starving..." Lewis explained as he chewed and swallowed quickly pausing briefly to wipe pancake syrup from his chin with the back of his hand.

"Yeah, we know that, Lewis," Jack reminded him, "but what we *don't* know is *who* you skipped dinner *with*. We can't recall which of the girls was missing from the mess hall last night. Was it... Rebecca...? I'll bet it was Rebecca, Sam."

"You'd lose that bet, Jack," Lewis said as he sliced a sausage link in two and then swallowed the halves in two quick bites.

"Okay... then who was she?" Jack whispered loudly over the din of the mess hall roar. "Was it Suzanne?"

"I'm not the type to kiss and tell," Lewis announced.

"So it *was* Suzanne! You dog... you *lucky* dog you!" Jack proclaimed.

"Believe what you will but I'll tell you this much, mates; I'll be walking like a saddle-sore cowboy the rest of the day."

Jack and Sam gazed over at the women's table. They surveyed the selection of the fine, fairer sex and easily found the blonde and buxom Suzanne sitting like a Hollywood movie starlet among her less-glamorous girlfriends. Ivana happened to meet the boys' gaze. She smiled at them both.

"Suzanne *is* quite the looker, Lewis, but do you know who I wouldn't mind bedding down with?" Sam asked him.

"Who?" Jack interrupted.

"Ivana," Sam announced.

Lewis froze for an instant as he processed Sam's sudden and unexpected confession.

"Ivana, Ivana the nurse?" Jack objected. "Be serious now, Sam, she's old enough to be your mother!"

"Maybe so, Jack, and say what you will, but there is something very sexy about that woman. I just can't put my finger on it," Sam said, a bit flustered.

"Oh… I'll bet you *could* put your finger on it, mate. All you'd have to do is ask her. A woman like that would jump at the chance for a fresh piece of boy-meat such as yourself," Jack suggested. "What do you think, Lewis?"

"I'm too busy eating to think right now," Lewis lied as he looked up in Ivana's direction, caught her eye and then smiled. "Ask me again later," he suggested as he snatched two slices of toasted butter-bread from a tin platter and then grabbed a jar of apple butter from the mess hall's varnished barn-wood table top.

"That Robbie Roberts sure is a looker isn't he, girls?" Wendy asked her friends around the table as they took turns glancing indiscreetly in the direction of the men's table.

"I'd say so," Rebecca agreed.

"He may be a looker but rumor has it, Robbie prefers boys to girls," Suzanne reported.

"No…!" Rebecca said, astonished.

"Tis true, Becky, or so says that cute dishwasher who works in the kitchen. Robbie flirted with him just last week."

"Frankie told you that, Suzanne?" Wendy asked.

"Well, not directly, but I heard it through the grapevine."

"I don't believe it, Suzanne. I've spoken to Robbie privately myself, many times. On one occasion he touched my wrist affectionately as we did so," Wendy claimed.

"I'm afraid that proves nothing, dear girl. Boys like that are affectionate to everyone; boys *and* girls. Am I right, Ivana?" Suzanne asked her.

"I suppose that homosexuals *might* be more affectionate than their heterosexual counterparts, but I wouldn't be so quick to judge anyone based on rumors alone," Ivana warned.

"Well, handsome or not, homosexual or not, he's not my type anyway," Suzanne said, haughtily.

"So, who *would be* your type, Suzanne? Jack...?" Wendy guessed.

"Jack is nice, and he *is* funny that's for sure, but he's such a boy, such a typical boy," Suzanne said.

"Sam?" Rebecca suggested, adding, "Personally, I like Sam. He reminds me of a dear boy I dated my junior year of high school; the all-American, take home to meet your father type of boy."

"Sam is nice too, but he's too run-of-the-mill for my taste," Suzanne claimed.

"So, who then, Suzanne? Which of those nine, eligible bachelors suits your discreet taste?" Wendy challenged her.

"For some reason... the older guy does something for me. I don't know what it is exactly but he seems strong and vigorous and sexy in some mysterious way. I'd bet he'd know *exactly* how to treat a lady and make her feel like a *real* woman inside."

"My word, Suzanne, you're causing me vapors!" Rebecca cried as she blushed and then took a long sip of ice water.

"I assume you're referring to Lewis?" Wendy assumed.

"Why yes I am; Lewis is his name. We've only spoken once

but I've thought of him often since then. I've even thought of him more deeply on occasion while lying in bed at night," Suzanne confessed.

"Suzanne, Dear Lord!" Rebecca cried out as she choked on her drink.

Wendy laughed and then she flipped her long brown hair and shook it in jest as she winked at Suzanne. Ivana patted Becky's back gently at first but then more sharply as the poor girl continued to choke. Ivana kept patting the girl's back until Becky finally cleared her throat and resumed breathing.

"What do you think, Ivana?" Suzanne asked. "You've been married before right?"

"I have, twice in fact. My first husband was killed in the war while I sat home crying. My second husband was also killed in the war while I served as an army nurse."

"How tragic!" Rebecca cried as she laid her and on Ivana's wrist.

"I'm so sorry," Suzanne said sadly.

"As am I," Wendy added.

"Oh girls, thank you kindly but I was so very young in those days. It seems now, like such a long time ago. I'd seen things in army medic units back then that would either break a person or make them stronger. Fortunately, they made me stronger. I've had many years to overcome my grief and have led quite an enjoyable life much of that time."

"So you didn't remarry?" Wendy asked.

"I've been a widow ever since," Ivana said. "But I haven't often been alone."

"Well, I'd say that's quite the right attitude," Suzanne said smiling; "see the world, enjoy life, dine wherever you choose and enjoy a variety of men for desert."

"Dear me, Suzanne! What *have* you been *reading* lately, *Hollywood Confidential?*" Becky asked astounded.

The other women giggled and smiled and continued eating their breakfast, pausing occasionally to see if any of the men were looking their way. As they were just about finished eating, Suzanne asked Ivana, "I assume that you've given all of those eligible men their physicals so tell me, Ivana, which of them would you recommend as suitable lovers?"

Rebecca gasped out loud. She went white in the face and fainted head first onto the table. Ivana, Wendy and Suzanne immediately jumped to her rescue. They pulled the poor girl off the table and got her quickly standing up on her feet. They walked Rebecca slowly toward the front door and then led her outside into the fresh and cool morning air. In the typically boisterous melee of the mess hall, none of the two hundred grade school campers had even noticed that Rebecca had fainted. All nine of the male camp counselors however, *had* noticed and they watched as the women left the building. When Lewis had stood up to offer his assistance, Ivana looked in his direction, smiled, and then gave him a thankful and reassuring nod. Suzanne, having noticed some sort of connection between Lewis and Ivana, gave Lewis a mischievous wink and a sexy smile. She then licked the upper row of her pearly white teeth slowly. Jack elbowed Sam in his ribs. They had both witnessed the vixen Suzanne flirting with their lucky friend Lewis. Envious, they let out a simultaneous sigh and then watched as Suzanne's fine hips swung and sauntered away.

"We're confused, Lewis," Jack announced as the three cabin mates lay on their bunks the following evening.

"How's that, Jack?" Lewis asked by the light of his oil lamp as he continued to write in his journal.

"Well... may I be blunt, Lewis?" Jack asked.

"By all means, yes you may. We're all friends here," Lewis suggested as he turned a page and continued writing.

"Well, don't get me wrong, Lewis, because I wouldn't want to hurt your feelings in any way whatsoever but... if I may be so bold... and honest..."

"For God's sake, Jack, ask the question already," Sam complained.

"I *am* asking the question, knucklehead! If you'd just shut up and listen and let me finish," Jack retorted and then he continued as Lewis laid his journal down to rest on his belly. "Let's be honest, Lewis, you're no Clark Gable or Cary Grant, but then again... neither are Sam or I, so we were just wondering, just curious is all, how it was that you got that knock-out Suzanne Sheppard to sleep with you?"

"I didn't," Lewis replied.

"You didn't sleep with Suzanne Sheppard?" Jack asked.

"No, I didn't," Lewis insisted.

"Okay, so you didn't *sleep* with her so to speak, but did you, you know... have *sex* with her?" Jack pressed.

"No sleeping and no sexing with her either," Lewis said.

"*Sexing*, that's a new one on me. I like it!" Sam announced as he sat up enthusiastically on his bunk.

Jack became anxious as he continued his interrogation, "Okay, now I'm *really* confused, Lewis. Who was it then that you slept with?"

"I can't tell you, Jack. Sorry, boys, I just can't break that personal trust. I *can* tell you though that it was fantastic! It was out of this world, wild and wonderful, indescribably delicious!" Lewis teased his friends.

"Wow… *delicious,*" Sam repeated aloud, wondering to himself in what way exactly, would sex be delicious?

"Fair enough, Lewis," Jack conceded, "at least our confusion over the subject of Suzanne has been settled. So you slept with another girl. You said earlier that it wasn't Rebecca and say now it wasn't Suzanne so that leaves, let's see… four or five other girls, and Nurse Ivana and… Rosie in the kitchen… you didn't sleep with Rosie did you, Lewis? Please tell me that you didn't have sex with Rosie!"

"No, Jack, I am not hot-to-trot for Rosie," Lewis reported.

"Thank God almighty! I'd lose all respect for you if you were," Jack warned.

"And I'd hate to lose your respect, Jack," Lewis said as he set his journal down on his mattress, swung his legs over the side of his bunk and then stood tall and stretched. "I think I'll get some fresh air before I turn in, mates," he announced as he pulled on a pair of trousers and slipped into his moccasins.

"Tell Rosie we said hi!" Sam said jokingly as Lewis stepped out through the cabin's screen door.

"I will if I see her on the way to Suzanne's cabin," Lewis promised his friends.

Sam and Jack both, hurled their pillows in Lewis' direction and then looked at one another, at first astonished but then confused and jealous.

"I say he *did* sleep with Suzanne and he's just trying to protect her reputation is all," Jack concluded.

"Uh, I don't think Lewis would lie to us though. He's such a stand-up guy," Sam said in defense of his friend.

"Well, mine would stand-up and throb for Suzanne," Jack insisted. "Can you imagine it, Sam? My God almighty!"

The two young men lay on their bunks that night trying to imagine it. Neither of them came close. It drove them both wild with lust while attempting to do so. Jack bit his lip and then yelled, "Oh, Suzanne!" to himself as he quickly finished his intense fantasy and then fell asleep exhausted. Sam on the other hand, succumbed more slowly, more romantically, before his thoughts drifted off to less-exciting topics of major league baseball and his upcoming classes the next semester.

"You're out late this evening, ladies," Lewis said to Suzanne and another girl he came upon along the camp's gravel road a few hundred paces from his cabin.

"Well, hello there... Lewis... it is, as I recollect?" Suzanne asked as she swept stray strands of hair from her face.

"Lewis it is, Suzanne, and... I'm sorry...?"

"This is my friend Marsha," Suzanne interjected, flattered that Lewis had already known her own name.

"Hello, Marsha. I've seen you down at the swimming pool. You are quite the springboard diver."

"Why thank you kindly, Lewis," Marsha said in a charming Southern drawl. "I swim nearly year round in Mississippi so I've ample opportunity to practice my diving as well."

"My heavens, you're quite the aquatic athlete. What brings you up North this summer?"

"My uncle arranged this job for me. I've been staying with him and my aunt up here these past few summers between semesters so momma can run around with her boyfriends unfettered," she said matter-of-factly.

"I see," Lewis said, a bit taken aback by the girl's candor.

"It seems to me perhaps, that your momma's behavior might suggest that Southern Belles aren't what they used to be," Suzanne said snippily, having felt that she'd been ignored and left out of the conversation.

"I blame *that* on her good-for-nothing, philandering drunk of a husband, her ex-husband, my so-called father," Marsha said in her mother's defense. "A woman has the right to live her own life too. Don't you agree, Lewis?"

"As a matter-of-fact I do, Marsha, and I admire your fortitude at such a young age," Lewis said with a smile.

"I'm not really that young you know," Marsha said shyly as she stepped a little closer to Lewis and gazed up admiringly into his kind, brown eyes. "I'll be a senior at Mississippi State this year. After I earn my degree in education, I plan to work a few years before I find a nice man to settle down with, unless of course, something were to change those plans. One never can tell."

"Right you are, Marsha," Lewis agreed. "What grade would you like to teach?"

"I hope to teach either second or third grade because I absolutely adore kids that age. These feisty little campers running around here all day long have given me delightful experience that I hope to utilize in the classroom. But it sure would be nice to take a break from them for a while and spend time with a grown man for a change... or so I'd imagine," she said bravely but then thought better of her bravery as she became embarrassed by her forwardness.

"It's just..." she continued a bit flustered, "well it's just *hard* on a girl my age to ignore those feelings altogether and do nothing but study nine months out of the year and work all summer long."

"So you don't have a boyfriend in college?" Lewis asked, sensing her embarrassment and hoping to put her at ease.

"No one special. Southern boys tend not to suit me. I blame *that* on my father as well," Marsha explained.

Lewis smiled at the pretty, innocent young woman; a delicate fawn he thought, but one who was not afraid to speak her mind. He liked that about her. He had noticed her before in the mess hall, but only from a distance. He'd gotten a much better look at her at the swimming pool. She was wearing a one-piece bathing suit and a swim cap. He recalled enjoying what he'd seen. Standing there then, she looked even more beautiful; long silky, strawberry-blonde hair, bright bluish-green eyes, delicate shoulders and a slender but shapely figure. It was hard to imagine her as such a good athlete. It was much easier to imagine her in other ways.

"Well now… maybe I ought to leave you two love birds to your selves," Suzanne said in a huff as she turned and then began to walk away down the road.

"Suzanne, please," Lewis pleaded, "let me walk you two back to your cabin, okay? It's much too dark for pretty ladies such as you to be walking alone in these woods."

Suzanne stopped, turned around, smiled at Lewis and then extended her hand toward him. He and Marsha caught up with her. Suzanne grabbed Lewis' hand firmly in her own. The trio walked along the road toward the girls' cabin. Suddenly, an owl hooted loudly from the branch of a tree overhead. Suzanne shrieked and wrapped her arms around Lewis' waist. She pressed her breasts tightly to his chest and buried her head on his shoulder. Marsha giggled softly, not having been spooked at all by the owl. As Lewis looked up through the tree's branches and into the starlit night sky, Marsha slipped her hand into his. Lewis returned his gaze back down to earth where it was met by Marsha's warm, sparkling eyes.

"Rosie says hi!" Lewis announced as he burst through his cabin's screen door but then moved about quietly after having realized that his bunkmates were sleeping.

Sam snored loudly. Jack, startled, quickly tossed his blanket over his exposed self and the *Hollywood Starlet* magazine he'd been ogling. He pretended then to be asleep. Lewis lit his oil lamp and settled into his bunk. He opened the cover of his journal and thought immediately of Ivana. As he did so however, his subconscious thoughts drifted. Marsha was such a beautiful and delightful young woman. He'd felt totally at ease with her from the very first moment. It was as if they'd known each other for a very long time. He imagined her in her bathing suit as she removed her swim cap adorned with pink rubber flowers. He watched as she shook sparkling water from her hair. He imagined her silky hair in his fingers. He imagined her lips pressed against his own, her wet swimsuit pressing firmly against his chest. He felt the sweeping curve of her back and the gentle curves of her hips. He felt the warmth and shape of her body beneath the cool, damp fabric of her bathing suit. Her lips tasted like roses and chlorine as she pressed them against his mouth. He felt himself suddenly mad with desire. He had just recently experienced first-hand, the incredible intimate pleasures a woman has to offer and they had far exceeded his wildest expectations. It was at that very moment that he longed for Ivana. She could satisfy him easily in a matter of shuttering moments. He would tremble with joy inside her and collapse gratefully into her arms. Lewis thought then again of Marsha. He imagined that she too could do the same for him. He wondered in which ways it might be different with her. She didn't resemble Ivana at all on the outside, would she feel different on the inside as well?

Lewis thought that she wouldn't but he realized then, that he would love to know for sure.

Ivana lay awake on her warm soft bed. She missed Lewis madly and wished that he'd come back to her that night. They had decided earlier that day though, to play it safe. They would rendezvous again after that week's campers had gone home. And when that time would finally come, at that very moment, they would enjoy each other again and again until a new wave of campers invaded the next day.

"May I help you?" Nurse Lovue asked, glancing over the top of her reading spectacles as she sat behind her desk, pen in hand.

"I have dull ache in my chest," the patient who had entered her office announced.

"I see. And how long have you had this ache?"

"It's been three days now."

"I'm sorry to hear that. Please unbutton your shirt and take a seat. I'll be with you in a moment."

Ivana completed the pharmaceutical requisition form she had been filing out by signing her name in graceful, flowing loops. She folded the form and slipped it into an envelope. She licked the envelope's flap, sealed the flap closed, licked a stamp which she patted down atop the envelope's corner. She stood up from her desk then, facing her patient.

"You seem quite adept at licking things," he remarked.

"Thank you. It is one of my many talents."

She sat down on a chair facing her patient and pressed the cold end of her stethoscope on his warm bare chest.

Their eyes met.

"Breathe in deeply," she told him.

He breathed in deeply. As he did so however, he slipped the fingertips of his right hand across her left knee and then slowly up and under the hem of her starched white dress. As he took a second breath per her instructions, his hand slid further up and along the smooth silk stocking that stretched tightly around her leg.

"Good, and again please," she instructed.

Her patient breathed in deeply again as he slipped his left hand as well, under the hem of her dress and slid it up and along the top of her right leg. Both of his hands found her soft upper thighs. It was there that they gripped her. He pressed his thumbs downward and inward, one toward the other until they reached the point where her legs met. Nurse Lovue sighed but remained motionless. Her patient spread his hands slowly across her lower belly and then gripped her hips firmly. He pulled her and her chair closer.

"Very good," she whispered as she bent forward pressing her chest against her patient's warm lips.

"I love the way you smell," he said in muffled tones.

"Thank you," she said, sighing. "You feel warm. I'm afraid that you may be running a fever."

He slipped his right hand off her hip. He reached around her and then under her where he found her soft backside. He pressed up against her bottom with the underside of his wrist. The fingers of his left hand on her belly, slid slowly in between her legs. They pressed further beneath her until they reached the fingers of his right hand. He cupped her and lifted her up and then down again slowly. She became warmer and wetter and more willing as she slid to the edge of her chair rising up on her toes. She moaned and spread her legs further apart. His fingers pressed inside her. She closed her eyes and bit her lower lip as she held her patient's head to her chest. He bit a button on her blouse and pushed his face into her bosom. She reached down with one hand and pulled her patient's belt buckle toward her. She slipped her other hand deep inside his trousers. The couple writhed against one another and sighed. They became warmer and wetter as they moaned in unison. The bells on Ivana's alarm clock rang loudly as the hammer between them struck repeatedly without mercy. Ivana pulled her hands out from between her quivering legs and reached for the obnoxious clock. Its hands pointed six and twelve; time for a new day. Ivana lay back down for a moment to catch her first, waking breath. She exhaled slowly and smiled as her quivering finally subsided. Soon thereafter, she became anxious.

Five bright yellow school buses rumbled into the gravel turnabout in front of the camp's mess hall. The bus drivers shut off their engines and waited patiently for the onslaught. Two of the drivers smoked cigarettes while two others leafed through magazines. The fifth cleaned his fingernails with a pocketknife. None of the drivers had to wait very long. Soon after they'd arrived, the mess hall's double screen doors suddenly burst wide open expelling some two hundred screaming campers onto the building's broad porch.

With bellies full of morning pancakes and eyes filled with home-sick excitement, the campers' screaming intensified as they scrambled toward the busses. The drivers held up signs as they stood aside their bus doors. They asked for and then checked off from the lists on their clipboards; the names of the children who stepped aboard their busses. The process that particular week had gone unusually smooth. No campers were left crying and standing alone and confused on the camp's gravel road. By the time that the busses had been loaded with campers and their rucksacks, the camp's staff had assembled along the mess hall's porch railing for the ceremonial farewell. The staff waved goodbye to most of the campers and good riddance to more than a few trouble-makers. The campers waved back through the open bus windows until the busses belched and then roared away in loud clouds of sun-bleached dust.

The staff smiled en masse and let out a collective sigh of relief. Not a word was spoken. A strange and wonderful silence engulfed the campground for the first time that week. The birds in the trees could actually be heard singing that wonderful summer morning. The staff dispersed slowly from the wood plank porch. Their footsteps echoed across the tranquil campgrounds.

Most everyone quickly gathered up into cars to head into town for a quick afternoon and evening of freedom; a good restaurant-cooked meal, a first-run movie, a trip to the five-and-dime for a new bottle of shampoo, a few beers and games of billiards at the local tavern. Lewis and Ivana lingered behind, waiting anxiously. As soon as the campgrounds had become all but deserted, they ran laughing hand-in-hand to Ivana's cabin.

"So... how is your book coming along, dear?"
"Not bad. I hope. I've finished the first chapter."
"May I read it?"
"You may, my love."
"I bet it'll be wonderful, like all of your books."
"Let's hope so. It'd be nice to pad the kids' inheritance."

"Oh they'll be just fine, dear. Your talent and dedication and success have guaranteed that. So what is *this* book about?" his wife asked as she leaned over her husband's shoulder to peer at the page resting in his typewriter.

"Actually, it's semi-autobiographical. It's based on the life and times of my first lover."

"Oh my, that sounds exciting!"

"Parts are I suppose."

"Will I be jealous when I read it?"

"That's up to you, but since you've never been the jealous type, I'll guess no."

"Well, I think I'm *already* jealous; a book about your first lover? You've never written a book about me."

"Not yet anyway. Maybe I'm saving the best for last," he teased as he swiveled around in his typing chair and wrapped his strong, aging arms around his wife's soft, narrow waist.

She bent down and kissed him. He held her silky hair in his hands as she did so. He looked lovingly into her eyes and then said, "Actually, you're in *this* book, my love, although you make just a few cameo appearances I'm afraid."

"I'm in your book?" she asked excitedly as she jumped up to snatch the typewritten pages from the top of his desk.

"You are, my love, and in the first chapter no less."

- The Beginning -

Less is More

Lester Gives became the red-headed stepchild of Grayson Morehead who was a full-time Appalachian coal miner and a part-time undefeated amateur Saturday-night boxer. Grayson also happened to be a full-time drunkard who would, with or without provocation, beat anyone who got in his way and that included his own wife and children. Any man, woman or child unlucky enough to cross Grayson's drunken path or those foolish enough to seek subsequent revenge against his drunken tirades, would feel the full force and fury of his punishing jabs if not his deadly roundhouse knockout punch.

Lester's biological father, Neville Gives, ran off with his pregnant wife's younger sister shortly before Less was born. Lester's mother Betty turned to certain, illicit drugs; "pep pills" as they were called, in an attempt to battle the deep depression that she suffered as a result of her husband's abandonment. No matter her condition though, she always cared for her only-child and did her best to protect, provide for and comfort him. Betty worked full-time as a waitress at the local diner and cleaned the houses of the few wealthy folk in town on her days off. She took her son to church every Sunday where she prayed for her son's future while Lester prayed that his mother would be happy again someday.

After church, Betty and Lester would change into their dungarees for a picnic down by the river. They'd laugh and eat peanut butter sandwiches and then walk along the riverside trails enjoying the sunshine and each other. They'd save bread crumbs from their sandwiches to feed to the fish and then they'd skip flat stones across the flowing water.

"I love you, Less," his mother would often say.

"I love you more, Mom," Less always replied with a laugh.

Before they were married, Grayson Morehead often ate at the diner where Betty worked, leaving his kids home alone to fend for themselves. Grayson always smiled at Betty and asked her out several times but to no avail. One afternoon though, when Betty was in an unusually good mood, she finally agreed to go out with Grayson. One date led to another and before she realized it, Betty was finally happy again. Lester was happy for his mother as well. At first, Grayson treated Lester kindly and bought the boy ice cream cones. Lester loved watching Grayson box on Saturday nights. He never once saw the man lose a fight. Betty however, always stayed home alone on Saturday nights because fighting of any kind terrified her. After the fights, Less would return home to his mother and play cards with her while Grayson would run off with his pals to drink and get drunk and chase women. Betty and Lester continued on with their usual Sunday rituals while Grayson would be sleeping off his hangovers in bed with a loose woman or two all day long. Grayson's kids, as usual, were left at home alone to fend for themselves.

After six months of dating Grayson, Betty finally said, "yes," to the last of his numerous marriage proposals. She married Grayson on the courthouse steps where she became Mrs. Betty Gives Morehead. She had to say, "I do," twice because a passing fire engine had drowned out her first response. She moved herself and Lester in with Grayson and his seven children. Betty's renewed happiness lasted about a week because by the end of it, Grayson had begun beating her and Lester both and anyone else who happened to be within reach. Once again, Betty became drug-dependent and shortly thereafter was unfairly convicted of narcotics distribution when she was caught purchasing pep pills in the alley behind the diner where she worked. The actual drug dealer; a sheriff's nephew, was released without charge. Betty Morehead was tried, convicted and sentenced to fifteen years in the Anthrax County State Penitentiary where she languished in sorrow and regret. Lester wrote letters to his mother faithfully every week and visited her on the first of each month for the allotted twenty minutes allowed him by state law. He'd bring his mother cigarettes and magazines that he'd buy with the money he earned selling newspapers and shining shoes at the local barber shop. On Mother's Day and on her birthdays, Lester would bring his mother flowers. Those beautiful flowers brightened her prison cell and her spirits as well when she'd place them next to Lester's photograph. Less would make his mother a handmade greeting card every Christmas and he'd bring her favorite chocolates tucked away in a brand new pair of cozy red socks. Betty would wear and admire those socks while she'd lie on her bunk at night nibbling her chocolates. Lester did his very best to keep his mother's hopes alive and in so doing, without even knowing it, he kept her thoughts of suicide at bay.

Aside from his hair lip and slight limp, Lester was just like any other twelfth grade boy at Anthrax High School until that is, when he decided to come out of the closet and announce that he was homosexual. He did it suddenly and unexpectedly in welding shop class while the teacher was demonstrating the proper blending of oxygen and acetylene.

"I'm gay," Lester announced to his teacher and classmates.

Luckily for Lester, his best friends in the class intervened when the other boys and the shop teacher immediately began beating him mercilessly with welding rods and welding torches and with uncoiled lengths of gas hose. Lester's friends may have saved his life when they hustled him quickly through a back door of the classroom and into the safety of the school's parking lot. It was there that a security guard intervened between Lester's frightened contingent and the angry mob that was pursuing them. None of the mob's members were ever punished for what they had done but the school's welding program was suspended when the instructor was dismissed without pay for fondling one too many under-age girls at the school. No other certified welder in the area was willing to take a pay cut to teach their trade to young men at the high school so the welding shop was converted into a dumping ground for broken desks and bent lockers.

When Lester's stepfather returned home late one night, drunk as usual, Lester announced to him; "I'm gay." Upon hearing the news, Grayson Morehead began beating his red-headed stepson mercilessly. Lester's seven stepbrothers and stepsisters may have saved his life when they quickly hustled him outside and through the cobblestone alleyway between their apartment building and the tavern next door.

Lester never did return to the Morehead household after he announced to Grayson that he was gay. He turned instead to the U.S. Army where he enlisted and kept his big mouth shut.

Lester hated abandoning his mother while she sat in prison but she insisted that he go and live his own life. Less continued writing to her every week and he sent her cigarettes and magazines and flowers and at Christmastime; a handmade card and chocolates in cozy red socks.

Despite the slight limp in one of his legs, Lester was in excellent physical condition and as a result, he excelled in the daily rigors of boot camp. After basic training Less went on to basic killing when he was sent to fight in a God-forsaken war. When Lester was captured by the enemy he drew on past experience and told his captors that he was gay. He figured that his captors would simply beat him and then leave him alone not wanting to deal with anyone who was gay. Lester was right. His captors beat him severely and then left him for dead in the bushes outside the prison gate. During his beating Lester sustained an injury which caused his "good leg" to develop a limp. Since both of his legs had limps they served to cancel each other out. As a result, Less was able to run faster than ever and so, he did so, back to his platoon. The next night, under the cover of darkness, Lester guided his platoon back to the prison camp. They overran the camp and claimed it as their own. The good guys were freed, the bad guys sat in chains. The guards who had beaten Lester had been shot and killed during the melee.

After serving his two years, Lester left the Army wearing medals for bravery on his chest. He returned to civilian life where he was reunited with his mother on the first of May at Anthrax County's State Penitentiary. She cried when she saw him and he did the same. Lester took a job as a school bus driver. He discovered quickly that it was much tougher than the Army had been. He could often be heard shouting, "Sit down!" or "Shut up!" or "Leave me alone, I'm gay!" While working as a bus driver Lester attended night school on the G.I. Bill. He studied hard and eventually earned his welding certification and a degree in secondary education. Less went on to teach the reinstated welding class at his very own Anthrax High School where he also taught piano. The whole time, Lester lived alone, never having taken a lover. Although he was gay, Lester remained celibate his entire life. The only organ that he ever played with was the Hammond at the Anthrax Baptist Church where every Sunday he would serenade the faithful sinners with hymns of devotion and redemption.

Lester spends his weekends and all of his spare time now with his aged mother. She lives with him and he looks after her like a good son should. He buys her cigarettes and magazines with the money he earns. His mother's depression has long since passed and Lester is very grateful for that. He takes his mother to church every Sunday. He prays for her while she mostly just stares off into space. After church Betty and Lester change into their dungarees for a picnic down by the river. They laugh and eat roast beef sandwiches and then walk along the riverside trails enjoying the sunshine and each other. They save bread crumbs from their sandwiches to feed to the fish and then they skip flat stones across the flowing water.

"I love you, Less," his mother often tells him.

"I love you more, Mom," Lester still replies.

Luck For Rent

Last Saturday morning I went down to my favorite beach; Jagged Rock Cove. It's my favorite beach because I'm usually the only one there. For some reason, sharp jagged rocks and bare skin isn't a combination that entices a lot of people. On rare occasion though, wayward tourists can be spotted there but those encounters are usually brief and often feature blood-curdling screams from bloody-legged tourists limping back to their rental cars. I often wonder what goes through their minds when they read the weathered, hand-painted sign at the exit of the gravel parking lot; Thanks for Visiting Jagged Rock Cove - Please Come Again! I may be the cove's only repeat customer.

Oddly enough, I wasn't alone on the beach last Saturday morning. Two other guys down a ways from me were throwing a fluorescent yellow Frisbee to what looked like a mix of Labrador Retriever and Wolverine. Since I wasn't alone I decided to hide my brand new fifty dollar sunglasses in my sneakers where nobody would ever think to look. I beefed up my security system by laying my towel on top of my shoes.

Unbeknownst to me at the time, as I ran into the cold and frothy surf, I had apparently stepped on a jagged rock that cut my foot deeply enough to draw blood but not quite deep enough to cause me pain and alert me to my injury. As I was floating on my back bobbing atop the waves, I noticed a curiously growing number of seagulls circling directly over me. I then noticed a patch of red fanning out in the water at my feet. "I wonder what *that* is," I thought to myself when suddenly, the water all around me erupted violently in a thrashing foamy froth. I lowered my legs, raised my head high and began treading water as I spun myself around to search for the source of the commotion. Moments later, I noticed a huge dark shadow circling in the water beneath me. Seconds later, fin tips broke the water's surface. I gasped a gulp of saltwater as a beast from the deep slashed its enormous head through the water toward mine. I stared into its cold, lifeless, menacing black eye as the beast cruised by. Judging from the distance between its head and tail fin, I realized then that I was about to become the main course for a sixteen foot long hammerhead shark.

The shark jerked around and swam toward me. I thrashed the water and pissed my shorts as the shark raised its hideous head out of the water. Its jaws stretched open sucking in gallons of seawater in the process. Wicked rows of jagged teeth thrust toward my midsection. As I was about to be sawn in half by that man-eating-machine from hell, a huge explosion cracked out of the blue sky above. A sizzling bolt of blinding white lightning nailed the shark right between its eyes. As thunderous echoes rolled off toward the distance, I regained my senses. I searched frantically for the shark but found it dead, floating belly up; its singed carcass steaming having been flash-fried by the megawatts of electricity. It had been the shark's intention that my last moments on earth were to be spent as its bloody screaming meal. As my rare luck would have it though, the shark's last meal was instead; a deadly bolt of lightning that had saved my life.

I floated on my back motionless, relieved and exhausted. I noticed then, an even larger number of seagulls assembling in the sky above me. The birds began to twitter high-pitched excitement. They cawed and squawked as they dipped down ever closer to their recent discovery; a fresh seafood buffet. With every torn morsel the famished gulls above and the schools of fish below stole away, the shark's hulking remains became evermore severed and diced. Before long the shark's brilliant white cartilage skeleton was picked clean. It drifted out to sea as it fell apart.

During all of the commotion a storm-induced rip tide had carried me five miles offshore. By that time the beach was barely visible as I bobbed atop the growing swells of what had become a stormy sea. As a seasoned swimmer I knew well enough not to fight the currents and so, I drifted even farther out into the deep and darkening sea. Several hours and many half-remembered, poorly-recited prayers later, I managed to float and drift and swim my way back to what was by then, a darkened shore. As the last of the sun's rays sank below the storm clouds on the horizon, I began trudging the miles of rocky shoreline back to the cove. I shivered in the cold night air and limped along on my throbbing foot; the gash upon which had been cauterized by hours of immersion in the ocean's saltwater.

When I finally reached my belongings, I collapsed in a heap face down aside them sucking a mouthful of sand in the process. As I struggled to sit upright, I reached for my towel and then buried my cold numb head heavily into it. After a short while, when I'd regained enough strength with which to leave, I reached for my old ragged sneakers to prepare for the long walk home. As I did so however, I discovered that my shoes were completely and utterly empty. "Damn!" I shouted aloud to the darkened heavens above, "What Rotten Luck!" Those lousy blokes had stolen my brand new sunglasses.

Mayhem in Cactus Gulch

The coyotes was howlin' louder than usual the night the cactus came alive in 1855. We was sittin' 'round the campfire 'bout an hour past sundown, just me and Frank, and Dallas from Houston, and his lady friend Phoenix from Tucson, and her brother Houston from Dallas, and Buffalo Bob the Kansas City hog farmer, and Tex from New Orleans, and Injun Joe the Chinaman, and ol' Denver from Cheyenne, and Pedro the Frenchman, and Pedro's lovely wife Suzette Dubois from Idaho, and their eldest young'un Pedro Jr. and his adorable baby sister Antoinette, and the rough-and-ready Johnson brothers: John, Johnny, Jon, and Jonathan, and the rough-and-tumble Johnson sisters: June, Julia, Julie, and Jill, and the Johnson's parents: Jack and Joan, and *their* parents: Grand Pap and Grannie Jonas, and the Burton gang was there: Bill, Biff, Bart, Bert and Burt along with the two women they shared amongst themselves: Bonnie and another Bonnie who between the two of 'em had eight young'uns: Inky, Dinky, Dotty, Doe, Otto, Oscar, Omar and Ralph. As I recall, Gabby was there too. He was sittin' alone, quiet as usual, listenin' to the Carson twins: Slim and Tubby, fussin' over the last stick of beef jerky. It was one *HELL* of a big campfire and could be seen glowin' in the night sky over the ridge line beneath which we were camped, for miles and miles or more, or so I'd imagine.

Later on that night, before it all started, everyone had fallen asleep. Well... everyone 'cept for me and Buffalo Bob and Denver and John Johnson and Jack Johnson and Bert Burton (not to be confused with Burt Burton) and Gabby and Slim

Carson that is. We few was still wide awake, mostly b'cause way off in the night, the coyotes (pronounce that "ki-oats" so's it sounds more authentic-like) were howlin' somethin' fierce makin' it nearly impossible for us light sleepers to get *ANY* shut eye. So as I says, we was still wide awake or near to it when Buffalo Bob said, "You pokes hear somethin' rustlin' out thar?"

So's we all sat still and quiet and listened for a spell but we didn't hear nothin'. Moments later though, the night air grew ice cold and a strange swirlin' wind kicked up all around us. The campfire flames jumped high in the air sendin' embers into a sparklin', flashin', whirlin' frenzy. We sat there hypnotized and confused. And then... the air went dead calm. And then... the rustlin' sounds that Buffalo Bob had heard started up again.

"Shush!" I shouted, "Buffalo Bob is *right!* Thar *is* somethin' rustlin' out thar and I aims to find out what it is after I gets me a good night's sleep that is. Night y'all."

While I was brushin' my teeth and puttin' on my long-john-jammies and clippin' my toenails and sayin' my prayers (I'd been multi-taskin' long before it became popular) I overheard Gabby say absolutely nothin' to which Bert Burton replied, "Okay then, *I'll* go and have a look-see but iffin' you hear me screamin' you'd better all come a runnin'!"

Not two minutes later, from somewhere out in the cold dark night, ol' Bert let out a blood curdlin' scream that sent the rest of the gang a runnin' all right... in the opposite direction (pronounce that "die-rection" or "dee-rection" so's it sounds more authentic-like).

The next mornin'; a cool, somber, misty-gray mornin', all's we found of good ol' Bert Burton was a sad pile of bones where he last stood. There was not a stitch of his clothes to be found nor any sign of his sidearm or holster or boots or spurs or raggedy black hat. There wasn't a cloud or a bird in the sky nor a dry eye in the bunch that mornin' as we stood there sad and dumbfounded around them pile of bones. We was how you say; plumb mystified as to what on God's green earth could've possibly picked Bert's bones clean like that without scatterin' 'em across the desert. No wolf or bear or coyote or mountain lion could have done such a thing. No outlaw or Injun we'd ever encountered could've done so either. Bert was a good ol' poke and would be sorely missed by all who knew him, including us.

For the longest time we just stood there completely speechless, droppin' a tear or two and remained as such until Johnny Johnson rang his cowbell and yelled, "Pancakes...! Pancakes...! Come and Get 'em While They's Hot!"

We all starts hootin', "Yessiree! Yeah Buddy! Yahoo!" and other hungry stuff like that as we high-tailed it to the chuck wagon where a pile of tin plates awaited stacks of pancakes smothered in fresh-tapped maple syrup accompanied by a fine pair of hot 'n' greasy, spicy pork sausages. Even though we had ta drink condensed OJ because we'd runned out of fresh-squeezed sixteen hundred miles back a ways outside Fargo, it was nevertheless one heck of a *FINE* breakfast and one we all knew that good ol' Bert Burton would surely have enjoyed, if he hadn't recently become a sad pile of bones that is. Luckily for me, since I was waitin' my turn at the tail end of the chow-line, I got ol' Bert's leftover sausage portion which made me a lil' extra gassy that day. Ironically, that apparently insignificant detail would later prove to have saved my life as you will soon discover.

After such a large and satisfyin' breakfast it would've been difficult at best for any of us to accomplish all of the back-breakin' work we faced that day but that work needed to be done and so, I slipped away quiet-like to take a nap. Have I mentioned yet that I was a trail boss and therefore didn't need to do work much? Well I was and anyways, while I was considerin' exactly where to commence my post-breakfast siesta, I discovered a giant pile of sagebrush which I managed to slide myself into. Once comfortably inside its cool and shady interior, unbeknownst to me, I had apparently laid my head down to rest atop the soft coils of a sleepin' six foot long diamondback rattle snake. Have I mentioned yet that I was nearsighted, farsighted and just plain poor-sighted? Well I was and anyways, to my delight (and despite the snake's dual sacks of deadly venom) the coils of that sleepin' viper proved to be one hell of a comfy pillow. As I began to drift off to sleep, or maybe shortly thereafter, I heard what sounded like the gently twinklin' keys of a saloon piano (pronounce that "pie-annie" because it's just too funny not to). As the music grew louder and the fuzzy scene came into focus, I found myself transported back in time to the year 1848. I was standin' outside my favorite waterin' hole west of the Mississippi; the Red Devil Saloon in the town of Cactus Gulch which lay a mere forty miles from where I was sleepin' at the time of my sleep-induced teleportation...

I swung the saloon doors open and stepped inside; my spurs a clinkin' as they shone brightly in the high noon sunlight that poured in behind me. The saloon doors swung shut, bumpin' my backside in the process. I drew my sidearm and swung around quick but decided to let the doors live. Once inside the saloon, I was temporarily blinded in its dim lamplight. A lazy blanket of cigar ("see-gar") smoke swirled 'round in the warm and fragrant air. I took a long deep satisfyin' breath of it. Havin' just ridden four hundred hot and dusty miles in two and a half days deliverin' deeds for Wells Fargo, I was grateful to finally be off of my dog-gone fast but bony-backed horse and walkin' on solid dirt again. I was holdin' a handsome pay at the time; twenty-five silver dollars that weighed down my saddlebag just fine and a twenty dollar gold piece that was workin' up a blister in my left boot. I thanked my lucky stars for that desert oasis that was spread out before me but I remember wonderin' at the time, *What on earth am I gonna spend my hard-earned money on?* Whiskey was cheap and so was beer. A plate of pork 'n beans cost a nickel. As it was, I was holdin' the most money I'd ever had before. I shuttered at the prospect of losin' it all in a crooked poker game. While I thought those thoughts a lil' bit longer, I turned toward one of the saloon's side rooms in which I quickly recognized the most delicious example of a female to have ever graced God's green earth or Louisiana's bayous; the impeccably gorgeous, Miss Veronica La' Rue. I also recognized the fact that she was gazin' straight in my direction ("die-rection" or "dee-rection").

At the very moment that our eyes met, gravity grabbed a good hold of my saddlebag and pulled it straight down to the clapboard floor spillin' a rollin', spinnin', clinkin' pile of sparklin' silver dollars in the process. As classy as Miss La' Rue was though, she didn't laugh a bit at my embarrassin' clumsiness. She didn't even budge an inch or bat an eyelash. She simply turned that perfect pair of sweet Cajun French lips of hers into the most friendly and invitin' of smiles that I'd ever seen before. And so, I bent myself down, gathered up my fortune from the floor, took a deep breath and then approached the red velvet chaise longue upon which she lay.

The saloon's floorboards (or maybe my knees?) creaked in anticipation as my slow and steady steps brought me closer to her side. Upon arrivin' in the majestic presence of her, I removed and then lowered my sun-bleached hat politely. As I did so however, bits of caked trail dust blew off of my hat in her direction. The dirt fell like brown snowflakes and then landed gently atop her silky smooth garments and person. I gasped out loud but then immediately got the better of myself as I attempted to gently brush away the bits of dirt from her petticoat and bosom with my grubby fingers.

"You know, Mr. Rhodes," she began with a frown, "I usually charge a handsome fee for that pleasure. But since it is *such* a delight to see you again, my dear, let's call this one; on the house," she announced with a heart-meltin' smile and a mischievous wink.

"So, now then," she continued as she raised an empty glass and tapped its ringin' rim with a perfectly manicured, long ruby red fingernail, "what does a girl have to *do* to get a drink around here?"

Her question tickled my fancy somethin' fierce and tickled my memory as well as I recalled our very first, heavenly encounter a few years earlier...

"Excuse me, sir... Mr. Rhodes? Mr. Rockefeller Rhodes...? Rocky...!" an anonymous voice called out in my direction.

I turned around slowly to identify who on earth was announcin' my name to the world. The only soul on that otherwise empty dirt street who coulda called out my name was the hound dog lyin' on the porch of McEwan's dry-goods 'cross the way. I was not convinced however, that that *particular dog* was smart enough to have remembered my name since we'd only met once or twice b'fore. As far as I could tell, the remainder of the town was plumb deserted as folks had apparently sought refuge from the God-forsaken heat eleswheres. I squinted in the white hot sunlight to adjust my vision in the dog's direction and once havin' done so realized that the dog was in fact, fast asleep. *So who was it then?* I wondered, that had hollered my name. It was then that I noticed and recognized, approachin' me fast from the opposite direction, none other than my pal Pokie Magillicutty.

"Is that you, Pokie...? Well, I'll be... it *is* you, Pokie!" I hollered, "My, my, how you've grown, lil' sidewinder! Come on over here and let me get a good look at ya, boy!"

Pokie stepped closer and smiled as he stood tall and proud smack-dab in front of me. I stared into the very same eyes of that sweet lil' boy I'd once known; his body by then all growed up and full-size. I set my hands on what were once his narrow, child-size shoulders. In my absence them shoulders had widened nicely into broad, man-size shoulders. I grinned from ear-to-ear and said, "What a fine young man you turned out to be! Who'd a figured?"

"Thanks, Mr. Rhodes!"

"Rocky," I said.

"Rocky," he repeated.

"How's your Ma?" I asked him.

"Not bad, Mr.... Rocky."

"And your Pa?"

"Not good, Rocky," the boy said as he cast his eyes down toward his boot tips. "He... he... passed on late last year. Doc Hartman said it was some kind of virus. It was horrible, Mr. Rhodes. Pa was always so strong. He worked so hard around the ranch year-round, sunup to sundown most days. During his final days, he could do no better than to sit up in bed. By the end, he couldn't even lift his head."

"Oh my heavens, Pokie. I'm so very, very sorry," I offered as I placed my hands on each side of the boy's face.

"Did he go quiet?" I asked him in a whisper.

"He did do," Pokie replied. "He just looked at me and Ma one last time, smiled, then closed his eyes for good, Rocky. I was sitting on his bed at the time. Ma was in Pa's favorite rocking chair right next to him. We three sat looking at each other holding hands for what seemed liked hours until Pa just closed his eyes one last time. As the room went dark his hands went cold. Ma and me didn't move around much 'til morning. By that time, sunlight had filled the room and there was Pa; just lying there, in eternal sleep, eternal peace I pray."

"I'm sure the good Lord's lookin' after your pa, Pokie. He's prob'ly got your father settin' fence posts and paintin' barns and breakin' broncs 'cause you know how plumb *lazy* those Saints can be don't ya, Pokie?"

Pokie looked up, stared straight into my eyes, and then burst out laughin' through his tears.

"It sure is good to see you, Rocky!" he said. "You can always make me laugh, even in the worst of times."

"I reckon that's why the Good Lord put me here, Poke. I'm not much of a book-learner or a letter-writer or much of anythin' at all. I *can* ride a horse and shoot with the best of 'em but what I can always seem to do good is ta help folk get through the rough waters. Speakin' of which... I'm plumb parched, how 'bout you?"

"Yes, sir, me too!" Pokie agreed.

"How 'bouts I buy you a sarsaparilla then, Poke?"

"A beer sounds better, Mr. Rhodes," he suggested, testin' his luck.

"A beer it *shall be* then! But for God's sake, Pokie, if we is ta become drinkin' buddies, you gotta start callin' me Rocky!"

"Rocky it is then and Rocky it will always be," he said smilin'.

And so, I led Pokie down toward the Red Devil Saloon at the far end of town. It was my favorite waterin' hole in them parts, I reckon b'cause it was the *only* waterin' hole around.

We sat down at the bar as the saloon's lone customers. The bartender was busy spit-shinin' whiskey glasses so I cleared my throat to grab his attention, "Uh humph...!"

"Rocky!" the bartender hollered as he set a glass down on the shiny shellacked bar top and looked our way. "What brings you ta these parts?"

"My horse and my thirst," I announced to my ol' pal Red, the bartender and owner of that fine establishment.

"Well, it's good to see's ya both! Didn't know you was a friend of Pokie's."

Pokie raised a kind hand of greetin' to ol' Red who'd been one of his pa's best friends in that small part of the world.

"Me and Pokie's been friends for a long time now, Red. I knew his pa well when I worked his ranch, remember?"

"Doggone it, right you are, Rocky! I don't remember things like I used ta anymore, not since that bullet ricocheted clean off my thick skull, see...?" Red turned sideways to show us the long nasty scar that ran from the top of his left ear and clean across the back of his bald head. "When it happened, Doc Hartman shaved my head to prevent infection so I just kept on shavin' it ever since. The ladies think it's sexy. They like to rub their pretty little fingers along my silky smooth hat stand they do. But 'nuff 'bout me, you's two look thirsty as sawdust. What's your pleasure...?"

"A double-iced beer for the both of us, Red," I requested.

"Comin' right up," he said and then he shuffled his nearly seven foot tall, three-hundred pound frame out the back door to his subterranean icehouse where he frosted the beer mugs and chipped ice that he'd pack around the beer kegs. Red returned to the bar with two frosty mugs, hit the keg tap twice and then walked back our way with two overflowin' mugsful.

"First beer?" I asked Pokie as he sipped a bit from his mug.

"It is so, Rocky."

"Well, partner... what do ya think? Better'n sarsaparilla ain't it?"

"I didn't really know what to expect, Rocky, but I'm thinking that I could get used to this real fast. It's pretty darn good!" he said as he took another cautious sip and then a real big gulp. "Yep," he said, slammin' his mug down as he wiped foam from his lip, "it's *darn* good!"

"Yes siree, it shore is pretty darn good!" I said, raisin' my mug high in the air. "To beer!" I toasted.

"To beer!" Pokie agreed, and then he added, "To Rocky!"

"To Rocky," I said, addin', "I hope you're referrin' to *me* and not some other Rocky."

"Course not, Rocky, you're one-of-a-kind," Pokie laughed, "one-of-a-kind," he repeated, I imagine b'cause I'd been one-of-a-kind on more than one occasion.

"I ain't much of a poker hand though am I, Pokie? A pair of deuces beats one-of-a-kind every time," I reminded him.

We both laughed out loud, spittin' a lil' beer on one another in the process. That made us laugh even more b'fore we drained our mugs in two simultaneous satisfyin' gulps.

"Hit us again, Red, we're dyin' of thirst over here!" I hooted, happy to have reintroduced those fine suds to my grateful gullet again. I hadn't done so for two weeks or more on the trail. There weren't nothin' 'tween San Antonio and Cactus Gulch 'cept fer prickly cactus, miles of dust and constant thirst. Tepid canteen water might keep a man alive but ice-cold beer makes him glad to be that way.

"Ya know, fellas... ya picked a real good day to stop on by," Red said as he set two more mugsful in front of us.

"How's that, Red?" Pokie asked.

"B'cause, if you stick around long enough and that doggone stage is on time for once, you'll gets the chance to meet my brand-new barmaid, that's how come," he announced.

"Where's Louisa?" I asked Red, noticin' for the first time that she was nowhere to be seen.

"She upped and got herself hitched to a city-slicker last month; a rich old geezer from St. Louis. He's maybe twenty-five years older than she is but he's got deep pockets and a sweet-talkin' sophisticated way about him. The judge married them two the day after they met, right here in this ol' place. Not more than two shakes after the happy couple said their 'I dos,' the ceremony ended and the celebratin' commenced in a fury of pistol shots and hollerin'. And then it got loud when Louisa's new husband bought rounds for everyone. Word spread 'round town quick that he was buyin'. By sundown, pert near everyone in Cactus Gulch and beyond had packed my place to the rafters. I made more money on that one single day than I did the next three months put together. And the groom paid for it all in cash, I say! He even tipped me twenty dollars personal b'cause I had to do most of the work myself, what with Louisa bein' the bride and all she couldn't help me out much."

"It's too bad I missed the hootenanny and missed wishin' Louisa all the best. She was one, great gal. She'd make a fine wife for *any* man that's for sure," I said, winkin' to Red havin' known her myself in a personal, affectionate way.

"Don't I knows it, Rocky," Red said, winkin' right back at me b'cause he'd known her in the same way too.

"And that's why I've had ta replace her with a brand new gal. She's all the way from N' Orleans she is. Word is, Rocky..." Red said, leanin' in close to me, "she's a real looker. They say she sings and plays pianee to boot but as long as she's not mule-faced, I could care less if she's musically inclined!" he said laughin', and then I laughed and then Pokie laughed and then we all three laughed together.

"I hate to say it, fellas," Pokie announced, "but I got to run along now. I need to send a telegram for Ma and then get on back to the ranch. I was supposed to be back by now so I guess I'll be missing the new gal, doggone it."

"Guess you will, Poke, but you know where you can find her, right?" Red asked the boy.

"Sure do and I *will* stop back soon enough to cast my eyes," he said, standin' up a bit wobbly-legged havin' just drunk his very first beers.

"Don't be fallin' offa your horse now, boy!" Red shouted as I walked Pokie out of the bar and onto the blazin' hot porch.

"Tell your momma I'll stop on by later this evenin' or tomorrow mornin', okay, Pokie?"

"Will do, Mr. Rhodes, and thanks for the suds, they sure was fine," he said, shakin' my hand.

I pulled Pokie tight to my chest and bear-hugged him best I

could. "Your poppa is proud of you, Pokie. I know for sure he is," I offered the boy.

"Thanks, Rocky," he said, and then I watched him walk off tall and proud down the long dusty street toward where his horse was hitched. Pokie may have been a young man at the time, but he was already a finer man than I ever was, or ever would be.

"What on earth does a girl have to *do* to get a drink around here...?" she asked me as I took her soft hand in mine and then helped her through the stagecoach door. As she stepped down, her silky red dress slid up and along her slender leg until it snagged on her black lace garter preventin' me from gettin' a better look at things that I shouldn't've been lookin' at in the first place. I gave a quick glance down the street and thought about yellin', "Hey, Pokie... come take a gander at this *fine* lookin' woman!" but he was either in the telegraph station or was long gone by then. And so, there we was; just me and her, lookin' straight into each other's eyes.

"Well, hello there, stranger," she said with a smile that changed my life forever as she stood there b'fore me on the dusty street, "name's Veronica... Veronica La' Rue."

"Rocky Rhodes at your service, ma'am," I said, tippin' my hat and bowin' my head like I thought might be proper.

"Are *all* the men in Cactus Gulch as *fine* and *handsome* as you are?" she asked, promptin' me to fall head-over-heels in love with her. Truth be told though, I'd already fallen in love with her from the very moment I first set eyes on her.

"Not sure, ma'am, I'm not from around these here parts," I said, wonderin' if I could've said somethin' better.

"Well then, we have something in common," she said with a

sly sexy smile that nearly stopped my heart before it got to beatin' even faster. "I'm from back New Orleans way myself," she said. "After I get settled in maybe we can explore this fine metropolis together. If you're not busy that is..."

"My time is yours, ma'am," I offered, and by that I meant; every single minute for the rest of my life.

As I took her bags down from the driver, I wondered what in tarnation a metropolis was, but she headed off quick-like so I stopped my wonderin' and follered her into the Devil where she approached the bar and introduced herself to Red. She made it clear to him that she'd start workin' the next day as she was too road-weary and dusty after her five-day journey to begin work that same evenin'. Red had no choice but to consent as we'd both come to realize that no man could ever refute anythin' that came by way of those luscious red lips of hers. And so, after I'd toted her bags up to the second floor of the saloon and after Red had showed her around a bit, she settled into her room. She gave Red and me both, a peck on the cheek and a nice warm hug of gratitude. I don't know about Red's, but *my* hug was one I'd never forget. It was definitely worth writin' home about, if I'd had one that is. A short spell later, Red and I sat starin' at one another while we was sippin' whiskey down at the bar. Die-rectly above us we heard Miss La' Rue pourin' buckets of hot water from the wood burner that served to heat the second floor on cold winter days and apparently, her bath water as well on hot and sticky days such as that one. Red and me sipped our whiskeys in silence. We was both hypnotized by the sounds of water bein' poured into her bathtub.

"Did ya ever wish you was a bathtub?" Red asked me as we heard, right above us, the sound of soft bare skin squeakin' against hard white porcelain.

I smiled at ol' Red and then said, "Never gave it much thought before but since you asked, I'd rather be a bar of soap right about now."

He laughed out loud at first but then stopped abruptly. I suppose it was b'cause he too was imaginin' himself as a bar of soap right about then. We both downed our whiskeys havin' grown tired of sippin' 'em and then we poured ourselves a second round.

"What's a metropolis, Red?" I asked, a short spell later.

Red thought a bit, repeated the word out loud and then said, "It's some kind of ancient Greek word I reckon, or maybe Latin. I'd bet Pastor O'Leary would know, he's been schooled quite a bit. Why do ya ask?"

"No reason, just curious is all," I said and then I sat up straight and tall on my barstool when I heard my name called from above.

"Am I hearin' angels, Red?" I asked him.

"You devil, you," he replied.

"Rocky... Rocky Rhodes...!" Veronica called again. "Come on up here please, will you, dear?"

"Either an angel is callin' you home or you're about to be tested," Red suggested and then he added, "What the hell ya waitin' for, boy? Git now! Show that fine woman some Texas hospitality."

"But I ain't a Texan," I joked as I stood to walk away.

"Even better yet then, boy, even better!" he said.

"Rocky?" she asked, as she heard my footsteps approachin.'

"Yes, ma'am," I said, standin' fast in her bedroom doorway not knowin' what on earth I should do next.

"Be a dear would you please and bring me my towel? I'm

such a scatter-brain I'm afraid I've left it in my bedroom," she said as I noticed the white cotton towel folded neatly atop her feather bed.

"I don't want to catch cold or drip water all over the floor," she explained.

I entered Veronica's bedroom, picked up her towel and then walked slowly toward the adjoining bathroom where I stopped short of the open door. She looked up at me from a seated position in the bathtub. Her long black hair was tied into a neat wet knot atop her head. Her beautiful bare shoulders glistened with bath salts. I took a step closer.

"Don't be shy now, come on in," she said. "I was raised with six brothers in a three-room house. I'm not shy at all."

She surely was not, by any means at all shy, as she stood straight up in that tub drippin' wet and standin' there for me to see her everythin' from head to knees. She looked like some sort of Greek goddess statue, or maybe Latin?

"Come quick now, I'll catch a cold like this," she declared.

I approached the tub and then wrapped the towel over her shoulders and around her tall and slender, perfectly shaped body. She wiggled around a bit in that lucky towel and then gave me her hand and stepped out of the tub. She stood in front of the vanity mirror where she untied her wet hair and let it fall limp on her back and shoulders. She slipped out of the bath towel and wrapped it around her head. She rubbed her towel-covered head vigorously to dry off her hair. I watched as she wiggled and bounced nicely right in front of me; her hips swayin' back and forth hypnotizin' me. My knees grew weak and my dungarees grew tighter. She removed the towel from her head, wrapped it around herself and then commenced to comb her beautiful, long black hair. I jumped a bit when she asked me, "Did you enjoy the show, dear?"

"Oh, I did indeed, Miss Veronica," I may have said and then I confessed, "you gotta be the most beautiful woman I've ever seen," or somethin' like that.

"Well, three dollars will get you a much closer look," she suggested as she reached out for my hand.

We lay on her bed and flew through the clouds. We soared above them into clear blue skies. We dove fast and low into a deep and narrow canyon. We sailed along a river and landed softly on its bank. We walked hand-in-hand up a ridge and looked down upon a meadow. Fields of crops before us stretched across the horizon. Dozens of farmhands were tending crops in bright sunshine. They chopped, bundled and stowed stalks of grain onto ox carts. A man with a whip cracked it high over their heads. With loud snaps he shouted commands and fired his pistol into the air. The workers toiled on steadily as the daylight grew dimmer. Three dollars later, the sun set below Veronica's bedroom window sill.

"That was quite a ride!" she said, still a bit breathless. She sat up then against the headboard and rolled a cigarette. She handed the smoke to me and then rolled another for herself. We sat there puffin' and blowin' smoke in the air as the room grew darker. She lit an oil lamp on the bedside table and turned over toward me. "Shall we sleep now or do another three dollars?" she asked me softly.

"I promised to show you 'round the metropolis," I reminded her, figurin' that she'd let me know what that meant.

"Oh, you showed me something much more exciting, Rocky," she said laughin' sweetly as she slipped her arm across my bare chest, "besides, Cactus Gulch will still be there when we wake up tomorrow, won't it?"

"To be honest, Miss La' Rue, it don't matter to me one way or another if it is, or it isn't, as long as you're here," I said as I rubbed her soft belly.

"Oh my heavens, that feels nice, Rocky. Will you rub my back for me please?" she asked me and then she rolled over on her belly and pulled her long black hair up high over her head. "That stage coach made me so very sore down there."

And so, I rubbed her neck and her shoulders and her back. I rubbed her hips and her bottom and the length of her long beautiful legs. I did it all gladly for an hour or more as she sighed and kept sayin', "Oh, that's nice, Rocky!"

I rubbed Veronica's ankles and her feet then we rubbed up against one another again. When I took another three silver dollars from my saddlebag and handed them to her she said, "Two of those belong to Red, Rocky. Will you be a dear and pay him his share for me now before he gets too nervous about us being up here all this time?"

"Will do," I said and then I pulled my britches up and over my tired but happy hips.

"And bring us back a couple of whiskeys, okay?" she asked me as I turned to leave the room.

"My pleasure, Miss La' Rue, will do."

Thirty minutes into my hour-long, post-breakfast nap, trail hands hollerin' nearby woke up the rattlesnake. It rattled its gosh-darn tail right in my ear. I awoke starin' straight into the viper's cold black eyes. I froze in fear when it raised its head and stretched its ghastly pink jaws agape to show me its drippin' wet fangs. I lifted my head slowly off of the snake's warm belly as it prepared to strike me towards heaven or hell. In my state of absolute terror, I accidentally let out a long, loud sausage-fart that turned out to be quite a stinker. The snake's nostrils flared. It snapped its jaws shut, wrinkled its nose, furrowed it eyebrows and then quickly slithered out of the sagebrush for a breath of fresh air. I thanked my lucky stars for ol' Bert Burton's spicy breakfast sausage that had fueled my extra-gassy condition. That previously insignificant detail had miraculously saved my life and so, I promised to thank Bert personally when I finally did meet my maker. Havin' started gaggin' myself like the snake had done, I crawled out of the sagebrush for some fresh air of my own. As I stretched out my spine I thought, *Well... I guess it's time to get back to work.*

"Load up them mules and do it quick now! Stow that gear tight and make haste as you do it! Water them horses and bridle 'em good! Tighten those wagon wheels lest they spin off in the dust! Round up them cattles and get 'em in line!" I shouted to the fellas scamperin' about who would've done all of those things anyway whether or not I had told them to. But after all, I was a trail boss so a boss I would be.

I shouted more orders and even lent the boys a hand or two. We was haulin' dry-good freight from way up north in the Dakotas to way down south at the mighty Rio Grande. It was there that we'd load river barges with goods and cattles just outside Cactus Gulch. Teamsters we was and good ones at that but we also served as armed escorts for families relocatin' from north to south or vice versa. For the sum of three dollars a wagon, we'd ensure the settlers that no band of renegade Injuns or highway outlaws would catch 'em and rob 'em and skin 'em alive or worse. Them three dollars included a big ol' breakfast and a plate of pork 'n beans when we camped at sundown. The settlers that signed up with us came and went along the route. Families would drop out of line near their new claims while others would join in along the way. And so it was that our wagon train was always changin', but we trail hands mostly stayed the same.

The company paid us well but most of us spent it in haste. Whenever we was in Southeast Texas, I'd bring my crew to the Red Devil Saloon. Red appreciated the business I brought his way. He'd pour me drinks on the house as a thank-you. We'd return to the Red Devil once again that very same night, after we'd help load the river barges. Later on we'd all load up on Red's hot Texas chili, double-iced beer, Tennessee sour mash, and soft, sweet-smellin' women if we was lucky. Under such alcohol-induced situations (pronounce that "sit-chee-ations") no love was lost between we trail hands and the locals. Hootin' and hollerin' would signal the point where bottles would start flyin'. Fist fights would break out and teeth would be lost but it was mostly in good fun. Weapons were rarely drawn let alone fired, except into the ceiling. Red would always put a quick end to that nonsense though. The boys'd just be havin' their fun while Red and me mostly just sat by and enjoyed the show, unless things got out of hand that is. I always looked forward to seein' my ol' pal Red again and drinkin' his good beer and his throat-clearin' whiskey. Whenever I was in town I'd ride out to the Magillicutty ranch where I'd say 'howdy' to Pokie and get a real nice hug from his momma. But mostly of all, when I was in Cactus Gulch, I looked forward to spendin' time with Miss Veronica La' Rue.

And so, as we drove the wagon train on down toward the river in hundred degree heat, we didn't it mind none knowin' that our long journey would soon come to an end. We'd shake the hands and slap the backs of our river-folk pals who'd bridle mules to the barges while we unloaded the wagons. The heavy barges would sit low in the muddy Rio Grande and make way at sunset in the cool night air. They'd return again in ten days' time with Mexican goods that we'd haul up north. In the meantime, our time was our own. When the trail captain handed out the sliver we'd earned for the haul, we'd hoot and holler and ride away quick to spend it.

"Rocky Rhodes!" Red shouted over the roar of the Saturday night crowd as I walked into the Red Devil with most of my crew in tow.

"Red!" I shouted back, wavin' a hand high in the air.

The place was really jumpin' - I'd never seen it quite that way b'fore. Red went on to tell me that a few prospectors had found chunks of gold along the Rio Grande while others were prospectin' for somethin' called "crude oil" that was buried deep in the ground. As a result, business was boomin' seven days a week. Red had hired three more girls. I noticed them weavin' their way through the crowd. The girls held trays of dinks high up in the air while men grabbed their sweet behinds from behind.

"That ain't free!" one gal shouted.

"Just samplin' the merchandise!" some cow poke yelled, winkin' his good eye her way.

Red told me that night that Veronica didn't need to serve drinks no more. She'd taken charge of the new girls and taught them to be respectable whores. When I'd finally found Veronica she was ticklin' the ivories. She was singin' a song and I just stood there lovin' every sweet note of it. I'd never heard Veronica sing before 'cept under the sheets when I'd hit her sweet spot. When she finished her song and grabbed her glass from the piano top I strolled up to her and asked, "Can I fill that up for you, ma'am?"

I filled up Veronica's glass and later on filled her up with love. She refused my silver and said, "You're not just another paying customer of mine anymore, Rocky. I lie down with you now because I just want to and miss you and always enjoy you when I do. At a certain point a woman needs to start thinking about settling down. The girls down stairs work really hard for Red and me. They earn ten dollars a go now and we each take a two-dollar cut. As for me, I've been charging thirty or forty dollars for a roll in the hay. Wealthy businessmen and the occasional judge or congressman visit me when their wives are too tired to make them smile and lately, that's been quite often. I have a big ol' bank account now, Rocky. I've been thinking about heading back to New Orleans and buying a place of my own."

Veronica rolled us tobacco and we blew smoke in the air.

"It sure is good to see you again, Rocky," she said, slippin' a soft hand across my bare chest.

"It's all that I live for," I told her because it was true and then I leaned in for kiss.

That started it up again real quick-like as we flew off into the clouds. We soared above them into clear blue skies. We dove fast and low into a deep and narrow canyon. We sailed along a river and landed softly on its bank. We walked hand-in-hand up a ridge and looked down upon a meadow. Fields of crops before us stretched across the horizon. Dozens of farmhands were tending crops in bright sunshine. They chopped, bundled and stowed stalks of grain onto ox carts. A man with a whip cracked it high over their heads. With loud snaps he shouted commands and fired his pistol into the air.

The workers toiled on steadily as the daylight grew dimmer. In the black of the night a demon soared through the sky. He searched for his next victim and found him in the desert. The demon touched down on the ground and transformed itself into a cactus. It stood there unflinching; its thorny arms outstretched waiting for its prey. A trail hand approached the cactus unaware. It reached out and grabbed the man who screamed in horrendous pain as thousands of thorns punctured his flesh. The cactus returned then to its demonic state. It lifted its prey off of the ground and up into the air. The demon ripped the man's soul from his body and tossed his lifeless bones back down to earth. A sad pile of bones remained where the man had last stood. I had witnessed it all myself, in Veronica's eyes as I lay atop her. I shook my head in disbelief as my heart nearly burst open. Veronica's lips met mine as she tried to calm me. She kissed my ear softly and then whispered, "Welcome to the Netherworld, Rocky."

She pushed me off her abruptly and jumped atop my chest. She pinned my arms against the bed with her knees. She bent over me, pressing her face close to mine and then said, "As reigning queen of the Netherworld, I welcome you gladly and wish to keep you by my side. I could have you enslaved, Rocky, for my demons are many, but I choose you alone as my lover if you come with me willingly."

"Am I dreamin'?" I asked her as I stared into her eyes.

Her usual sweet lavender fragrance had given way to a scent of burnt roses. The earth beneath us began to shake as a wind howled and swirled. Fire erupted all around us. The room had suddenly burst into flames. She wrapped her arms around me. We lifted slowly off the bed. I sailed in her arms above the town in flames far below. I witnessed her demons grabbing up the townsmen and then tossing their lifeless bones back to earth. The men's souls were swept deep into a canyon where the earth had cracked open. We dove down through flames and followed the demons to green meadows. Lush croplands stretched out before us across the horizon.

"I treat the souls of my subjects quite well, Rocky," Veronica claimed as we stood upon a grassy hillside looking down upon them. "I never order them tortured or destroyed. I simply engage their services and demand their devotion once they've been released from their lives in your world and transported to our realm. Should they refuse to comply, or if they fight hard enough to regain their old lives back, I simply return them to their bones whence they came. But once they arrive here, most find what they need and even more so than that which they've left behind in your world. Most do not complain. They work hard here 'tis true, but no more so than they did in their old lives. They have here; food and shelter, women and whiskey. They can drink and fight and sin as they wish after their day's work is done. What more could mere mortal men desire?" she asked me.

I was a captive of her voice. I had listened to her closely. I felt dark, comforting truth in her words. I recalled having the same visions before as dreams but suddenly realized then that I only experienced those dreams when I was with *her*. Could it possibly be that Miss Veronica La' Rue was in fact; the reigning Queen of the Netherworld? And if she was in fact a queen, and I wasn't just dreaming, what could she possibly want from a simple trail-ridin' cow poke like me?

"I hear your thoughts clearly, Rocky, and I can tell you this much; I desire a mate and have chosen one carefully. I wish to bear children but cannot do so without a man; a mortal man such as you. I've rejected the sheriff, the marshal and the mayor, businessmen and trail hands and cowboys and such, but it was only you, Rocky, who could chill my burning desires; desires much deeper than mere mortal love. I will make you my king if you stay with me now and I will share you with my fine sister whom you may remember quite well."

"Welcome, Rocky," Louisa said as she appeared before us. "I am recently widowed since my poor rich husband shot himself in the back just a few days ago. I've missed you terribly and I too desire you. My dear sister Veronica reminded me how heavenly your devilish backrubs are."

The two women, or queen demons, or whatever they were, laughed as they both wrapped their hot arms around me.

"You won't regret staying here," one of them said.

"You'll never grow cold if you share our warm bed."

"You'll never grow cold and you'll never grow old. You'll never grow bored we promise you that much."

"But, Veronica, what of your bank account and your plans to return to New Orleans and buy a place of your own? Were those merely lies that you told me?" I asked her.

"Heavens no, dear Rocky, they're all true. I would never lie to you, my love."

"Nor I," Louisa said. "You see, Rocky, Veronica and I live in both realms. We come and go as we please. We find Earth and humans so primal and uncivilized, but it's all quite entertaining to us as well. After all, Rocky, Earth is where we found you. Earth is where we both fell in love with you; your human soul and human flesh as well."

"Unlike our subjects, you are still whole in body and soul, Rocky. As a result, you will also have the opportunity to enjoy both realms as we do," Veronica explained. "But it must be of your own choosing. We could force you to join us but we cannot force you to love us."

"So... demons love like humans do?" I asked them.

"Not so much, silly boy," Louisa laughed, "but demon *goddesses* do. It's what we do best as you know quite well."

"They tell you no lies," a booming voice called out, "for they are *my* goddesses and I've taught them quite well."

I spun around quickly and sucked my breath in with fear, for before me stood Red, with tail, horns and a spear. His flesh was bright red, from the top of his bald head to the sharp tips of his clawed toes. Flames danced from his fingertips as he blew smoke through the ring hanging from his nose. The ground shook as Red approached me ominously. I trembled inside and out. I felt the searing heat of his flames. He raised his enormous right hand high above me and then swung it down hard to offer me his open palm. "Welcome, Rocky," he bellowed, "Red Devil I *am,* my good friend!"

- The Bitter-Sweet End -

Nine O'clock Noir

Driving rain poured from buckets that night and the empty metal buckets banged and clanged as they crashed across the wet city streets in loud explosions that resembled thunder. The rain rushed down the city's storefront windows in pulsing veins of reflected red and blue neon light. Cast from the headlights of passing automobiles, a steady barrage of rain-streaked beacons pelted the windows like flashbulbs and then swept across them. Wind-driven raindrops were thrown violently against the glass. They clung there momentarily and sparkled star-like in the bright pulsing light before they too slid down... to join their comrades. A middle-aged man sat alone in a red vinyl booth at the Nine O'clock Diner; his cheek pressed up against a cool comforting windowpane. He slid up the sleeve of his second-hand grey tweed jacket to check the time on his stolen gold watch; it was nine o'clock. *It shouldn't be much longer,* he thought. At nine minutes past nine an umbrella entered the diner. It was immediately snapped shut and then tossed with a head-first bang into a brass umbrella stand by its owner whose heels clicked slowly and steadily across the white tile floor. The dame approached an empty booth next to where the man was sitting.

"Care to join me, Gloria?" the man asked her casually.

"Alright then," she decided and then she slipped elegantly into his booth facing him for the first time.

The woman sat in perfect posture; her hands folded atop the white linoleum table. Ten glossy red fingernails and a dazzling diamond ring adorned her forty-year-old hands that looked half their age. The black felt sleeves of her coat rose up toward her broad padded shoulders. The top four buttons of her starched white blouse were unfastened allowing it to plunge into a deep and suggestive "V" between her lapels. A string of pale pink pearls appeared from behind her chestnut colored hair and swooped down to lay resting across the base of her neck. Despite the driving rain from whence she came, the length of the woman's shiny hair rested on perfect swept-under curls at her shoulders.

"Care for a cigarette?" the man asked.

"I suppose," the woman acquiesced.

She leaned forward and pursed her ruby red lips. He placed a cigarette gently between them and then lit the tip of the cigarette with a diamond accented lighter that sparkled in the dancing orange flame. Gloria drew on the cigarette with her right hand and then snapped the lighter closed with her left taking it from his hand abruptly. She inspected the initials "G.G." engraved on the lighter and then said, "I believe this is mine." She slipped the lighter into her purse. Her deep green eyes studied her handsome companion.

"Do you always take chances?" he asked her.

"I always take what's mine," she responded calmly and then added, "while *you* apparently, take what's *not* yours."

He lifted the brim of his hat and stared at her coldly. He reached into his coat pocket and pulled out a bundled handkerchief which he placed on the table between them.

"I believe this belongs to you as well," he said as he slid the handkerchief toward her.

Gloria laid her cigarette into a glass ashtray and then carefully unfolded the white linen cloth. She didn't flinch when its contents were revealed; a bloody severed finger adorned with a man's gold wedding band. She held the finger down with her right hand and slipped the ring off of it with her left. She brought the ring up close to her eyes to confirm the initials "G.G." engraved on the ring's interior. She replaced the ring onto the finger, refolded the cloth carefully and then slipped the bundle into her coat pocket.

"There's more where that came from," he said coldly.

Gloria stared calmly into his eyes and studied his Hollywood good-looks carefully. She drew on her cigarette slowly and blew the smoke directly into his face. He grinned slightly but remained silent. She told the man that she had something for him as well as she dropped both of her hands into her lap. She slipped a revolver out of her purse and then aimed it at his midsection under the table. She pulled the gun's hammer back with a click.

"If you pull that trigger you'll never see your husband again," he advised her.

"And I'll never have to see you again," she said calmly.

"Nor I, you," he said as he pulled the hammer of *his* gun and tapped the underside of the table with its barrel. "It just so happens that I've been shot before. I know what to expect. I can tell you that it's not very pleasant at all. Have you ever been shot before, Gloria?"

She released the hammer on her gun, slipped it back into her purse and then placed her hands atop the table. She looked into his eyes and said, "If you harm my husband any more than you already have, I will gladly exchange bullets with you. I will watch you bleed and watch you die and will spit on your pathetic corpse."

"Fair enough then," he said, "but if you keep jerking me around or call the cops or have me tailed, my associates will bring you to me kicking and screaming. I'll show you no mercy whatsoever while I have my fun with you after which time I'll watch you die slowly. Am I clear?"

"You've made it quite clear that you're a pig," she said. "But it's also clear that you happen to have the upper-hand. I will bring you the money but only after you return George to me unharmed."

"Ain't gonna happen, sweetheart. You'll get the key to where your husband is being held only *after* the money is in our hands. No money, no George, no negotiation."

"Why the hell should I trust you?" she asked sternly.

"Because you have no other choice, Gloria. Yeah, I *could* kill George *and* take your money but why would I? He's no good to me dead or alive after I've been paid so I'll keep him alive as a favor to you because that's the deal."

"I want to speak to my husband on the telephone before I give you the money," she demanded.

"Fair enough, we can do that," he said, and then he pointed toward the wall by the cash register. "That phone will ring tomorrow night at nine o'clock. You answer it, you speak to your husband, I hand you a key and an address and walk away with the cash. We part ways and everyone's happy."

Gloria slipped out from the booth. She stood tall and turned her back toward him. She walked across the diner's floor, paused, and then stepped out the door. Ted watched as she popped her umbrella open under the diner's awning and then walked elegantly across the wet city street. He stared through the rain running down the cold glass window.

Ted Nixon had tailed George and Gloria Gordon for six weeks before he and his cohorts decided to make their move. The Gordons lived in an upscale apartment building guarded by private security personnel disguised as doormen. Before he began watching the couple, Ted's intention was to nab Gloria. He figured that a woman would be more manageable in the long run. The problem became that Gloria was rarely in a situation where an abduction would go unnoticed. She took taxis in public, went shopping in crowds and spent leisure days at a country club that would be difficult at best to gain unnoticed access to. Her husband on the other hand, was more accessible. He drove his own car to his bank job, spent many evenings in taverns or restaurants with clients and friends and enjoyed long, so-called "lunches" with various lady friends. He spent his weekend days at the club with his wife or alone at a cheesy midtown massage parlor near the docks. Most Friday and Saturday nights he was out on the town with his wife at the theatre or in a fine restaurant with other well-dressed, well-to-do couples. At sixty years of age, George Gordon was more vulnerable. He was twenty years older, six inches shorter and fifty pounds heavier than his tall, athletic wife. He was often alone in parking lots or on dark city streets late at night. He was often drunk or nearly so. He would be abducted and kidnapped in broad daylight from an empty industrial parking alley after spending two relaxing and exhausting hours in the skillful hands and legs of an exotic South Pacific masseuse.

"Got a light?" a man in work dungarees carrying a metal lunchbox asked George Gordon as George bent over to unlock the door of his Buick.

"I don't smoke but my wife does," George told the man. "As I recall, she keeps a lighter in the glove box."

"Much obliged, pal. I just got off the graveyard shift and a smoke would be nice while I wait for that goddamn weekend bus that rolls around once an hour if I'm lucky."

George opened his car door. He slid onto the bench seat and then leaned over to pop open the glove box, nearly lying down in the process. Ted Nixon ducked into the car and drove both of his bent knees into the back of George's kidneys. The impact forced all of the air out of George's lungs. As Ted's elbows came down hard on the back of George's shoulders, the victim kicked his feet and thrashed his pinned arms in vain. Ted grabbed George's hair and pulled his head back cracking the man's neck in the process. Ted reached around George's face and pressed a chloroform-soaked rag over his nose and mouth. George snorted and squealed like a pig destined for an Easter Sunday table. He was out like a light in seconds, lying flat on his face across the car seat. Ted slid out of the car, closed the door quietly and then walked briskly to a seedy tavern across the empty street. Once inside, Ted pretended to slip a dime into the tavern's payphone as he held the phone to his ear. A patron sitting at the bar took the cue. He tossed a dollar bill onto the bar top and then stood up to leave.

Ted and Lenny slumped George into the trunk of the victim's Buick and then drove out of the city smiling.

"Did he put up a good fight?" Lenny asked.

"It was like changing a baby's diaper... only easier," Ted reported. The two men laughed as they sped onto the highway toward a cabin waiting in the woods an hour away.

The night after Gloria first met Ted, the diner's pay phone rang at exactly nine o'clock. Gloria rose from the counter and answered the call. She spoke for a few moments, hung up the phone and then joined Ted in his booth by the window.

"Well, Gloria... does your hubby miss you?"

"He does indeed."

"And did you tell him that you miss him too?"

"I did not."

"And why would that be?"

"Because, Mr. Nixon, it's not true, that's why not."

"With all due respect, Mrs. Gordon, you are one, cold bitch. It's a wonder why he misses you at all."

"He misses me because I'm the only one who can save his pathetic life."

"So... are you *going* to save his life?" Ted asked, teasing her unmercifully.

"I don't think so," she replied casually, catching Ted totally off guard. "I've decided that you can keep him," she lied, staring calmly into Ted's eyes.

"I'll cut his throat wide open," Ted warned her as his mind raced through the current situation which he was by no means, prepared for.

"So be it then," she said. "He's not worth sixty thousand dollars to me. He's nothing more than my sugar-daddy, just as he's been the entire ten years we've been married. If you cut daddy's throat... I still get the sugar. It's in the will."

"Then I'll cut your throat too, Gloria," Ted threatened her. He lit a cigarette and blew the smoke in her face.

"You don't frighten me, Mr. Nixon. You're no powerful mobster. You're a second-rate thug, a two-bit loser. You're just some street creep who picks on the weak and vulnerable; like George. I on the other hand, Mr. Nixon, am strong. I'll blow your balls off right now without blinking an eye if you make a move. I can afford even more security than I already have. Do you see that gorilla that just walked in? He works for me. He packs a really big gun and he uses it quite nicely I might add. He really enjoys the extra perks and I pay him handsomely for his services. He does whatever I ask, whenever I ask him to. He'll twist your neck like the chicken you are if you so much as wink at me. Are we clear?"

"What do you think your husband will say about this?"

"I imagine he'll piss his pants when you tell him that you're going to cut his throat but the truth is, Mr. Nixon, you'll be doing me a favor. Do you see that now? Do you see what a fool you've been and still are?"

"I'll have him revise his will," Ted warned her. "He wouldn't need much convincing when he learns that you *want* him dead. He'd suddenly become valuable to you again, wouldn't he?"

"I'll call that bluff in a heartbeat. What are you going to do, Mr. Nixon, walk him into an attorney's office with a gun at his back? You're pathetic don't you know?"

"I'll tell the police that you were in on it. I'll tell them that it was *your* idea and that *you* hired *me* to stage it all," he suggested, thinking out loud as fast as he could.

"Even if they *do* believe you, which they won't, you'll still end up in prison, Mr. Nixon. I can afford the best trial lawyer in the city, can you? I think not. You'll end up with some bumbling public defender and spend the rest of your miserable life behind bars whether I get convicted or not which is highly unlikely. Besides, what evidence do you have that I was in on it? None, I'd imagine."

She was no fool, Ted thought. In her opinion, she had him in the palm of her hand. He realized then why she never made a threat to call the police. She either wanted her husband dead or could care less if he actually was. If she had *any* feelings at all for her husband maybe she would agree to less ransom. George was still making money hand-over-fist for her at the bank. His investments and client accounts were keeping her in furs and diamonds and caviar; surely he was worth something to her alive. On the other hand, if George *was* in fact worth more to her dead than alive, maybe he could make sure that her husband ended up that way and collect some kind of disposal fee from her. He had nothing to lose either way and so far, the way things were going, he had absolutely nothing to gain.

"Let's say then, that we turn the tables, Mrs. Gordon," Ted began.

"In what way," she asked with curious indifference.

"Let's say that I work for *you* now, Gloria. Let's say that I can help you achieve your immediate goals. Let's say that, given your current position, I am at your disposal. What can I do for *you*?" he offered.

She considered his proposal carefully. She considered her options and weighed the benefits and risks. So far, aside from not reporting the kidnapping to the police, she was clean. Her defense would be her undeniable, terrible fear that George would have been killed if she had reported his abduction because after all, that was exactly what Ted had told her. George was a good provider, a very good provider. He loved her deeply in his own imperfect way but he ran around on her like most married men do. Gloria had always tried to make herself sexy and desirable to him. She was blessed with inherent good looks and a lasting youthful appearance that made all but her best girlfriends jealous. But over the years, Gloria had to rely on sexy lingerie and silly sex toy novelties in order to grab her husband's attention in the bedroom. Her efforts had not always been successful. Gloria may not have been able to accept and forgive her husband's indiscretions with who knows how many younger or prettier gals, but she did at least understand his temptation and subsequent weakness. After all, she herself had enjoyed her own flings on occasion. George may even have been aware of her affairs. How could he not suspect? George was no dummy. He never said a word though, never made an accusation and never gave her any grief whatsoever. Gorge was a kind and comforting teddy bear when she needed him to be. He wasn't all that much to look at but he could be a tiger in the sheets and could always make her laugh. He was well-liked by anyone who ever met him and was adored by all of his friends. George had never laid a violent hand on her and had always allowed her the freedom to come and go as she pleased. Did he deserve such a horrible and terrifying end? Gloria was suddenly much more fearful for him than she had been. She reminded herself that George had given her ten decent years of marriage. Before that, he'd been her best friend and companion near the end of her first marriage. She had acted tough with this two-bit, jackass criminal in order to give him notice of her toughness but through it all, she had hidden her fear and kept a soft spot in her heart for her poor husband. She had no doubt that George had been and remained terrified every second of every hour during the last five horrible days.

"Whatever happens, it needs to happen quickly," she said at first, postponing any decision or commitment. "George's bank is currently under the impression that he's out of town for a family funeral. Come Monday, they'll start wondering what's up if he doesn't come back to work or phone in."

"I move quickly, Gloria. You're the one who's dragging this out. You're the one stalling and changing your mind. I'm trying to work with you but my patience is rapidly wearing thin. I don't give a damn that you have a gun and a gorilla. I've hunted gorillas before. They bleed like all animals do. And due to your stonewalling, Gloria, you'll find me much more dangerous now than I was just five days ago. If I'm going to prison it won't be before you and your husband and your goddamn gorilla have bled out dead. It may very well start right here right now, or later tonight... or tomorrow... or at any other goddamn time and place that I choose but know this, Gloria; I'm ending this soon. It's your call as to exactly *how* it will end. If you *really* don't care if your husband is dead or alive then we have something in common, Mrs. Gordon, because I really don't care one way or the other if the *both* of you live or die. I can easily imagine you dead, Gloria, and I won't hesitate to make it so."

"Get this straight, Mr. Nixon," she shouted and then she lowered her voice, "I don't want *anyone* killed. I didn't *choose* to have anyone killed, Mr. Nixon. You brought this shit on us because you're nothing more than a worthless piece of shit. The sooner I'm no longer forced to look at you, to talk to you and to think about you, the better. I have twenty thousand dollars in my purse. I can't get another forty thousand without my husband's signature or without his verbal request to his bank over the telephone. I am not however, simply going to hand you the money that I *do* have and watch you walk out of here. My husband and I may be comfortably well-off but we're not rolling-in-dough rich, Mr. Nixon. If you weren't so goddamn stupid you'd have realized that by now. Twenty thousand dollars is a lot of cash. Sixty thousand may be out of reach unless my husband has liquid assets I'm unaware of. Most of what we have is tied up in stocks and bonds that would require both of our signatures to liquidate. If you take me and my gorilla to George right now, I'll hand you the twenty thousand and walk away. That is my best and final offer."

Ted considered her proposal. Twenty thousand split three ways wouldn't go very far. He'd been banking on twenty thousand apiece. He could take Lenny out easily enough but that would leave him with a measly ten grand. He could take both of his partners out and end up with twenty grand all to himself. He tended to believe Gloria when she said that she needed her husband to access more money. Ted decided to play along for a while and see where the cards fell.

"I won't ride with the two of you in one car. I'll need a car of my own," he lied. Lenny had dropped Ted off near the diner earlier in George's car and was lying low with it at the cabin. But Ted figured that the Buick was too risky to move around much more. A new car wouldn't be reported stolen until it actually *was* stolen. By that time he could be three states away with a relatively clean set of wheels and ten or twenty grand in his pocket.

"A second car can be arranged," Gloria said.

"Show me the money," Ted ordered quietly.

Gloria lifted her purse onto the table and spread it open. She reached in and flipped open a thick envelope wedged against her revolver. The envelope was stuffed with two hundred, hundred dollar bills.

"Bring your gorilla over here."

Gloria rose and walked over to the diner's counter. She spoke briefly to the huge man who was sipping coffee as he sat balanced on a relatively tiny stool like some kind of circus act. The gorilla stood up on two legs and then walked with Gloria back to the booth. She slid into the booth as far as possible to allow room for her companion. He barely fit in beside her.

"We're all going for ride," Ted began. "An hour away, my associates are entertaining your dear Mr. Gordon. Aside from the necessary sampling of his finger, he's been well cared for. I imagine he'll be happy to see you when you enter the building, Gloria, but *you* my friend, will remain in the car at all times is that clear?"

"No good," the talking gorilla said.

"And why would that be?" Ted asked.

"We both wait outside. You bring Mr. Gordon outside. If you don't like that I break your neck right now, okay?"

"Well now, that won't be necessary, my good man. Besides, if that should in fact happen, my associates will hunt you down and gut you like the animal you are while you scream like a pregnant woman giving sudden birth to your bloody organs. Is *that* okay with *you,* you son of a bitch?" Ted asked in restrained, quiet anger. Not waiting for a reply, Ted stood up and pointed his gun discreetly yet directly at the gorilla's huge head. "Meet me here in one hour with a second car, Gloria. And calm this beast down in the meantime if you want to see your Georgie-boy in one piece again. Is that clear?"

"I promise he'll behave himself," she said, placing her hand atop her companion's giant paw. "Unless of course I tell him to rip your head off," she added as she leaned her head against the gorilla's mountainous chest and stroked his thick, muscular leg under the table. Ted left the diner. Gloria kissed the gorilla. The gorilla grunted.

The gorilla followed the glowing red taillights of the nearly invisible black Mercury that Ted was driving. Gloria had borrowed the car from a friend. She'd driven it herself the five blocks back to the diner where she waited with the kidnapper for the gorilla who finally showed up half an hour later in his own car. Gloria handed the Mercury's keys to Ted at the curb outside the diner and then slipped into the gorilla's car parked behind it. As the Mercury pulled out and into the night, the couple followed. For the next half hour Gloria sat quietly beside the gorilla on the soft leather seat of his smoothly humming Hudson. She had recently hired him as her personal bodyguard and impersonal lover. As is the case with most gorillas, hers wasn't much of a talker. And so, Gloria sat in silence and listened to herself worry nervously about things to come.

Weeks earlier, Gloria's biggest problem at the time had been rectified when she'd switched to a more reliable drycleaner. She was now involved in a life and death situation for which she had no experience and for which she was totally unprepared. Why on earth hadn't she called the cops when Ted Nixon (if that was in fact his real name) first phoned her apartment nearly a week ago? The police are trained in such matters. Detectives would have tracked her husband down and rescued him by now. Or... they would have moved too quickly or carelessly and would have instead, brought a lifeless body to the morgue where Gloria would've nodded her head "yes" when asked if the body was her husband's. The latter was a chance that Gloria refused to take. Her decision to not risk getting the police involved was made easier when Gloria confided in her best friend Suzanne. Suzanne agreed wholeheartedly with Gloria's decision to keep the police out of it and went on to tell Gloria about a kidnapping that she had personal knowledge of. It had gone horribly wrong. Suzanne shared the gruesome details with Gloria who immediately became scared to death for George. Gloria was, for the most part, just playing with Ted Nixon when she told him that she didn't care about George. The truth was, she still loved him deeply and she desperately wanted him back safely. But after taking what she had thought at the time was the wisest course of action, she then realized that she was taking extreme risks with her own life. Nevertheless, due to the sudden subconscious exhilaration she was feeling, Gloria was either ignoring or was unaffected by the potential danger she was in. As a result, adrenaline rushed through her veins. It infused her with an exhilarating zest for life that she hadn't experienced in years. Gloria's entire life to date had been one of stress-free leisure made possible by the continuous attention of doting men. Her father had spoiled her since birth. He bought her the best things that money could buy. After her mother's tragic death, Gloria's father hired nannies and servants to pamper his daughter's every waking hour. He sent her away to exclusive private schools and showered her with gifts during holiday breaks. Gloria never had to wash a load of laundry or cook a single meal. She never operated a sewing machine, a steam iron, or for that matter, a dustpan and broom. Why on earth would she when others were paid to do those things for her? Up until the time that her first husband was indicted, tried and convicted for tax evasion, he also, had treated her like a princess. He continued spoiling her, even from prison, using hidden assets via third-party accounts administered by his banker; George Gordon. During her husband's second year in prison, Gloria's loyalty to him first faltered after she and George had enjoyed one-too-many, post-dinner cocktails. After a wild night of drunken sexual gratification, the couple finally fell asleep at sunrise the next day. Gloria divorced her husband while he remained in prison. With George's help, she took sole ownership of her ex-husband's hidden assets after he had slashed his wrists with a butcher knife in the prison kitchen. And so it was that gorgeous Gloria became happily married then to the least likely of suitors, the barely-attractive but extremely-charismatic, Mr. George G. Gordon. Because of her good looks and her husband's good nature, it wasn't long before the odd couple became a crowd favorite among the many high society circles in which they found themselves spinning. George and Gloria became regarded as fun and fashionable and entertaining. They were invited to parties virtually every weekend. They attended the weddings, funerals, birthday parties and bar mitzvahs of people they barely knew by virtue of the fact that they would spice up any guest list. They spent weekends with wealthy businessmen and their wives at extravagant seaside resorts. They attended parties in countryside villas nestled away unseen by the lower classes. Gloria ate, drank and remained merry, morning, noon and night while George's savvy investment skills made the board members of banks and corporations even wealthier. George earned an excellent salary himself but he facilitated obscene profits for his clients who showed their gratitude by lavishing George and his wife with tax-free gifts and vacations which the couple gratefully accepted. Over the years, George and Gloria had seen most European countries and many South American capitals. Their upscale apartment became lavishly appointed with fine furnishings and art. They held small parties of their own that became the talk of the town when celebrities and politicians alike made impromptu appearances just to be seen with the couple. But over the years, the couple's popularity began to fade; some say that it burned itself out as new faces arrived on the scene to take their place. The Gordons however, didn't seem to mind. They willingly surrendered their whirlwind lives to ones of quiet respite. They had drifted well under the social radar when Ted Nixon saw his opportunity.

Gloria paced her apartment when she'd received the news of her husband's kidnapping. She didn't necessarily need George specifically, but she couldn't imagine not having a man in her life. The gorilla gave Gloria immediate substitute comfort. He, the mighty Jason, was the antithesis of George; physically strong, intellectually weak, exciting to look at, but extremely boring to talk to. Gloria quickly learned to enjoy Jason's physical prowess while mostly ignoring his mundane intellect. He was just what she needed and she needed him quite often. He had come highly recommended to her by her best friend Suzanne who had herself, thoroughly enjoyed his services. Suzanne vouched for his discretion and loyalty when she gave Gloria his phone number. Jason was a bodyguard first and foremost. He had reportedly saved clients' lives and had taken a few himself in the process. He'd been shot, stabbed, choked with piano wire and buried at sea but always rose from the dead to exact revenge on those foolish enough to believe that he'd been properly disposed of. The specific facts of Jason's feats were never made public but they became legendary to those private clients who'd either experienced them firsthand or sought his services because of them. As a result, Jason didn't come cheap but according to Suzanne, when he did come, it was worth every penny. Gloria banked on him to help her see things through.

"Jason darling," she said.

"Talk to me, Gloria."

"Are we doing the right thing?"

"So far."

"Does this Ted character worry you?" she asked.

"Not a bit."

"Who do you imagine is working with him?"

"I'm guessing additional criminals."

"Do *they* worry you?" she asked.

"Not a bit."

"Darling, how can you say that when you don't even know who they are?"

"It's easy to say when I don't give a damn *who's* working with him. If they're working with him they're obviously idiots. Idiots don't worry me. Idiots make mistakes. It's the smart ones that cause problems."

Gloria admired Jason's confidence but was not impressed by his less-than-profound observations. In her estimation, he may not have been an idiot, but he was no genius either. What if he was reading the situation all wrong and George ended up dead? Gloria opened her purse and pulled out her gun. She spun the cylinder checking the chambers for rounds.

"You may not want to point that in my direction," Jason suggested, keeping his eyes straight ahead on the road. "If it should go off accidentally my driving skills might suffer."

Gloria laughed embarrassedly having noticed that her gun was in fact, pointing directly at Jason's midsection. If it *had* accidentally discharged there would've been little chance that the bullet could've missed such an enormous target. She re-directed the gun toward her feet and took a deep breath.

"Have you ever fired that thing?" Jason asked her.

"Not yet," she confessed.

"Have you ever fired *any* gun?"

"Not yet," she repeated.

"Well, roll down your window and fire the damn thing."

"Should I?"

"I'm not asking, Gloria."

As ordered, Gloria cranked her window down. Fresh night air filled the car with sudden cold refreshment. She raised her gun with one hand and pointed it out the window toward the blackness rushing by along the side of the road.

"Hang on tight with both hands, Gloria. Bend both of your elbows slightly and squeeze the trigger slowly. Let the gun recoil to your left or right but never straight back against your pretty little nose."

Gloria held her breath and followed Jason's instructions verbatim. She sat there wondering what she'd done wrong.

"It works a little better if you disengage the safety first," he suggested.

"Well, why didn't you tell me that?" she asked.

"I just did," he said as the gun exploded and she screamed out in fear and delight.

"Again," he said. "Empty all of the chambers so our buddy Ted gets good and scared."

Gloria fired five more rounds. Jason watched as Ted's car swerved nervously ahead of them.

"That was fun!" she squeaked.

"Party's over. Engage the safety and put it away now."

"Are you proud of me, Jason? I did good right?"

"You're the best I know, Gloria."

Moments later, with its turn signal flashing, the Mercury slowed to a crawl as Ted searched for the un-marked access road to the cabin. Soon thereafter both cars turned off of the two-lane highway and onto a bumpy dirt road. Gloria had quickly and skillfully reloaded her revolver in the dark while Jason was preoccupied with following the Mercury. She had never fired her gun before but she loved playing with the bullets. She liked the way they felt in her fingers and the way that the gun itself, felt elsewhere. She'd sit at home sipping wine while loading and unloading her gun. She'd bring it to bed with her on occasion or when she or George was in the mood to be handcuffed. She'd slip a bullet between George's lips and then lick it and suck it like candy. Having finally fired her gun, she was suddenly willing and able to come to her husband's rescue with her sexy gun a-blazing.

The tandem of cars plowed ahead slowly through the pitch-black woods. The deep sound of crunching gravel was accompanied by a high pitched chorus of frogs and crickets. The Mercury's headlights illuminated a small wood cabin ahead of it. Ted hit his car horn loud and long causing Gloria to pee herself a tiny bit as the unexpected shock of sound rang out. Ted parked the Mercury to the right of the cabin's front door. He stepped out of the car, paused briefly to give Jason a five-finger "wait right there" sign and then proceeded to enter the cabin. Once Ted was inside the cabin, both of its lit windows dimmed as he drew their curtains. Gloria sat still, her gun in her lap. Jason drew his own gun from its holster.

"Is that your husband's car?" Jason asked her, pointing the barrel of his gun toward the Buick parked to the left of the cabin door.

"It is," she said as she pressed her gun between her slightly damp legs. She squirmed at the thought of walking up to the cabin to use its bathroom, "Um… excuse me, Mr. Kidnappers, I'll just be a minute…" Had she done so however, she would have been directed to a gully behind the cabin over which hung; a well-used but never-cleaned outhouse.

With his car still running, Jason cracked open his door to switch on the car's interior dome light. He switched off the dome light at the dashboard and then did the same to the headlights. He engaged the parking brake, opened his door all the way and then stood up behind it.

"Hand me the money," he told Gloria.

Jason took the envelope from her and then slipped it into his pants pocket. The back of his head cracked open as a single shot rang out. Gloria screamed as she watched Jason sink to his knees. Lenny approached the rear of the idling car more closely as he swung his rifle toward the cabin. He thought that he'd take Ted out next and then pump a few rounds into George. He'd teach them all once and for all, not to steal a man's finger. He would save the dame for later; maybe have some fun with her. Gloria held her breath and her screams as she stretched out her arms. She held her gun tightly in both hands and aimed it toward the open driver's side door. She heard footsteps on gravel approaching from behind the car. She watched as a man ducked his head down past the car's open door.

"Give me the money," the man hissed, keeping his gaze and rifle directed toward the cabin.

Gloria held her breath and squeezed a shot into the side of the man's head. She screamed as he was blown sideways. She fired again but her second shot missed. The man slumped to the ground. Lenny's lifeless body landed atop Jason's. Gloria swung her door wide open. She jumped out of the car and bent down behind the door. She was shaking terribly but felt immediate relief as she began to pee.

"What the hell?" Ted yelled as he ducked out of the cabin and squatted down in front of the Mercury.

Gloria remained crouched behind the car door. She followed Ted's voice blindly with the barrel of her gun as she held it above her head through the car's open window.

"Lenny, you there?" Ted yelled and then waited. "Jason, you there?" he yelled.

Gloria wondered immediately how it was that Ted knew Jason's name. She didn't recall his name being mentioned at the diner. Her mind rushed in waves as her heart pounded in her chest. Her breasts rose and fell with each short anxious breath. She swore that Jason's name hadn't been spoken.

"Lenny's dead..." Gloria yelled, assuming that the man she had just shot was Lenny. She quickly debated herself whether or not to announce that Jason was dead as well. She could not decide quickly enough if it would be an advantage or a disadvantage to her so she ignored the fact that he *was* dead and yelled, "...and you'll be dead too if you don't bring my husband out this instant!"

Gloria reached inside the car and accidentally pulled the dome light on. She quickly pushed it off again and then pulled the knob next to it. She grinned as the Hudson's headlights shined on Ted's face.

"Calm down now, Gloria!" Ted yelled as he squinted in the bright beams. "I never told Lenny to ambush you. That jackass took it upon himself to get himself killed."

"Bring George out!" Gloria demanded.

"Okay, okay, I'll do what you say, Gloria, but put your damn gun away," Ted said as he wondered what in the hell had happened to Jason.

Gloria held her gun steady as the cabin door opened. She watched as Ted pushed her husband through it. George was handcuffed. He held his arms bent in front of him as if he were praying. George squinted in the Hudson's headlights. He yelled, "Gloria…?"

"George!" she yelled. "Stay calm and do what he says."

"Where's my money?" Ted yelled as he shoved George closer toward Jason's car.

"Your money's in Jason's pocket," Gloria said loudly but calmly. She could see both men clearly by then as they were directly in front of her.

"Well… give me my money or I'll blow your husband's head off!" Ted yelled.

"Get your own damn money, Ted. Your asshole friend Lenny shot Jason and is lying on top of him right now. I'm not touching either of them so get your own damn money yourself!" she screamed.

Ted shoved George in front of him past the Hudson's headlights toward the driver's side of the car. They shuffled around the open door. Ted pushed George and then pushed him again harder down to the ground.

"Get my money!" Ted yelled as he held his revolver against the back of George's head.

"It won't be easy with these handcuffs on," George complained as he twisted his head around to look up at Ted from his knees.

Ted searched for the key to the handcuffs in his pants pockets as Gloria stood up slowly. In one deliberate motion, without grinding the gravel beneath her feet, she swiveled her hips toward Ted and swung her gun up and over the top of the Hudson. She held her gun firmly with both hands and let the heels of her hands come down to rest atop the car's roof. She aimed steadily at Ted's ear as he tossed a key down to George. Ted caught a glimpse of Gloria out of the corner of his eye. He turned to confront her and raised his gun. A single shot rang out. It drove through the bridge of Ted's nose and out the back of his skull. It echoed loudly through the woods. Ted stared in disbelief and into her bright green eyes before he sunk lifeless to his knees.

Gloria ran around the back of the car and dove atop her husband. She wrapped her arms around him and kissed the top of his head. "Is that all of them, George?" she asked as she scanned the cabin and the dark woods surrounding it.

"Yes, Gloria, just those three," George said as he hugged his wife having finally managed to unlock his cuffs.

"Three?" she asked him. "What do you mean three?"

"The three guys that you just shot dead, Gloria. That's all of them," he said.

"But I didn't shoot Jason. This guy Lenny shot Jason," she told her husband, confused.

"Why would Lenny shoot Jason?" George wondered out loud. "They were all in it together…. unless Lenny was trying to take Jason's share of the ransom."

George hugged his wife tightly as the couple sat on the front seat of the Hudson. Gloria continued to wonder how it was that both her husband and Ted knew Jason.

"What I really want to know, my love, is… when on earth did you learn to shoot like that?" George asked his wife.

"About ten minutes ago," she said blankly as she shrugged

off her husband, pulled the keys out of the ignition and then jumped out of the car. She walked immediately around to the back of the car and opened its trunk. She stood there, staring into the dim light of the trunk as George came to her side. Before he had a chance to ask her what was wrong, he couldn't help but notice the trunk's contents.

"Looks like they tried to clean us out as well," he said as the two of them tossed through Gloria's fur coats and discovered her jewelry boxes and George's bank bonds buried beneath them. "How the hell did they break into our apartment without you knowing, Gloria?"

Gloria stormed around the car and confronted the pile of corpses. She stared into Ted's dead eyes briefly and with the toe of her shoe, flipped him over face-first. She bent down and jerked his wallet out from his back pocket. She sat down on the driver's side of the Hudson, pulled the dome light on and began rifling through Ted's wallet.

"What on earth are you looking for, dear?" George asked as he slid in beside her on the passenger side.

"This..." she said as her shaking hand held out a photograph of Suzanne.

George took the photograph from his wife with his right hand and took both of her hands in his left. Her hands trembled while George examined the photograph. Having easily recognized who it was in the photograph, George asked his wife, "What the hell is going on, Gloria?"

"Your hand! My God, George... your hand... they brought me your finger with your wedding band wrapped around it!"

"Oh, sweetheart... you poor thing!" George said as he reached his arm across her waist and pulled her toward him. "That was Lenny's finger. The stupid fool whacked it off with an axe when he was trying to split firewood. He begged Ted and Jason to take him to the hospital so it could be sewn back on. They refused! They said it was too risky. So Lenny tried to bandage his own finger back on his bloody hand with a sock. He drank half a bottle of whiskey to kill the pain. I got to admit, it was quite a pathetic sight. When Lenny had finally passed out drunk, Ted yanked off my wedding ring and then pulled Lenny's severed finger out from the bandage. He shoved my ring on Lenny's finger, wrapped them both up in his handkerchief, left me with Jason and then drove off! While Lenny was still passed-out, Jason re-wrapped the poor fool's hand so he wouldn't even realize that they had stolen his finger. I had to bite my tongue to keep from laughing. Jason would have blown my head off if I had. So how was your week, dear?" George joked.

"Terrible!" she said, slapping her husband's arm. "I was worried sick over you! And now I've come to learn that my best friend stood by as we both got fucked-over and nearly killed!"

"Well, you can stop worrying now, my love. Suzanne's not going anywhere... we can deal with her tomorrow. Look on the bright side; you saved your beloved husband, you watched one nasty thug get his just reward and sent two others straight to hell yourself. You are quite the extraordinary woman, Gloria. As a reward... may I show you into my cozy cabin by chance, and offer you a cocktail or a cock in your tail?"

The couple wrapped themselves up all warm and snuggly in Gloria's furs. They took turns sipping Lenny's whiskey straight from the bottle. The furs felt divine on Gloria's naked body and the whiskey and George felt divine inside her. The couple rolled around laughing as they pounced upon each other repeatedly. Gloria shouted and then shuttered and sighed as George celebrated his release from captivity inside her. When the sun rose the next morning, the couple strolled outside for some fresh air. George puked when he saw the gunshot corpses he hadn't seen very well the night before.

Suzanne Smits entered the Nine O'clock Diner as invited; promptly at nine o'clock. She looked around quickly and then waved her hand high in the air to Gloria who was sitting in the back booth. Suzanne walked proudly and briskly past the customers sitting at the counter on her way to join her friend. Suzanne was a country club hostess by day but you'd never guess it by the way that she dressed at night. She was all about style; looking her best and attracting men who could improve her situation. Her too-many-to-mention men often showered her with gifts after she'd showered with them. Her previous beau was none other than Jason James Jackson; a gorilla of a man who could care less if she saw other men. Suzanne was fine with that because it prevented her from becoming bored to death in a monotonous, monogamous relationship. She had never been the marrying type, although she could've been swayed if a tycoon had happened along. Unfortunately for her though, most of the wealthy men she'd been with, bored her in the end, and in the front. The few wealthy men she *did* happen to like, tired of *her*, and so, she'd run back to Jason. She and Jason had often made big plans together but they could never quite see them through. Jason finally decided that he needed a couple of thugs to help him pull off his latest and most brilliant, infallible scheme. So he recruited Ted Nixon and Lenny Cobb. Lenny gave Suzanne the creeps but she took an immediate shine to Ted. Ted didn't disappoint her. Suzanne ended up spending more time with Ted than she did with Jason. When Jason told Suzanne that Gloria's husband was in the their sights, she made him promise that no harm would come to George. At times, George himself had been very generous to Suzanne and she ended up liking him a lot more than most of her other flings. But Suzanne felt bad using Gloria's husband in that way and truth be told... Suzanne actually preferred Gloria to George. The two women could often be seen in one another's company. They'd shop and have lunch and pick up men and swap men between themselves and then dump them and end up in bed together. They'd roll around and laugh and get drunk and talk about men or shoes or parties they'd been to or parties they hoped to be invited to. When Gloria didn't have George or another man by her side she could always rely on Suzanne for entertainment. They'd often have wild spontaneous sex with one another whenever men weren't around or didn't seem to be worth the trouble.

"So how's it going with Jason?" Suzanne asked excitedly as she slid onto the seat across from Gloria. "Is he everything that I told you he was?"

"More or less," Gloria said as she pushed a bundled handkerchief across the table toward her so-called friend. "But he's much *less* of a man now, as is your Ted."

- The End -

Nine Won One

While the Gods play billiards an errant shot wreaks havoc…

It was 11:11 p.m. on the eleventh day of January, 2011, when I called 9-1-1…

"What's your emergency?" an anonymous voice asked me.

"I just witnessed a giant, nine-ball of fire crash out of the sky!" my anonymous voice announced excitedly.

"Did you say a *nine* ball of fire, sir?" the woman asked.

"Yes, an enormous yellow ball of fire with the number nine emblazoned on it."

"Can you spell emblazoned?"

"Uh, no. Don't you have spell check?"

"Oh yeah, sorry…. My supervisor's been on my case about spelling. I tend to forget to use spell check because I'm a pretty good speller to begin with so I usually just assume that I'm spelling everything correctly but when you said, *emblazoned,* I knew that I'd mess that one up. Here it is; emblazoned, e-m-b-l-a-z-o-n-e-d, emblazon; to ornament with heraldic or other devices. Heraldic? What the heck is Heraldic? Let's see… heraldic; of heralds. 1). An official in former times who made announcements and carried messages from a ruler. No… that doesn't sound right. 2). A person or thing indicating the approach of something, i.e. heralds of spring. Well that makes sense. You've apparently witnessed the approach of something. I wonder what it could be?" the dispatcher asked me.

"How about… a giant nine-ball of fire?" I suggested.

"Well now we're getting somewhere!" she replied and then asked, "Where did you say your present location was, sir?"

"I didn't."

"Okay then. Where *is* your present location?"

"I'm not sure. I got lost so I stopped to ask for directions."

"So, can you ask somebody where you are?"

"I would but there's nobody around here right now. I'm all alone."

"Okay... who then, were you planning to ask for directions if there's nobody around you?"

"Anyone I could find," I answered.

"But you didn't find anyone at your present location?"

"No! I mean, Yes, I didn't find anyone here! That's exactly what I've already told you!"

"There's no need to get snippy with me, sir, I'm just trying to help you."

"Sorry," I offered, slightly embarrassed.

"That's all right, um... what did you say your name was, sir?"

"I didn't. You didn't ask me my name and to save time and expedite this process I'm going to give you my name right now. Are you ready, ma'am?"

"I am."

"Ted E. Bear," I said, at which point I no longer remained anonymous.

"Can you spell that?"

"Yes, I can."

"Well, will you spell it for me then?"

"T-E-D, capital E period, B-E-A-R; Ted E. Bear."

"Ted E. Bear. Teddy Bear? Are you joking with me, sir? Do you realize that it is a serious crime to place a fictitious, non-emergency, crank phone call to the 9-1-1 system under any circumstance and that it is punishable by six months in jail or a thousand dollar fine or both, Mr. Ted E. Bear?"

"No, I'm not joking, yes, I know the laws and the penalties for not obeying them, and please call me Ted."

"Okay, enough of that for now, Ted. Can you identify any road signs or describe your surroundings?"

"No, I'm standing in the center of a giant ball of fire and it's so bright, I can't see beyond it."

"So, you're in immediate danger?"

"Yes, that's why I called you."

By that time the searing flames had nearly reached me. The laces of my sneakers were igniting like candle wicks.

"Can you hurry? I begged her. "I'm catching on fire!"

"Drop immediately to the ground, Ted, and roll around to extinguish the flames!" she ordered, to which I did but which resulted in my entire body being engulfed in flames that charred and melted away all of the skin and flesh from my blackening brittle bones.

"What lousy advice," I thought out loud.

"I beg your pardon, sir?" I heard from my cell phone which by then was also melting away in the flames.

And so, while my charred and brittle bones vaporized in the flames, the Gods above laughed at my misfortune. As one of the Gods bent over to pick up the errant nine-ball he'd sent flying off the table and crashing to Earth, my defiant soul made a loud farting sound. The other Gods laughed at him uproariously. The embarrassed God turned blood red, roared loudly and then immediately vanquished my soul to burn in eternal Hell from where I tell this, and other tales. But since Hell hast no fury (nor humidity) I find it quite pleasant indeed. Take That - Ye Omnipotent Gods!

Nuts About You

Summer

Like the heading says, it was summer, and it was Zippy the squirrel's very first summer. Zippy celebrated his very first summer by scampering happily up and down every tree that he saw, in search of delicious acorns. When Zippy would find an acorn he'd become even happier until he had either eaten the acorn or had hidden it away for later, at which point he would immediately set out to look for more acorns. One morning, while he was busy scampering and searching, Zippy spotted another squirrel. That particular squirrel however, was somehow different from the other squirrels that Zippy had seen. The squirrel was the same age as Zippy but was, he believed, a girl squirrel. He thought so because she was a lot prettier than the boy squirrels were and she reminded him of his momma who was also a girl but was more like a mother to him. At first, Zippy was intrigued when he saw the girl squirrel, but then he became hungry and forgot all about her when he set off to look for acorns. Throughout the course of Zippy's first summer, his schedule remained much of the same; look for acorns, eat some acorns, hide some acorns, look for more acorns, eat some more acorns, sleep when it got dark, wake up when the birds started singing and then start looking for more acorns. Zippy never tired of his routine because he had so much fun running through the trees and eating acorns which he considered quite tasty indeed. Near the end of that first summer, Zippy met a friend his age and the two became best buddies. Zippy's best buddy's name was

Fast Eddie because he was the fastest young squirrel in the forest. Zippy and Fast Eddie loved to race one another through the trees but Fast Eddie was much faster than Zippy was and would always win those races. One day, Zippy asked Fast Eddie, "How come you can run so fast, Fast Eddie?"

Fast Eddie replied, "I don't know, Zippy, I just do is all."

"Well I don't know either, Fast Eddie, so that's why I asked," Zippy said, and then the two of them took off running through the trees.

One day, a messenger squirrel named Lucky, came by to call Zippy and Fast Eddie and all of the other young squirrels to a young squirrel orientation lecture that was being held by Whiskers, the eldest squirrel in the forest. When the young squirrels arrived at the meeting, Whiskers was sitting stoically in the crotch of five huge branches in the center of the biggest tree in all of the forest. The young squirrels chatted amongst themselves as they gathered around Whiskers and sat upon smaller branches. Zippy and Fast Eddie arrived at the lecture late so they got bad seats in the back of the tree. Before the lecture began, Zippy happened to notice a really cute girl squirrel sitting ahead of him in the front row. The girl squirrel looked familiar to Zippy. "Had he seen her someplace before?" he wondered. "It could be," he thought but he couldn't quite put his paw on it so he asked his friend Fast Eddie, "Fast Eddie, do you know who that cute girl squirrel is, way up in the front row?"

Fast Eddie looked through the crowd in the direction that Zippy was pointing his paw and asked him, "Do you mean the one with the really nice bushy tail?"

Zippy confirmed, "Yes, that one."

Fast Eddie replied, "Nope," at which point all of the young

squirrels became suddenly frightened by a loud noise. It was Whiskers clearing his throat in preparation for his speech. "Beware the Hawks in Summer and the Owls in Winter," Whiskers bellowed and then he said calmly, "You may go now."

"That's it?" Fast Eddie asked Zippy.

"I guess so," Zippy guessed.

"So, Zippy... what do you think Whiskers meant when he said, "Beware the hawks in summer and the owls in winter?""

"I guess he meant that we should avoid getting snatched by hawks in the summer time and by owls in the winter time," Zippy surmised, as best as a young squirrel could surmise.

"Well, why didn't he just say so?" Fast Eddie wondered.

"We shouldn't question our elders," Zippy reminded his friend and then he said, "Darn! She's gone already!" because the pretty squirrel who Zippy liked had already left with her less-pretty friends. "I wanted to say hello to her, Fast Eddie, but I missed my chance, darn!"

"Better luck next seminar," Fast Eddie replied.

"I hope so too," Zippy said with a frown.

Late that same summer, while Zippy and Fast Eddie were taking an acorn-hunting break on a branch of their favorite tree next to the sunny meadow, they watched as a young squirrel ventured out into the meadow in search of stray acorns and tasty flowers. All of a sudden from out of the blue, a giant hawk swooped down out of the sky. It dove toward the ground, pounced atop the pour squirrel, snatched it up fast and swooped it away! Zippy and Fast Eddie were so horrified they couldn't speak until Zippy finally said solemnly, "Beware the hawks in summer."

"I'm glad that summer's almost over," Fast Eddie replied.

Autumn

Well, summer finally ended and autumn began soon thereafter and Zippy and Fast Eddie spent every day looking for acorns. The acorns were easier to find in the trees because the green leaves were turning to bright colors and were beginning to fall. But the acorns were also harder to find on the ground because the falling leaves often covered them up. As a result, Zippy and Fast Eddie would have to dig under the leaves which, as time passed, were beginning to form huge piles. Zippy loved those piles of leaves because he could hide in them and then jump on Fast Eddie when his friend wasn't expecting it. Fast Eddie liked the new game that Zippy had invented. The two of them would take turns scaring each other and then chase one another up a tree. Zippy may have been slower than Fast Eddie was but he was much better at hiding. One day, Fast Eddie asked Zippy, "How come you can hide so good, Zippy?"

Zippy replied, "I don't know Fast Eddie, I just can is all."

"Well I don't know either, Zippy, so that's why I asked," Fast Eddie said and then the two of them took off running through the leaves.

One day, while Zippy was hiding in the leaves, he thought that Fast Eddie was running toward him so he jumped right on top of him. The funny thing was though, the squirrel that Zippy had jumped upon wasn't Fast Eddie at all. The squirrel that he had jumped on was different from the other squirrels Zippy had seen. The squirrel was Zippy's age but was, he believed, a girl squirrel. He thought so because she was a lot prettier than the boy squirrels were and she reminded him of his momma who was also a girl but was more like a mother to him. The squirrel that Zippy had accidentally jumped atop was very soft indeed, much softer than Fast Eddie for sure.

"That wasn't funny at all!" the girl squirrel complained to Zippy. "You frightened me terribly, do you know?"

"I'm so very sorry! I thought that you were my friend Fast Eddie," Zippy explained. "We always hide in the leaves and scare one another because it's fun."

"Well, if you think that I resemble Fast Eddie you are sadly mistaken, mister, and for the record... you will *never* be my friend," she announced in a huff and then added, "so go frighten another poor, unsuspecting squirrel," she said and then scampered away.

Zippy felt really, really bad that he had frightened her. He felt even worse when he finally remembered her as the very same squirrel that he'd seen in the springtime and had seen a second time at Whisker's lecture. She was so very pretty and had such nice long eyelashes that she batted quickly when she had become angry with him. When Zippy fell asleep that night he dreamt about her instead of the acorns that he usually dreamt about. He dreamt that she was no longer angry with him and was instead, his friend.

One day, a messenger squirrel named Fuzzy, came by to call Zippy and Fast Eddie and all of the other young squirrels to a young squirrel orientation lecture that was being held by Whiskers, the eldest squirrel in the forest. When the messenger squirrel spoke to Zippy and Fast Eddie, Zippy asked him, "I thought that Lucky was the messenger squirrel, Fuzzy. Why are *you* passing messages instead of Lucky?"

Fuzzy hesitated a bit but then finally said, "Because Lucky can no longer deliver messages. He was swooped away by a hawk last summer."

Zippy and Fast Eddie immediately remembered witnessing that very same event with their very own terrified eyes. They were so disturbed by the horrible news that the squirrel who'd been swooped away was Lucky, they were the first to arrive at the lecture. Because of that, they got really good seats right up in the front row. As the two of them sat quietly waiting for the lecture to begin, the other young squirrels filed in slowly and filled up nearly all of the branches. It was standing room only when someone tapped Zippy's shoulder and asked him, "Excuse me please, is this branch taken?"

"No, it is not taken. You may sit next to me," Zippy replied before he realized that it was his favorite girl squirrel who had asked and who was then sitting right next to him! Zippy summoned all of his courage and then turned slowly toward her and said, "You may not remember me but... I was the one in the pile of leaves who accidentally scared you. I just wanted to say that I am still very sorry."

"I forgive you," she said quickly.

"You do?" Zippy said, happily surprised.

"Yes, I do. I know that it was a mistake on your part to have frightened me. I was mean to you when I said that we would never be friends but I was so very frightened at the time that it made me angry with you. That was no excuse to be mean to you though. And so, I am sorry to you as well," she said as she batted her beautiful eyelashes.

"So... does that mean that we can be friends?" Zippy asked her and then he held his breath.

"Maybe," she replied.

All of the young squirrels gathered about were suddenly frightened and silenced as Whiskers cleared his old throat really loud and then began to speak. "Beware the Owls in

Winter and the Hawks in Summer," he bellowed and then he said calmly, "You may go now."

"I saw *that* coming," Fast Eddie said to Zippy.

Zippy replied, "You and me both, buddy," and then he shouted, "Wait!" to the cute girl squirrel who had been sitting next to him but was preparing to leave.

"My name is Zippy. What's your name?" he asked her.

"My name is Bushy," she replied with a smile.

"That's a *beautiful* name for such a *beautiful* squirrel!" he told her with glee and then he continued, "Your name is perfect for you because yours is the nicest and bushiest tail that I have ever seen!"

"Thank you!" she said. "You are so sweet to say so."

"Can I see you again?" Zippy asked and then held his breath.

"Maybe," she said and then she scampered away.

Yes, dear reader, even girl squirrels play hard to get.

Winter

The leaves had all fallen and the sky had turned grey. All of the squirrels had hoarded acorns away. The winters were cold and often were cruel. The squirrels huddled together for they had no warm fuel.

Like the other squirrels, Zippy slept a lot in the winter time. When Zippy slept he often dreamt and when he dreamt he dreamed of his true love Bushy. One fateful night however, Zippy was suddenly awakened by a bad dream that had frightened him terribly. He jumped out of his nest, climbed quickly down his tree and ran as fast as Fast Eddie to Bushy's tree. In the glow of the moonlight Zippy spotted an owl circling above the nest where Bushy was sleeping! Zippy gasped all of a sudden as the owl began diving straight down toward her!

Zippy ran up the tree trunk as fast as he could. He jumped at the owl as it dove on his love. He bit hard on the owl and he wouldn't let go. The owl screeched and took flight with Zippy in tow. The bird's talons scratched Zippy so he bit all the harder. The owl finally let go. Zippy fell, a brave martyr. He crashed through the treetops and right past his love. Zippy landed on a big branch and held on from above.

When Zippy regained his senses, he saw Bushy sitting on a branch right above him. With her tiny trembling paws held in prayer she asked him, "Oh my dear, Zippy, are you hurt?"

"A little bit I guess," he replied.

Bushy jumped down to his branch and then knelt down beside him. She licked his wounds clean and then said to him, "Come now, Zippy, let's get out of this cold wind."

And so, they climbed up the tree and into her warm nest. They held one another and got some good rest. The owl was long gone, it had learned its hard lesson; if you attack sweet Bushy, with Zippy you'll be messin'. A short while later, when the two had awoken, they gazed at each other, but no words were spoken.

A longer while later, Bushy smiled and said, "You are so very brave, Zippy. You are my true hero!" She kissed him, oh so very sweetly and then asked him, "Zippy, will you promise me that you'll never leave my side?"

"I'll stay with you always, my love, except to look for acorns of course," he said with a smile.

Bushy laughed out loud for the first time that cold winter and then she gave Zippy another nice, warm kiss.

The winter was freezing but those two kept quite warm. They held each other at night and played in the snow in the sun. Zippy had many acorns stored up for the season. He gave Bushy the best ones. He did so for good reason.

One winter day, Fast Eddie stopped by Bushy and Zippy's tree to say hello to his friends. Fast Eddie was lonely because he missed his good pal Zippy. One day soon thereafter however, Bushy introduced Fast Eddie to her cute sister Tushy and in no time at all, Fast Eddie was happy again.

Spring

When the tree buds began to sprout there was still snow on the ground. But the days finally grew longer and warmer and the nights suddenly became much more fun for Zippy because he had found something that he loved doing even more than hunting acorns, and her name was Bushy, and she had such a nice soft tail.

One late spring morning as summer was fast approaching yet again, Zippy suddenly became a proud father. He'd chase his cute little offspring around as far and as fast as he could and then he would chase their mother back to their nest. Whenever Zippy lay down to rest with Bushy he'd tell her, "I'll love you always, my dear."

Bushy would smile at him and then whisper in his ear... things that only squirrels truly understand, things that it's best you not hear.

- The Happy Ending -

Old Fart Young at Heart

I was walking through a quiet city park one warm summer afternoon when I noticed ahead of me; an old grey-haired man in an old brown dapper suit sitting alone on a park bench in the shade. The old man was mumbling to himself, or to the old polished brown shoes on his feet. Whatever the case, he seemed somewhat distressed which compelled me to stop near to him and ask him if something was wrong. When I did, the old man snarled a reply.

"Hell yes, somethin's wrong!" he said, staring at his shoes.

"What's wrong...?" I asked him.

"Kids is what's wrong," he said as he looked up at me.

"Kids?" I asked.

"Yeah, spoiled rotten kids," he claimed.

"Did some spoiled rotten kids come along and hurt you?" I asked as I examined the man for signs of trauma.

"No, you knucklehead!" he scorned. "Kids in *general* are spoiled rotten."

"In what way?" I asked as I cautiously took a seat next to the man.

"In *every* damn way, that's what way!"

"And this upsets you why?"

"Because it's *wrong* that's why!"

"So... what can we do to correct the situation?"

"We can stop *spoilin'* 'em, that's what!"

"Well, I don't have any kids to spoil so you can't blame me," I offered.

"I wasn't blamin' *you,* knucklehead. I'm blamin' the spoiled kids' parents!"

"As well you should, spoiled kids are usually the product of parents who spoil them," I agreed.

"I already know that, knucklehead! I'm tryin' to figure out how to *un-spoil* kids because their parents sure don't know how to, or don't want to!"

"I definitely have my hands full with this one," I thought to myself. I often wonder why I even bother to get involved in the first place. I'd wonder, and then I'd usually ignore the possible reasons as I'd get even more deeply involved.

"So, do you have a plan as to how we can un-spoil kids?" I inquired, holding my knuckleheaded breath for his response.

"I got ideas…" he began, waiving my knucklehead title.

"Such as…" I queried.

"Well for one… we can tear down those playgrounds at Mac-Donald's," he suggested and then continued, "When I was a boy we didn't have playgrounds to jump around in when it was supper time. And we didn't get *toys* in our meals either. Hell, we was lucky to even *get* a meal. We was happy to get a spoon full of beans on a tin plate. That was *our* idea of a happy meal. And toys…? We didn't get no toys in our meals," he repeated. "We was lucky to get a toy at Christmas time. If we got a top or a rubber ball for Christmas we was happy, happy I say! Nowadays, kids get piles of presents for Christmas and a week later they want more!"

"It does seem a bit excessive," I agreed.

"Damn right it's excessive, it's obscene is what it is!"

"Okay… so we tear down the playgrounds and eliminate the toys in meals. Anything else we should do?" I asked.

He thought hard but not for long. "The other day I saw a kid in a minivan watchin' cartoons on a seat-back screen. Can you believe it? Kids watch TV all damn day long, do they have to watch it in the car too? What the hell is wrong with this planet?"

"A lot," I suggested.

"Damn straight, a lot," he agreed. "When I was a boy the only cartoons we saw was in the movie theatre. We didn't have ta carry 'em around with us all damn day long on those portable gizmos. We watched them once, memorized them and that was it, we were done with them! We didn't need no cartoon video tapes to watch over and over and over again a hundred times. Are kids so stupid they can't even remember a simple cartoon?"

"Makes you wonder," I said.

"Damn right, it does," he agreed. "Which reminds me of another reason why kids are spoiled... minivans! Do kids not have legs anymore? Are mommas these days personal chauffeurs? When I was a boy we'd walk ten miles to school, bare foot across broken glass and railroad tracks. Half the time we'd get chased by rabid dogs with white foam drippin' off their snarlin' teeth. And we didn't need no fancy backpacks for our books. We carried 'em with a book strap slung over our shoulder. And we didn't ask our mommas to do our homework for us neither; we did it our damn selves. Nowadays, moms and dads run all over tarnation gettin' supplies for their kids' science projects; from over-priced fancy-pants hobby supermarkets. We built our own science projects ourselves with sticks we dragged out of the woods or with rusty metal scraps we'd snag from the junkyard. Now that's *real* science I tell ya!"

"Sure 'nough is," I agreed, sounding a bit like my new-found friend and hero.

"I see kids gettin' shuttled to school, shuttled to soccer

practice, shuttled to karate or judo or whatever it is they do nowadays. When I was a boy we boxed bare-fisted. We didn't need no kimono or rubber mats. We'd knock each other straight down in the dirt need be," he recalled with gusto.

"Good for you!" I declared.

"And it *was* good too; made us boys into men real quick I tell ya. We didn't need no cellular phone stuck in our ear all damn day long to be a man. That's for sissies if you ask me. We had tins cans and waxed strings to talk on. We passed hand-written notes in class. We wrote real love letters to our sweethearts and made our own birthday cards. These stores nowadays are ridiculous I tell ya! They sell everything ready-made now so kids don't have to learn how to make things for themselves. I suppose it gives 'em more time to watch their cartoon tapes over and over again."

"And don't forget video games," I suggested.

"Don't *even* get me started on that junk!" he complained.

"I wouldn't dare," I said, and then hoped he'd forget I'd mentioned it.

"Grandpa...! Grandpa...!" tiny voices shouted in our direction. We turned our heads to see who was coming our way.

"Grandpa!" a tiny boy yelled as he jumped up on my friend's lap.

"Easy now, Cody! Grandpa's leg is still bothering him," Cody's mother warned the boy.

"Nonsense, Christine, I'm fine," my friend said as his tiny adorable granddaughter and her mother approached us.

The granddaughter joined her brother on her grandpa's lap and then asked him, "Did you bring me anything, Grandpa?"

"I sure did, Angel," my friend said as he took a cellophane

wrapped sucker from his shirt pocket; the old-fashioned kind of sucker with a white cord loop for a handle. "Hope you like strawberry," he asked the tiny girl.

"I sure do! Thank you, Grandpa!" she said.

With strong shaky hands, her gramps tore the plastic off for her. The happy girl popped the sucker into her tiny mouth.

"Do I get one too, Grandpa?" Cody asked.

My friend looked into his shirt pocket and then frowned like a sad circus clown. He hunched his shoulders in exaggerated regret. The boy suddenly turned sad.

"Wait a minute..." Grandpa said as he searched his other shirt pocket. "Here it is!" he announced as he revealed a purple sucker. "I hope you like grape," he said as he tickled his grandson.

"I *love* grape, Grandpa, thanks!" the boy giggled as he kicked his tiny sneakers excitedly.

"Are they twins?" I asked the woman.

"Yes they are, but at the moment they're triplets," she said smiling. "Thanks for looking after my dad," she whispered to me as I stood up to give her my seat.

I waved goodbye to my friend and then winked at him. He winked back and almost smiled. He shrugged his shoulders and confessed to me then, "I guess I like to spoil 'em is all."

Out at First

"How's your job going, Jake?"

"I had to quit, man."

"You quit your night-watchman job at the daycare center? You quit a cakewalk job like that?"

"It was the clowns, man... those clown pictures on the walls at night, they were creeping me out big time. I couldn't take it anymore!"

"Oh yeah... the clown pictures. They're creepy enough in broad daylight."

The boys bent their knees and sat down carefully in their seats. They did so in deliberate slow-motion so as not to spill any of the draft beer from the super-flimsy, super-size cups that they gripped gingerly in each of their hands; four beers, twenty-eight dollars. What an insult to blue collar America! The Wall Streeters up in the glass-enclosed club level boxes were sipping ice cold, twelve-dollar imports right out of the bottle. Those rich punks didn't even have the good sense to pour their beer into a doggone glass to let it breathe for God's sake! Life ain't fair, that's for sure.

"So... what are you going to do about work, Jake?"

"Look for some I guess."

"Good luck, man. It's tough out there."

"Yeah I know, I *live* out there remember?"

"Hey, check 'em out, Jake... twelve o'clock, ten rows down... sweet!"

"Yeah, Buddy! You gotta love summer, man. If those shorts were any shorter they'd be belts!"

"If those shorts were any shorter I'd get tossed out for

corking my bat!"

"Ha-ha-ha-ha! Man... that makes no sense at all but it's damn funny!"

"Yeah I know, right?"

"Please Rise For The Singing Of Our National Anthem," the P.A. announcer announced on the P.A. system.

"Too late, my corked bat already did, ha-ha!"

"Hey man, show some respect for Old Glory will ya?"

"Always do, Jake, always do."

"Oh... Oh... Say Can You See... Blah, blah, blah... blah, blah... blah..."

"Who's pitching today, Jake?"

"I'm guessing the dude on the mound is."

"Well, we shall soon find out... Hey, you're right! The dude on the mound is pitching!"

"Told ya, man. Never doubt the Jake."

"You know, I'd watch a lot more baseball if they had cheerleaders."

"Damn straight! That's a brilliant idea! Cheerleaders would definitely fill a few more of these empty seats," Jake agreed.

"Hey, look...! There's three empty seats on each side of the hotties down there, shall we...?"

"Yes We Shall! But let me finish one of these beers first. I'd hate to spill expensive watered-down cheap-ass beer all over their tight and tiny t-shirts."

"And why not, Jake? We pay good money to see wet t-shirts beachside."

"I don't think they'd appreciate warm sticky beer in their bras at the top of the first inning, numb-nuts."

"Maybe they're not wearing bras, Jake."

"You can see the straps, dude, look..." Jake said, pointing to the girls' backs.

"Yeah, you're right, Jake. Let's wait 'til the seventh inning stretch to give 'em an *accidental* bath. Maybe they'll take off their t-shirts to dry 'em off."

"That's cold, man! And besides... watch your mouth, that blonde down there just may be my future ex-wife."

"The blonde? The blonde's mine, Jake. You get the tattoo princess."

"Let's just say we both share 'em for starters and see what happens."

"Actually, the black-haired girl with the barbed wire ink is damn hot!"

"Change your mind already?" Jake asked.

"I have no idea. I'm like a kid in a candy store."

"Well come on, kid... *kill* that beer, time's a wastin'."

"Okay... *gulp-gulp-gulp*, ready! Let's Do This...!"

"Let's do this? What the hell are you; a D.E.A. agent bustin' a meth lab?" Jake asked.

"Bite Me!" his buddy replied, non-sarcastically.

Ten rows later... the boys approached their prey. Carefully orchestrated pre-meditated maneuvering on Jake's part placed him inboard; an empty seat away from the girls. Pretending as if the numbers on their new seats actually matched those on their ticket stubs, the boys proceeded to sit down. The girls were leaned into one another in an attempt to continue their conversation over the ear-rattling din of the P.A. system.

"BATTING FIRST... LEFT FIELDER... JOSE' JESUS..."

"Boo! Boo! Boo!" the home crowd announced as it welcomed the visiting batter to their fair city. The visiting batter responded to the warm welcome with a lead-off single. "Boo! Boo! Boo!" the crowd responded, but in truth, was glad that the game wasn't going to end up as another boring pitchers' duel. Nevertheless, the crowd booed the next batter twice as loud as the first. The second batter hit a bad pitch (the taboo *first* pitch) into a quick and easy double-play and the game was on... "Yay! Yay! Yay!"

"That's more like it, right?" Jake asked the tattoo princess sitting next to him.

"Excuse me...?" she asked with a quizzical smile.

"The double-play..." Jake said, pointing toward the field, "...nice play, right?"

"Oh sorry, I didn't see it," she said and then she turned back to her friend.

"Smooth... Jake; ultra-smooth," his buddy whispered loudly.

"Hey, man! Whose side are you *on* anyway? At least I'm breaking the ice."

"Yeah, you broke the ice alright and got a cold shoulder and a cold shower. Let me show you how it's done, Jake, swap seats with me..."

As the buddies stood up to swap seats, two heavily bearded sasquatch biker dudes the size of storage sheds came lumbering down their row toward the girls. Both of the hotties stood up to let one of the monsters pass by. Dejected by the new arrivals, Jake's buddy decided not to swap seats after all and sat back down where he was. Jake remained standing; at eye-level then with the biker dude who had already sat down. The dude looked Jake straight in the eyes and then bellowed, "Did We Miss Any Action?"

Jake hesitated at first; hypnotized by the fact that the super-size beer in the monster's paw looked like a Dixie cup by comparison.

"Double play, two outs," Jake finally reported.

"Good For Us, Boy... Good For Us!" the dude rumbled.

And from his other side, Jake's buddy warned, "If you're taking the tattoo princess home tonight, you'd better not piss off her boyfriend... he looks mean!"

"Bite Me!" Jake barked to his buddy.

"Say Again?!" the bearded monster roared.

"Uh... I was talkin' to *this* looser," Jake replied in a plea of self-defense as he pointed to his ex-best friend.

"Yeah, I know you were kid... I was just messin' with ya. Sit down... relax, enjoy the game! Our daughters here were just sayin' they think you guys are kinda cute. Now ain't that just adorable!" he laughed. "Play your cards right and you might end up with their phone numbers," he added.

"A reprieve from the Governor! Halleluiah - Halleluiah! The game was *on!*" Jake thought to himself.

"What's up, Jake?" his friend prompted, not having heard the recent conversation.

"Calm down, buddy... their dads like us," Jake whispered loudly as he retook his seat.

"Dads...? Dads! You kiddin' me? Sweet! So is the blonde mine or the tattoo princess?"

"Keep cool and shut the hell up for once, will ya?"

"Okay, Jake, whatever you say, man."

The End
(for now)

Pandora's Attic

The very first thought that popped into his head that sleepy June morning as he walked to the curb for his newspaper, was that someone was watching him. But as he looked along what was apparently an empty street and then yawned, his second, more compelling thought; coffee, nullified the first.

He decided to leave his favorite coffee cup in the kitchen cupboard that morning and drink straight from the stovetop percolator instead. As he scanned the front page headlines for any signs of extraordinary news, he began to sip what would have been his second cup of coffee when his doorbell chimed. He rose from his kitchen table, placed the coffee pot back on the stovetop and then walked barefoot across his parlor's creaking wood floor to his front door. He unlocked the heavy oak door and then opened it slowly. He was met immediately by overwhelmingly bright morning sunlight and the dark silhouette of a petite figure partially eclipsing the sunshine beyond.

"Can you help me please?" a delicate voice inquired anxiously through the blinding glare.

"I imagine so," he offered, squinting, "but let me put some pants on first..."

"There's no time for that, please come quickly!" the voice of a young woman begged.

She turned away abruptly and left. And so, for the second time that morning, he slipped his bare feet into the work boots lying atop a doormat in his kitchen. He burst through the side door, strode down his driveway and then scrambled to catch up with the woman before she scampered away.

As his un-tied laces slapped the sides of his leather high-tops, he followed her stride for stride diagonally across the otherwise silent street. At 1111 Mystic Lane, the couple entered a house perched above stone steps. The first floor of the house was shaded by a wide wrap-around porch as it had been for the past one hundred and eleven years. After entering the house they began climbing three narrowing flights of creaking wood stairs. They arrived at last breathless, atop a small landing facing a miniature, four foot high door. The young woman turned around to face her companion for his first recognizable encounter. Her nose was at the level of his chin. Her head was draped with wavy ribbon-like white hair. As she raised her chin, her head bent slowly backwards revealing to him; her pale white forehead, her thin white eyebrows, delicate cheekbones and then suddenly, her eyes of sparkling blue diamonds which met his in one remarkable moment that would change his life forever. His heart stopped beating, his breath stopped breathing, his thoughts vanished defenseless in the presence of her; an incredibly beautiful creature, an exquisite goddess surely not of his mundane and unworthy world. He stood motionless in stunned silence. The front of the woman's white robe rose up as her delicate arms extended slender fingers to each side of his head. Her long soft fingernails raked ever so slowly through his hair. She pulled his face gently to hers. Her angelic voice whispered through delicate, pink rose petal lips, "You must promise..."

Startled by voices, Rachael turned around suddenly. In the process, she nearly knocked over the ceramic floor lamp she'd been dusting. Luckily though, Rachael grabbed the lamp quickly in both hands before it toppled over and smashed to pieces. Having jumped to save her lamp while attempting to process the strange voices she'd heard, Rachael's adrenalin reached its peak. She glanced around nervously in her otherwise empty guesthouse. Her heart pounded heavily in her chest.

"You must promise me..." the young woman continued, "that what I'm about to tell you will remain our secret for if others were to find out, they might consider me delusional if not totally mad."

"But of course," he replied, suspending both thought and judgment.

"I hear voices at night," she began, "voices I tell you, coming from beyond this very door and they frighten me while I lie alone in my bed at night. I become frozen with fear and cannot sleep or rest at all until the morning light shines and the voices subside. I have not yet ventured past this door. I have not dared come up here at night when I hear the voices. I am embarrassed to say that I am too much of a coward to even come up here alone during the day when the voices are silent. I fear that the voices belong to those who are sleeping during the day beyond this door. If I were to come up here alone and awake them, there is no telling what fate might befall me for there would be no one to come to my aid. That is why I asked you help me. I happened to notice that you were home this morning when you came outside to pick up your newspaper. You gave me the impression of man who might help a woman in need. I am so very afraid to come up here alone but I feel much braver now with you by my side."

"How long have you been hearing these voices?" he asked.

"I began hearing them on the second night after I took

residence here nearly a week ago. I've not enjoyed a sound night's sleep since."

"You poor thing, you must be exhausted."

"I am quite fine despite it all as I sleep during the daylight hours. I do however, so very much wish to lead a normal life again amongst my new neighbors... to enjoy the sunshine, to hear the birds singing. As it's been, I hear only crickets at night and then... the voices."

"Well, that explains why I haven't seen you at all until this morning. You've done the right thing seeking help. There's no point in taking chances these days. I'll help you in any way that I can. I imagine you want me to have a look around in the attic to find the source of the so-called voices?"

"So-called voices? Do you doubt me already?" she asked quietly and calmly although understandably dejected.

"No, not at all, I *do* believe you. I believe that you've been hearing *something*. But chances are, my dear, you've been hearing the creaking and moaning sounds of a hundred year old house cooling off during the night and settling in upon itself. When old houses such as ours heat up during the day they expand, the wood in them expands, mainly along the roof lines and in the attics where temperature changes are greatest. When a house cools off at night the wood shrinks or contracts and the nails in the wood pop while the wood framework can sound as if it were groaning. My own house does the very same things but I'm so used to it that I simply ignore the so-called moaning voices. You, my dear, are obviously not used to those types of sounds and have simply mistaken them for voices."

"But I *do* hear those sounds you describe; the popping and creaking sounds. I hear them at night when the house cools off and then again during the day when the house warms up while I'm trying to sleep. The other sounds that I hear are different. They are voices I tell you. I hear spoken words."

They gazed at one another. She saw a tall, fairly handsome man with brown, slightly disheveled "morning" hair and dark green eyes. She saw a kind and caring man but one who obviously doubted her word. He saw a bright and beautiful but frightened and vulnerable young woman. He saw a woman that he would walk through fire for. He placed his hands on her soft shoulders and directed her gently out of the way to the side of the landing. He looked again into her eyes and smiled kindly. He bent down and turned a tarnished brass doorknob which creaked quiet objections. He pulled on the stubborn door. Its frame and hinges cracked and popped in an attempt to resist but then finally surrendered. The door opened with a rush of cool musty air.

"I'll go first," she said with a sudden burst of bravery.

She stooped lithesome under the cobwebbed doorway and then vanished into the attic. She had disappeared right before his eyes but then, in the dim brown light of the landing's antique wall sconce, he caught a fleeting glimpse of her white robe as it flashed beyond the doorway. He bent down and proceeded through the tight doorframe, scraping the back of his head and then his shoulder and tailbone as he did so. He stood up slowly and deliberately and found the woman standing in the darkness. He approached her from behind and placed his hands on her shoulders yet again. His breath fluttered the hair on the top of her head. The woman reached up and pulled a dangling chain which clinked against a suspended Edison-era light bulb that came back from the dead, lit and swinging. The attic was revealed to them in the dim glow of the bulb's rhythmic, pale orange waves. Sloping roof trusses danced above them like an ancient gargantuan spider. The couple stood there hypnotized until the light stopped swinging and the beast stopped dancing.

They'd entered the attic at its center. The load bearing walls of the stairwell through which they had climbed extended above them to the underside of the roof. A rough river stone chimney hugged one of the walls and extended above it. The chimney passed through the sloping roof deck above and rested squarely that day in bright morning sunlight. The attic's dusty wood floorboards creaked as the couple took slow and cautious steps in the dimly-lit darkness.

"There's not much up here," he observed, "not much at all," he repeated as he left the woman's side to explore beyond the opposite walls of the stairwell. "We could really use a flashlight though," he suggested from around a corner.

"I have a flashlight, in the pantry," she said. "I used it just last night to search for Tom."

"Tom?" he asked as he rejoined her.

"My cat," she explained.

"But of course," he said, smiling to himself.

"He vanished the first night we moved in," she reported sadly.

"Well, maybe Tom's just exploring his new neighborhood at length," he offered in consolation.

"I can only hope that is the case," she lamented.

As his eyes slowly adjusted to the dim light, he realized that during the day, a flashlight wouldn't be necessary. The attic's feeble light bulb did little to aid sight beyond the stairwell but its soffit vents did. Along all four exterior edges of the flooring, strips of bright morning light poured up and into the attic. Like floor-level lights do in a dark theatre, the soffits provided adequate light while the couple explored the attic in search of the voices or for those from whence they came. As it was however, the only thing in the otherwise empty attic that sparked the couple's curiosity was an old and dusty, metal-strapped wood steamer trunk. It lay in state in the attic like an ancient tomb awaiting the first tourists of the day; tourists who would walk around it slowly while whispering to one another so as not to disturb or offend the tomb's revered contents. The couple approached the dusty trunk and walked slowly around it. They talked quietly so as not to disturb or offend its contents, after all, they both reasoned to themselves to differing degrees, the source of the voices might be contained within it.

"Is it locked?" she asked in a whisper.

"I don't see a padlock but there *is* a keyhole. Let's see if it's locked," he said and then he stooped down toward the trunk.

"Be careful!" she warned quietly.

"Be careful of what?" he asked, slightly amused.

"I'm not really sure but be careful just in case," she pleaded.

"Will do then, I promise to be careful," he agreed and then he carefully slid the latch buttons near each end of the trunk simultaneously. The buttons cooperated nicely. The latches themselves resisted at first but then suddenly jumped up in unison with a loud *Snap!*

"No key or crowbar necessary," he announced as he grabbed the front corners of the trunk's lid.

"No, wait!" she begged as he began to lift the lid upward.

"Okay then, I'll wait," he agreed. "Just let me know when you're ready and I'll stop waiting."

"Okay… now I'm ready," she decided mere moments later.

He pulled up on the stubborn lid raising it slightly but was only able to create the smallest of gaps between it and the front wall of the trunk. He let go of the lid, stood up, walked around the attic briefly and then returned with a scrap of plank board. He handed the board to the young woman and instructed, "When I crack open the lid, shove the end of the board into the gap, okay?"

"Of course," she said and then did so.

He released the lid onto the board and then told her to let go. He grabbed the end of the board in both hands and twisted it. Despite the hinges' squeaking objections, the lid began to rise. Suddenly, the trunk's hinges freed up and snapped loudly. The lid jumped up and then slammed down on the board, raising a cloud of dust in the air.

"That should do it," he announced, dropping the board to the floor.

He grabbed the trunk lid again and began to lift it but then stopped abruptly to ask, "Are you ready, my dear?"

"I am indeed ready, sir, and thank you for asking."

And so, as he ignored the rusted hinges' persistent squeaking complaints, he raised the trunk lid to its upright position. As he let go of the lid it fell backwards and slammed against the backside of the trunk. A larger cloud of dust arose and lingered briefly in the attic's diffused light. The couple stood over the trunk not quite believing what they saw; the bottom of the trunk was missing and sat directly over a cutout through the attic floor. They bent down slowly to inspect the void but saw only darkness. They looked at one another in search of an explanation.

"Care to hop down there? I'll hold your wrists," he teased.

She shrieked and then ran off, clambering down the stairs.

In a few minutes' time, the young woman returned to the attic breathing heavily. She was holding a flashlight which she handed to him. As they knelt down in front of the trunk, he lit up its interior. They leaned in to get a better look.

"Well I'll be… it's a tiny, empty room," he reported. "Can you tell which room in the house it is?"

"I don't recall a room like that on the floor below," she said. "Shine the light further to the left please."

He shined the light to the left and then to the right. He splashed light across all four walls of the room but to their surprise, there were no doors or windows whatsoever.

"That's odd," she said.

"*Very* odd I'd say, but I'm guessing that it's just an old closet that someone walled over for some reason. Apparently, they cut a hole in the attic floor to access the room," he surmised.

"But why?" she asked.

"That, my dear, is the sixty-four thousand dollar question."

"Sixty-four thousand dollar question?"

"Sorry, it's just a saying, it's from an old 1950s TV quiz show, obviously *way* before your time," he explained.

"So, what would be your best guess then?" she asked. "Why would anyone do this?"

"Well, obviously, someone wanted to conceal the space. Maybe they were hiding valuables down there," he guessed as best he could.

"Or maybe… someone was *keeping* someone down there!" she suggested anxiously.

Although he doubted it at first, he couldn't dismiss her theory entirely and the more that he thought about it, the more that it seemed like a definite possibility, albeit a macabre and gruesome explanation. He began then to feel, some of the woman's anxiety himself.

"I've got it!" she shrieked suddenly, grabbing his arm and startling him in the process. "Someone *was* keeping someone hostage down there and that poor tormented spirit haunts this house to this very day. The voices I hear at night are those of the victim and the captor!" she concluded as she buried her trembling head in the crook of his arm.

"There, there now," he said, stroking her hair and rubbing her shoulder. "In my opinion, the original owner of this house was most likely eccentric, but I seriously doubt that he was an evil monster. I'll bet that we'll find a far less terrifying explanation for the voices you hear."

"Do you think so?" she asked, looking up into his eyes.

"I do," he said, gazing back at her. "I see no evidence of a hostage situation here or in the room below, but I'll bring a ladder up and have a closer look down below just to be sure, okay?"

"Okay," she agreed as they broke their embrace and then looked once again into the room below.

As she was doing so, he noticed four bolts in the bottom of the trunk's four corners which apparently held it fast to the attic floor. He then noticed a loose sheet of wood standing upright against the back wall of the trunk.

"Watch yourself now…" he said as he gently pulled her out from the trunk by her shoulders. He tipped the sheet of wood forward and then let it fall with a bang against the frame of the bottomless trunk.

"A false bottom," he announced, "quite clever indeed. No one would have suspected a hole in the floor beneath the trunk, unless… unless they would have tried to *move* the trunk, in which case… because of the concealed bolts, they would have wondered why an empty trunk wouldn't budge an inch."

"But why would anyone want to move an old and dusty, empty trunk?" she asked.

"Exactly!" he said. "Even if it weren't bolted to the floor, this thing must weigh a hundred pounds empty. It would be more trouble than it's worth to try and move it. It may have served as the perfect foil but we, my dear, have uncovered it for what it truly is."

She reached a hand up to touch his cheek. She looked into his eyes, smiled and then said, "Thank you so very much for not laughing at my silliness. I might blame it on my abnormal sleep habits as of late but to be honest, I've always been a bit over-emotional about things."

"There's no need to explain. If I had experienced those same things myself, all alone in this house, I'd probably have reacted the very same way. Now then, do you have a ladder? If not, I've got one across the street."

"There is a ladder in the garage. It's splashed with dried paint but it's quite long. I'm not sure that we could manage to get it up here around the corners of the stairs. Let's see... oh, yes! There is another shorter ladder in the basement!" she announced.

"Perfect, care to show me the way to the basement?"

They made their way to the basement where they found the ladder; an old, eight foot high, step ladder. He looked around the basement, which had a decent compliment of tools scattered about, in search of things that he'd need. As he found them, he dropped them into a bucket.

"What's all of that for?" she asked him.

"Wrenches to loosen the bolts in the trunk," he explained as he grabbed the bucket's handle and the wide, bottom end of the folded step ladder. "Shall we?" he asked her.

She grabbed hold of the ladder's narrow, top end and then led the way slowly up the basement steps. They passed through the kitchen and its adjoining mudroom. They turned a tight corner past the parlor and up three more flights of stairs back into the attic. They were barely able to maneuver the ladder through the short access door but did so by turning it diagonally to the door frame. After having finally wrestled it in, they set the ladder down on the attic floor and then sat atop the trunk short of breath. Having accomplished their initial tasks, they felt good and were enjoying a well-deserved break until their moods suddenly changed when she asked him, "Wasn't the trunk open when we left?"

"Um... I thought it was," he said, "but I *could* be wrong."

"Well, I am *sure* that it *was* open," she claimed.

"Okay, so... the lid fell closed then."

"But we would have heard it slam shut," she insisted.

"All the way in the basement?"

"Well, maybe not from down there, but wait a minute...! How could the lid have fallen closed when it was opened up all the way and lying flat against the back of the trunk? How could it have possibly swung up before it fell closed?" she asked him, and then she stood up immediately and stared down at the trunk.

"Then the only obvious answer is, the trunk lid *was* closed when we left it," he suggested as he stood up to join her and then began to doubt his own assessment.

The more that he thought about it, the more he believed her. And the more that he believed her, the stranger he felt about it. He bent down in front of the trunk and then grabbed the sides of its lid.

"Wait!" she cried out. "Be careful!"

He lifted the lid slowly as its hinges creaked and cracked and popped. Once again, he raised the lid up past vertical and let it fall backwards with a bang. They looked into the trunk and gasped. She grabbed his arm with both hands and shrieked. He held her tightly as she began to shake. He gazed into the trunk at the neatly folded clothes packed amongst shoes and hats and old framed photographs. He looked around the attic as he held the woman in his arms. "Surely someone had come up there while they were downstairs," he thought.

"*Now* do you believe me?" she asked, not daring to look into the trunk again.

"I believe that something strange is definitely going on that's for sure," he said. "But I'm also sure that there is a logical explanation for it. Are you sure that you're living alone in this house?"

"I'm not so sure anymore," she said as she continued to shake.

"Okay, first thing's first," he suggested. "Whoever did this is either long gone, still in this house somewhere, or in the room under the trunk. It's unlikely that they could be in the room beneath us and have covered themselves over with this stuff, so that leaves either long gone or in the house somewhere. I say that we search every single room in this house right now just to be sure, okay?"

"I say we call the police," she suggested.

"Well, we *could* phone the police but they usually want to know what's been stolen, what crime has been committed or what kind of danger we're in so, what would we tell them;

somebody filled your empty trunk with junk and then left?"

She couldn't help but laugh at the thought of it. He was pleased to have eased her anxiety. He began their search by investigating every nook and cranny of the attic with the flashlight. As he did so, having regained a bit of her bravery, the young woman removed one of the old framed photographs from the trunk. She gazed at the handsome couple who had posed for the portrait some hundred years ago. She wondered then, if they were to speak, would she recognize their voices.

"Shall we?" he called out, offering the young woman his hand as he stood by the attic door waiting for her to join him.

They searched the house from top to bottom; every room and closet, under every bed, behind the window drapes and shower curtains. As he had totally expected, they found no sign whatsoever of an intruder. The prankster was long gone by then, but *damn,* what was his motive? Would he return? Was he deranged, was he dangerous, or was he just some local kid with a sick sense of humor? They returned to the attic and carefully removed the trunk's contents. They stacked it all neatly on the floor. With wrench in hand, he leaned into the trunk to loosen its bolts.

"That's strange," he said, his head buried in the trunk.

"What's strange?" she asked.

"I can't seem... to lift up the false bottom... it's like it's stuck or something..."

As he continued to try to find an edge of the bottom with which to get a grip, he stretched further into the trunk leaning more heavily against its front wall. Suddenly, the trunk shifted on the attic floor. He stood up immediately and looked down upon the trunk, wondering. He bent down again in front of it and then pushed it with all of his might. The trunk slid on the floor and came to rest a few feet away from him. He shoved it two more feet in another direction and then two more feet in yet another. She gasped. She held her hands to her mouth. There was no sign whatsoever of the hole through the attic floor. Furiously, he tipped the trunk up on its back side and then kicked the trunk's bottom as hard as he could.

"Solid as a rock," he announced, bewildered.

His companion fainted and fell to the floor.

He would have carried the petite woman downstairs to her bed had he been able to maneuver her safely through the half-size attic door. Since that was not possible, he made her as comfortable as possible on the attic floor. He placed folded clothes from the trunk under her head and covered her chest and hips with an old coat. As he stroked her hair with one hand he gently tapped her cheek with his other. She came to, groggily, a few minutes later. She blinked slowly as her eyes struggled to re-focus.

"Are you alright?" he asked her, relieved.

"I think so," she whispered.

She sat up with his help and then stood up slowly beside him. He led her out of the attic and then down two flights of stairs into her bedroom where she sat upon her bed. With his help, she leaned back on her bed and lay down. He made her comfortable with pillows. He left the room briefly and then returned with a glass of cold water.

"Drink it slowly," he advised. She took his advice.

"What else can I do for you?" he asked her.

"Well... since you asked, I would feel much safer if you slept with me this evening," she suggested.

"Here? I mean, in this *house?*" he asked, as he thought to himself, *in bed with you?* "You're welcome to stay with me at my house if you're frightened here," he offered.

"I'm not really frightened per say, at least not while you're with me. I'm more confused and bewildered than anything else," she explained.

"As well you should be, because I am *totally* confused," he confessed.

She laughed at his honesty and felt relieved to have an ally. She trusted him completely and was quickly becoming more attracted to him.

"I want you to hear the voices with me. I want you to lie next to me and hear the voices so that I can be sure I'm not crazy."

"I think it's already been established that you're not crazy, my dear. There are inexplicably crazy things going on in this house and you haven't been imagining any of it. I totally believe you now, about the voices that is."

"So you *didn't* believe me at first?"

"As I've said, I believed that you *thought* that you'd heard voices when you were actually hearing something else. But now... I'm not so sure. Now, given all that has happened, I tend to believe that you've been hearing *actual* voices."

"So you'll stay with me then, to find out?"

"As you wish," he agreed. "If sleep with you I must, then sleep with you, I shall do."

"Oh, thank you so much! I'm so very grateful!" she said.

She sat up then and hugged him enthusiastically in her soft and grateful arms.

"It is my duty and pleasure to help whomever and wherever I can but I have one request," he said, sitting beside her, his chin resting atop her head.

"Anything," she said as she drew away from him.

"If I am to sleep with you this evening, my dear, I must first know your name."

"Oh, silly me! I'm so very sorry! My name is Pandora, and yours…?"

"Peter," he announced. "It's been quite a pleasure meeting you… *Pandora.* Well, as much as it *could* be under such strange circumstances. Now then… shall we run over to my house for some dinner before nightfall? I for one, am totally famished."

"As am I!" she agreed. "We've spent the entire day running around my house and I didn't even offer you anything to eat or drink. I've been such a bad hostess, I fear. In my defense though, I *do* have good manners. I simply lost them along with my appetite until you reminded me of them just now."

"There's no need to apologize. I've been too busy being tricked and confused and downright stumped to high heaven myself to even think about anything else. So, shall we…?" he asked as he rose from her bed and offered Pandora his hand.

The few neighbors out and about that late afternoon stared curiously at Peter in his boxer shorts and work boots as he clopped across the street holding Pandora's hand. Pandora's long white robe fluttered in the breeze as Peter waved a kind hand of greeting to Fred Franklin who stopped trimming his hedges and to Mrs. Capriati who was unloading groceries from the trunk of her Buick. Out of spontaneous courtesy, both of Peter's neighbors waved back to him but then stared at one another and then at Peter and Pandora as the giggling couple entered Peter's house.

"Let's see... I've got some left-over pasta salad and some frozen fish fillets," Peter announced as he took stock of his refrigerator and freezer. "Or... I could fire up the grill and toss on a couple of steaks," he suggested.

"Pasta salad sounds wonderful," Pandora decided. "I don't really eat much red-meat I'm afraid."

Peter was about to ask her in jest why she was afraid of red meat but then thought better of it. "Okay then, I'll broil a couple of fish fillets and two ears of corn. Would you mind slicing up some of that French bread while I get it started?"

"Sounds delicious, Peter," she said as she threw her arms around him from behind.

"What's that for?" he asked her, not really caring what her answer might be.

"Just a gesture of thanks is all. You've been so kind and patient with me."

She let go of Peter after one final squeeze and set about slicing bread and setting the table. After Peter had prepared the food and slid it into the oven, he excused himself to his bedroom where he pulled off his work boots and pulled on a pair of blue jeans, socks and sneakers. He popped into his bathroom where he dowsed his hair at the sink and then ran a quick comb through his unsightly mop.

"Well, you clean up nicely," Pandora noticed.

"Ha-ha, thank you, m' Lady," he said, bowing playfully.

They sat down at his kitchen table and dove into the pasta salad with forks a 'blazing. They tore into the slices of French bread and swallowed it in chunks. They looked at one another and laughed as they excused themselves silently for their lack of table manners. Peter poured two tall glasses of milk which they gulped half-empty in seconds.

"We'd better both slow down lest we give ourselves tummy aches," Pandora suggested.

"Right you are, my dear, besides the main course still awaits us."

Peter popped open the oven door and portioned their plates. They ate their fish and corn on the cob in the manner of civilized adults.

"So how did you come to live across the street from me, Pandora?"

"By way of a classified ad for a live-in housekeeper; I mailed my resume and references to the P.O. box listed in the newspaper. A week later, I received a letter of employment and a set of house keys in the return mail. The home owner instructed me to tidy-up the place and make myself at home in advance of his return on July 1st. Do you know the owner, Peter? He never mentioned his name in the correspondence and there was no return address on the package he'd sent."

"That house has been vacant since I've lived here, Pandora. On occasion I'll see a cleaning service van in the driveway or a landscape truck parked out front when a couple of guys cut and trim the lawn during the growing season, but I've never seen or met any occupant or owner of the house."

"And how long has that been; how long have you lived here?"

"Let's see... it will be five years this July."

"Well, I guess I'll be meeting my new boss and you'll be meeting your neighbor for the first time next month then."

"If not sooner," Peter suggested.

"Why do you say that, Peter?"

"I have a feeling that we may have already met this mystery man, or at least, have fallen victim to his shenanigans."

"Peter! Do you think…? Could it be him?"

"Who else could it be, Pandora? He knows well enough that you are a young single woman living alone. For whatever twisted reasons he may have, he has set the stage to frighten you, if not torment you or worse."

"But if your theory is correct, Peter, he runs the risk of scaring me off completely. I have no obligation to stay there, especially through such circumstances. How would he benefit from driving me away?"

"Maybe he just wants to watch you squirm, Pandora. There are a lot of sick people in this world."

"But where would he be watching me *from*, Peter? We searched the house but found nothing unusual, remember?"

"He may not be actually watching you per say, Pandora, but he knows what you must be going through. People who make crank phone calls don't see their victims, but they get kicks out of it nevertheless."

"But he must be nearby *someplace* to have snuck inside, changed the trunk like he did and then leave the house unseen."

"I agree and I think it best if you stay away from that place for now. You're more than welcome to stay here until the first of the month. Come July 1st I'll meet him right along with you to make sure that he's legit and isn't responsible for what's been happening; if he shows up at all that is."

"Okay, Peter, you win. But can we at least stay there one night, tonight, so you can hear the voices with me? I really need to know if they're real and not just some figment of my imagination."

"As you wish, my dear. The sun will be setting in a few hours. Night will be upon us soon. I'll grab my toothbrush and baseball bat and we'll be on our way, okay?"

The couple decided to take turns bathing in Peter's shower before they headed back across the street. They caught accidental glimpses of one another as their wet towels were exchanged for dry clothes. They smiled at one another having enjoyed their quick peeks. The couple ran across the street and into Pandora's house before Mrs. Capriati could identify through her drapes; the source of the giggles outside her window. They then upon Pandora's soft bed with satisfied bellies and light hearts. The potential gravity of their situation was easily trumped by their blossoming excitement for one another. As they lay on Pandora's bed, the couple exchanged abbreviated versions of their life stories accompanied by a few tears and several bouts of laughter. They didn't notice that the evening light had long since surrendered to darkness.

"So, Pandora my dear, do you feel better tonight with me by your side?"

"No," she replied.

"No?" he asked, surprised and a bit dejected.

"No," she repeated. "To be honest, I'd feel much better with you *this way*," she explained as she threw herself atop him.

Their eyes crossed briefly as their noses touched lightly. Their heavy breaths fluttered her silken robe which had sailed over her head and had fallen atop their faces when she pounced. Under the white glow of their silk tent, their breaths became heavier still, exchanging between them the unspoken announcement of their imminent first kiss; a kiss that pressed heavily upon their impassioned lips locking two against two, their eyes never closing but instead gazing deeply into each other's heart and soul which had suddenly grown wild with flaming desire. Their arms and legs battled for attention while the couple rolled about; one atop the other and then back again. His heart pounded in his chest as hers pounded beneath her breasts beating in concert while their lips and breaths and embraces became evermore driven until her soft angelic sighs transformed suddenly then into low deep moans that at first excited Peter but then gave him cause for concern. He froze, motionless, and then asked her, "Pandora dear, are you alright?"

She herself had also become suddenly frozen, but with fear. Pandora blinked as she stared into his eyes and then whispered, "Peter, that wasn't *me* moaning."

Bearable weather permitting, Peter ran every weekday evening after work. He ran because it was the antithesis of sitting at his office desk. He also ran because apparently, exercise was good for one's health. He had begun his run one Friday evening as usual but two miles into it, for no apparent reason, he deviated from his routine five-mile route through the neighborhood. As a result, he found himself on a tree-lined residential street that he'd never run on or driven down before. He couldn't even recall ever noticing the street at all before then. The street that he found himself running on was in a less-affluent, more rural area than that in which he lived. The street had no curbs or sidewalks. The houses along the street represented a wide-range of architectural styles built decades apart by owners of various means. The houses were spaced further apart, sat deeper on their lots and were more obscured by trees and landscape than those in a typical suburban neighborhood. Drainage ditches served as storm sewers, moonlight served as street lights. Rabbits, raccoons, opossums and deer felt right at home along that wooded street and were all well aware of Peter's presence from the very moment that his rhythmic, tapping footsteps announced it. Whereas Peter's street would typically see heavier traffic on a Friday evening, aside from the sounds of his running shoes, the street he was on that Friday night was dead quiet.

"Help...! Help me please!" a woman screamed from a distance behind him.

Peter stopped dead in his tracks and turned toward the voice. He searched his field of vision expecting to see a woman but he saw no one. He continued to listen but heard nothing. He waited for what seemed like minutes but then began jogging slowly toward the direction from whence the voice had come in a matter of seconds. He searched left and then right and continued doing so as he scanned every driveway and front porch and side door that he passed. He stopped in an area that he best thought that the woman had called out from. He stood in the middle of the road and with his hands cupped around his mouth called out, "Hello...! Is anybody there...?"

He turned around a moment later and repeated louder, "Hello...! Is anybody there?"

He searched for porch lights in the advancing dusk. There were no lights whatsoever in any window along the street. He heard not a sound. He walked up the driveway nearest to him and then approached the house that it served. He stepped up to and then knocked on the front door. While he waited he turned back toward the street; he saw only evergreens and maple trees and thick green grass. He gazed at the dark houses across the street and watched as the night settled in rapidly. He considered knocking again but walked away from the house slowly. Halfway back down the driveway he looked left and then right down the long and darkening street. He stood once again in the middle of the right of way, out from under the thick canopy of trees where the night sky was brighter. He considered knocking on another door. He considered running back home as fast as possible to phone the police. The entire time that he'd been on the street, he found it strange that there hadn't been any sign of human activity at all. He called out once again, twice as loud as before. He stood in the darkness and waited.

"Peter… it's the voices!" Pandora whispered as softly as she could. "You heard them too didn't you?"

"I heard *something*, Pandora," Peter said.

He pushed her gently way from him by her shoulders and then sat up on the edge of the bed.

"Oh… oh… oh…," they heard again; the voices louder and more anguished.

Peter stood up and slipped his feet into his sneakers. He grabbed his baseball bat in his left hand and a large flashlight in his right. He stepped slowly into the hallway.

"Peter, wait, don't leave me!" Pandora insisted.

She followed him barefoot into the hallway and then up two flights of stairs onto the attic landing.

Peter switched the flashlight on. He handed it to Pandora and then opened the attic door slowly. He motioned to her to shine the light past him. He crouched through the attic door clutching his bat.

"Help me...! Please...!" the woman's voice called out again.

Peter turned toward the voice as a woman came running up to him from across a front lawn. He jogged toward her and then took her by the shoulders as she ran straight into his arms.

"What's wrong?" Peter asked the woman.

"I hear voices..." she said frantically, "strange voices in my guesthouse. It's been empty for weeks. I only go in there occasionally to tidy up, but they were shouting..."

"Slow down," Peter suggested to the breathless woman as their eyes met. "My name is Peter, what's yours?" he asked, attempting to calm her nerves.

"Rachael," she said, staring blankly into his eyes.

"Okay, Rachael, are you in any danger?"

"I don't know..."

"How can I help you?"

"I'm not sure."

"You said that you heard voices in your guesthouse. I assume that you live alone in the main house?"

"Yes."

"Do you want me to take a look in your guesthouse?"

"I'm afraid to go back in there."

"Okay... so do you want me to take a look in your guesthouse while you wait outside?"

"I'm afraid to be left alone right now."

"Do you want me to go with you to your house and phone the police?"

"They've already been here, last week that is."

"The police came to search your guesthouse last week? They came and found nothing but now the voices have returned?"

"How did you know?" she asked, smiling, slightly confused.

"I *don't* know, Rachael. I was just trying to evaluate your situation, call it; a lucky guess. Do you have family or friends in the area?"

"I live alone. I don't really know my neighbors. I don't have much family to speak of."

Peter felt sadness in her statements. He felt compassion for the woman and felt her fear and confusion. "I'll do whatever you'd like me to do, Rachael... to try and help you. What would you like me to do?"

"Honestly?" she asked, hesitating as she considered his offer.

"Yes of course, honestly," Peter agreed.

"Will you stay with me tonight?" she asked abruptly.

Peter crept into the attic. Pandora followed closely directing the flashlight's beam past him. Peter snapped the chain hanging from the attic light but the bulb did not respond. They approached and then stood at the spot where the trunk had last been. Peter took the flashlight from Pandora and swept its beam across all four corners of the attic. He scanned the attic a second time in search of the trunk. It was nowhere to be found. There was no sign of a hole cut through the attic floor. Peter and Pandora were too stunned to speak. The couple gasped as the sound of voices rose up from the floor below them. They turned toward the attic door at the very moment that it slammed shut. Pandora screamed.

Peter stared at Rachael and into her deep, dark eyes. She smiled nervously at him while awaiting his reply. He considered her request and, recalling that it was Friday night, was reminded of the fact that he wouldn't have to go to work the next morning. He had no other obligations that he could think of.

"As you wish, Rachael," he said, wanting to add that it was dangerous to invite a total stranger into one's house, but he decided that the poor woman was frightened enough as it was.

"Thank heavens!" she said, taking his hand in hers. She led him away then and into her house. She left him standing inside her front doorway as she left the room.

"Make yourself comfortable," she suggested cheerily from the next room, "I'll be right with you."

Peter looked around the comfortable living room. He noticed a comfortable looking chair upon which he made himself comfortable.

"Lemonade?" she asked, handing him a tall, frosty glass.

"Perfect!" Peter said as he took the glass from her with both of his grateful hands. "Just what the doctor ordered."

"Your doctor prescribes lemonade?"

"He does indeed, for post-run rehydration."

"So that's what you're doing around here... jogging?"

"Yes it is," he said, after having taken a long and satisfying gulp of his drink.

"Well, that explains the jogging outfit then doesn't it?" she said with a laugh.

"You're quite astute, Rachael," Peter said, laughing right along with her.

"I may be astute as it were, but I'm also quite the coward I'm afraid," she confessed.

"I seriously doubt that, Rachael. If I'd heard strange voices I'd go running myself," he offered.

"But at least you'd be dressed for the occasion," she said, to which they both laughed themselves silly until Peter coughed, choked and then took a long, slow sip of his drink.

"Be careful now, Peter, you'll get one of those ice cream headaches if you drink too much at one go," Rachael warned.

"Right you are," he agreed, licking his lips. "I've had more than my fair share of that self-inflicted torture."

She laughed and smiled and gazed at him affectionately. "Feel free to take off your running shoes. Like I said... make yourself comfortable," she reminded him.

Peter pried off a shoe by the heel with the toe of his other shoe. He then pushed his other shoe off with his stocking foot. "Now that's comfortable!" he announced, wiggling his toes and rubbing his hot and tired feet against one another.

"Would you like a massage, Peter?" she asked him.

Peter hesitated, not quite believing his recent good luck.

"I'm a professional massage-therapist... it's what I do," she explained, legitimizing her offer, "but it would be pro-bono of course, what with you helping me out and all."

"I can't possibly think of anything better than a massage right now," Peter announced but then did.

"Did you have to think very hard?" she asked him to which they both laughed.

Peter ran toward the attic door and kicked it with the sole of his shoe. The door flung open banging against the stairwell wall. It bounced back half-way shut as Peter pushed his way through it. Peter yelled for Pandora. She followed him closely as they stepped down the flight of stairs. They turned a corner and walked slowly down the hallway. They stopped and waited, and listened for the voices.

"Is there any chance that I could shower first? I'm a bit on the disgustingly sweaty side in case you hadn't noticed," Peter asked the woman.

"But of course, Peter. Finish your drink. I'll put out a clean towel," Rachael said and then she left the room touching his shoulder in the process.

The ice cubes in Peter's glass banged against his nose as he drained the last drops of his lemonade. He heard Rachael humming sweetly and then he heard a shower head blast open. He rose from his chair and followed the sounds. He met Rachael in her bathroom. She passed by him casually and suggested playfully, "Enjoy yourself now... take your time... I'll be waiting..."

Peter enjoyed the hot water while he contemplated his incredible luck. He lathered his hair with exotic shampoo and his body with exotic soap. Cool night air wafted through the tiny bathroom window. It swirled the steam vapor as he toweled himself dry. Using Rachael's pink hairbrush, he tamed his wild wet mop in the bathroom's foggy mirror.

"You clean up nicely," she observed, poking her head into the bathroom, "need anything?"

"I'm good, thanks."

"I have pasta salad and fruit salad if you'd like. The only protein I can offer you is locked up in a can of tuna or nestled inside eggs but I do have fresh, five-grain bread. You must be famished... shall I lay it out?"

"You read my mind, Rachael, do you tell fortunes as well?"

"As a matter of fact, I *can* predict your future, but I'm afraid that I'd only be guessing," she laughed.

Peter laughed. "Your guess would be as good as mine."

"Oh, I think my guess would be *much* better, Peter."

"And why would that be?"

"Because I have inside information," she claimed.

They both laughed yet again, although Peter wasn't quite sure why he was laughing.

"Peter, did you hear the laughter?" Pandora whispered as she held onto him tightly.

"I did," he agreed, "but I have no idea where it came from."

"Nor I, but It feels as if it's right here with us."

"I can't deny that, Pandora. I'm beginning to believe that we aren't dealing with an intruder... a *physical* intruder that is."

"Do you mean ghosts, Peter?"

"It's the only logical explanation I can think of for these illogical events, Pandora. We've witnessed the results of things but haven't seen them actually happening."

"You mean the trunk?" she asked.

"Exactly, it's there and then... it's not there."

"And the room below it... the room somewhere on this floor?" she asked him.

"Yes, the room should be here somewhere but it doesn't seem to be. We've seen both the trunk and the room below it and then... we've *not* seen them both. The situations are exact opposites. We've witnessed two, separate realities but haven't witnessed the transition between the two. It's possible though, that we haven't seen those things actually happen because those things didn't *actually* happen. We've heard voices but haven't identified their source. It could be that the voices have no physical bodies associated with them. It's possible that what we've seen and heard are merely illusions, or figments of our imagination."

"So what now, Peter?" Pandora asked, taking his hand.

"We wait and see I suppose. We aren't in any apparent danger. We haven't actually been threatened by anyone... or anything. We may be confused and frightened but we don't seem to be in any immediate danger. We are frightened by our own fear, Pandora. We are afraid of the unknown... but not without reason."

"You haven't had a reason to use your bat yet," she joked.

"Exactly!" Peter chuckled as he imagined himself swinging away at a ghost; swinging right through it while it laughed at him. He dropped his bat to the floor and pulled Pandora into his arms. They returned to Pandora's bed where she pulled Peter into her arms.

"So, why did you become a masseuse?" Peter asked as he finished devouring the delicious omelet that Rachael had whipped up for him.

"I took it up to put myself through college. Oddly enough, my degree became all but useless while my temporary occupation became a permanent career."

"Good for you!"

"Yes, it has been. I rented out my guesthouse for several years to supplement my fledgling income but now I'm in a position where I don't need the extra money. I plan to convert the guesthouse into a massage studio. Luckily for me, city zoning tends to leave us alone around here. I've been working out of a spare bedroom since I bought this place five years ago. Before that it was out-calls and slave labor in a few studios around town. I worked the country club for a while. The money was good but it wasn't worth suffering the pretentious egos and propositions."

"Wealthy businessmen and corrupt congressmen?"

"Their wives were even worse!"

"Ha! Now, wait a minute... did their wives come on to you or did they just suffocate you with their egos?"

"In some cases, both."

"Interesting, interesting but not surprising," Peter thought out loud.

"And why would that be?" Rachael asked.

"The interesting part or the surprising part?"

"The, *not* surprising part."

"Well, I'm not surprised that a client would expect an innocent massage to turn intimate."

"Have you experienced that firsthand?"

"Well, I have had a massage before, and it *was* intimate. I mean after all, she *was* rubbing my naked, oily body with her hands; how could that *not* be intimate?"

"And did that intimacy escalate?"

"Only in my involuntary imagination," Peter confessed.

"So, you fantasized that your innocent massage would turn sexually intimate?"

"Not voluntarily. When she told me to roll over onto my back under the towel, it was obvious that I was sexually aroused. It was embarrassing. I apologized to the woman."

"And what did she say?"

"She said there was no need to apologize because it was a completely natural reaction."

"Have you had another massage since?"

"No, I can't handle it. It feels too good. It's too much of a tease."

"You could try a male masseuse."

"Yeah right, and if I had the same involuntary reaction I'd probably freak out."

Rachael laughed playfully. She stood up to clear the dishes from the table. As she placed them gently into the sink, Peter couldn't help but to admire her adorable shorts. Rachael turned around then to face him. Her weight shifted from one beautiful leg to another as she leaned back against the sink.

"So, do *your* male clients become aroused?" he inquired.

"Most definitely," she said.

"And how do you react?"

"I usually ignore it."

"Usually?"

"Yes, usually."

"And what happens during those unusual times?"

"Well... you'll just have to wait and see, now won't you?" she said, surprising him yet again. "Would you care for a coffee or a glass of wine before your massage?" she offered.

Peter's thoughts had drifted. "Wine would be nice," he said involuntarily.

"Good choice," she said, "I don't have any coffee."

"I smell coffee," Peter said, smelling coffee.

"How do you take it?" Pandora asked him.

"Internally," Peter announced as he rubbed the sleep out of his eyes and then settled into a chrome frame, vinyl-topped chair at Pandora's vintage kitchen table.

"You, m' Lord, are much too humorous this soon after sunrise," she laughed as she placed a piping hot mug of coffee in his majestic and immediate presence.

"And your radiance, m' Lady, eclipses the day's sunrise."

"I am so very humbled by your remarks, m' Lord. Do I detect a hint of satisfaction in your voice this morn?" she queried.

"Last night's satisfaction has not yet ceased satisfying."

"I trust then, that m' Lord will spare me the gallows?" Pandora hoped.

"For now 'tis true, fair damsel, ye shall sing another day."

"And another night, I pray?"

"Another night cannot come soon enough, m' Lady."

"More wine?" Rachael asked.

"May I take it to go?" Peter asked.

"Indeed," she said, pouring his glass half-full before she led Peter down a short hallway to her massage room.

"It's... incredible!" Peter remarked as he admired the stark, effervescently lit room. "It's so... it's so...?"

"Exotic?" Rachael suggested.

"Well, not exactly exotic in ways that I'm familiar with. To be honest, it's more exotic than exotic. I'm at a loss for words."

"I opted for a Zen-like, minimalist feel in lieu of a western knockoff of Asian decor," she explained.

Peter sipped his wine methodically as he attempted to absorb the atmosphere.

The room was dimly illuminated by five, glowing, blue glass orbs. Four of them were mounted in the dead-centers of the pale raspberry-colored walls. The fifth light hung from the center of the similarly colored ceiling directly above the massage table. What may have been most striking about the room was that the top of the massage table was perfectly level with the floor that surrounded it. A set of steps at the head of the table led down to a narrow pit which surrounded the table. The walls and the floor of the pit were painted dark slate grey. The earth-tone tiled floor, upon which Peter stood, shined deeply below its surface as if the tiles themselves had three-dimensional depth. Tiny, glistening, glass marble chips suspended in the tile, sparkled at Peter's feet like diamonds.

"The table is at floor level so that the client can rest upon the earth's surface," Rachael explained. "The table is white because it represents birth and rebirth and the quest for purity and truth that occurs subconsciously between such events. The dark pit represents death and the void. Notice that it surrounds the table of life. It does so because the delicate balance between life and death is ever-present and precarious. Death; the inevitable transition that marks the end of one's sum total life experience, also marks the beginning of something else yet to be explained."

"Wow... I'm with you so far... I think," Peter said as he attempted to absorb the symbolism. "So, if I understand you correctly, your pit of death facilitates rebirth and a better back."

"Exactly!" Rachael laughed and then continued. "The red walls and ceiling represent fire; the fire of our sun. This fire, the physical source of heat, warmth and comfort, burns also in one's metaphysical realm as the engine of life's energy, the fire in one's belly, the flame in one's soul," she explained. "The cool blue lights represent ice which is simply water in its most serene state. Locked in that ice, are the nutrients essential to all life. Without water there is no life. Without light, there is only darkness."

"Wouldn't it be more appropriate if the lights were red, representing the fire of our sun?" Peter asked.

"Watch, Peter..." she said and then she turned a dial on the wall. The lights dimmed at first but then brightened and as they did so, they transitioned from blue to red. Peter found the effect pleasing but was not particularly impressed by it.

"So now we have red lights and red walls," he observed.

"Do we, Peter?" she asked.

Peter noticed then that the walls; which, though difficult at first to distinguish from the red glow of the lights, had somehow transitioned from red to blue.

"Okay, *now* I'm impressed! How on earth…?"

"Effervescent paint, Peter."

"Home Depot?" he asked.

"Ha-ha funny, but not hardly. The paint contains deep-sea, negative-ion, effervescent enzymes. The enzymes react in a way opposite to their environment; blue light results in red walls, red light results in blue walls."

"So if I scratched the walls would they react and say, *a little lower please?*"

"That would require a second coat of paint to enhance the enzymes' awareness, Peter."

"Ha-ha, quick on your feet, Rachael, I like that. Do you have an answer for everything?"

"Not for the voices, Peter."

"Right… the voices, the inexplicable voices. Would you care to elaborate?"

"Let's save that for later shall we? We've massaging to do."

"We?" Peter asked.

"Well… I *do* love a good massage myself," she confessed.

"So, this is where you heard the voices?" Peter asked as Rachael unlocked the door to her guesthouse; bright morning sunlight filtering through the trees.

"Yes, inside, a man's and a woman's voice, they spoke softly and calmly but scared the dickens out of me every time that I came in here after she moved out."

"She?" Peter asked.

"My last tenant, a young woman," Rachael began, "after she finished her bachelor's degree in town here, she accepted a job offer out of state."

The couple entered the guesthouse and stood in its front room. "I've never heard the voices during the day though, Peter, only at night."

Moments later, a cat burst into the room from outside and wrapped its tail around Rachael's ankle. "Late night, Tom?" she asked, bending down to stroke the cat's chin.

Rachael looked up at Peter. "Last night, just before we met, I came in here... to listen for the voices. Crazy I know but I'm very much in-tune with the spiritual world, or so I thought. Having witnessed it firsthand though, I became frightened. But I was also intrigued and extremely curious. Last night was something entirely different though. The usually calm voices suddenly sounded anguished and terrified. There were screams. I became so frightened that I ran out into the street yelling like some kind of lunatic I'm afraid."

Peter looked around the small, nearly empty guesthouse. He noticed a tiny kitchen pantry past one side of the main room and a small bathroom past the other. He glanced over a ceramic floor lamp standing in a corner but then stared steadily at a solitary steamer trunk lying in the center of the otherwise empty room. He'd seen that trunk somewhere else before, or so he thought.

Rachael noticed Peter staring at the trunk. "That's the only thing that Pandora left behind. Well, that and Tom here. She thought he'd run away. I've left phone messages for Pandora to let her know that Tom came back but she hasn't returned my calls. I guess Tom is mine now. I thought I could use the trunk as a bench in my studio. What do you think, Peter?"

Peter didn't know what to think. He approached the trunk, bent down slowly, pushed the trunk's latches open and then raised its lid. He stared down into the empty trunk and then further still, beyond it.

"Hello..." Peter called out to a couple busily working their yard sale.

"Hi there, are you looking for anything in particular?" the man asked as his wife chased after their toddler who was running toward the street.

"Well actually, I'm looking for the woman who lives here," Peter said.

"You've already found her. That's her... my wife Jill chasing our adorable, albeit overly-energetic little rascal," the man said, pointing toward his wife and their son who had scampered half-way down the driveway.

"No, I mean the housekeeper here," Peter explained.

"No such person I'm afraid, although I do wish we could *afford* a housekeeper. Unfortunately, this place is costing us a fortune, but when my wife falls in love with something, there's no stopping her. This yard sale is but a small part of the bigger plan to afford this place. The larger part involved the recent sale of my beloved best friend; my thirty-foot sailboat. They say that the happiest day of a man's life is the day that he buys a boat and the second happiest day is the day that he sells it, but not in my case."

"Well, that explains the life jackets," Peter said absently as he surveyed the wares, half-dazed. "So... you don't know Pandora at all?"

"My daughter?" the man asked, a bit surprised. "You know

my daughter?"

"You have a daughter named Pandora?" Peter asked.

"A step-daughter actually, my wife's daughter; she lived in the area but moved out of state after she finished college. Jill and I found this place during a visit with her. We're starting a new life here together with little Jack; our little rascal."

"I was referring to a housekeeper named Pandora who was looking after this place," Peter explained.

"We've never met her I'm afraid. Do you live around here?" the man asked.

"Across the street, diagonally," Peter said, pointing toward his house.

"Well, I guess we're neighbors then. Pleased to meet you. I'm Jack, Jack Martin senior, and you are…?" he asked, extending his hand.

"Peter," Peter said, shaking Jack's hand aimlessly as he noticed over Jack's shoulder; a trunk lying on the floor of the man's garage.

As the busy garage sale got even busier, Peter left the company of his new neighbor and walked further up the driveway toward the man's garage. As Peter stood in front the familiar steamer trunk, the hair on the back of his neck stood on end. He bent down slowly, pushed the trunk's latch buttons and then raised the lid.

"Strong enough for a circus elephant," Jack announced, startling Peter a bit.

"Pardon? Oh yeah… I imagine it is," Peter agreed.

"It's old and dusty but it's got potential," Jack suggested and then added, "Make me an offer. In fact, make me an offer on anything or everything. We need to clear out all of this old stuff before we start moving our own things in."

"I'll think about it," Peter said, not really thinking about it. "I was just looking around and looking for... well, thanks, Jack. I'll see you later."

As Peter turned to leave, he nearly tripped over a cat that had come slinking out from between the piles of goods stacked in the garage.

"I see you've met Tom," Jack apologized.

"Tom?" Peter asked.

"That's what his nametag says; no address, no phone number, just Tom. He was our one-cat welcoming committee when we moved into this place. He scared the dickens out of my wife when he came charging up the basement steps at her. But, she fell in love with him and so did little Jack so I guess he's part of the family now."

Peter smiled distantly at Jack. He watched as Tom's tail disappeared through the hedges toward the neighbor's yard.

"Stop on by later for a beer!" Jack offered cheerily as Peter walked away in a daze down the driveway, passing Jill and Jack Junior in the process.

Peter's run slowed to a jog as he neared his home and approached Jack's house. A moving crew was wrapping up their day's work. They climbed exhausted into their truck and pulled away. Jack was out in his front yard. He was off-loading cardboard boxes of junk from his handcart onto the curbside for the next morning's trash collection.

"Hi ya neighbor!" Jack announced, as Peter stopped to say hello.

"All moved in?" Peter asked.

"We sure are. It'll be nice to finally sleep in our own bed again."

"Do you need a hand?" Peter offered.

"Thanks but no, Peter. The moving guys put everything exactly where we wanted it. They even set up our beds for us. We'll be unpacking boxes for weeks to come but we're in no hurry. This stuff here is unsold garage sale leftovers and some other things that we found tucked away in the attic. Feel free to dig around and take what you want. There are some really nice, old picture frames in one of the boxes. I'd bet they'd be worth something if anyone took the time to clean them up."

"The neighborhood pickers will probably clean you out by sundown, Jack," Peter told him.

"I hope so. I've seen enough junk lately to last a lifetime. Now, *my junk*, that's another story altogether because I only save *good junk*. At least that's what I'm always telling my better half. For some reason though, she still insists that twenty-five years' worth of old sailing magazines aren't worth keeping around. Go figure, right?" Jack laughed.

"Go figure," Peter agreed.

The men smiled at one another casually and then went their separate ways.

As Peter dropped his half-full trash can onto the curb, he watched as a picker's beat-up station wagon belched to a smoking curbside stop down the street. For reasons that he could not explain, other than maybe there *was* something that he could use, Peter walked over to Jack's tree lawn and casually pulled open the lids of one of the boxes. He squatted down next to the box and removed a dusty, antique picture frame. He blew off most of the dust and then held his breath. He wiped the frame's convex glass hurriedly and as cleanly as he could with the sleeve of his shirt. His heart skipped a beat.

Peter stared at Pandora in the old sepia-toned photograph. She was dressed in a short sequined skirt and a matching low-cut sleeveless top. One of her gorgeous legs was poised stepping into a trunk. Her left arm was extended gracefully. A handsome magician in a tuxedo and top hat held her wrist as he helped her inside the trunk. Pandora smiled at Peter from the photograph. He stared back at her. Peter looked up toward Jack's house. All of its windows were dark. He held the framed photograph in his arms and returned home.

Peter lay flat on his back on top of his bed covers; his neck resting in his palms atop his pillows, his elbows pointed toward the far wall. The room was dark except for a narrow strip of street light that slipped through his curtains and bathed Pandora's bright shining face. She smiled at him from the photograph on top of his bureau. He smiled back and then closed his eyes. He felt her soft warm body climb lightly atop him. She kissed him deeply and then whispered in his ear, "I miss you, Peter."

"I miss you too, Pandora," he replied as he opened his eyes and gazed deeply into hers.

"You know where to find me, Peter," she suggested.

Peter slipped his bare feet into his work boots and stepped outside for a breath of fresh air. He walked half-way down his driveway toward the street; bare-chested in his boxer shorts. He looked past his hedges toward his neighbor Jack's house. The pickers had taken everything it seemed. Jack's house was totally dark but its front door was wide open. Peter crossed the street and strode up Jack's driveway. He stepped up onto the porch and then into the house.

"Hello?" he called out softly.

"Hello...?" he called out louder.

"Up here," he thought that he'd heard.

"Up here, Peter..." he heard for certain.

Peter climbed the familiar stairs. He entered the ominous silence of the attic. He knelt down and opened the trunk slowly. A glowing effervescence spilled out into the darkness. Pandora gazed up at him from below as she offered Peter her hand. He took her hand in his. He stepped into the trunk and down into her loving arms. The lid of the trunk slammed shut. It did so for the very last time.

Rachael rang Peter's doorbell for the third time. She waited but to no avail. *He must be out jogging,* she thought.

"Hello...?" Jack asked the woman on Peter's front porch as he walked up Peter's driveway.

"Hello," Rachael said as she turned to face him.

"I noticed a car behind Peter's in his drive and then saw you standing at his door. Are you a friend of his?"

"I am, yes. Actually, we just met a few days ago. I assume he's out jogging so I thought I'd just wait for him here."

"I see. Please, sit a moment will you?" Jack asked her.

They sat down next to one another on the steps.

"I don't know how to tell you this so I'll just say it," Jack began quietly. "Peter was struck and killed while running last night. It was a hit and run. They didn't even stop."

Rachael gasped. She began to shake. She looked at Jack in disbelief. Tears fell from her eyes. Jack placed a hand on her shoulder and held her. A cat cried at their feet.

Ruth: Chapter 7 Verse 7

Ruth was losing faith fast. Roger would be there in five minutes and she was running *at least* twenty minutes late. And she *really* liked this guy! What's he going to think when he shows up to find her *still* in her bathrobe and with no makeup on for God's sake? Was it *her* fault that her boss made her stay late for no good reason? Was it *her* fault that the parking garage gate stuck and she had to sit and wait for the attendant to finally show up and raise it? Was it *her* fault that her kids had asked to stay over at a friend's house half-way across town and she was too nice to say, no? Ok... maybe that *was* her fault but was it *her* fault that traffic had been an absolute nightmare on a Friday night as usual? Was it *her* fault that her last decent pair of nylons decided to run and Mr. Chin down at the Zippy Mart took fifteen minutes to find her favorite shade in the stock room? What on earth was he *doing* back there anyway, eating chop suey? Was it *her* fault that the left heel of her black pumps broke off in her hands and she had to totally re-design her evening outfit from scratch? Ruth didn't think so. Ruth thought that the evil forces of bad luck were conspiring against her. They didn't *want* her to make a good impression on a really nice guy; a guy she really, really liked. They didn't want her to be happy after twelve months of dating not-so-nice guys and weirdoes and riff-raff and whatnot. Well, Ruth didn't care *what* they wanted. Ruth *knew* what *she* wanted. Ruth wanted Roger. Maybe Roger would understand? *Surely* Roger would understand. Roger is after all, a *really* nice guy so he's *bound* to understand... won't he?

Ruth's phone rang.

"For God's sake what now?" she cried out loud as she looked toward the heavens, set her curling iron down and then ran off to the phone.

Did her boss forget where Ruth had put the files? Because if he'd forgotten she'll remind him, and not too nicely, that the files are in the same darn place they always are. Or, was it her kids wanting permission to go to an R-rated movie that they knew well and good that she would never allow, at least not for a couple of years anyway. Or, was it Sheila about to ask her what she was up to on a Friday night and then go on and on and on about how poor Sheila *never* gets to have any fun anymore because her best friend and only friend in the whole wide world; Ruth, started dating again?

"Hello?" Ruth asked, breathless and flustered as she picked up the phone, smearing a freshly painted fingernail in the process.

"Roger... Hi...! Oh, you're running late...? Thirty or forty minutes...? Oh no, no, that's fine, Roger, see you then!"

Ruth returned the phone to its cradle and then screamed, but it wasn't a scream of fear or disgust or disappointment. It was a scream of extreme relief and ecstatic joy; a scream that would be repeated later that evening and not soon forgotten.

Sandy Shore

I met an amazing woman while walking on the beach one summer day. Her name was Sandy Shore. Given where we had met, I attempted to stifle my laughter when she told me her name but I inadvertently laughed out loud nevertheless. Her immediate reaction was to laugh right along with me and then one thing led to another until we ended up lying on the sand next to each other with tears of joy in our eyes and washed-ashore seaweed between our naked toes. When our hysterics had finally subsided, I remember experiencing a strange sensational feeling that those tears of laughter might be signaling the beginning of a beautiful esoteric relationship.

"Would you like to come over to my house?" she asked me.

"Sounds like fun," I replied as I envisioned a quaint island cottage, a white picket fence, wind chimes chiming on a cozy porch facing the sea.

And so, we took off on foot up a narrow sand trail through lush vegetation. As I followed her along the winding path, I kept a close watch on her tight knee-length sweatpants which did very little to disguise what was beneath them. It appeared as if the pants were simply a faded grey version of the figure inside them; nicely curved swaying hips, toned hypnotic buttocks and shapely striding legs. My companion's long sandy blonde hair fluttered to and fro across her shoulders as we strode along for what seemed like miles. About half way through our trek she stopped suddenly, turned to face me, and then offered me a long wet swig of water from the canteen slung across her shoulder. As the refreshing water cascaded down my dry and grateful throat, my eyes became fixated on her tattered and tightly shrunken t-shirt which did very little to disguise what was contained therein; a pair of perfectly shaped breasts that rose and fell with each of her steady breaths. The faded yellow smiley-face on the front of her shirt definitely had good reason to be happy; or maybe he was smirking at me for staring too long?

"Had enough?" she asked me.

"Pardon?" I asked.

"Has your thirst been quenched?" she clarified.

"Oh yes, it has been, thank you," I replied, handing back her canteen. As she slung the canteen over her shoulder, its strap bounced across one of her breasts and then came to rest snugly in her cleavage. In so doing, the strap had stretched and twisted the front of her shirt. It was then that I noticed that the smiley face's frozen smile had suddenly transformed into what appeared to be a stern scowl, or maybe, he was warning me to keep my distance.

"Stay close," Sandy suggested.

"Will do," I agreed, ignoring smiley's warning.

We made our way along another meandering mile of pathway and then finally came upon a clearing and a crude hand-painted sign which read; Warning! Private Property - Keep Out! Below the message, furrowed eyebrows sat above a pair of piercing painted eyes and a menacing frown. Had I seen that ominous face before?

"Welcome!" Sandy announced giddily as she half-turned in my direction and extended her long tanned arm toward the entrance of her home.

As I ducked inside the shade of the entryway, I realized that what I had come to expect as a quaint beach cottage turned out to be a sand-floored, driftwood-walled, thatched-roof hut in the middle of an untamed tropical jungle. It was both slightly disappointing and incredibly exciting all at once. I felt silly kicking my sandals off near the entrance of the floorless hut, but I followed her lead and then stood motionless as I took in the surroundings.

"Very tropical," I offered.

"Thank you kindly! You must be exhausted, have a seat," she suggested, directing my attention toward an old suitcase upon which I gratefully rested my weary legs.

"Would you like a nice cup of tea or a blowjob?" she asked.

"Tea would be nice," I said.

"Sugar?"

"No."

"Lemon?"

"Please."

As I continued sipping my tea some five minutes later, I sat wondering if I had made the right choice because for some reason, the lemon seemed unnecessary.

"What kind of tea is this?" I asked her.

"Seaweed tea, do you like it?"

"As a matter of fact I do. It has an interesting... seafood flavor," I suggested.

"It always does but even more so today because last night I steamed scallops in it. I have to conserve what little fresh rain water I have you see."

"But of course," I agreed, sipping my tea a bit slower. "How long have you lived here?" I asked her as she sat down next to me on the suitcase with a cup of tea of her own nestled in her long slender fingers.

"I'm not quite sure," she replied after some consideration

and then added, "I do believe I've lost track."

"Well, that's understandable," I said without understanding.

"Yes indeed," she agreed.

"Please forgive me if I'm mistaken, Sandy, but earlier, when you offered me tea, did you also offer me... offer me... a... a..."

"A blowjob?" she said matter-of-factly.

"Uh yes, a blowjob as it were."

"I did indeed, why, are you ready for one now?" she offered excitedly, swiveling her hips toward mine.

"May I take a rain-check for now?" I asked her.

"Of course, dear, I was just trying to be a good hostess is all. Just let me know when you're ready for one," she suggested cheerily but then added in distress, "Oh, my heavens...!"

"What is it, Sandy?"

"Are you married...? Because I would never have offered you a blowjob if I'd known that you were married. I am so sorry, I just assumed..."

"No need to worry, Sandy," I said, touching her wrist gently. "I'm not married. Me and my cock are both single."

"Well that's a relief!" she said happily. "I don't often entertain men and I'd be terribly disappointed if you were both spoken for."

"Well, rest assured, Sandy, nobody speaks for us but me."

She laughed, I laughed and then we both laughed and cried tears of joy together. After our hysterics had finally subsided, I remember experiencing a strange sensational feeling that those tears of laughter might be signaling the beginning of a beautiful esoteric relationship.

"Would you like to taste my mangos?" Sandy asked as she sat up more erect; her beautiful breasts following suit.

"Okay!" I said a bit too enthusiastically, but in my defense, I had no idea what to expect.

"Well come on then!" she said as she stood up and pulled me up by the hand along with her.

We walked hand-in-hand, side-by-side and stride-for-stride through her long and narrow hut to the end opposite from where we first entered. We ducked under the rear entrance, or exit as it might have been, and came out into a beautiful natural courtyard garden that swept in a giant arc around us. In the middle of the courtyard, a small wood fire burned in the center of a circular ring of stacked sandstone rock.

"As you can see... I have coconut palms, banana plants, a few lemon trees and of course, my favorite of all... mangos!"

"Your mangos are beautiful!" I remarked.

"Aren't they? And so juicy too!" she added with pride. She ran up to a tree, twisted off a bright yellow-orange fruit and then ran back to me holding it up to my nose. "Smell it."

"Wonderful!" I said. "Your mangos are so aromatic, they are heavenly indeed!"

"Just wait," she suggested. She pressed into the fruit with her long fingernails and then peeled back its skin. She held the mango up to my lips and said, "Bite it."

I bit into her mango. Juice ran down my chin. The fruit's sweet flavor erupted on my tongue. My teeth ground the magnificent morsel into pulp that slid down my throat in an exquisite river of juices. We took turns biting and chewing and enjoying the fruit until nothing remained but a pit that rested between our juicy lips. As the pit fell to our feet and disappeared into the sand, our lips met one another and introduced our tongues. Our arms held us tightly as our legs pressed firmly against one another. We kissed deeply and passionately but then slowly and gently as we both gazed into each other's eyes.

"Are you busy this evening?" she asked me in a whisper.

"I have no plans," I reported.

"It's settled then, we will dine by moonlight if you have no objections."

"Moonlight dining it is!" I agreed enthusiastically.

"Smashing!" she said gleefully. "But we have work to do first. Come now..."

She led me back into the hut where she handed me a sheathed knife similar to the one that she herself carried as she led me through a gap in her courtyard garden and onto another narrow sand path. A short distance later we came upon a rocky coast on the opposite side of the island from where we first met. She removed her clothes and then hung them in the branches of a wind-swept tree. She suggested that I follow suit so I hung my shorts and shirt next to her clothes. She un-sheathed her knife and I did the same with mine. She laid both sheaths on a large rock beneath our clothes which fluttered like flags in the ocean breeze. She led me then by the hand, slowly and carefully between wave-washed boulders as we entered the warm blue ocean and stood facing one another in waist-deep water.

"Shuffle your feet in the sand less you step on a stingray," she warned. "Trust me, 'tis better to scare them off than to feel their sting."

"Okay, will do," I consented.

"The saltwater might sting your eyes at first but you'll get used to it," she promised and then she dipped below and disappeared beneath the water's surface as I watched and waited...

A minute later Sandy re-surfaced holding a large scallop in each of her outstretched hands. "Woo-hoo!" she shouted past the knife blade clamped tightly between her teeth. She tossed the pair of scallops ashore and removed the knife from her mouth. "Your turn," she directed, but then added, "look in the rock crevices. When you find a scallop, insert your knife behind it and then twist the shell free from the rock."

"I'll do my best," I promised and then I sank down into the ocean. I found a scallop easily on my first attempt but my cloudy vision and limited skill with the knife prevented me from loosening it completely free. I made two more quick dives before I too shouted, "Woo-hoo," and then tossed my bounty ashore. Sandy dove through the surf toward me and then gathered me up in her arms. She kissed me quickly but deeply as reward for my success. Her salty lips tasted like heaven, well, heaven with a dash of salt that is.

"Twelve is quite enough," she decided a short while later. "And now... for the main course," she announced as she tossed her knife ashore and then disappeared yet again beneath the water's surface.

I watched as she re-surfaced half a dozen times at ever-increasing distances away from me before she ended her hunt abruptly and held up our prize high above her head shouting, "I hope you like lobster!" She waded her way through the water toward me holding the greenish-brown beast by its shell upside down; its legs twitching, its giant claws and tail thrashing against the cloudless blue sky.

"Oh, I do indeed like lobster, but not nearly as much as I like you!" I replied, having become completely awestruck by such a remarkable woman.

Sandy Shore

Sandy wrapped the lobster up snugly in her t-shirt while she instructed me to knot the leg ends of her sweatpants. We washed the sand from the scallops in the surf and then dropped them into her pants. I pulled the waist string of her pants tight and then slung the bundle over my shoulder. I thought about putting my shorts and shirt on, but as Sandy started back down the path stark naked with our lobster in tow, I decided against it. I snatched up my clothes and our knives in my free hand and scrambled to catch up with her. When we arrived back in the courtyard, Sandy dumped the scallops out of her pants and into a large dented pot of saltwater. She unwrapped and rolled the thrashing lobster into the same pot and then slid a large flat stone atop it.

"If he was any bigger he wouldn't have fit," she remarked.

"I guess not," I agreed.

"I usually grab smaller ones, but I have company tonight. It's so exciting!" she squeaked with delight.

"I'm excited too!" I agreed, smiling happily.

"Yes you are, I can see that quite clearly," she remarked as she noticed my aroused condition that had developed while I was watching her bend over the pot.

We both laughed and then hugged and then kissed a bit as we pressed our hungry bodies against one another.

"Shall we dress for dinner?" she suggested.

"But of course," I agreed.

"Do you care to bathe first?" she asked me.

"Sounds delightful," I remarked.

"I'm afraid that all I have is shampoo," she announced as she came out from her hut with a large green bottle in hand.

"Shampoo it is then!" I shouted with joy as I followed her back down the path and then out into the surf.

As she held my wrist steady she squirted several drops of shampoo into my open palm and then did the same in her own hand. We lathered up our hair and then we lathered up each other. We rubbed our soap-bubbled hands vigorously across each other's backs and then up and down each other's fronts. We held each other tightly as we slid our slippery soapy bodies across one another repeatedly to and fro in the rocking surf. We watched a beautiful sunset dip toward and then sink below the horizon as we dipped under the water's surface slowly and repeatedly to rinse off. As we re-surfaced one final time, we kissed in the early evening moonlight.

"Are you hungry?" she whispered in my ear.

"I'm famished for you," I confessed.

While sitting on an old suitcase in her garden courtyard, Sandy and I dined on lemon, banana and mango fruit salad, fresh steamed scallops and succulent coconut lobster. Bright moonlight sparkled on her exquisite sequined evening gown and on my fine Italian suit.

"You look beautiful in that dress, Sandy," I remarked.

"Why thank you kindly, kind sir. Luckily for me, the woman who owned it was close to my size. When her suitcase washed ashore I prayed that it belonged to a woman before I opened it. The two others before it had belonged to men which reminds me... I have cigars if you'd like! I tried one myself months ago but I nearly choked to death."

"I'll bet you inhaled the smoke," I wagered.

"You win that bet," she announced.

"Therein lies the problem; a cigar is not to be inhaled, it is to be lightly puffed and savored," I explained.

"Care to teach me how it's done?" she asked. "I'm willing to give it another go."

"By all means, Sandy, we can share one if you'd like."

She left my side and then returned with a cigar, a diamond accented lighter and four, tiny, shot-size bottles of vodka.

"Party-time!" she announced jubilantly as she held her booty aloft. She sat down then beside me and proceeded to tell me her story.

"While I was a stewardess, the possibility of a crash always lingered in the back of my mind," she began as I lit our cigar. "I never really thought that it would actually happen though because if I had, I couldn't possibly have done my job properly. When the airliner I was working on developed engine trouble and then actually *did* crash into the ocean, I felt lucky... I felt lucky that I had survived! I was so happy to be alive! When an airline service cart washed ashore shortly thereafter, I couldn't help but feel even luckier and now that I have *you* to share the contents with, I feel like the *luckiest* woman in the world!"

"And the best part is, Sandy... you get to share it with the luckiest *man* in the world," I declared.

"So, what's *your* story?" she asked me.

"I was sailing solo in the South Pacific when pirates shot across my bow and boarded my craft. They tossed me overboard with a life vest and two bottles of water. I thought for sure that I was headed straight for Davie Jones' locker but three days later... here I am!"

"Well, it's time to celebrate then, now isn't it?" she asked.

She didn't have to wait long for my reply which I sealed with a kiss and a light squeeze of her hip.

We sat happily in the moonlight, puffed on our cigar, sipped our vodka, made silly jokes and laughed and then ripped off one another's borrowed clothes. We jumped straight into the fishing net hammock that was strung up between two palm trees and sent it rocking and swinging until we rolled right out of it laughing.

"I've grown to love cigars!" she said breathless.

"And I've grown to love you, Sandy."

"Why yes, I can see that quite clearly," she said, giggling at my persistent condition.

We climbed back into our cozy hammock, kissed in the moonlight and fell asleep hours later in each other's arms.

"Are you still with us, mate? Mate... are you still with us?"

"Sandy?" I asked as my eyes opened to blinding white light.

"Yes, sir; Lieutenant Sandy Shore, Her Majesty's Royal Navy, at your service, sir."

"Where on earth are we?" I asked the young man standing above me staring into my eyes.

"Presently, we are one hundred and sixty-five degrees west longitude, fifteen degrees south latitude, sir."

"No, I mean this room, where is this room?"

"It is not a room, sir, it is a cabin; a medical berth aboard H.M.S. Buckingham. We found you unconscious on the shore of an uninhabited island. You were near-death, sir, some three days ago. So good to have you back with us, sir."

"And the woman... is she alright?" I asked.

"Woman, sir?"

"Yes, the woman... Sandy... Sandy Shore, is she alright?"

"You were alone when we found you, sir. I'm afraid that we found no one else. But I can assure you that our landing party did a thorough search of the island."

"I see," I said groggily before the cabin went dark.

I awoke the next morning and kissed her beautiful sleeping lips. So as not to awake her, I climbed slowly and deliberately out of our gently rocking hammock. I lit a fire and placed a pot of tea on the crackling flames. The low morning sun shined on Sandy's beautiful mangos. The clear blue sky above announced yet another wonderful day ahead.

Not surprisingly, Sandy remained sound asleep; we'd had quite an exhilarating evening. To pass the time, I wandered wobbly-legged down the path in search of firewood. As I leaned into the brush to grab a dead branch, I suddenly realized that the branch was in fact; a large leg bone. I dropped the bone and cleared the brush away; before me lay a bleached human skeleton. Its skull was adorned with a pilot's cap. The skull's jaws and teeth were clenched in a hideous scream. The skeleton's hands clutched a sharpened stick that had been thrust through its ribcage. Hands wrapped around my waist from behind.

"I see that you've found Captain Clark," Sandy whispered.

"Captain Clark?" I asked, as I stared into his eye sockets.

"Yes," she confirmed. "He and the others were fun for a while but over the months and years, they became desperate and downright grouchy. They weren't suited at all to island life. I can't tell you how nice it is to have fresh meat again. I've had *such* a craving."

I awoke broiling and bathed in sweat; my arms and legs bound tightly together. The hot high noon sun beat upon me through the trees. I struggled to free myself.

"Here… let me help you, Mr. Sleepy Head," Sandy said as she untangled me from the frustrating hammock and helped me to my feet; a captain's hat shading her dazzling eyes.

Sara Sahara

Sultan X, the Tenth Sultan of the Kingdom's Tenth Province, came into the world on October 10th in the year 1010 A.D.

After three days and nights of perpetual and unforgiving winds, the walls of the Sultan's tent fluttered mildly in the forgiving evening breeze. The winds had generated piercing sandstorms that wreaked havoc throughout the province and beyond. The entire region was forced into a temporary state of desert hibernation. But not all were idle during the storm.

"Take *her*," the lead marauder ordered, "and *her*, and *her*," he commanded as he pointed out three terrified girls huddled amongst other girls and elderly women in the Bedouins' tent. Amidst the howling winds, the persistent screams and cries of the women and girls remain unheard by their tribesmen sleeping in neighboring tents. No men would come to their aid and rescue on that horrible night. The elder women's attempts at resistance were easily quelled by the six sword wielding marauders who laughed heartedly at the soft yet defiant blows thrown their way. During the struggle, the chosen girls were ordered hooded by the lead marauder in order to protect their soft young flesh from the sandstorm raging outside. The elder women pursued the abductors outside but watched in horror as their granddaughters were ridden away on horseback and then disappeared into the dark curtains of swirling sand. The women turned then and trudged through the sand in agonizing slow motion toward the tents of their tribesmen. Relentless headwinds knocked the women to their knees and into the deep flowing sand.

"Exquisite indeed!" the lead marauder announced as he inspected the captive girls lined up along a torch-lit cave wall.

"The Sultan will be pleased with our gifts," the leader predicted. "Tomorrow, on the fiftieth celebration of his birth, Sultan X will reward us handsomely. We will have good food to eat and fine wine to drink," he promised his men as they gazed wantonly at the beautiful girls.

"Can we keep a girl for ourselves?" a marauder asked him.

"If the Sultan should refuse a girl, we will keep her. Until such time, do not lay a wandering hand upon them!" he ordered his men. The leader then brandished a short curved sword which he brought down hard and repeatedly upon a melon. His men hand-fed morsels of the fruit to the trembling girls as they stood chained to the cave wall; their hands bound behind their backs.

As night turned into day the raging sandstorm turned calm at last. The marauders were temporarily blinded by bright sunlight when they left their cave on the morning of the Sultan's celebration. Four of the six rode into the village to scout the offerings in the temple grounds. It was there that the Sultan's subjects were preparing for his celebration. Water was being drawn from wells, bread was baking in earthen ovens, livestock were being slaughtered and gutted and prepared for the spits. Young women and girls were washing garments and grinding grain while young men and boys erected tents and hauled charcoal to the pits. The altar in the temple grounds was becoming covered with gifts of fruits and flowers, live caged birds, elaborate woven rugs, jars of fine wine and olive oil. The Sultan already had everything that any man could ever wish for and yet, his subjects gave him even more each and every year on the anniversary of his birth. In return, the Sultan ordered his warriors to remain vigilant and defend his subjects against nomadic savages who would otherwise slaughter the weakest among them and rob them of what little they had. And so it was that the Sultan's subjects were forever grateful and loyal to him.

The marauders were pleased that no beautiful women were among the gift of slaves chained to the walls of the temple. The Sultan would therefore be pleased with the marauders' unique gifts. The Sultan himself was generous to his devoted subjects but to those less-than devoted, he would bestow the harshest of punishments. Maiming was commonplace for unlucky liars and thieves who would spend the rest of their days without fingers or hands, toes or feet, tongues or eyes. Executions of fellow tribesmen were uncommon but were often enjoyed by those in attendance when enemies were captured and then tortured to death.

Marauders themselves acted independently of provincial rulers but were often favored by those Sultans to whom they were most loyal. Those marauders who fell out of a Sultan's favor were considered enemies of the province. If captured and fortunate, they would be enslaved. If captured and unfortunate, they would be doomed to horrible torture. Those so doomed were often impaled through the groin on the sharpened end of a long vertical staff upon which they'd scream in unbearable agony as they'd slide down slowly to their gruesome demise. Other unfortunates would be stood upright in a pit and then buried to their necks. As the day would progress the scorching desert sun would broil their scalps and bake their brains. Those unlucky enough to survive until nightfall would fall prey to the wild dogs and jackals that would trot in from the desert to tear off the ears and noses and lips of the condemned before ripping into their throats. At times such as those, blood-curdling screams would pierce the night and awaken all from their sleep.

Should the Sultan find himself in a compassionate and sympathetic mood, those so condemned would be relieved of their heads quickly by the sharp blade of the Sultan's sword. According to tradition however, on the day of the Sultan's celebration, there would be no quick executions or slow and torturous deaths to enliven the festivities.

"If you surrender your virginity to us, the Sultan will refuse you. And when he does, you will be released to return to your families," two young marauders claimed as they lied to the girls they were guarding.

The girls looked to one another but remained silent. They considered the advice of their captors while the marauders waited anxiously and lustfully for the girls' reply.

"And if we are given to the Sultan as virgins," the eldest girl asked boldly, "what then will become of us?"

"You will remain his property until he tires of your worn flesh at which point you will be enslaved if you are lucky or executed if you are not. You see..." the marauder said as he caressed the girl's soft cheek, "the Sultan already has seven wives. He has no permanent need for any others."

After having scouted the temple grounds, the four elder marauders bartered for provisions. They received loaves of bread, strips of dried meat and jars of wine in exchange for the three gold pendants they had taken from their captives. The eldest girl had bitten the marauder who had felt beneath her tunic and discovered there, between her breasts, the first of the three gold pendants. The younger girls did not resist when their own pendants were ripped from the woven wool strings around their necks.

Come mid-morning, the marauders regrouped in their cave where they filled their bellies with bread and meat and their heads with wine. At midday, all six marauders rode into the village on horseback. Three of them clutched a girl by the waist in front of them.

When the marauders entered the temple grounds, shouts of admiration erupted from the crowd for the gifts they were bearing were quite beautiful indeed. Elderly women adorned the girls' hair with desert flowers before they were paraded on foot toward the altar. The Sultan would surely be pleased with his fine gifts of young virgins. Unbeknownst to most however, the eldest girl was herself, no longer virtuous, for earlier that day she had sacrificed herself willingly to both of the young marauders. After the men had their way with her, she stole a knife while they lay sleeping exhausted. As she stood bravely then at the altar awaiting the Sultan, the knife she had stolen remained hidden in the folds of her tunic.

As the marauders had hoped, the Sultan was pleased with his young and beautiful gifts. He caressed the girls' cheeks and then smiled. Cheers erupted from the crowd.

The Sultan's lively celebration continued well past sundown. After the night air had turned bitter cold and the celebration had subsided, the Sultan retired to his tent with his gifts; glorious gifts that were sure to keep him warm.

"Three beautiful young women..." the Sultan remarked, "you are virgins I trust?" he inquired, smiling.

The frightened girls remained silent.

The Sultan startled the girls when he broke the silence by demanding loudly, "If any of you have been with a man you must tell me now!"

"I am not a virgin," the youngest girl lied.

"Nor I," the second youngest lied.

"Very well then, be still there 'til morning while I enjoy this one who is," the Sultan ordered.

Sultan X directed the eldest girl to disrobe to which she did so willingly. The Sultan was pleased for the girl's figure was exquisite indeed. "Do not be afraid, dear one," he told her.

"I am not afraid, my Sultan. I wish only to please you in any way that I can," she promised him.

"And I am sure that you will!" he laughed and then he himself disrobed and lay back upon his pillows.

The young woman jumped playfully atop his belly, knocking the breath from his chest in the process.

"You seem as anxious as I am!" the Sultan gasped and then he gasped again as her blade sliced his throat open.

Sara gripped the bloody knife in both of her hands then and plunged it deep into the Sultan's heaving chest. She pulled the knife out of him, wiped it clean on his pillows and then dressed quickly while the other girls stood watch.

The girls crept from the Sultan's tent and then across the empty courtyard. They made their way to sandstone hills and to bluffs beyond where a vast plain stretched to the horizon. They followed a dry river bed and made their way slowly and steadily along it toward home. The next day, the relentless desert sun scorched them for hours on end as vultures circled high over their heads. Day turned to night. They followed the stars. As dawn broke, the girls gasped as they were suddenly gathered up, in their grandmothers' loving arms.

The days following the Sultan's celebration were black days indeed as the village mourned the loss of their beloved leader. Women and children wailed as their elders made burial preparations. The six marauders remained motionless for their bruised and broken bodies were bound and buried upright, shoulder-deep in the sand. The six terrified men stared in disbelief as six starving wild dogs were brought toward them on leashes. The dogs sniffed hungrily. They growled and snapped in the faces of their unfortunate meals. A large crowd gathered. One by one the dogs were released. When the first doomed marauder began screaming, the vengeful crowd cheered its approval.

A province away, a young woman was honored as a heroine and was showered with gifts. Sara was sad however, because having sacrificed herself to the marauders, she knew that no man would ever take her as a wife. She was soon thereafter taken by surprise though when she was made the favorite wife of her tribal leader. He so admired Sara's exquisite beauty and the strength of her courage that he couldn't help but to fall in love with her.

And so it was that Sara Sahara reigned with her husband for many years. After his death, Sara herself led her tribe. She ruled all of her subjects fairly but gave particular preference to the women of her expanding province who were at long last accorded the respect they deserved. When her long life came to an end, Sara was laid to rest in a gold sarcophagus. Her anointed body was entombed in the cave in which she had sacrificed herself to save her friends. To this very day however, that cave, her tomb, which had become a shrine to her and to all women, has yet to be rediscovered.

Sex and Violence and Salad

The biker known as Snake by virtually anyone within a hundred mile radius of wherever he happened to be at the time, swung his tree-trunk-size leg off his '62 Panhead Harley, stretched his spine straight, grabbed a sawed-off shotgun from his saddlebag and then marched his leather boots across the wide gravel berm of the desolate desert highway. Snake's cohorts Dart and Spike waited for him with handguns at their sides. They faced Paco and Lucia as the farmer and his daughter stopped working their roadside stand that was partially shaded by the only tree that could be seen for miles around.

Snake approached his fellow gang members and then stood tall between them providing nearly as much shade as the tree. He lowered the muzzle of his shotgun to the ground alongside his dusty, size fourteen black boots. An eight foot long rattlesnake slithered up Snake's arm. Its tail end coiled tightly around the man's left forearm. Its rattle lay motionless and silent across his wrist like a handcuff. The serpent crept up and under the sleeve of the biker's black t-shirt and then stretched unseen across the man's wide barrel chest. The snake's body became visible where it wrapped around its owner's thick neck but then vanished again where it slithered down inside the man's shirt. It reappeared out from below the opposite sleeve where it coiled around the man's massive bicep. The snake's lower jaw pressed against the biker's thick forearm; its menacing upper jaw stretched wide open. The snake's fangs, dripping with venom, threatened to strike. Lucia's eyes fixated on the snake's wicked forked tongue.

Although she'd seen the biker's elaborate tattoo many times before, every time that she had, it had given her both chills and thrills. Many a night while lying in bed, Lucia thought about Snake and the snake wrapped around him. She'd wonder if the snakes would ever rid the desert of rats.

The bikers who'd come to visit Paco and Lucia that day weren't holding their weapons against the farmer and his daughter, they were carrying them as insurance against the possibility of a roadside ambush. The god-forsaken territory through which they rode was unclaimed. It was up for grabs. Highway patrolmen and sheriff's deputies were fewer and farther between than trees in those parts. Beautiful desert flowers such as Lucia however, were even rarer. They were considered endangered.

Paco may have been locally famous for his delicious naturally-grown fruits and vegetables but his stunningly beautiful daughter Lucia was the main attraction for men lucky enough to happen upon her. She was the sole reason why many of those men became regular customers. An eye-full of luscious Lucia was motivation enough to improve one's diet with fresh fruit and healthy vegetables.

Lucia stood stoically at the produce stand that day but her outfit screamed for attention. Tight, faded denim shorts rested low on her nicely curved hips and tugged snugly between her long, gorgeous brown legs. Above the girl's bare bronze midriff, a skimpy pale yellow top stretched tightly across her shapely chest plunging low at her cleavage where tiny droplets of perspiration glistened.

"I like the look of those melons, Lucia," Snake remarked.

"Thank you," Lucia said shyly.

"Are they sweet and juicy today?" he asked the girl.

"They're sweet and juicy every day," she replied innocently.

"Be a good girl then, and toss four in a sack for me," he asked with the softest growl that his normally booming voice could muster. He turned then to Lucia's father Paco and in his usual terrifying tone requested; "Six heads of lettuce, one bunch of radishes, a bunch of green onions, six red onions, one bunch of carrots and let's see now… oh yeah, three bunches of that beautiful asparagus."

As Paco began filling Snake's order, the biker turned again to Lucia and said, "Nice looking tomatoes, Lucia. Are they sweet and juicy today?"

"They're sweet and juicy every day," Lucia said shyly.

"Be a good girl then, and pick out a dozen for me, okay?"

"Si, Señor Snake," she said and then she carefully chose fifteen of her father's finest tomatoes.

Dart and Spike collected the heavy sacks from the farmer and his daughter. They returned to their bikes where they stuffed full, all six of their saddlebags.

"How much do we owe you, Paco?" Snake grumbled as he reached through a chain for the wallet in his hip pocket.

"Ju owe us nothing," Paco said, "ju protect us," he added as he stared into Snake's jet black eyes.

"So the rats haven't been bothering you?" Snake asked.

"We see no rats for two months now," Paco reported.

"Good to know. We exterminated two more of them just ten miles from here a week ago Friday," the biker announced. "Let us know if you see any others crawling around."

"We will," Paco promised, "we will, señor."

The biker slipped two thick fingers into the breast pocket of his leather vest. He withdrew a twenty-dollar bill and offered it to Lucia. "Buy yourself some earrings," he suggested.

Lucia looked at her father. Paco nodded his head, yes.

Lucia took the money from Snake and gave him a shy, glistening white smile in return.

Snake turned to leave but before he did he said, "I wanna see you wearin' 'em the next time I stop by, Lucia."

As the enormous man lumbered away and the earth beneath him shook, Lucia read the familiar name stitched on the back of his vest; *Demon Vegans*. Her thoughts drifted then as she stared at the colorful arrangement of fruits and vegetables stitched beneath the gang's name.

Lucia wondered if she were to sit behind Snake on his motorcycle and press herself tightly against his broad back, would her arms be long enough to reach around him. She assumed that she wouldn't be able to reach his belt buckle but knew for sure that she would love to try to someday. She wondered what it would be like to glide along the highway with him, free as a hawk, her long black hair dancing in the desert wind. She thought that it would be heavenly. She wondered if her father would ever allow her to ride with Snake, if she could summon the courage to ask his permission that is. And then she thought that her father just might agree to let her ride with him and if that were to happen she knew in her heart that Snake would gladly give her a ride. Dart and Spike often brought girlfriends along with them but for some reason, Snake always rode alone. Lucia often wondered if Snake had a girlfriend, but she was much too shy to ask him. Maybe he *did* have a girlfriend but preferred to ride solo.

Maybe he *didn't* have a lover and slept alone at night like she did. Lucia imagined Snake holding her in his strong, tattooed arms. She envisioned herself wrapped up in his rattlesnake hug at night. It frightened her and thrilled her and gave her chills just to think about it. No boy during her high school days had ever made her feel that way. She felt deeper desires now though. In bed at night Lucia could almost feel Snake lying beside her, slipping inside her. She shuddered at the thought and then shuddered again as motorcycle engines suddenly roared alive awakening her from her daydreams. She watched as Snake sped off onto the highway. She watched as he vanished in the hot shimmering distance.

Left abandoned, Lucia's thoughts drifted off to her elder brother Francisco. He'd been shot to death right in front of her three months earlier. His killer was a member of the Road Rats gang. They had knocked her father to the ground and started ransacking the stand. Her brother swung at the Rats with a tire iron. He hit two of them hard before two others knocked him to the ground. A fifth Rat lowered a pistol and shot Francisco twice in the chest. Her brother died in the exact same spot in which Lucia was standing. As she recalled that dark sunny day, tears fell from her cheeks and dropped sadly onto her father's beautiful blood-red tomatoes. Ghosts of the gunshots that had taken her brother's life haunted her every night since his death. They'd ring in her brain until she'd wake up screaming and shaking in her bed.

Three days after her brother's murder, Snake delivered the shooter's severed head to her father at the stand. When Snake pulled the head out by its hair from the blood-stained burlap sack, he asked Paco, "Is this the Rat?"

Lucia ran away screaming and hid sobbing in her father's truck. Paco replied, "Si," and then shook Snake's hand.

"That's good, Paco," Snake said as gently as he could. "It'll save me another trip."

On this day though, Lucia walked calmly to her father's old worn out truck. She pulled the creaking passenger side door open and then slipped up and onto the hot vinyl seat. She opened the glove box and removed a tattered envelope. She slipped a small photograph of her brother out from its folds and gazed at his portrait lovingly. As was often the case, a tear or two dropped onto Francisco's beautiful smile. Lucia wiped the photo dry on her breast and then held it to her heart. She slipped the photograph and the twenty dollar bill that Snake had given her into the envelope. She wiped her eyes dry with the backs of her hands and then jumped quickly out of the truck as a roaring Greyhound bus came grinding to a halt in front of her father's stand.

Lucia ran to the back of the truck, whipped off the tarp that covered its bed and then lowered the truck's tailgate. She pulled a huge yellow lemonade jug that outweighed her to the edge of the tailgate. She slipped cellophane down from a column of white plastic cups. The loud popping hiss of the bus' airbrakes suddenly shot through the air startling her.

The passengers stepping out of the bus were temporarily blinded by the bright noonday sun. They cringed in the stifling desert heat made even hotter by the bus' idling diesel engine. As they recovered from the initial shock of the inferno, the passengers began swarming the stand bringing with them their hunger and thirst. By the time the westbound bus had lumbered away, Lucia's lemonade jug was all but empty.

Passengers onboard the air-conditioned coach unwrapped and devoured egg-salad on freshly-baked flatbread. Others dug into mixed-green salads or chomped on juicy fresh fruit. The fruit salad cups however, were the crowd favorite and sold out fast to parents of sweet-tooth children. As they watched their kids enjoying healthy food for a change, the mothers onboard the bus were glad that there was no junk food to be had at Paco's stand. Paco was happy for the good business that day. It would be two more days before the same bus traveling in the opposite eastbound direction would return to the stand. For now as it were, all of the peach crates lay empty. Paco and Lucia tossed them easily into the truck bed atop half-empty crates and empty ice chests. As the tired sun began to rest low on the horizon, Lucia's father lifted the truck's squeaking tailgate and then pushed it closed. He and Lucia drove away from the two-lane highway on a dry riverbed dirt road that few besides themselves even knew existed. Their heavy wood tables were left in place to stand alone for the night. Desert lizards would lick them clean of juices and crumbs. They'd fight over the rinds and seeds left behind leaving the sand swept and furrowed by the angry arcs of their battling tails.

Paco's truck rose slowly out of the flat desert valley toward a summit and a beautiful sunset. He coaxed the truck forward over rocks and through ruts. His daughter's head bobbed back and forth as she bounced about sleeping. An hour later the truck's headlights swept across their green valley home. Paco parked his truck alongside the farm's weathered barn and turned off its tired motor that simmered and sighed in relief. The cooling engine pinged and crackled the otherwise silent night air. Paco placed his hand gently on his daughter's soft knee. He sat still for a moment and closed his tired eyes. Screams pierced the silence as Paco's baby boy scampered excitedly toward the truck. Paco's wife, dressed in a knee-length white smock, stood watching in the open doorway of their mortared stone home. The warm soft glow surrounding his wife and spilling out onto their stone walkway beckoned to Paco. He would spend the night in his wife's loving arms and sleep with her in heaven. Lucia awoke suddenly and snatched up her noisy baby brother. She tickled the boy mercilessly as she carried him laughing and squirming into the house. Paco strode solemnly beneath the farm's largest shade tree; cave-like and dark then under the cover of night. In his hands he carried a colorful bunch of freshly-picked desert wildflowers. He knelt down and placed the flowers gently onto his eldest son's grave. Paco's tears washed over the flowers as he prayed to the saints.

"Rock and Roll, Demon Vegans!" Snake shouted as he raised a dripping wet bottle of ice-cold beer high in the air; a gesture that triggered bedlam on a nightly basis. And so it was on Snake's cue the Demons' hangout, a previously abandoned hilltop horse barn, erupted in mayhem. A three piece band, two electric guitars and a drum kit, blasted notes and chords and shrieking sounds that resembled music. Off-key vocals and screams of utter nonsense were exchanged between the wild band members and the boisterous crowd. A trio of tattooed women danced like happy witches around a wood burning brick oven. Men in the crowd grabbed women and more booze and each other as they smoked home-grown herb and devoured fresh-picked fruit like mountain gorillas. The lead guitar wailed something resembling Hendrix that

stirred the wild crowd into an even wilder frenzy that got quickly out of hand. Gunshots were fired up into the barn's ancient rafters prompting Snake to yell at the top of his massive lungs, *"Cut That Shit Out!"* before he resumed his business of chopping carrots, slicing radishes and snapping long, crisp, fresh green onions in half. He diced tomatoes and peppers and squash with deft skill. He licked his chef's knife clean and savored the juices. With the back of his knife he swept all of his efforts into a huge bed of ice cold lettuce. He then tossed the ingredients and dowsed them liberally with his locally-famous homemade secret-recipe salad dressing that everyone called; "Snake Juice." The dressing's secret ingredients featured six different types of exotic peppers that Snake himself lovingly cultivated in the gang's communal garden. The garden's most popular crop grew incredibly high and got everyone who smoked it even higher. Any gang member, at any time, could help themselves to most of garden's wonderful bounty but nobody who valued their life would ever dare lay a hand on Snake's peppers. He treated those rich and colorful plants lovingly as if they were his very own newborn babies because perhaps, he had no kids of his own to pamper let alone a steady girlfriend.

The so-called "salad bowl" that Snake used to mix up his concoction was in fact; a huge, lidless, insulated cooler. The gang member known as "Fat Dude" had cracked the once, brand-new cooler's lid in half, busted its hinges and cracked its sides earlier that summer when he tried to sit on it. His enormous ass and incredible bulk rendered the vessel useless as a beer cooler for which it was originally intended. Fat Dude was subsequently saddled with the responsibility of driving the gang's beat-up pickup truck a hundred miles into town to fetch a new cooler for the gang's beer. The Dude didn't mind the trip though because it presented him the opportunity to break the gang's main sworn rule by pigging-out on two pounds of delicious, greasy, char-grilled meat. Three teenage girls who had witnessed the comical irony of a fat man in a Demon Vegan leather vest devouring four huge hamburgers at Harold's Roadside Grill that day, giggled madly amongst themselves.

When Snake finally yelled, *"SALAD!"* the mob attacked en masse like a heard of drunken starving goats. Men's beards and mustaches dripped with hot pepper salad dressing that burned their tongues and mouths and watered their eyes. Giant swigs of ice-cold beer tamed the pain between each delicious bite. Women as well shoveled forkfuls of the salad into their hot and hungry mouths. A trio of girls deliberately and repeatedly dropped bits of the salad into their cleavage tempting the waggling tongues of hungry men to lick the oily women clean. Mere moments after Snake had slid six vegetarian pizzas out of the huge brick oven they were immediately devoured by the crowd. *"Thanks for saving Me a slice you Filthy Coyotes,"* Snake bellowed before he began tossing dough for six more pizza pies. His sexy assistant, bare-chested beneath her chef's apron, spread a thick layer of sauce across the skillfully shaped dough. She and Snake dressed the pizzas with toppings and then slid them carefully into the red hot glow of the oven's interior. Beer ran in rivers while the pizzas baked and filled the barn with irresistible aromas. Two army-size pots of vegetarian chili that had been simmering on the cast-iron stove for hours were scooped dry in minutes. As they ate, most in the crowd drank heavily. Many of those chased their beers with shots of Tennessee sour mash or with Mexican tequila. A few too drunk or foolish to know any better, drank all three.

After the feast, a trio of half-naked women in the barn's loft beckoned to potential bunk-mates below by hooting and twirling their tops. Those in the crowd who remained upright continued to drink and get drunk and smoke and get high. Through it all the band rocked on. The barn's sticky dance floor remained occupied by writhing sweaty bodies. In one corner of the barn a group of guys and gals took turns firing a Daisy b-b-gun at Dart's bare back. Tiny red welts peppered the dartboard tattoo inked on the biker's back from shoulder to shoulder. Based on the welts, the shit-faced marksmen kept serious score. Before a champion could be crowned however, Dart took a hard errant shot to the back of his head and the tournament ended abruptly in a fistfight brawl. Dart himself was the recipient of ten blows, a few of those straight to his jaw. He shrugged them all off though and knocked his three attackers (one of whom was his own younger brother) flat on their backs. Snake watched the entire melee while laughing from afar in the comfort of his leather recliner. He couldn't decide if he was witnessing the Keystone Cops or the Three Stooges in action. Either way, he looked on at the comical carnage with a satisfied grin. He loved each and every one of those crazy knuckleheads to some degree or another but he wasn't exactly sure why. It may have been because any one of them would take a bullet for him as he would do for them. As they say, blood is thicker than water and all of them were blood brothers and sisters. Around two o'clock in the morning the latest runaway kid to join the gang gathered the nerve to approach Snake for the very first time.

"Hey there, Mr. Snake sir. My name's Zack. What cha think

of my new ink?" the kid asked his leader as he showed off his brand-new, naked lady tattoo.

"She's hot, kid. I think she's giving me a boner."

"Really?" the kid asked.

"I wouldn't kid ya, kid," Snake said and then he grabbed the kid's skinny arm in his grizzly bear paw and leaned in for a better look. "Is that iceberg or romaine she's lying on?" he asked the boy.

"Actually, it's arugula," the kid answered politely.

"Oh yeah... *arugula*... I can see that now," Snake agreed with a smirk as he released the boy's arm. "You must have a lettuce fetish... I love it! And speaking of boners... hey, Trixie... come here a minute, girl..."

"What's up Doc?" a sexy, mature, long-legged woman asked as she stopped in her tracks and then pranced over to the guys.

"This here's Zack, Trixie. He's our newest, youngest, slightly bruised, member. The boys roughed him up pretty good last night during his initiation but there's one thing left he needs to do before he's a full-fledged Demon Vegan."

"He needs to fuck a Demon Vegan girl," Trixie said, finishing Snake's sentence for him.

"Sexy *and* smart," Snake said with a grin and then added, "I thought that since you tend to like 'em young, Trixie, you might wanna do the honors... if you don't mind that is."

Trixie looked the boy up and down, apparently uninterested when she said, "Well... I don't know, Snake... he's kinda..."

"He's kinda what?" Snake asked her.

"He's kinda cute," she teased. "I'd love to fuck him for ya."

"I thought you might, Trixie. Zack my man... you're in for one *hell* of a ride... if you want to fuck her that is."

"I sure would, sir, she's smokin' hot."

"Well, don't tell me, tell her..."

Zack turned toward Trixie and announced boldly, "I wanna fuck you, Trixie."

"Not *that,* boy!" Snake bellowed, terrifying the kid. "Tell her she's hot."

"You're hot, Miss Trixie," the kid said as romantically as he could.

"And you wanna fuck me?" she asked him.

"I sure do," Zack confirmed.

"Why?" she asked, torturing the poor boy.

"Because you're smokin' hot," he repeated nervously.

"Do you think you can handle it?" she teased.

"I'm not sure. I've never done it before."

"You're a virgin?" she asked, both surprised and delighted.

"So far, but I'm ready to learn."

"I can tell you're ready from that big bulge in your britches," she said and then she approached the boy and gave his big bulge a big squeeze.

"Zack just got himself vegan inked, Trixie. Why don't you show him your radish and strawberry tattoos, see which one he likes best," Snake suggested as he winked at the woman.

Trixie pulled her top up to her chin. Her beautifully aged breasts and juicy-red nipples bounced playfully in the process. There were no tattoos to be seen.

Zack stared at her nipples, swallowed hard and then asked, "Which one is the radish and which one is the strawberry?"

"That's my boy!" Snake hooted.

"Well, you'll just have to taste them both and decide for yourself," Trixie teased the boy and then lowered her top.

"So it's settled then; you two run along now and play,"

Snake suggested as he slapped Trixie's smokin' hot ass.

Snake watched as her smokin' hot ass climbed the loft's wooden ladder. The boy watched as well, up close, directly beneath the woman as he scampered up behind her. Zack's anxious feet slipped off a rung half way up. He grabbed the sides of the ladder hard in order to save himself from falling. Snake hollered up at the anxious boy, *"Slow Down There, Cowboy... You Got All Night!"*

Zack stopped at the top rung. He turned around and looked back down at Snake. The kid smiled like a hungry coyote with a tasty bunny in its jaws. Snake smiled back recalling his very own first sexual encounter thirty years ago. According to her nametag, his delicious bunny was named Darleen. She was a sexy seasoned truck stop waitress. He could still taste her.

As the morning sun rose, no one on the hilltop beneath it stirred, so it continued on by its lonesome self. How anyone could have slept through all of the snoring and burping and farting and the orgasmic operas that sprung up every hour or so from one corner of the barn or another was a testament to the anesthetic properties of home-grown marijuana and store-bought alcohol. The dogs that hung out with the gang rarely chose to sleep in the pungent and noisy barn. After their successful jack rabbit hunt and subsequent feast the night before, the dogs and their full bellies settled in under the stars in the cold and quiet fresh air. The coyotes came trotting in around three a.m. At first, they circled the sleeping dogs from a tentative distance but became bolder and moved in closer with every pass. Two of the coyotes grabbed one of the sleeping dogs by its hind legs. The dog kicked free and then jumped up quickly to brace itself for a second attack. It barked loudly alerting the pack. The pack chased the coyotes off of the hill and down into the desert brush where skirmishes ensued. An hour later all but one of the dogs returned home. The weakest among them had been cleverly and skillfully separated from the rest. It was lost and left behind having been dragged away yelping into the cold and unforgiving night.

Paco picked heads of lettuce an hour before sunrise. He chased away four coyotes while he was loading the crates into his truck. By dawn he had also picked two crates of peaches and three crates of tomatoes. His wife rewarded his efforts with fresh delicious flat bread and marmalade jam. He kissed her goodbye and then awoke his daughter. Lucia splashed water on her face but its affects wore off quickly as she fell asleep again in the truck. An hour later Paco looked down in disgust upon the remnants of his tables lying scattered across the road. Tracks in the sand where his tables last stood were those of motorcycles. A dead rat impaled lengthwise on a wooden spike left little doubt as to who had smashed his tables overnight. It was the Road Rats' calling card; a sick joke in Paco's mind. As he kicked the rat down and then buried it in the sand with the toe of his shoe before Lucia would see it, he wondered why a rat would kill one of its own.

Paco managed to hammer together wood scraps from the road and salvage one makeshift table while Lucia sold produce to a few locals from the back of their truck. Lucia wore her grandmother's earrings that morning. Her mother had given them to her the night before after they'd slipped Snake's twenty dollars into Paco's cigar box bank without him knowing. Lucia promised her mother that she would be careful with the earrings. She hoped that Snake would be pleased with them and would say nice things to her. She feared the man somewhat but that apprehension was tempered by wild the affections she held for him. He was a beast and a blessing rolled into one; a man who would never let any harm come to her. Lucia's borrowed gold earrings shined brightly in the hot noonday sun. They flashed brilliant gold tribute to the desert spirits.

Well into the boredom of a slow business day, Lucia heard the faint rumble of distant bikes approaching. While her father tossed broken lumber into the bed of his truck, Lucia smoothed out her top, combed her fingers through her hair and then awaited whoever was coming their way. The closer the motorcycles got to the stand, the louder and louder they roared. Paco was convinced that there were many bikes. The Demon Vegans rarely came in such large numbers so he expected the worst.

A battalion of motorcycles encircled Paco and his daughter and washed a cloud of sand and dust over them as the pair scrambled to their truck. Paco read "Road Rats" on the backs of their black leather jackets as he pushed Lucia across the driver's seat and then jumped in behind her. He turned the truck's key and gunned the engine. He ground the truck into gear and swung onto the road. The sand and dust that kicked up in the process flew in the faces of the two bikers in pursuit. They fishtailed after the truck and then rode up along each side of it. The biker outside Lucia's door banged his fist on her window. She screamed and yelled, *"Papa!"*

Paco crossed the centerline sharply and sent the bike on his side of the truck into a skid that laid it down flat. The Rat aboard the bike bounced hard across the road. The rest of the gang, having witnessed the wreck, took off after the truck in serious pissed-off pursuit. The first two gunshots missed their mark but the third or fourth blew out and shredded one of the truck's rear tires. Paco struggled to keep the truck in control as he drove on the bare, sparking steel rim. Bikes lined up behind the truck and filed along each side of it. Two other bikes sped ahead surrounding the truck. Passengers riding on the bikes in front turned and aimed shotguns at Paco and Lucia who held on for dear life and sank low for the shots. They cringed in unison when the first gun blast shattered their windshield into a shower of flying glass. Lucia screamed, *"Papa!"* as she ducked below the dashboard. She lay on the floorboards and grabbed her father's knee. A second shot sounded. Fragments of it found her father's shoulder. Paco groaned as he grabbed his arm while steering with one hand. He slammed on the brakes and then u-turned as hard as he could. Bikes scattered. Some crashed but most stayed fast on the hunt. The truck's rear window exploded. Paco's head hit the steering wheel knocking him out cold. He'd been hit a second time near his spine. Lucia realized that he was hurt badly when the back of his white shirt turned blood red. She pulled on her father's shoulders and laid him back upright against the seat. She grabbed the truck's wheel with her left hand. With her right hand she pulled up on her father's pant leg lifting his foot off the gas pedal. The truck coasted to a stop as it ran off the road.

"Papa, Papa!" Lucia screamed. She grabbed the sides of her father's head in her hands. She watched between her arms as his chest heaved while he tried to breathe. She pressed her right hand on his bloody shoulder wound and slid her left

hand behind his back, feeling for the wettest spot along his shirt. Having found it, she pressed hard.

"Papa, please don't die," she whispered; her father's blood running down her wrists. Blood of her own trickled into her eyes from the cuts on her forehead. Lucia heard a loud bang and jumped. She thought that she'd been shot. She prayed to the saints, sobbing as she waited for death.

Lucia's door had been yanked wide open. When its hinges snapped, the door banged loudly against the truck's front fender. A gloved hand reached in and squeezed her arm. Other hands wrapped tightly around her ankles. As Lucia was being dragged out of the truck, she grabbed in vain for her father. She tore open the buttons on his shirt. Lucia screamed and kicked and bit down hard on a leather glove. Another hand grabbed the front of her shirt as the bit hand slapped her across the face. A second slap sent her falling backwards and hard to the ground. Lucia sat up quickly and spat blood in the sand between her legs. She looked up into the cloudless blue sky. Ten silhouetted men stood around her in a circle. They stared down upon their prize. Lucia jumped to her feet, her fists flailing. She kicked a man square in the crotch. The other nine laughed loudly as they shoved her back down on the ground. Lucia screamed, *"Papa! Papa!"* as she tried to stand up again but was pushed back down by dirty boot heels. On her last attempt to stand up, the man she had kicked in the crotch knocked her out cold.

Lucia awoke suddenly and screamed, *"Papa! Papa!"*
Paco slammed on the brakes as he reached across his daughter and grabbed her soft knee.

"Lucia, Lucia, it okay, sweetheart, we almost home," he told his daughter as he held her head in his hands. "My good girl have bad dream. It okay now."

Lucia sobbed in her father's arms. The stars shined down upon them like diamonds. The cold desert air breathed new life into her but she trembled with chills. Her father wrapped a thick blanket around her. She pulled it tightly to her face and fell asleep trembling.

Lucia awoke suddenly and screamed, *"Papa! Papa!"*

"You're papa ain't gonna help you now," a deep voice in the darkness told her.

Lucia sat up slowly on a dirty mattress. A dark haze filtered through her eyelashes. A halogen lantern was clicked on. It filled the room with bright obnoxious light and danced on her retinas. A tall unshaven man approached and then stood over her; his lean muscular arms folded in front of him. The man had nothing to say. Neither did Lucia. She felt groggy and weak and dizzy with dope. The bad bruise on the crook of her arm ached. She felt it with her fingers and cringed. The needle had hit a nerve hard when the bikers doped her the night before. Outside, the noonday sun shined brightly but none of its light found its way into the room. The windows in the motel where Lucia was being held had been blacked out a year prior to avoid calling attention to the place. The Road Rats called the motel "headquarters." They parked their bikes behind the abandoned units, out of sight from the desolate road a hundred yards away. When they moved into the place, the Rats installed back doors in the motel's two end units and cut an open passageway that linked all of the rooms' interiors. They tack-welded the front doors shut and installed bars in the window frames. The Road Rats had converted the abandoned motel into a bunker against anyone who might challenge them. The motel hadn't had electricity or running water for years so the occasional car that passed by had little reason to suspect that anyone was living there. The Rats had cut skylights through the ceiling and roof of one end unit in order to grow marijuana plants indoors. They had to squeeze themselves through the bushy plants whenever they used that backdoor. An old well behind the motel sucked up ground water for the first time in years when a Rat had replaced its pump and juiced it with a portable generator. Whenever a patch in the water line failed, the Rats would run bucket brigades to fill sinks and bathtubs and to irrigate their cash crop.

From time to time, the Rats entertained guests in the motel. Those drifters, junkies, hitchhikers, runaways and hookers unlucky enough to be brought willingly or unwillingly through the back doors soon discovered to their horror that the Road Rat motel served as a prison, torture chamber and morgue.

Lucia sat trembling on the tattered and sunken bed in room number six where two runaway girls had been gang-raped and murdered days earlier. Her brain battled the effects of the heroin swimming through it but her body remained lost in limbo. Lucia opened her eyes slowly and then stared at the man sitting on a lawn chair across the room from her. She made sounds resembling words through her cracked and dry lips. The man looked up from his light slumber. The handcuffs on Lucia's wrists and ankles were linked by a chain that clinked with her every movement. As she attempted to slide off the bed she was held back by the end of the chain that was locked to the bedframe.

"If you behave yourself I'll take those off," the man said.

Lucia remained silent, staring blankly but directly into the man's eyes.

"Suit yourself," he said and then he closed his eyes.

"I have to pee," she said meekly.

"What's that?" the man asked, and then he stood up and approached her.

"I have to go to the bathroom," she said.

"Fair 'nough then. Your wish is my command, princess."

He pulled her toward him by her ankles to the end of the bed where he unlocked the handcuffs binding her legs together. "Fair warning now," he said, "if you kick me or hit me or spit in my face you *will* regret it. Do you understand me?" he asked quietly.

Lucia had understood most of what the man had said. She nodded her head, yes. He reached around her and unlocked the cuffs on her wrists freeing her from the chain that bound her to the bed. She rubbed her sore wrists briefly and then pushed her hips to the edge of the bed. Her feet touched the ground for first time in thirty-six hours. With her arms behind her, Lucia pushed against the mattress and rose slowly up and onto her feet. She took one step before falling forward, limp into the man's arms. She hung there motionless with her head on his chest. She heard his heartbeat. She closed her eyes and prayed to the saints.

Lucia woke up naked and frightened partially submerged in tepid bath water. She yelled, *"Papa!"* The man in her room entered the bathroom and sat on the toilet. Lucia wrapped her arms tightly around her cold bare breasts. Shivering and shaking, she looked up at the man with tears in her eyes.

"You didn't make it in here fast enough, princess. I cleaned you up best I could though. Come on now," he said, standing up as he grabbed a dingy bath towel, "Let's dry you off before you catch pneumonia."

The man held the towel out in front of him like a curtain and said, "Come on now, princess, I promise not to peek. If you can't stand on your own I'll give you a hand."

"I can do it!" Lucia shouted loudly, startling the man.

She shifted her weight in the bathtub but not having moved an inch on the hard tub for the past hour, she cringed from the pain of horrible cramps. She slipped twice but caught herself and eventually rose and snatched the towel from the man's hands. She wrapped the towel around herself, tucked the end and then pushed the man away square in the chest.

"Take your time in here," he said, closing the door behind himself. "I'll wait out here 'til you're done," he promised her through the door.

Lucia looked at her ragged face in the dirty mirror. Her mind raced feverishly, *Who is he? Where am I? Where is my father? Papa! My God he was shot! My God, did they kill him?*

Lucia prayed to the saints and sobbed in her hands. Her towel dropped to the floor as she screamed out loud. Her caretaker rushed back into the bathroom. He picked up the towel behind her and then wrapped it around her trembling shoulders. She flailed her arms and tried to spin around. He hugged her tightly from behind and held the towel firmly in place between them. He whispered in her ear, "Calm down now, princess. Fighting will just get you beaten to a pulp around here or killed quickly if you're lucky."

Lucia stopped struggling. She opened her terrified eyes and looked at his in the mirror.

"Who are you and why am I here?" she asked as calmly as she could, her voice shaking.

"My name is Frank but the Rats call me Razor. You can call me whatever you want. You've been kidnapped. Any other questions?"

"Where is my father?"

"I have no idea."

"Is he... is he... dead?"

"I don't know."

"What are you going to do to me?"

"As far as I know, nothing. Until that is, when they sell you."

"Sell me? What the hell do you mean?" she asked him directly, having spun around to face him.

"Consider yourself lucky, princess," Frank said, holding her at arms' length fully expecting a knee to the groin. "If you weren't so absolutely gorgeous or weren't a virgin, they'd probably just rape you until they got tired of you. And then, they'd bury you out back with the other less-pretty, less-virginous girls who weren't nearly as lucky as you are."

By that time Lucia's eyes were nearly bulging out of her head. She began to tremble and shake and then she fell forward fainting into his arms.

When Lucia awoke again on the bed two hours later, she immediately realized that she wasn't chained up. She found herself dressed in a fairly clean pair of baggy sweatpants and a man's white t-shirt. She sat up terrified and confused but sober and alert. Frank waited for her to speak her piece but Lucia wasn't sure what to say so the two of them just stared at one another in silence. Frank decided then that it would be best to try to calm her down.

"What's your name?" he asked her.

"Lucia Sanchez," she said quietly after she had decided not to lie.

"A pretty name for such a pretty girl. Are you hungry?"

Lucia realized at that very moment that she had never been hungrier. She said, "Yes."

"I can take care of that," he promised and then he walked to the dresser, raised the lid of the cooler sitting on top of it, reached in and selected a sandwich before closing the lid. He walked over to the bed, handed her the wrapped submarine sandwich and returned to the cooler for a drink. He offered her a can of Coke but noticed that she was ripping into the sandwich like a starving dog so he popped the can's top and set it down on the bedside table.

"If you eat it all you win a prize," he teased.

She looked up directly into his eyes without stopping her chewing and swallowing as if to ask, "What would that be?"

He read her eyes and then said, "Your prize will be another sub." He reached into the cooler and then held up a second sandwich for her approval.

Lucia swallowed hard. She wiped her mouth on the back of her hand and then blindsided Frank by asking him, "So why didn't you rape me when you had the chance?"

"Good question," he said, considering his response.

"So what's your answer?" she asked him impatiently.

"First off, you and I are the only ones in this motel right now. You've been left in my custody because I'm one of the few Road Rats that Jessie could trust *wouldn't* rape you. A half dozen guys were gettin' ready to last night. They had your panties down around your ankles when Jessie walked in and all hell broke loose. You see, Jessie, the leader of this gang, plans to sell you to a client of his. If you'd lost your virginity last night you'd be worthless to him, or... I should say, as gorgeous as you are, significantly less-valuable. Jessie says the sex slave trade is booming right now. He expects you'll fetch six figures so as valuable as you are, no harm is to come to you."

"Six figures?" Lucia asked. "What does that mean?"

"Six figures means a hundred thousand dollars or more. Get it... six numbers in a row... six-figures? Who knows, you might be worth a quarter of a million to a Saudi oil sheik or a U.S. Senator or a born-again Christian mega-church minister."

"So you're going to sell me as a sex slave, is that it?" she asked defiantly as the last bite of her sandwich disappeared.

"What happens to sex slaves?" she asked him.

"Well, sex slaves provide sexual gratification to whoever buys them."

"I can assume *that* much, I'm not totally stupid you know."

"I never said you were but you asked so I told you," he explained.

"What I meant was, *after* the sex part. What happens to me then?" she asked.

"It depends."

"Depends on what?"

"It depends on the client I guess, what do I know? I'm not a sex slave client. Hell, I can't even afford new tires for my bike let alone a beautiful young virgin to satisfy me."

"Do they kill the sex slave girls?" she asked matter-of-factly.

The answer that he thought to be true was; sometimes, but he thought better of admitting it, not wanting to freak her out any more than she already was. "Why would anyone want to waste six figures like that?" he asked her instead, satisfied with his convincing lie. "You'll probably become some married rich dude's pampered mistress living in a penthouse suite with your own maid and butler."

"Or with my throat slit lying dead in a drainage ditch," she countered, not buying his bullshit version.

"I really don't think so," he offered. "Drainage ditches are for crack-whores, junkies and drug deals gone bad. It says so right on the signs; No Dumping by Police Order except for dead crack-whores, junkies and wannabe dope dealers."

"So, Frankie, do *you* rape and kill girls around here?" she asked, catching him off guard having unknowingly called him by the name that only his mother used.

"Me...? No," he lied, embarrassed that the truth was that he *had* participated in the rape of a girl once; a girl who was eventually choked to death by the fifth of six rapists. And here he was now, lying about it to a girl brave enough to ask such questions.

"So, you're a good boy then, is that what you're telling me, Frankie?" she challenged.

"*I really don't need this shit!*" he said, standing up angrily and then pacing the room. "I'm no saint, princess, if that's what you mean. Yeah, I've done shitty things, plenty of shitty things but who hasn't? Have I ever caught a break? No! Have I ever been able to earn a decent living doing the right thing like all of those other fine, upstanding citizens out there cheating on their wives, cheating on their taxes, beating their kids, joining the Army and blowing away civilians and earning goddamn medals for it? No! I'm not that goddamn good or that goddamn lucky if that's what you're asking," he said breathless and spent.

"I think you're *better* than those people," Lucia said, further testing her approach.

"Yeah, I'm the greatest that's for sure," he said, finally sitting down to relax a bit.

"You've treated *me* with respect, Frank. It's hard to believe that a man such as yourself who might kill me if I tried to escape would actually treat me like a lady in the meantime," Lucia said, thinking out loud but carefully considering every single word that came out of her mouth.

"I ain't gonna kill you if you make a run for it, Lucia. First of all, I'd catch you in a heartbeat. Second, even if you did run there's no place whatsoever out there to run to unless you want to bury yourself in the sand and hide. You'd die of dehydration before sundown."

"What time is it now, Frank?" she asked, not having a clue due to the black enamel paint covering the barred and curtain-less windows.

"I'm guessing two in the afternoon," he guessed.

"So... the gang will be back here soon then?"

"Hell no, we only come and go under the cover of darkness. It's the law around here and has been for almost a year now."

"You've been living here for a year; no electricity or running water?" Really?" she asked, genuinely surprised.

"Pretty much," he said. "Where else are we supposed to hang our hats; the Las Vegas Hilton?" he laughed.

For the first time in almost two days Lucia felt herself almost smile. And then she asked him, "So... you're stuck here until... sundown? You're on guard duty for six or seven more hours until the others get back?"

"Pretty much," he agreed.

"Can we get some air, Frank? It's freaking hot in here," she asked, for more reasons than she let on to.

"Yeah, I know," he agreed. "The back doors are wide open but we're gettin' no breeze whatsoever through here. I could try to crack the window open a bit but most of 'em are frozen or rusted shut after sittin' closed for so long. There's no way I can take you outside though. Jessie would skin me alive."

"Jessie's not here right now and won't be for a long time," she reasoned.

"True, but he could ride by and not pull in. If he saw me outside with you in broad daylight he'd blow my head off and I'm kinda sentimentally attached to it."

Lucia smiled at that and almost laughed. Frank noticed and smiled at her warmly and then said, "You are *really* good looking, Lucia. And I ain't just sayin' that either. You just may be... the prettiest damn woman I've *ever* seen."

"Well, thank you, Frank, even though you're obviously exaggerating."

"No, it's true, Lucia, and I ain't just sayin' it to get in your panties because as you know, I've already seen that part of you; I've seen *all* of you. Do you have any idea how hard it was for me to slip off your pissed-soaked shorts and panties and your puke-covered top and then carry you naked into the bathroom when I set you in the tub? I washed you from head to toe while you were passed out. It's an absolute miracle that I didn't just throw you on the bed and rape you after all of that tempting torture I went through."

"So you didn't touch me that way at all?" she asked him.

"Nope, but I touched myself damn good though; three or four times while you were sleeping or passed out. I sat on the toilet looking at you in the tub and frosted the bathroom floor pretty good because you are, as I've said; one irresistibly hot woman. I laid down next to you on the bed a few times and shot loads clear across you onto the wall," he reported, becoming suddenly embarrassed having both done those things and then confessing them in such ridiculous detail.

The room fell silent as they both thought to themselves in six different directions. They each admired the other in some way, for one reason or another and truth be told, they were both starting to actually like one another as human beings. There was no doubt that Frank was in love with Lucia's body but he was surprised by the fact that she wasn't some kind of self-centered, stuck-up bitch with no sense of understanding or compassion. Lucia was grateful to still be alive at that point. She had relaxed considerably in Frank's company but felt that come sundown, no matter what Frank might have been led to believe, her throat would be sliced wide open and she'd bleed out dead in that disgustingly filthy place. Either that, or she'd be shipped away somewhere else where a similar fate would await her compliments of some deranged sex addict with no regard for human life. Lucia was preparing herself for the worst. She was testing her own internal strength; testing her will to live. She was desperately trying to save herself but she saw little way out as her mind raced in circles searching for any viable option. She felt that Frank was right about running. If she *could* outrun him, which seemed impossible to her, where would she run to? Maybe she could bash him over the head but then what; run to the road and wait for a ride? Run into the desert? She had no idea where she was or where she would go. She needed desperately to either get outside and look around or try to get more information from Frank somehow. As far as she knew, he wasn't holding anything back from her so far.

"Where are we, Frank?"

"We're in the desert."

"But where in the desert? The desert is a big place."

"We're in the middle of nowhere in the middle of the desert," he said convincingly.

"How far is the nearest town would you say, just out of curiosity?" she asked.

"A hundred miles give or take. There's a gas station and sub shop about half way into town half an hour away. Aside from that, it's sand and cactus. Why do you ask? You wanna buy lotto tickets? Feelin' lucky are you?"

Lucia began to feel sick and disturbed over Frank's new-found sarcasm. She was losing him fast. She needed him. She needed to get him back somehow.

"Will you run away with me, Frank?" she asked him and then immediately wondered why on earth he would possibly agree to. Lucia noticed that Frank had no immediate response. He hadn't flat out rejected the idea from the get-go and so, she shot in the dark and offered him an incentive.

"If you run away with me, Frank, I'll fuck you after we do." Lucia held her breath for his answer, trying not to imagine what might happen if he said, no, or what might happen if he said, yes. She prayed to the saints. She asked them to forgive her for doing what she desperately needed to do to stay alive. Above all else, she sure as hell wasn't ready to die. She refused to die a helpless victim and would fight to the death need be by any means necessary.

Frank sat up straight in his chair and looked into Lucia's dazzling dark eyes. He shook his head ever so slightly and then raised his eyebrows. He buried his face in his hands and then rubbed his eyes. He stood up and took a deep breath and walked into the bathroom. He splashed water on his face from the rusty metal bucket on the floor. He came back into the room and then sat back down in silence.

"Well?" she asked. "Do we have a deal, Frank?"

He looked at her then for the first time, not as a captor with ultimate authority over her, but looked at her instead as if he was *her* victim, as if *she* had power over *him*, as if she was in control because truth-be-told she was in total control of his libido. To Lucia, Frank seemed suddenly vulnerable. They stared at one another is search of answers.

"They'd hunt me down and kill me, princess," he finally said. "They'd hunt me down and kill the *both* of us. As sure as shit we'd both end up in a ditch."

She had got him back. Her hope was restored. He had thought over her proposal seriously and he seemed eager to say, yes. It seemed to her that he wanted to say, yes.

"If we had protection they wouldn't hurt us, they couldn't hurt us," she claimed.

"What the hell are you talking about?"

"Take me to the Demon Vegans, Frank."

"Oh yeah sure, that's just perfect, Lucia! I take you to the Demon Vegans and *they* cut my throat. Either way, Frank ends up a loser as always. I got a better idea, princess," he said, pulling a straight razor out of his hip pocket startling her. He opened the razor, held onto the blade end and then handed the handle to her. "There you go, princess, why don't *you* just cut my throat right now? Put me out of my goddamn misery, okay?"

"You're acting like a fool, Frank. All I want to do is get the hell out of this god forsaken place and then willingly fuck you gladly for helping me. As you know, you'd be my very first fuck so I'd probably want it again and again," she assumed or lied, trying to make her proposal sound even more irresistible to him. "We walk up to the Demon Vegans, you throw your Road Rats leather down on the ground and say, 'Whatever you guys want to know about the Rats I'll tell you because I'm through with those assholes.' You give up this hideout, the Demons exterminate all of the Rats once and for all because those goddamn assholes killed my brother and may have killed my father so, *Fuck Them All!*" she screamed but then immediately calmed herself down and continued, "You walk in there with me safe and sound and I guarantee you that Snake will give you sanctuary. Hell, he'd probably make you a full-fledged Demon Vegan right on the spot."

"You know Snake?"

"We're *damn* good friends," she fibbed, but then she spilled the truth in detail. "He brought my father the head of the Rat that shot and killed my brother."

"Holy shit!" Frank said. "That was *your* brother?" he asked not waiting for a reply. "I'm so goddamn sorry, Lucia. That freak Curveball deserved what he got that's for damn sure. It was only a matter of time before somebody gave *that* crazy-assed Rat his just reward. He's probably headin' straight to hell and goin' there without a head." Frank laughed out loud at his own sick joke and then elaborated, "Can you imagine it, Lucia... a headless dumbass... wandering around hell... wondering, *where the hell am I...?*"

As the joint he'd been smoking singed his fingertips, Frank suddenly broke out into spastic laugher. He jumped around the room slapping his thighs. He wiped tears from his eyes with the backs of his hands. Lucia laughed nervously right along with him. She thought it best that she did. Despite Frank's near-hysterics, Lucia sensed then that she may have won him over to her side. Despite rekindling her anguish over the anointed body of her dear brother, she was beginning to see glimmers of hope for her own desperate situation. She needed then to reset her standing with Frank and do so when he and his spirits were high. As soon as he had calmed down enough to hear what it was that she wanted to tell him, she quickly repeated her offer, "Will you run away with me, Frank, and make love to me after we do?"

"You're not just *teasing* me with that smokin' hot body of yours are you, Lucia?" he asked, smiling seriously.

"Tonight, Frank... I'll be yours, I promise. I would lay down for you right now I swear, but I'm so stressed-out and terrified that I'd probably start screaming or pass out or something. Is that what you want, Frank; a rape victim kicking and screaming under you?"

"Of course not, Lucia, I prefer candlelight and violins," he joked, refusing to imagine himself raping her.

"Well then..." she laughed, "we'll just have to order some tonight. But if we hang around here much longer, Frank, you'll have to bring Jessie along too," she said, attempting to get her plan into immediate motion but unwittingly striking a raw nerve in the process.

"Fuck Jessie!" Frank yelled and then he paced the room defiantly. "What has *that asshole* ever done for me besides push me around and kick my ass?"

Lucia realized then that she finally had him. She'd won him over to her side. She thanked the saints and nearly burst into tears as it dawned on her that the only decent, half-way sane person in the entire gang of criminals holding her hostage was left alone to guard her. She rose up off of the bed and walked over to Frank. She took him by the wrist. She pressed his open palm against her warm soft belly. She pushed his hand lower guiding his fingers under the waistline of her sweatpants and then further still, into her panties. His fingers found her quickly; a slice of heaven he could never have imagined. She grabbed his bulging jeans with one hand as she swung his razor up and behind him with her other hand. She pressed her breasts against his chest and with a desperate desire to finally seal the deal and escape her inescapable hell, she whispered in his ear, "Have you ever made love to a virgin before, Frank?"

"I'm not sure," he said honestly, not giving her question much thought at all.

"Would you *like* to be sure?" she tempted, squeezing him even harder.

"Absolutely," he said, not hearing his own reply.

"So tell me, Frank," Lucia whispered, "do we have a deal?" She released her grip on his crotch and reached her hand around his waist. She pulled him closer, pressing her hips firmly against his. She kissed him gently and licked his lower lip. She raised her right hand up and along his back tightening her grip on the handle of his razor. She kissed him again and then whispered, "Do you want me, Frank?"

Frank's razor glistened behind his ear awaiting his response.

Super Average Man

John Doe seemed like an average Joe with a different name. John was married to an average woman named Jane. The Doe's lived in an average-size house and had two average-size kids; John Jr., age eight and June, age six. Both kids were born in the middle of the year in the middle of the month on June fifteenth. As newborns, the Doe children were in the fifty percentile for both weight and length and maintained average height and weight as they continued to grow. Both of the Doe kids did well enough in school. They earned average grades and were average athletes. John Jr. played centerfield on his little league baseball team while June played center for her school's intramural basketball team. The Doe's had an average-size dog named Mutt who chased their average-size cat Mittens on average; twice a day. John Doe earned an average salary at a mid-sized company in the Mid-American city of Middlefield. John's job was located a nation-wide average commute time of thirty minutes from the Doe's residence in the town of Centerville. John was a loving father to both of his children and loved his wife dearly. Although he was basically happy, John began to wonder if there was something missing from his life; a little pizzazz perhaps.

"I think I need a little pizzazz," John told his wife one night while she was reading a book in bed beside him.

"But we just had pizzazz last night, John. Married couples our age have pizzazz twice a week on average. We've already had our pizzazzes for the week. Are you asking for an advance on next week's pizzazzes?"

"Not that kind of pizzazz, Jane, a different kind of pizzazz."

"Well, I'm not about to start experimenting with you now, John. I'm comfortable with things just the way they are."

John rolled over toward his wife. He took her book gently from her hands, memorized the page number she was on, closed the book, placed it on the bed beside him and then asked her, "Do you ever get the feeling, Jane, that our lives are just a little bit too average, a bit too normal, too predictable, too safe and secure?"

"Yes, John, every single day, and that's why I read murder mysteries, vampire novels and letters to the editor in your Penthouse magazines. We have kids, John; safe and secure is the way to go according to most experts on child rearing."

"But, Jane, we don't have to put the kids in jeopardy to enjoy a little pizzazz ourselves do we? We could slip away together, just the two of us. We could go... oh, I don't know... we could go skydiving or mountain climbing or whitewater rafting, something, anything that would spice up our life," John suggested.

"Or not, John. I don't want our darling children sent off to an orphanage. Do you?"

"They still have those?"

"I think so. Where else would they send the children of parents who died in the pursuit of pizzazz?"

"I suppose you're right, Jane. I don't want our kids sent to an orphanage either."

"That's a good boy. Now give me my book back and read your Penthouse magazine. A new issue came in the mail today. I put it in your night stand drawer."

John handed his wife her book and then told her, "You were on page a hundred and fifty."

"I know, John. I submitted it to memory when you took it

from me."

"How long is that book, Jane?"

"Let's see…" she said, thumbing to the end of the book, "it's three hundred pages long. Why do you ask?"

"Just curious," John said, not at all surprised that she was exactly half-way through her book.

About ten minutes after John had begun staring at the June Penthouse Pet of the month, his wife noticed and remarked, "You're going to burn a hole in that girl's bellybutton if you keep staring at her that way, John."

Jane turned back to her reading. She expected a response from her husband but when none came she tried again, "John dear, did you hear me?"

She waited a bit, staring blankly at her book. "John," she said, turning to look at her husband. "John, are you alright, dear?" she asked, becoming a bit concerned.

Rolling over closer to him, Jane peered over the top of her husband's magazine and gazed into his blank, unblinking eyes. She placed her hands on his ribcage and felt his chest rise and fall as he breathed. "John," she said. "John!" she repeated louder.

"Was he in a coma?" Jane wondered. Her husband's blank stare was freaking her out. She became alarmed.

Jane slipped the magazine from her husband's hands and laid it aside on the bed. She placed her hands on the sides of his face and rocked his head gently from side-to-side. "John?" she asked. "John darling… can you hear me?"

Suddenly, John sat straight up in bed, rolling his wife to the side in the process. She let out a shriek and asked, "John, what's wrong! Were you having a nightmare?"

"No, dear, I wasn't having a nightmare but I'm afraid there

is trouble. I must go now," he said and then he jumped out of bed, walked quickly to the bedroom window, removed his pajamas, slid the window wide open and then dove through it headfirst soaring up and into the night sky.

"Well, I wish he would've told me that in the first place," his wife said aloud. She picked up her book, resettled herself atop her pillows and resumed her reading.

SAM streaked through the night sky at warp speed low to the ground rising quickly when he encountered traffic as he flew along the streets. He pulled up sharply near mid-town Middlefield and landed softly on his feet. He shot through the dark like lightning as he streaked to the end of a dead-end alley. It was there that he confronted a pair of gang-bangers banging the head of their victim while a third gang member held back the victim's girlfriend.

"Stop that!" SAM shouted to the merciless thugs as they continued to pound the nearly-unconscious teen. "Stop, I say or you will regret it!" SAM demanded and then he grabbed the two thugs and raised them up and over his head; their fists flailing, their feet kicking the air. The third thug released the girl and ran out of the alley screaming.

"It's Super Average Man, Tony, we're saved!" the relieved girl announced to her bruised and bloodied boyfriend.

"Call me SAM for short if you'd like, little lady."

"Okay, Mr. SAM, I will! Thanks so much! You are my hero!" the girl said, hugging his chest and then laying her head on the letters S.A.M. emblazoned across it.

The girl's bruised and bloodied boyfriend moaned. And then he moaned again when she accidentally stepped on his hand.

"Farewell, SAM!" the girl waved as SAM flew off with the thugs and then dropped them in the middle of a swamp.

The next day, while Jane and little June were busy baking in the family's kitchen, John and John Jr. returned home from their shopping trip in mid-town Middlefield. As John pulled the family's mid-size car into the driveway he tooted its horn to announce their arrival to the girls. Jane and June ran to the kitchen window and waved to the boys who stayed outside to play. It was an average summer day; partly cloudy with a fifty percent chance of rain.

When the five hundred degree oven reached two hundred and fifty degrees, Jane slid an average-size baking tray of portioned cookie dough (half chocolate chip / half oatmeal raisin) into it while little June added red and blue sprinkles in equal proportions to the frosted cupcakes that she and her mother had baked earlier that morning.

"Good job, June! You're half-way done already!" her mother said with a smile.

June returned her mother's smile and then continued her task in earnest; her tiny pink tongue sticking half-way out between the center of her lips.

"Well I'll be... it's midday already!" June noticed as she checked the kitchen wall clock. "I'll ask the boys what they'd like for lunch. Don't touch the oven, dear, it's very hot," June's mother warned.

"I won't, Mommy," her daughter promised as Jane stepped out the door; her mid-length dress fluttering in the mild summer breeze.

At the very moment that Jane spotted her husband, he was suspended in midair; his arms and legs flailing before he crashed flat on his back in the middle of the driveway. John Sr. let out a loud moan as he grabbed his midsection. John Jr. looked on with concern but when his father started laughing the boy laughed right along with him.

"Are you crazy, John? You'll break your neck!" his wife scolded as she stood over her husband.

John sat up and watched as his brand-new skateboard went rolling down the driveway and into the street where it was run over and crushed by a passing steam roller.

John looked up at his wife and said, "John Jr. was teaching me how to skateboard. I was just starting to get the hang of it when I hit a rock or something and went flying."

"So that's what you two bought at the store this morning; an adult-size skateboard for my juvenile husband?"

"That's not all we bought, Mom," John Jr. announced. "We bought you a new book to read. It's called *Vampire Mid-Life Crisis.* I left it in the car. I'll get it for you," he said and then he ran toward the garage.

"Thank you, honey!" his grateful mother called out to her son as she bent down beside her husband. "Are you alright, dear? You look ridiculous," she laughed.

"I'm fine, Jane, thanks. I was just trying to add a little pizzazz to my life is all."

"Well, I'd wish you leave those wild skateboards to the kids. If you promise to give it up, I promise to give you a little extra pizzazz this week. Do we have a deal?"

"And such a deal it is!" John agreed. "It's an offer that no average man could possibly refuse!" he said as he pulled his wife gently toward him and then kissed her sweetly. Jane sighed as she rubbed John's chest. She felt her embroidery; the letters S.A.M., beneath his shirt. She smiled lovingly and then kissed her super-average husband.

Tale of Swan and Sumo

"Eat, Puwki, eat! You nothing but skin and bones and some fat. You want to be Sumo you need *more* fat! So eat, Puwki, eat!"

"Yes, Momma, I eat more."

"That my good boy," Puwki's mother said as he proceeded to shovel ladles of lobster stew into his mouth which he washed down with huge gulps of eggnog.

"If you eat whole pot of stew, Puwki, Momma give you yummy desert; whole cherry pie, *homemade* whole cherry pie. Momma take cherry pits out so you no choke on cherry pits this time. Okay, Puwki?"

"Okay, Momma."

After Puwki had finished his pot of lobster stew and his jug of eggnog and his entire cherry pie (which had only one cherry pit that he accidentally swallowed) he did an hour of third grade algebra homework, an hour of third grade physics homework and an hour of third grade economics homework before he brushed his teeth, squeezed into his pajamas and then laid his three hundred pound carcass down to sleep on his overburdened futon which groaned every night at eight o'clock. Puwki would always leave his bedroom light on because he knew that his mother would come in to kiss him goodnight.

"Hi-lo, Puwki," his mother said from his doorway. "I come in to kiss you goodnight, Puwki. You such good boy today Momma bring you bedtime treat, okay?"

"Okay, Momma, thank you, Momma," Puwki said, taking the pitcher of chocolate milk from her tiny hands.

Puwki drained the pitcher dry in four gulps and then wiped the milk he had spilled on his chins with his pajama sleeve before he handed the empty pitcher back to his mother. "All gone, Momma, thank you for chocolate milk."

"You welcome, Puwki, sweet dreams now," she said, kissing his melon-shaped cheeks lovingly before she turned off his bedroom light. Puwki's mother left his bedroom door slid open a bit so he wouldn't be afraid of the dark and scream like a lunatic banshee in the middle of the night and wake up their grumpy neighbor Mr. Homohito again.

An hour later, after his mother had fallen asleep, Puwki snuck out of his bedroom and tip-toed to the bathroom where he stuck his sausage-size finger down his throat and threw up in the sink. He rinsed out the sink and his mouth with cold tap water and then returned to his bed.

Puwki's mother was right, Puwki *did* have sweet dreams that night, the very same dream that he had every night; he was dancing with his true-love Lilly in the third grade ballet. You see... Puwki did not want to be a Sumo as his mother wished him to be. His only wish was to dance with his true love Lilly in the third grade ballet.

"Wake up, Puwki! Wake up, Puwki! It time for school now so wake up," his mother urged him the next morning. "But first, jump on weight scale here," she instructed him. "There you go... let me see now, Puwki... Oh my! You lost ten pound! How could it be you lost ten pound! You never become mighty Sumo if you lost ten pound! I suppose Momma need to feed you more."

Puwki got dressed then in his school uniform and walked briskly into the kitchen. Puwki loved going to school. He could hardly wait to arrive. Puwki always ate his breakfast on school days as fast as he could so that he wouldn't miss the bus. He had to get to school on time in order to see his true love Lilly before the headmaster rang the bell. This morning was no different. Puwki ate his stack of six syrup-smothered buttered pancakes, his six-egg cheese omelet, his six slices of bacon and his six pork sausages in six minutes. He chugged his gallon of orange juice dry on his way to the kitchen sink into which he carefully placed his empty platters and pitcher. He went into the bathroom, brushed his teeth, grabbed his knapsack of books from his desk and then kissed his mother goodbye as he rushed through the kitchen and out the door.

Because Puwki couldn't fit through the school bus door, he had to enter the bus through the wider emergency exit in the back of the bus. It was there that he stood, wedged between the rows of seats, on his way to school. As soon as the bus arrived at school, Puwki jumped through the emergency exit and ran to the school bathroom where he closed himself in a stall, stuck his sausage-size finger down his throat and threw up into the sparkling white toilet bowl. Puwki did not want to be a fat Sumo. He wished only to dance the ballet with his true love Lilly. After he had rinsed out his mouth with cold tap water, combed his hair nice and neat and straightened his tie, Puwki went off to find his true love Lilly.

Puwki found his true love Lilly easily enough, as usual, near the fountain in front of the school's entrance. There she was; in the center of a half-moon circle of friends in the center of the perfectly manicured circle of cheery trees that encircled the circular fountain. Lilly was often the center of attention at school and was always at the center of Puwki's attention.

"Hello, Lilly!" Puwki said to the beautiful girl surrounded by her gang of adoring friends. Lilly's gang was known as the Half Moon Gang. It was the most popular gang of all at the Fushiama School for Gifted Students and Gangs.

"Hello, Puwki!" Puwki's true love Lilly replied with an angelic smile and a wave of her lovely hand. Puwki always loved talking to his true love Lilly that way every day before school. Suddenly, from the top of the school's steps, the headmaster rang his brass bell three times. All of the children immediately formed a line and then walked one after another up the school's steps. Puwki filed in line behind his true love Lilly and watched as her lovely skirt swayed to-and fro.

Puwki's Algebra teacher handed back the test he had taken the day before; A+ was his grade. Puwki leaned over to his friend Jito sitting next to him and asked, "Did you do well, Jito?"

Jito said, "Yes, Puwki, I earned an A+ and I am happy. Did you do well?"

Puwki said, "Yes Jito, I also earned an A+ and I am also happy."

"I am happy that we both did well and are both happy. Are you, Puwki?"

"Yes Jito, I am also happy that we both did well and are both happy."

The teacher then announced to the entire class, "I am very pleased with each and every one of you in this class for all of you have earned an A+ on your test. You should all be very proud and happy."

Puwki looked over to his friend Jito and Jito looked over to his friend Puwki. Both of the boys extended a thumb into the air and smiled at one another because they were both very happy and proud.

Puwki's Physics teacher handed back the test he had taken the day before; A+ was his grade. Puwki leaned over to his friend Oko sitting next to him and asked, "Did you do well, Oko?"

Oko said, "No, Puwki, I earned a B+ and I am sad. Did you do good?"

Puwki said, "Yes Oko, I earned an A+ and I am happy that I did well but I am also sad that you earned a B+ and are sad."

"Even though I am sad I did poorly and have brought shame to my family, I am happy for you, Puwki," Oko replied.

The teacher then announced to the entire class, "I am very pleased with almost everyone in this class. Every student earned an A+ on their test except for one of you who earned a B+ and has brought shame to his family."

Puwki looked over to his friend Oko and Oko looked over to his friend Puwki. Puwki extended his thumb into the air and smiled but Oko pointed his thumb down toward his desk and frowned because he had brought shame to his family.

Lunch time was next and Puwki was happy because he would get to see his true love Lilly sitting like an angel with her friends at their table.

"Hello, Lilly!" Puwki said to his true love Lilly as he stopped by her table with a tray of food in his hands.

"Hello, Puwki!" Puwki's true love Lilly replied with an angelic smile as she nibbled on a piece of apple.

Puwki always loved talking to his true love Lilly that way every day at lunch time. He smiled as he walked away toward his table where he ate his rice and apple and drank his milk. Puwki's school lunches were the only meals that he truly enjoyed. He was always hungry at lunch time in school so he did not throw up afterwards.

Puwki's Economics teacher handed back the test he had taken the day before; A+ was his grade. Puwki leaned over to his true love Lilly sitting next to him and asked, "Did you do well, Lilly?"

Lilly said, "Yes, Puwki, I earned an A+ and I am happy. Did you do good?"

Puwki said, "Yes, Lilly, I also earned an A+ and I am also happy. But I am even happier because you are happy."

Lilly said, "Thank you, Puwki, that makes me happy."

The teacher then announced to the entire class, "I am very pleased with each and every one of you in this class for all of you have earned an A+ on your test. You should all be very proud and happy."

Puwki looked over to his true love Lilly and Lilly looked over to her friend Puwki. Both of them extended a thumb into the air and smiled at one another because they were both very happy and proud. Puwki's smile lasted longer than Lilly's did though because she was his true love.

After Economics class, Puwki went to Athletics class where he wrestled three boys and squashed them all flat.

"Hi-lo, Puwki, welcome home!" his mother said, kissing him on his melon-shaped cheek. "Did you have fun in school today?" she asked him.

"Yes, Momma, I had fun in school today. I earned an A+ in Algebra, an A+ in Physics, an A+ in Economics and squashed three boys flat in Athletics.

"Oh, Puwki!" his mother said, "I so very happy to have such good son. You bring great pride and joy for me! I hope you squash many more boys and become mighty Sumo. I make you special dinner tonight, Puwki, so wash hands and come eat."

After washing his hands, Puwki knelt down at the table, folded his legs and waited for his food. His mother brought out an enormous platter and placed it with pride in front of her son.

"If you eat all of that sturgeon you find caviar to eat inside!" his mother said.

"Okay, Momma, thank you," Puwki replied.

Puwki enjoyed the caviar more than the sturgeon. He enjoyed it even more than the entire birthday cake that he ate for desert. Puwki's mother worked in the village bakery where she baked for the village. At times, she'd bring home birthday cakes that dishonorable customers had ordered but never picked up. It didn't happen very often though because most of the bakery's customers were honorable.

Just like every other school night, Puwki did three hours of homework, threw up in the sink and then went to bed where he dreamt that he was dancing with his true-love Lilly in the third grade ballet.

Tuesday and Wednesday were good days for Puwki and Thursday was as well (he drew a funny picture of a kitty cat in Visual Arts Class that made his friends laugh) but this particular day was Friday so Puwki was very happy. Fridays were his special days at school because after third grade Biology lecture/lab, third grade Chemistry lecture/lab, and third grade Western Civilization/Philosophy, Puwki would attend his favorite of all classes; Performance Arts - Oh Boy!

Most Fridays were rehearsal days in Performance Arts class but on this particular Friday, the auditorium was filled with anxious parents awaiting the performances of their gifted children. The students in third grade Orchestra, third grade Drama and third grade Dance Class were very excited to have an audience. Unfortunately for Puwki though, his mother could not attend because she was busy at the village bakery baking for the village.

When Puwki had first begun his studies at the Fushiama School for Gifted Students and Gangs, he joined the orchestra where he attempted to play the flute. Unfortunately, he bent the fragile instrument in half while practicing. He did the same thing to a tuba that his teacher thought would be more appropriate for him (the teacher was obviously wrong). Puwki left the orchestra then and tried out for Drama Class but during his very first play he became so stage-frightened that he forgot all of his lines (and he only had one). Puwki's teachers became concerned that he would fail miserably at any form of performance art and would become sad and jump off a bridge. Puwki however, would prove his teachers wrong.

The parents in the audience that Friday applauded politely after the third grade orchestra performed an interpretation of Tchaikovsky's Pathétique Symphony. They also applauded politely after the third grade drama class presented their version of William Shakespeare's Jacobean tragedy; Troilus and Cressida. But the audience became instantly mesmerized when the dance troupe finally took the stage to perform Master Shitipupu's classic ballet; Tale of Swan and Sumo.

The stage curtains were slowly drawn open while ethereal orchestral tones announced the stunning arrival of eleven beautiful ballerinas who twittered onto the stage like delicate flowers in the wind or fairies on caffeine. The string section of the orchestra then dramatically introduced the troupe's twelfth dancer; the graceful Swan who took center stage by leaping and twirling and kicking her legs really high in the air like ballerinas do. The dancer was of course; the angelic Lilly, the school's prima ballerina. As she continued to dance she amazed everyone in the audience. She brought great pride to her family (and a measure of envy to the other parents). Suddenly though, the orchestra fell silent, the dancers stopped dancing and the houselights dimmed. The audience sat wondering what on earth could have gone wrong when the kettle drums sounded and rattled the walls. Out onto the stage leapt the amazing Sumo; Puwki! With a spot light upon him he spun on his toes and jumped higher and higher and higher up into the air like a really strong frog would (but even better). Puwki then took his true love Lilly in his arms and tossed her skyward into the electrified air where she spun and then stopped motionless in midair. She drifted then slowly and softly like a feather on a breeze back down into Puwki's strong and steady waiting arms. The couple then proceeded to dance with such wonder across the stage and then back again several times over that by the time they had finished their dance and taken their bows everyone in the audience was on their feet in a standing ovation that lasted about five minutes, give-or-take. After their performance, the entire dance troupe gathered together backstage to high-five and congratulate one another. Lilly was surrounded by her adoring fellow ballerinas but when she saw her partner Puwki approaching, she broke away from her friends and when no one was watching, she kissed him sweetly on his melon-shaped cheek. Puwki was so astounded by what his true love

Lilly had done that he decided to tell his true love Lilly that she was in fact, his one, true love. And so it was that Puwki whispered to his true love Lilly, "Lilly, you are my true love!" to which his true love Lilly replied, "Yes, I know that I am your true love, Puwki, because you are also *my* true love as well!"

Puwki was so shocked and amazed and surprised and happy and other stuff like that by what his true love Lilly had just told him, he got stage fright and forgot his next line which remains a mystery to this very day.

During the years that followed, Puwki and Lilly kept their love for each other a deeply held secret but later shared their secret with their entire village and a few wedding crashers when they became man and wife in a beautiful lakeside wedding ceremony with a majestic snow-capped mountain backdrop. Their reception featured a romantic classic rock band that cost Lilly's father way too much money because all of the wild band members drank like fish between sets. Puwki's mother baked the couple's wedding cake herself and although she loved her new daughter-in-law very much, she felt that Lilly didn't feed her husband nearly enough. Puwki lost so much weight he didn't even look like a chubby person anymore, let alone the mighty Sumo that his mother had always wished him to be.

Puwki and Lilly remained very happily in love even when they had to give up dancing because of Puwki's bum-knee. They took jobs as teachers at the Fushiama School for Gifted Students and Gangs. Lilly taught Performing Arts Ballet at the school and tutored a few fourth graders who struggled with differential equations. Puwki taught second grade Industrial Welding and coached Sumo wrestling to the growing number of chubby boys at the school.

Puwki's mother lost her job at the village bakery when it burned to the ground during a severe drought. Dry lightning had sparked wildfires in the parched foothills surrounding the bakery. The drought itself had dried up the pond where the firemen would normally fill their buckets. Luckily for Puwki's mother, she found employment at the Fushiama School for Gifted Students and Gangs just as her son and daughter-in-law had done. She worked in the school cafeteria kitchen where she became famous for her deep-fried meatloaf and her refried Mexican jumping bean burritos. All of her rich and delicious dishes became popular favorites among the growing number of chubby students at the school.

One of those chubby students was Lilly and Puwki's very own son, Momma's very own grandson; Achu. Momma was delighted to cook for her beloved Achu not only at school but at home as well. She hoped that he would someday become a proud and mighty Sumo. Despite his grand-mamma's wishes however, Achu had planned all along to major in Third-World Industrial Horticulture until he entered the second grade and developed an incurable allergy to most species of flowers. Achu's flower allergy became so chronic that he even sneezed when someone referred to his mother by her first name. He did however, show promise on the ballet dance floor where his true love Tiki held the honor of prima ballerina in the dance troupe.

Tiki was an exchange student from Tahiti. Even though she was very popular in the school, she was often reprimanded by the headmaster for failing to wear a bathing top during Aquatics Class. Tiki's mother; Mrs. Tatas, caused quite a stir when she came into the school to explain to the headmaster that bathing tops were not among the customs that Tiki was familiar with in her native Tahiti. Apparently, Mrs. Tatas herself was also not familiar with the custom of wearing a top because she entered the school without one. The headmaster became so captivated by Mrs. Tata's beautiful figure that he hired her on the spot as a model for the school's Life Drawing class which soon thereafter filled up quickly with boys eager to explore the visual arts.

Mrs. Tatas became very popular at the school, especially since she was unmarried. She had lost her husband in Tahiti when he was washed out to sea by a cyclone shortly after Tiki was born. And so it was that Mrs. Duyu Tatas began dating Mr. Oshi Simai; the Nuclear Physics teacher and volleyball coach at the Fushiama School for Gifted Students and Gangs. The happy couple married soon thereafter. Their elaborate wedding ceremony featured a beautiful dance performance by the mighty Sumo Achu and his lovely Swan Tiki.

After the performance was over, the happily married bride; Mrs. Duyu Simai Tatas, hugged her daughter Tiki lovingly.

As Puwki hugged his wife and son, he told them, "I love you Achu and I love you, Lilly," to which Achu sneezed and to which all three of them laughed. Or so as the tale is told.

- A Brass Gong Clangs -

Terror Tory

The jungle that night was darker than usual. A thick blanket of clouds cloaked the starlight. Torches went dark as driving rain poured upon them. Men stumbled and struggled in the darkness along a narrow, overgrown path. They pressed on through the stubborn curtains of wet jungle vegetation while thick mud sucked at their feet. A fallen branch tripped up a member of the king's landing party hurtling him face first into the mud. Another man fell forward against the man ahead of him. No one spoke for fear of discovery. Everyone hoped that the driving rain would drown out the sounds of their slow, yet steady progress. Leopards could see the men in the dark. Leopards could smell the men from afar. Leopards could hear the men from greater distances if leopards were in fact; nearby. Every man in the landing party knew those things. They also knew that given the circumstances, the ledges and caves that loomed ahead of them were their only chance for survival should leopards attack in the dark.

The king's landing party suddenly grew smaller when the last man in line was dragged away screaming. He grabbed in vain at slick branches and vines that slipped through his desperate hands. Horrible screams were heard in the distance and then; all was silent again, except for the rain.

The party assembled closer together and began again to plod ahead slowly. The thick mud at their feet gave way to firmer footing as the men rose out of the jungle muck and onto rocky slopes. The men's knees and elbows and chins slammed upon jagged rocks as they slipped and stumbled and climbed their way up the slopes as torrents of water rushed down beneath them. The rocky ledges ahead offered shelter from the rain but they also gave good vantage to those above watching the men below. One of those watching from above leapt and then pounced upon a man below, tumbling with him in its grip. The king's men swung their knives blindly in the darkness. One such swipe tore open the attacker's hind quarters sending it screaming human-like into the night. The First Lieutenant's life had been saved but he lay limp as two of his men dragged him by the wrists up and into the caves.

The king's men collapsed at last en masse upon the moss-covered floor of a large cave. With solid rock protecting their backsides and flanks from attack, the men breathed a collective sigh of relief. Torches were lit. Bandages torn from tattered flags were wrapped tightly around wounds. Swords and knives were honed on rocks as the men dared any beast of the jungle test its fate against them. The king's men slept in shifts in the damp cave while those who remained awake on watch kept a fire burning near its entrance.

A solitary figure stood guard at the mouth of the cave. As he pissed on the rocks below he caught glimpses of starlight that had begun to pierce through the breaking clouds above him. Unbeknownst to the man, a leopard approached his position. It crept slowly and cautiously as it climbed up the slope and then crouched in a rock crevice directly below the man's feet. As the leopard was about to leap, a loud pop sounded from the campfire at the mouth of the cave. The leopard cowered from the noise. Its claws scratched against the rock alerting the man to its presence. The man drew his sword and stood firm as he called out to his shipmates. With pistols in hand two men joined his side but no sign of a threat was found for the leopard had retreated. While legions of insects and frogs sang a deafening morning celebration, forty native tribesmen joined twenty others who had positioned themselves atop the caves the night before. The tribesman who had been wounded when he pounced on the invaders had made his way back to his village. It was there that the village chief assembled more warriors and sent them to join in the hunt.

As daylight filtered into the jungle, morning sunlight burned an eerie phosphorescent glow through thick curtains of fog. Towering trees stood like silent sentries as they rose through the mist from the valley below. One after another the king's men awoke while three others stood watch over the twenty.

Above the cave, a warrior cloaked in a battle-worn leopard skin raised his spear high in the air as silent signal for the hunt to begin. The tribesmen split deftly into ranks; twenty below the cave, twenty to its right and twenty more to its left. When all were in position the lead warrior signaled the attack. He roared like a leopard as he led his warriors up to the mouth of the cave. A wave of the king's men charged toward the attack but they were clubbed from behind by warriors on each side of them. The clubbed men sailed over the edge of the cave. Some were impaled as they landed on spears held upright. Others screamed where they had fallen as they were stuck and skewered. Flintlock gunfire erupted from the back of cave as more warriors charged inside. The First Lieutenant gasped as he grabbed ahold of a spear that had been thrust deep into his belly. Pinned against the cave wall, he watched in horror as a second warrior approached him. The warrior removed the Englishman's sword from its scabbard and then held the Lieutenant's head by the hair. The sharp blade sliced easily through the Lieutenant's windpipe and spine. The warrior held up his prize as blood poured from its neck and onto the headless body slumped below it. Fifteen heads were taken as trophies. Eight prisoners, pushed from behind by the tips of spears, led a procession through the jungle toward a village. Tribesmen in the rear carried three of their own dead.

Shortly into the trek, the procession passed a pair of eyes riveted fast upon them. The eyes peered out from beneath a leopard skin that had been plundered from a warrior stabbed to death the night before. The eyes watched intently as familiar captives passed by. The eyes watched in horror as the severed heads of the less-fortunate swung by the hair and knocked against one another. The eyes blinked as the Englishman contemplated a route back to his ship. They blinked again at the sound of cannon fire offshore in the bay. While fellow Englishmen slept warm in their beds two oceans away, blood ran in rivers across the deck of the king's ship.

In the days that followed, the bodies of the king's men who had been slaughtered were gathered up and eaten. Once the dead had been consumed, the tribe turned then to fresher meat. One-by-one, captives were dragged from their cages kicking and screaming. Fellow sailors and officers looked on in horror as their doomed shipmates were bound to spits and then roasted alive atop a carefully tended fire. Tribesmen and women danced around the flames. They thanked the Gods above them for their succulent meals. After each of the feasts, the bones of the king's men were sucked dry and were then put to good use as tools or as weapons or as skillfully carved tribute to the Gods. The eternal Gods of the jungle were pleased with their subjects while oceans away, yet another God, called upon his subjects to set sail for revenge. And so it went, and so it goes, and so it never shall end.

The Balcony is Best

The Wilsons returned home from their senior center's ninety-fifth annual summer picnic early that Sunday evening. The picnic was quite a shindig, as it usually was.

"That picnic was quite a shindig," Mrs. Wilson remarked as she rinsed out her empty potato salad dish and then placed it gently into the empty dishwasher.

"It usually is," her husband agreed.

"The wheelchair races were exciting," Mrs. Wilson said as she dried her hands on a flower pattern dish towel.

"I'll say. I took ten smackers from Stan thanks to old man Hennessey. That geezer can really motor."

"You didn't bet on the races, did you?"

"I did."

"You're bad."

"To the bone, my dear," Mr. Wilson said as he pulled his wife gently to his chest and then kissed her sweet lips. "Wanna fool around?" he tempted her.

"Don't you think we've had enough foolin' around for one day?" his wife asked rhetorically.

"I suppose so," he lamented.

Both of the Wilsons were tired but were not yet exhausted. Mrs. Wilson went upstairs where she washed up, dressed for bed, and then settled herself atop her pillows to finish the murder mystery she'd been reading the past four nights. Although she had a theory of her own, she was anxious to discover who had actually done it.

Mr. Wilson remained downstairs. He drank a cold bottle of beer at the kitchen table while he thumbed through the

Sunday paper one last time before he dropped it with a thump into the empty recycling bin next to the kitchen door. Instead of calming him down and filling his belly, the beer he drank just wound him up and made him even hungrier. He decided then to order a pizza. While waiting for the pizza delivery guy to show up, Mr. Wilson walked two leisurely miles on the treadmill that his daughter had gifted him and his wife the previous Christmas.

"Oh look…" he remarked to his wife and daughter on that snowy Christmas morning as he inspected the extravagant gift, "a cup holder for my beer!"

"My father the athlete," his daughter decreed and to which her mother just rolled her eyes as she so often did.

"But no ashtray for my cigars," he noticed, disappointed.

"Your cigars are still banished to the back porch," his wife reminded him.

"Your mother is trying to kill me," he notified his daughter. "Death by pneumonia; his body was found frozen, slumped in the snow with a cigar butt in his mouth. She probably got the idea from one of her murder books," he assumed.

When the pizza delivery guy finally showed up, Mr. Wilson noticed immediately that the pizza delivery guy was a girl.

"Hey, you're a girl," he remarked.

"Hey, you're right. You win a pizza for guessing correctly," she teased him and then announced, "that'll be ten fifty."

"Ten fifty? When I was your age, pizzas were a quarter," he grumbled and then he handed the girl eleven dollars and said, "Keep the change."

"Oh boy thanks, Pops," she cried, "a whopping fifty cents to fill up my gas tank and pay my babysitter."

"There's no need to thank *me*, Missy, thank *you!*"

He watched as the girl wiped out one of his wife's rose bushes and then knocked over their mailbox while backing out of the driveway.

"I *knew* I shouldn't have tipped her!" he mumbled, closing the door in disgust.

"I ordered a pizza... do you want a slice?" Mr. Wilson called up to his wife from the foot of the stairs.

"No thanks... my teeth are soaking," she called back.

"Okay then," he replied.

He sat down then at the kitchen table, popped the cap off a second bottle of beer and then bit into a slice of pepperoni. "Not bad," he thought and then he remembered his wife.

"I ordered a pizza... do you want a slice?" he called up to his wife from the foot of the stairs.

"No thanks... my teeth are soaking," she called back.

"Okay then," he replied.

Wally and Dolly had been mostly happily married for sixty-two years before they eventually broke their marriage vows and found themselves engaged in a steamy love affair. The affair began innocently and accidentally when Wally drove his '63 Plymouth through a plate glass window at Shop Mart. Apparently; he had stomped on the car's accelerator pedal instead of its brakes when he pulled in to park.

Wally's car came to a crashing stop mere feet away from Dolly who had been shopping at the store for half an hour prior to the wreck. The front bumper of his Plymouth had knocked over the woman's shopping cart spilling all of its contents (two cans of split pea soup and a box of unsalted soda crackers) across the store's shiny floor.

"Hey, you dented my soup cans!" Dolly complained.

"Are you okay...? You're not hurt are you?" Wally asked concerned as he forced his driver's side door open, toppling over a rack of jarred pickles in the process.

"I suppose I'm okay. I'm not hurt," Dolly decided adding, "It's a good thing you didn't break my brand new cane, Mister Stuntman," she said as she picked it up off of the floor (it had been hooked over her shopping cart handle and was thrown clear of the wreckage). "I was going to buy one of those new-fangled aluminum canes but decided to stick with good ol' fashion wood. What do you think?" she asked the man as she held up her cane for his approval.

"The wood tone compliments your age spots quite nicely," he noticed.

"Oh my," Dolly blushed and then asked, "Aren't you a bit too old to be flirting?" She snickered shyly and as she did, happy notes whistled across her sparkling white dentures.

"One's never too old to act younger," Wally replied and then he accidentally kicked one of the few jars of pickles that hadn't been shattered. As the jar rolled across the floor, Wally observed, "You know... they used to keep this store nice and tidy. Now look at it... it's a royal mess. This place has really gone down-hill lately."

To which Dolly agreed and then whispered to Wally, "I think the new owners are *hippies*."

"Or worse yet; college graduates!" Wally suggested to which the eighty-year-old couple burst out laughing like a couple of eight-year-old kids.

When their laughter had finally subsided, Wally dabbed tears of joy from Dolly's pink rouge cheeks with his handkerchief. As he returned his handkerchief to his pants pocket a thought occurred to him; "Hey now... I've got two dimes in my pocket. Let's say you and I blow this pop stand and catch a movie. Are you game, Doll?"

"How did you know my name?" Dolly asked the man.

"Lucky guess, I guess," Wally guessed and then he asked her again, "So... how 'bout it, Doll?"

"A movie sounds nice," she decided.

"It sure does, Doll, but do you mind if we walk? I'd hate to lose my parking spot."

"That'll be fine," Dolly agreed. "It'll give me a chance to break in my new cane."

"Shall we then?" Wally asked as he offered his date the crook of his arm.

"We shall," she said happily, taking his arm in her hand.

As Dolly stepped past her box of crackers, two stock boys who'd been tokin' a doobie out back by the dumpsters, stood at the far end of the wrecked aisle. "Clean up on aisle eight, dude," the boy in charge told the new kid.

"You gonna give me a hand?" the new kid asked to which his cohort applauded.

The store manager zipped up his pants and scrambled to his office window. As he peered through the one-way glass from the mezzanine level he hollered, "Holy shit!"

"What is it?" a cashier asked as she sat on the edge of his desk buttoning her blouse.

"Come quick!" he told her.

"I already did," she joked.

"No, seriously, Lorraine, come here," he implored.

Lorraine stood up from his desk and smoothed out her skirt before she joined her boss at the office window.

"Holy shit," she declared, "the earth *did* move!"

As they stared affectionately into each other's eyes, neither Wally nor Dolly noticed the express bus that came barreling down Second Avenue the moment they stepped off the curb. Luckily for them though, they were crossing Third Avenue.

"Do you like butter on your popcorn, Doll?" Wally asked.

"I sure do," she replied happily. "It makes movie kisses even sweeter," she said, her cheeks blushing the moment the words had slipped off her tongue.

"So who's flirting now?" Wally teased the woman as Dolly's cheeks became even rosier.

"Want to sit in the front row like when we were kids?" Wally suggested with boyish excitement.

"No, not really..." Dolly replied, "I much prefer the balcony. You know... in case the movie is boring," she said and then she winked at her new beau.

"Yes indeed," Wally agreed, "the balcony is best."

After the movie (which cost Wally an arm and a leg and wasn't even a double-feature and didn't include any World War II newsreels or cartoons for gosh sakes) the couple strolled arm-in-arm back to the store where they had met. As Wally and Dolly got closer, they noticed a half dozen police cars in Shop Mart's parking lot. Two of the cars were spinning brilliant blue and red lights into the early evening sky.

"I wonder what all of the fuss is about," Dolly wondered.

"Let's find out, Doll," Wally suggested and then he led his date toward the brightly lit storefront entrance where groups of people were talking to police officers.

As the couple approached to inquire as to what had happened, they heard a voice call out in their direction; "Mom..? Dad...? Oh my God...! Are you alright?"

It was the couple's daughter Lisa who immediately charged through the crowd and made her way toward her parents. Lisa wrapped her arms around her mother and father and hugged them dearly. She then held them both out at arm's length and scolded, "You two scared me to death! What on earth happened?"

Wally and Dolly, who were at first confused, were quickly prompted back to reality by the presence of their daughter. The couple came to realize then what had *actually* happened.

"Well, Lisa... I was picking your mother up at the store when I must have blacked out or something. I'm fine though... we both are. I guess we just wandered off a bit is all," her father explained.

"The police traced your license plate, Dad. They tracked me down at work," Lisa reported. "I was so shaken up I nearly wrecked my *own* car driving over here!"

"Oh my, we're so sorry, dear!" her mother apologized and then with a worried look asked her daughter, "I guess we're in some kind of trouble, right?"

"No, I mean yes, no, not really, Mom. I told the police what I thought might have happened but when they checked the hospitals they couldn't find you anywhere. As far as the wreck is concerned, the police said that criminal charges wouldn't be filed unless someone was hurt. Apparently, the insurance companies will handle the damages. I'm just so happy and relieved that you're alright," she said and then she broke down sobbing in her parents' arms.

"There, there, honey," her mother said. "It's okay now."

"Let's go home. I'm worn out," Wally suggested as he pulled his car keys from his pants pocket.

"Your car's been towed away, Dad," Lisa notified her father

through the tears she was wiping away with the backs of her hands.

"Don't tell me it was towed to the Plymouth dealer!" her father warned. "Those crooks charge an arm and a leg!"

"No Dad, they don't have Plymouth dealers anymore. I told the tow truck driver to take your car to your buddy Stan's body shop."

"That's My Girl!" her father shouted relieved and then he kissed his daughter gratefully and lovingly on both of her cheeks. "Can you give us a ride home, dear?" he asked her. "My car's in the shop," he explained.

"Sure can, Pops," Lisa said laughing.

"Do you mind if we do a bit of shopping first, dear?" Dolly asked her daughter. "We've run out of soup and crackers."

When Lisa pulled into her parents' driveway, her headlights washed across a smashed mailbox lying on their front lawn. Lisa's father, sitting shotgun, turned around to complain to his wife in the backseat. "Doggone it, Doll, look...! Some neighbor kid must have flunked his driving test!"

"Or maybe it was hippies, dear," his wife suggested as she peered through the car window.

"Whatever the case, Doll, I'm calling our insurance agent first thing in the morning."

The Ending Begins

Slate stone walkway, once straight and true, once tight joints parting ways for grass and weeds surrounding these listing, tilting, shoe worn, rain worn, time worn, slick old mossy-edged stones that lie still and silent while ribbons of sunlight pierce the ever fewer leafless gaps remaining in the thick oak canopy of two hundred wet springs, two hundred hot summers and two hundred leafless frozen winters. Gnarled ancient roots push patient escape beneath the evermore vaulted stones one of which I stand upon rocking a hollow and wobbling, "thump-thump-thump," to which a soft, muffled, "Hello…" rises up between my boots.

I stand still and silent, bewildered and then again, "Hello…" to which I return a moment following a, "Hello…" of my own.

My ears hear, "Come join us," as my mind pauses in disbelief. "Down here… come join us."

I kneel down slowly and then ask the stone, "Hello…?"

"Down here, come join us," this time another's voice and then again in unison, "Lift the stone," which compels me to step forward, forcing my full weight on one foot to which the stone tips up ever so slightly.

I reach down and grab ahold of the stone's edge and slide it easily enough across the adjacent stone with a quick, slick, lightly grinding scrape. I step aside the open pit and kneel down to inspect the earth beneath me which reveals two pair of glowing eyes staring up at me from the darkness below.

"We cannot climb out but you may step down," I am told.

And so I do, inexplicably and without hesitation, I descend slowly into the dark damp earth and then from twelve feet below the earth's surface I hear the stone above me slide back into place taking with it, the leaf filtered sunlight above.

I find myself then, in total darkness.

"Welcome…" the word echoes in random blackness and then fades softly to sounds of distant dripping water.

"I cannot see," I announce softly and cautiously toward the assumed direction of my unseen companions as I stand astride the four, tiny puddles of subterranean water I had mistaken for glowing eyes when sunlight struck them for the first time in eons.

"Welcome," is whispered in my startled ear accompanied by a soft and cold sensuous kiss to my opposite cheek as twenty strong, thin fingers suddenly rake my hips and my waist and my chest from four different directions interlocking then with one another in a soft yet firm, icy cold embrace that surrounds and chills my trembling body to a point of near frozen ecstasy. With eyes wide open I see absolutely nothing in the blackness but immediately begin then to revel in the icy embrace as fingernails comb sharply yet gently through my hair and then explore the curve of my brow and the corners of my mouth and the lengths of my thighs and then stop and become still as the dark silence is softly broken.

"We've been waiting for you forever," a strange feminine voice whispers and then a second adds softly, "We think you'll like it here," as they both begin then to slowly and gently disrobe me head to toe caressing me as it's done my ever warming body enjoying the cold air and cold hands I am once again embraced by my companions their soft cool bodies introducing themselves to mine through soft silken gowns I tremble yet again in ecstasy until one and then the other sink their cold sharp teeth deep into my neck.

My shock and pain rise quickly out of my heart and up through my throat in a silent scream not of torture but of total extreme nearly unbearable ecstasy. I fall limp into their arms and to the raw earth below as they feast on my soul which I willingly surrender while I sleep or die or am reborn it matters not for in this death, ironic though it is, I feel totally alive for the first time in my life as my body rises up into the air while my weary eyes close slowly to the darkness.

My eyes then again, open ever so slowly to the dimmest of light its halo illuminates my companions and their beautifully strange black eyes and their full wet black lips that sparkle as their blood red tongues dance about their ivory yellow teeth as they speak.

"Did you enjoy your death?" one inquires in a whispered hiss, her long sharp nails stroking my chest.

I sit up slowly between them. They push me back down the next asking, "Are you ready now, to live?"

Cold black lips lock themselves atop mine preventing any verbal response on my part while serving to invoke a much more convincing response in the affirmative that rises up between us as we introduce one to the other in a rush of internal flaming heat our dead hearts pumping the blood of others through our shuddering bodies as we pound against one another with a reckless fervor each new moment more intense than the last in nearly unbearable crescendos of lust and lascivious joy which suddenly freezes then between us simultaneously as we feel ourselves thrown full force flying over the highest of cliffs we hang motionless... embraced in midair... we shudder, paralyzed violently at first but then it repeats again and again and again and then fades as we fall headfirst together into a looming precipice far below.

Our weakened bodies spin as we plummet, helpless against the impending impact upon the jagged rocks approaching us faster and faster from a thousand feet below. White light flashes as my head cracks open. My lifeless body lies broken.

My eyes blink slowly. Sunlight glitters through my lashes. I roll my head to one side and with my cheek pressed against a cold flat stone damp with morning dew I stare upon the dead tree branch that had fallen from the sky and knocked me unconscious twelve hours earlier. I roll over onto my side and then rise to my knees and finally to my feet and begin to walk then slowly down the long stone path back to my cabin where page four of my story rests between the rolls of my typewriter while my famished cat lies in wait ready to give me a well-deserved lecture soon to be silenced by a fresh can of tuna followed by roaring purrs of satisfaction and faint muffled voices beneath distant stones.

- The Beginning -

The Old Man and She

"Have you caught anything yet?" I asked an old man sitting on a weathered wood stool at the far end of the pier.

"Hell No! Fish around here are cowards!" he complained, staring into the water and not bothering to look up at whoever had inquired, which happened to be me.

"What are you using for bait?" I asked him.

"Mermaid," he replied.

"Mermaid?" I inquired. "What's that?"

"Are you a knucklehead or somethin'? You honestly don't know what a mermaid is?" he asked as he turned around and looked up at me, squinting seriously through his sun-tanned wrinkled eyelids.

"Oh... you mean *actual* mermaid," I said apologetically, realizing immediately that I'd just implied that mermaids were real. "I thought that you meant some kind of fishing lure called a mermaid."

"Nope, I'm usin' cut-mermaid. The meat is sweet and most fish love it but not these damn coward fish. They're too scared to nibble, as much as they might want to," he said, turning back toward the sea where his fishing line stretched and then disappeared into ocean swells twelve feet below us.

As I bent over to look into one of the two buckets on the deck beside the man, I wondered, *Was it his empty catch bucket or his bait bucket?* I cringed in anticipation as I inspected the bucket for what might be; cut-mermaid. Fortunately, the bucket was empty, in apparent anticipation of the man's first catch. I shifted my position then to inspect the second bucket. I didn't know what to expect never having seen cut-mermaid before. I gasped as the bucket's contents came into view but when I realized that what I was looking at appeared to be cut-fish, I relaxed a bit. What was I expecting anyway, beautiful, sad mermaid eyes staring up at me? I shuddered at the thought.

"Do you fish here a lot?" I asked the old man, expecting to be lectured or slapped upside my head.

"Every day," he responded rationally.

"Did you catch anything yesterday?"

"Yep, and a real beaut too, ate him for dinner last night."

"Were you using mermaid yesterday?" I asked, wondering what he'd say.

"Nope, used squid yesterday. I got the mermaid early this mornin' from an old sailor down by the docks. He had an eye-patch and a peg-leg and he groaned, *Arrgh!* when I handed him two dollars so I figure it's genuine."

"Nothing worse than imitation mermaid," I declared.

"Damn straight, it's perk-near useless, just like this fishin' rig of mine."

The man was using what appeared to be an expensive rod and reel and so I said, "That looks like a real nice rig to me."

"Oh, it's okay I reckon. It was a gift from my sweetheart granddaughter. She drops me off here every day to fish for a few hours. If I don't use this here pole she bought me I might get all offended or somethin'. You know how lady-folk can be, don't ya?"

"Sure do, lady-folk can be damn sensitive that's for sure," I said, sounding exactly like my new-found friend who began then to reminisce.

"When I was a kid we didn't have any fancy fiberglass rods or monofilament line or sissy ball-bearing spinning reels. We fished like real men, I tell ya. We used *real* string and safety pin hooks and willow branches or bamboo poles, none of this fake and fancy crap they make nowadays."

"Fishing *has* gotten quite commercialized," I said.

"And fish were bigger back in those days too," he claimed.

"And less-cowardly," I added, happy to have done so.

"Brave fish taste better that's for sure," he proclaimed.

I stood on the pier contemplating the age-old wisdom of my companion. I was feeling a heightened sense of awareness. I was beginning to recognize things as they actually were while understanding the way that they *should* be. I found myself eager to learn even more. Who was I kidding? The old man was a crackpot. He was obviously messing with me. He had to be pulling my leg about the mermaid, right? Then again, what do I know? Maybe truth *is* stranger than fiction. As gruff as the guy was he was almost lovable, in an abrasive sort of way. I began to feel sorry for him, sitting there all alone, day-after-day, waiting for coward fish that were too afraid to bite.

I gazed back along the pier fifty yards to the shoreline and then along the beach; not a soul in sight. No, wait... two solitary lovers on the beach in the distance, rolling around on a blanket. Do they have no shame? Good for them!

My thoughts turned back then to the grumpy old man. Maybe I could cheer him up. "Gettin' any bites?" I asked.

"Hell no! Your constant jibber-jabberin' is scarin' all the fish away!" my dear friend insisted vehemently.

"It's almost *too* easy to scare away coward fish isn't it?" I suggested.

He laughed out loud. I actually cheered him up! Would hell be freezing over?

"Sit down and shut up will ya?" he demanded as he flipped his empty bucket upside down for me to sit upon.

So there I sat, quietly, on the bucket as instructed while we stared at the water waiting for something to happen. We sat and stared and waited for thirty minutes or more. My ass was getting cramped or bucket-pinched or both. The old man suddenly looked to his left. I leaned backwards and looked past him to see what had attracted his attention.

"Here she comes..." he announced. "The party's over."

I watched as she approached us. As I recall it now, I was mesmerized at the time. I'm not sure how long I was staring at her until I finally realized that I *was* staring at her. She looked as if she'd just walked out of a magazine ad for edible suntan lotion; short yellow shorts, tiny blue top, long shapely sun-tanned legs that reached all the way to the ground, swinging, swaying, long blonde hair that blew like golden angel dust in a photographer's fan.

"Your granddaughter?" I asked rhetorically.

"And a beauty at that," he said proudly.

"I hadn't noticed," I lied.

"Oh, you will," he promised.

"Ready, Pops?" she asked as the slowly setting sun bathed her lovingly in a caressing orange glow that lingered lustfully along the entire length of her stunning figure.

"Suppose so," Pops said, rising slowly off of his stool. "Goin' home empty handed," he reported.

"Who's your friend, Pops?" she asked him, looking my way as I stood up eye-to-eye with her.

"Don't know his damn name. He was trying to rob me."

"Pops! Behave yourself now!" she scolded, extending her lovely hand toward mine. "Stacy," she said smiling.

As I shook the woman's hand I envisioned the name Stacy tattooed on my arm.

"Chad," I said, thinking that Chad and Stacy sounded quite nice indeed. "Do you two live together?" I asked her and then wondered if it was too personal a question.

"She *tries* to keep me out of trouble," Pops interjected defiantly, "and notice I said, tries, ha-ha!"

"Oh, Pops is no trouble at all, and he's real good company for me. He's actually a sweetheart, isn't he, Chad?"

I noticed the woman's ring-less left hand when she laid it on her grandfather's shoulder. "Pops is indeed a joy!" I said, a bit too enthusiastically.

The three of us walked the length of the pier as the setting sun warmed our backs and my sore butt. I toted Pop's stool and tackle box and both of his empty buckets. He carried his fishing pole in one hand and held his granddaughter's hand in his other.

While Stacy and I were loading Pop's gear into the trunk of her car, Pops opened the driver's side door.

"Pops," she scolded, "you haven't driven for ten years!"

"That doesn't mean I forgot how!" he complained.

"But you don't have a license or insurance," she reminded him.

"When I was your age, Missy, we didn't need no damn license or insurance," *he* reminded *her.*

"We have this same conversation every night," she whispered to me.

"You're an angel to look after him, you know," I told her.

"So nice of you to say so, Chad," she said as I closed the trunk.

"A lot of families these days lose patience. They give up and pack the elderly away into zombie nursing homes," I said as sadly as I could.

"I know. I could never do that to my Pops though. I'm all he has, now that my parents are gone. My mother was his only child. She and my father were killed in a plane crash four years ago. I was an only child as well. Since I've no brothers or sisters to lean on, he's all I have now too," she said sadly.

"Such a heartbreaking tragedy, I'm so sorry for the both of you," I said, touching her arm with my sympathetic hand. "At least you have each other. He's a lucky guy."

"It really helps me to have him around too. You wouldn't believe it but, he's actually quite funny in his own way. We laugh all the time. Sometimes his teeth pop right out of his mouth. And the stories he tells... you wouldn't believe!" she said, but I believed her.

"What on earth are you two jibber-jabberin' about?" Pops complained from the passenger side seat. "Am I sleepin' in this car tonight or what?"

"So nice to meet you, Chad," Stacy said, smiling as she shook my hand again.

"And I, you. By the way, your grandfather loves his new fishing pole," I fibbed.

"Actually, he hates it," she corrected softly. "He may have *told* you he likes it but he only uses it because I bought it for him. It's *way too fancy* for him, or so he says. It really doesn't matter anyway, he hasn't caught a fish for months now, but he sure *loves* to try," she whispered and then smiled.

I waved to them both as they drove away in her car. Miraculously, Pops waved back to me! Or maybe, he'd given me the finger.

On my way home that night I stopped off at the twenty-four hour mega-mart. I was pleasantly surprised to find actual, genuine, bamboo fishing poles in their sporting goods department. I picked up two poles and a galvanized steel bucket. I went next, to the toy department in search of kites. A clerk pointed me in the right direction. I picked up a ball of sturdy, braided, white kite string and tossed it into my bucket. On my way to the cash registers I passed through the health and beauty department where I picked up a bag of various-size safety pins and then selected what I thought might be the most irresistible body-spray for men. I tossed my wares into my bucket and made it through the self-checkout in a jiffy. I made a mental note to keep the word "jiffy" handy for later use. I liked the way that it sounded and thought that Pops might like it too.

Tomorrow is Friday, I thought as I walked through the acres of parking lot to my car. I planned then and there to kick off my weekend right by doing a bit of fishing; the old-fashion, proper way of course. *And who knows?* I thought, *I might actually catch something worth keeping.*

The End for Now

>(((())'>

The Red Nose Gang

It was a hot and cloudless summer day in the desert. A gang of bikers, loaded for bear and looking for trouble, rolled two abreast along a deserted highway. Although they'd already made a hit earlier that same day, they were pumped up and eager for more action. As the gang rounded a wide, sweeping bend at the base of a barren, cactus-studded range, a potential target revealed itself up ahead; an isolated truck stop. The gang leader signaled the others from the head of the column and then turned off of the two-lane highway and into the truck stop's empty parking lot. The gang members followed behind him and rolled single-file around to the rear of the building where they parked out of sight from the roadway. The gang dismounted in unison, gathered together and then stormed into the building and up to the cashier.

"What do you clowns want?" the store owner asked gruffly as he stood firm behind the counter. The gang opened fire on the man with a merciless torrent of water that came squirting from the colorful, plastic novelty flowers pinned to their enormous floppy lapels.

"Stop! Stop! Please Stop!" the man begged as he quickly became soaked to the skin. "I'm drowning!" he gurgled as he sank to his knees and then fell face-first to the floor. The lead clown jumped over the counter, punched the "Sale" button on the cash register and then quickly emptied its contents into the enormous baggy pockets of his multi-colored pants. As he hopped back over the counter, the gang leader used the sole of his giant floppy shoe to mush the store owner's face into a deep puddle of water. Upon leaving the store, the lead clown discovered his fellow clowns clowning around in the parking lot. They were celebrating the heist with wild silent gestures as they tossed dozens of sucked-clean chicken bones across the pavement. Suddenly, the clowns' leader signaled to the gang; "Let's roll, you clowns!" at which point the clowns rolled. They left as quickly as they'd come; their tricycle wheels squeaking, a cloud of desert dust rising in their wake.

The store owner pulled his soaked t-shirt over his head, wrung it out best he could and then wiped off his dripping wet face. "Bozos!" he muttered as he grabbed the phone off the wall and then dialed zero for the operator.

"Operator, how may I assist you?"

"I've just been robbed by the Red Nose Gang!"

"Is that you, Clem?"

"Vicky?"

"Yeah, buddy. How's Darlene and the kids?"

"Okay I reckon. Lil' Clem's got a runny nose."

"Well doesn't he always that one?"

"Suppose so."

"Did Darlene decide what's she's bakin' for the church picnic?"

"Don't know, Vicky, you'll have to ask her yourself I reckon."

"I'll do that then. I'd hate to bake the same thang she does. You know how those church ladies can be; all a talkin' and fussin' about every little thang."

"Yeah... so what about my robbery, Vicky?"

"Oh that... the police are already on it, Clem," the operator reported. "The same gang hit the KFC up the road from ya, not less'n an hour ago. They got away clean with three buckets of chicken and three large sides."

"Well, that explains the chicken bones in my parkin' lot!" the owner retorted as he gazed through his office window at the mess strewn about the ground. "Let me know when the good guys catch 'em, Vicky. I've got a bone to pick with those clowns. As a matter of fact, I've got *several* bones to pick with 'em! Armed robbery is one thing but tossin' greasy chicken bones all over my parkin' lot is way over the line!"

"Will do, Clem, but please try to calm down, ya hear? It ain't no good for your ticker to get all riled up. The police have already sent a squad car to the area. They said they'd do their darndest to catch the crooks."

"Good 'nough then, Vicky, thanks."

"No problem, Clem. Give Darlene and the young'uns my best."

"Will do, Vicky, bye now."

"B-bye, Clem."

Further on up the road, the Red Nose Gang pedaled their way along County Road 69. Hidden well out of sight behind a stop sign, police officers: Boppo, Bippo, Bleepo, Bingo and Bongo sat crunched together in their tiny patrol car as they waited for the gang.

"Here they come, men!" Sergeant Boppo gestured. "It's show time!" he implied emphatically.

As the criminals approached, the officers frantically pedaled their tiny squad car directly into the path of the oncoming gang. The gang's tricycles squealed as they collided with the squad car in a skidding... sliding... tumbling heap. The unconscious gang members came to quickly and then jumped up in unison. They began running in various random circular patterns bumping into each other as they attempted escape. The officers, by then on foot, began a furious zigzag pursuit of the gang members but they too bumped into one another repeatedly in the process. After several more collisions and numerous trips and falls, the officers finally managed to corral the criminals. Despite the fact that the gang members had raised up their enormous gloved hands in surrender, the officers began pummeling them mercilessly with foam rubber night sticks sending them all to the ground in a tangled pile of brightly colored laundry. From across a fence, a lone rodeo clown who'd witnessed the entire spectacle waved his big floppy cowboy hat in joyous celebration.

As the officers pedaled their way back to the station, Sergeant Boppo turned around to face the gang members shackled together in the back seat of the tiny patrol car. He gestured to them silently, "It's the end of the line, boys. It's back to the circus for you!"

Suddenly, the tallest gang member stood up, raising the entire tiny patrol car up off the ground in the process. As he held the car up with all of his might he yelled silently to the gang, "Now's our chance... run for it, boys!"

The gang members took off running, freeing themselves from their plastic shackles in the process. The tallest gang member slipped out from under the car and dropped it hard on the road leaving the clown cops trapped inside. By the time the cops were able to squeeze themselves out of their car, the gang members had hopped back onto their trikes and were long gone down the lonesome desert highway.

To this very day, the Red Nose Gang remains at large. There have been reports that they show up at the circus from time to time; disguised of course. So, let it be known... Ladies and Gentlemen... Children of All Ages... Be on the Lookout!

Tiffany's Epiphany

An old but reliable table-top fan hummed and occasionally buzzed as it swung left and then right blowing hot August air around Tiffany's room as she lay on her bed leafing through last year's high school yearbook. She was anxious to begin her senior year and reunite with friends she'd lost touch with over the long and hot, mostly boring summer. She wondered what her friends had been up to over the summer months. She herself hadn't done much of anything at all except kill time with Jimmy when he wasn't busy working or looking for work or running around with his wild friends; friends that Tiffany's mother refused to let in the house. Tiffany's mother barely tolerated Jimmy as it was and only did so because her daughter took a shine to him.

As Tiffany flipped through the pages of her yearbook, she wondered what she'd be doing after graduation. Would she marry Jimmy and get pregnant? Or, would she get pregnant and marry Jimmy? The thought of those options scared her to death. Not so much the Jimmy part or the pregnant part but the part that would keep her stuck in her good-for-nothin' hometown for the rest of her long, miserable life. She began feeling a bit desperate and somewhat sick to her stomach when the pink princess phone on her night table rang and suddenly changed her mood.

"Hi, who's this?" she asked cheerfully.

"Hey, Tiffy, what's ya doin'?"

"Layin' on a hot and sticky bed talkin' to you, Jimmy."

"I figured as much. What I mean is... what's ya doin' *later* tonight?"

"I imagine I'll be layin' under you on *your* hot and sticky bed. Isn't that what you wanna do, Jimmy?"

"Yeah, baby doll, but I was thinkin' we'd do somethin' *better* first."

"And what might *that* be, Jimmy?"

"How'd ya like to get rich with me... get rich and leave this crappy-ass town once and for all?"

"Tonight?"

"Tonight."

"For good?"

"For good, baby doll."

"Should I pack a bag?" she asked, sitting up in a start on her hot and sticky bed.

"It's up to you, Tiffy. Fill a bag with your old crappy clothes if you want to or wait 'til tomorrow when I buy you all the brand new clothes you want, you know... the expensive kind you is always talkin' about."

"Seriously, Jimmy?"

"You know me, girl, I don't joke around too much, now do I, Tiify?"

"No, Jimmy, you *are* the serious type, at least you have been the two years we've been fuckin'."

"It's been two years? Seems like just a year to me."

"It was two years this past Fourth of July, Jimmy. Don't you remember... we missed the fireworks altogether that first year 'cause you was too busy explodin' all up inside me? Remember... I was in the tenth grade... I had to take that horrible trip to the free-clinic to set things right? I had to use your sister's name and driver's license so I'd be old enough to set things right without my momma findin' out. Don't you remember, Jimmy?"

"You mean that time we took your momma's bedspread down to the lake and she found out and nearly skinned us alive?"

"No, Jimmy, that was *this* year, our *second* Fourth of July. I'm talkin' 'bout the year before that, our *first* year together. You know... our very first time fuckin', at least *my* very first time anyways."

"Can't say I remember too much about all that, baby doll, but if you say so it's good enough for me. All I know right now is, I got big plans to wrap up so I'll be seein' you later, okay?"

"Okay, Jimmy."

"My new beau Carl is picking me up at eight, Tiffy. You be alright home alone tonight?"

"Jimmy said he might stop over later, Momma."

"Well, remember now, Tiffy, it's okay for a girl to spread her legs for a *good* man, after she finishes high school that is, but don't be givin' it away to no two-bit loser now."

"Jimmy ain't no loser, Momma. He makes *good* money paintin' cars and besides... we's just friends."

"Well, you two sure don't act like friends, Tiffy. I may have to wear these God-awful contacts but I ain't blind you know."

"I know you ain't, Momma, but me and Jimmy are just... we's just... well, maybe we *are* a little bit affectionate towards one another but we ain't in love or anything like that. We's just close friends is all."

"Well, I sure do hope it stays that way, honey, because I've heard things about Jimmy around town lately. Apparently, he's been runnin' around with that Gil Graham character. You know the Graham boy don't ya? The one who shot and killed that old man when he was all of twelve years old? Jimmy's wild-ass friends are bad enough but that Gil Graham weirdo scares me to death. When he looks at you it's like... it's like he's looking right through you or somethin' with those cold, empty black eyes of his."

"I heard about him, Momma, but I don't *know* him."

"And it better stay that way you hear me, young lady?"

"Yes, Momma."

"Oh listen, sweetheart... you got your whole life ahead of you. I'd hate to see you waste it away on a boy like Jimmy. You can do *so* much better. Look at you... my baby girl all grown up right in front of my eyes... at least parts of you is anyway. Aside from those big beautiful tits of yours though, the rest of you is skin and bones. Listen now, there's tuna casserole in the refrigerator and fresh cornbread in the breadbox so you make sure you eat some, okay?"

"Oh, Momma, you're skinny too. And in case you hadn't noticed, I got these tits from *you*."

"But yours sprouted out of thin air in the past six months, honey. Mine took two or three years to blossom. When you head back to school this fall the boys'll be all over you. In the meantime, keep your blouse buttoned, your bra fastened and tell Jimmy to keep his hands to himself, you hear me?"

"Yes, Momma."

"And I want you to eat, okay?"

"I will, Momma."

"Promise?"

"I promise."

"That's a good girl. Now zip me up please..."

Tiffany did as she was told and then watched from her mother's bed as Maggie touched-up the unnecessary coats of makeup on her naturally beautiful face. Maggie gave her puffy, bleach-blonde hairdo an extra sweep of hairspray and then spritzed three shots of breath freshener into her mouth and all while humming her favorite song; Aretha Franklin's *Natural Woman*. As Maggie adjusted the straps on her bra, her tune suddenly changed into a girlish squeak of delight when Carl's car horn sounded as he pulled off of the two-lane blacktop and onto their gravel driveway.

"Kiss, kiss," Maggie said; her ruby-red lips pursed in Tiffany's direction. Maggie grabbed her tiny sequined purse and then tiptoed in high heels out of the house as fast as her skin-tight dress would allow. Tiffany heard her momma yell, "Shit!" through the screen door as Maggie clopped her way down the trailer's steps. Tiffany assumed that her momma had either snagged her stockings or had picked up a splinter from the stair's weathered wood railing.

When Jimmy busted through the screen door an hour after her mother had left, Tiffany was sitting at the kitchen table nibbling on cornbread crumbs. As Jimmy bent over Tiffany from behind and slid his hot calloused hands up and under the front of her thread-bare t-shirt, the country radio station announced; "It's nine o'clock in the P.M."

"Guess it's time. You ready, baby doll?" Jimmy whispered through his warm whiskey-breath.

"You hungry, Jimmy? Momma said there's a casserole in the fridge if you are."

"No time for that, Tiffy, we's on a tight schedule so be a good girl and get your things quick."

"Care to explain what we're up to, Jimmy?"

"I'll fill you in on the way there. We need to be sittin' at the Bluebird Truck Stop in thirty minutes or the deal is off."

"What deal, Jimmy? Are you plannin' on doin' somethin' illegal?"

"Well, how else you expect us to get rich overnight; by strikin' gold... by strikin' oil? All the gold and oil's already been found, Tiffany. It's been found by rich folks. If you wanna be a rich folk too you gotta trust me on this."

"I don't want to end up in jail, Jimmy. And I don't want *you* to end up in jail neither."

"Nobody's going to jail, baby doll. We ain't gonna get caught."

"And how do you know that, Jimmy? Can you predict the future all of a sudden?"

"As a matter of fact, I can. I predict that tomorrow, you and me will be half-way to California with piles of cash just waitin' to be spent."

"And *I predict* that the cops will be right on our ass, Jimmy."

"So what's it gonna be then, Tiffy? You wanna take a chance and live the good life with me or sit here all safe and sound and poor growin' cobwebs all your damn life?"

"I wanna get out of here bad, Jimmy, *real bad* honest I do, but I'm scared is all."

With his chin resting atop Tiffany's freshly shampooed hair, Jimmy reached around and pulled a long barrel chrome handgun out from the back of his blue jeans and laid it on the table in front of the girl. He reached his hands back up under her shirt, gave her a firm squeeze and then whispered, "This here gun'll keep us good and safe, baby doll."

"Where on earth did you get that thing, Jimmy?" Tiffany asked, not ever having seen a handgun nearly that big or shiny before.

"Never you mind none, Tiffy. Time's wastin' fast. Just get

your things and get in the car."

"Are you askin' me or tellin' me, Jimmy?"

"Well, baby doll... at this point you know too damn much to be askin', so I reckon I'm tellin' ya."

"You look good enough to eat, Maggie," Carl said as he laid his menu down on the tablecloth and leaned sideways past the candlestick burning between them.

"Maybe you should skip dessert then. I wouldn't want ya ta spoil your after-dinner appetite," Maggie suggested coyly.

"I *never* skip dessert, Maggie, but in your case... I *will* postpone it 'til later."

"Ha-ha, later it is then besides, you promised to take me dancing."

"And I'm a man of my word, Maggie; dinner, dancing, dessert, it is!"

"Sounds delicious," Maggie said and then she searched the Rain Tree Restaurant's menu for steak and lobster.

Tiffany grabbed her overnight bag and purse and locked the trailer door for what she thought at the time might be the very last time. She hopped down the steps and into Jimmy's grey primer Chevy Nova. The couple took off in a loud cloud of dusty gravel that banged against the trailer's aluminum siding. Jimmy took a few quick swigs from the pint bottle of bourbon between his legs and then handed the bottle to the girl. She took a tiny sip just to try and calm her excited nerves. She winced at the taste of it and then handed the bottle back to her boyfriend. Jimmy took a good swig and then another a few miles later. He tossed the empty pint out the window and shouted, "Whooie, Baby Doll... Life Shore is Good!"

Gil Graham and Kent Clark (Kent's father Fred was a lifelong Superman fan) sat in Gil's beat up pickup truck in the Bluebird Truck Stop's parking lot waiting for Jimmy. The pickup's engine and radio were shut off. The boys sucked on cigarettes in silence. With each drag, the bright orange tips of their Marlboro's glowed in the dark like fireflies. Smoke wafted around Gil and Kent and then rolled lazily out of the truck's open windows. A choir of crickets shrieked for attention from the weeds that lined the perimeter of the parking lot. Neon signs buzzed and crackled in the distance. Swarms of stupid summer moths bombarded the parking lot pole lights that rose high above the asphalt toward the night sky above. Every now and then, a belching big rig would rumble in and then slow to a crawl as it chose a spot to cool off for a while. Girls for hire in hot pants and tube tops, clip-clopped across the parking lot in cheap high-heeled shoes to greet the new arrivals. In some cases, after a girl would hop up on the step of a truck cab, she'd disappear as tattooed arms helped her inside. While Kent stared off into space, Gil kept a sharp eye out for the tractor trailer of interest. If Jimmy didn't show up soon, they'd go it alone and split the take two-ways.

Jimmy arrived at the Bluebird right on time. If Jimmy was one thing in life, he was punctual and just to prove it he found Gil's Ford with five minutes to spare.

"Why the fuck did you bring *her* along?" Gil complained the moment he noticed Jimmy's girl sitting next to him.

"Don't you worry none 'bout her, Gil. She can handle herself, can't ya, Tiffy?"

Tiffany shook her head, yes, and then immediately wondered why she had. She had no idea that the boys were about to commit murder, but then again, neither did they. The plan was to knock the driver out cold when he asked for the drug money in exchange for the goods. None of the boys had any money to speak of, let alone thirty thousand dollars.

Carl and Maggie slow danced to a three-piece band at the Rain Tree Lounge as a steady procession of big rigs slowed down for the Bluebird Truck Stop next door. Chances were good that most people out and about in that half of the county were spending their time and money at one of those two places.

"So, Carl... can I interest you in a little late-night dessert at my place this evening?" Maggie whispered in his ear as she slipped her hand inside his sports coat and ran her polished fingertips along the gun holster hidden there.

Carl considered his wife in the neighboring county briefly but figured that a hot dish like Maggie was well worth the risk when he said, "Ready when you are, doll."

So as the music stopped and the band took their last break of the evening the couple headed out toward the lobby's double glass doors when Carl suggested, "You know, Maggie... we could just get a room here tonight if that suits you." He figured that he could make a quick, early morning getaway from there and arrive home before his wife woke up. It would save him the long haul to and from Maggie's place and would shorten his morning commute considerably. He'd leave Maggie a note and twenty dollars cab fare in the hotel room the next morning.

"That'd be just fine with me, Carl. I *love* those big ol' hotel room beds. It'll give us more room to stretch out... if you know what I mean."

"Oh, I know what you mean, doll... I'm planning to stretch you out *real* good!"

"Carl, you *nasty* boy, you!" Maggie complained as she pulled his face down to hers and slipped her warm drunk tongue into his willing mouth.

"What about your daughter, Maggie, will she be alright?"

"Tiffany's in high school, Carl. She can look after herself. You can meet her tomorrow when you drop me off in the morning. If she's up that is."

"Hard to believe that a woman as hot as you has a kid that age, Maggie. I was expectin' to have to pay your babysitter overtime."

"Well, I know you're lyin' 'bout *that*, Carl, but a woman sure does like to hear it anyway," Maggie sighed.

So the couple got a room key and two tooth brushes and one of those tiny little tubes of toothpaste from the front desk clerk and then headed for the hotel's elevator. An hour later they were lying naked on a king-size bed smoking cigarettes. Carl flipped through the cable TV channels while Maggie perused the room service menu. She was thinking about ordering something... maybe an *actual* dessert or some of those deep-fried cheese sticks with that spicy dipping sauce. Carl reached for his smokes again but crushed the empty pack in his hand and then tossed it toward the faux-brass trashcan. The shot bounced off the rim and then again as it rolled under the dresser where no vacuum cleaner had been able to reach since the inn's grand opening nearly thirty years ago.

"Be right back, doll, order whatever you want," Carl said as he left Maggie alone in the room in pursuit of cigarettes. As it turned out, the lousy selection in the Rain Tree's cigarette machine didn't include Carl's brand. He wasn't about to waste good money on some other nasty brand so he headed next door to the Bluebird where truckers and other smart smokers bought discount cigarettes.

Ten minutes after Jimmy and Tiffany had arrived at the Bluebird, their one-way ticket to California; a Trans National tractor trailer with a bright red cab and Alabama plates came rumbling to a stop six vacant parking spaces away from them. Gil and Kent and Jimmy got out of their rides clutching their handguns out of sight. Tiffany sunk low in her seat and hid below Jimmy's dashboard just like he told her to do.

Carl lit a smoke from the fresh pack he'd just bought. He was standing outside the Bluebird enjoying his first drag more than usual not having had one in twenty minutes or so. He watched from a distance as three young guys approached a rig across the parking lot. The truck's driver jumped down from his cab and greeted the trio. They all shook hands and then disappeared behind the ass-end of the trailer. Moments later, Carl noticed a man slumped to the ground under the back of the truck after which he heard the trailer's tailgate latch clink open.

Carl was unaware that the driver had just been gutted by Gil's eight-inch long hunting knife but he knew that something bad was going down. He ran into the Bluebird and hollered at the cashier to call the sheriff. He turned back through the doors, pulled his service revolver from his shoulder holster and then headed out across the acres of parking lot. As he wove his way through rows of parked cars, Carl wondered if the Jackson County boys would be as quick as his own men usually were.

Maggie opened her hotel room door a crack and then loosened the chain to let the room service boy in. He crossed the carpet and set her tray down on the table by the window. Maggie noticed the boy's cute butt as he did so and on his way back to the door the boy couldn't help but notice Maggie's sexy outfit. Her breasts were barely covered by the hand towel she held up to her chest and the only thing not covering her long shapely legs was a tiny pair of pink panties. Maggie was wondering where on earth her beau had run off to when she dropped her towel to the floor while handing the boy the twenty dollar bill that Carl had left for her. As the boy shoved his hand in his pants pocket for the woman's change, Maggie slipped a hand between the boy's legs and then gave him a good squeeze. The boy just stood there, breathless, frozen in place staring at Maggie's bare breasts. She squeezed the boy a little harder as she reached around him to lock the door's deadbolt with her other hand. Maggie knew that Carl hadn't taken the room key with him so there was no chance that she'd be caught red-handed with the boy. She figured that Carl was down in the lounge flirting with a stray whore. Two of them had been eyeing her man all night long and it seemed to her that Carl had noticed. What's good for the goose is good for the gander she reckoned. The room service boy serviced her just fine. He fucked her like a happy puppy for five wonderful minutes and was still long and hard when Maggie zipped him back up. She thought about going another round with the throbbing boy but figured she shouldn't press her luck with Carl. She imagined Carl getting a second key from the front desk and walking in on the two of them. Then she imagined Carl joining them. She hadn't had *that* kind of fun in over a year but remembered it like it was yesterday;

two brothers no less, some crazy shit that was.

"Well, thanks for the big tip!" she told the boy laughing and then added, "I should be the one tipping you!"

"Oh, you tipped me just fine, ma'am," the boy said as he stood at the door staring past Maggie's dark mascara and into her sparkling, experienced eyes. "Let me know if you need anything else, ma'am," the boy suggested to which Maggie replied, "You know… I just might do that. Who should I ask for?"

The boy pointed to the nametag pinned to his shirt and recited his name, "Robert Johnson."

Maggie laughed hysterically but then finally calmed down enough to say, "Silly me, Bobby! I ain't usually this drunk you know."

"Yes, ma'am," Robbie said and then he said goodnight as he closed the door behind himself. Maggie flipped the deadbolt and then wandered over to the window, still giggling to herself. She bent over the table and peaked out through the smoke-stained curtains. She watched as two, silent squad cars; their red and blue lights flashing and spinning, sped into the Bluebird's parking lot next door.

Carl heard men shouting and then gunshots. A girl shrieked screams from a car nearby. He held his weapon at the ready and sidestepped in a wide arc behind parked cars toward the back of the tractor trailer. The truck's tailgates were swung-open blocking most of his view but he could see two more bodies lying on the ground beneath them. Carl approached closer and shouted, "Police Officer; Drop Your Weapon!"

As he circled further back behind the rig, Carl noticed the dark silhouette of a man standing high above him inside the trailer. Red and blue lights flashed as two squad cars pulled up; one on each side of the rig. Four deputies jumped out of their cars and drew weapons on the rig as they crouched behind their opened doors. Carl raised his shiny badge toward the headlights of the squad car on his side of the truck. The deputy nearest to Carl shouted, "Police Officer!" to his partner across the front seat of the squad car. Carl's head exploded from the impact of a single shot. The deputies cringed as they watched him sail backwards and then slam to the pavement like a ragdoll. Jimmy jumped out of the back of the trailer breaking his left foot as he landed. He dragged himself and a duffle bag toward his car. The deputies who had witnessed the shooting emptied their weapons into him. The night air went silent. Tiffany started screaming.

At first, Maggie thought she'd heard gunshots outside, but then decided that it must have been the TV from the room next door. She considered getting off of her nice big bed to peek out the window just to be sure but then thought better of it. It had taken her five minutes to get comfortably propped-up on her stack of pillows and she wasn't about to mess that up. So she dipped another cheese stick into her marinara sauce and took a bite as the HBO movie she'd been watching suddenly turned violent. Her lobster tail at dinner that night had been delicious, although the steak was a bit tough for her liking. No matter how much she may have eaten beforehand, Maggie always worked up an insatiable appetite when she was out drinking and dancing and fucking. She was no cheap date by any stretch of the imagination but in her opinion; she was well worth it. Most of her lovers and two of her three ex-husbands held the same opinion of her.

When the police sirens began wailing, Maggie would have gone to the window had somebody not knocked on her door.

"Bobby!" she shrieked when she opened the door.

"Just checking to see if everything's to your satisfaction, ma'am," Robbie announced.

Maggie popped the end of her cheese stick into the boy's mouth and then pulled him inside her room for another quickie. Robbie came quickly and came back to Maggie's room a third time a few hours later after his shift was over. He had always wondered what actual sex would be like and having experienced it for the first time earlier that evening, he found himself wanting it even more. Even though the woman had eventually passed out on top of him, Maggie turned out to be an ideal and convenient source of fledgling sex for the boy.

As a new day was dawning, Robbie snuck out of Maggie's room quietly so as not to wake her. He chose to use the inn's discreet back stairwell and he did so, bowlegged and smiling, praying that the dayshift manager wouldn't catch him leaving the building six hours after his shift had ended. While his recently-purchased used car sat warming up in the morning chill, its radio reported the dreadful local news events of the night before; events that had occurred right next door. As the details of the blood-bath unfolded, Robbie was shocked when he realized just how close he was to it all. For him, it made that night all the more unforgettable.

Minutes after she had paid the taxi cab driver who'd driven her home from the Rain Tree Inn that morning, the phone on Maggie's wall rang; it was the county sheriff's office. They were phoning Maggie to come pick up her daughter.

"Oh my God, I'll be right there!" Maggie yelled into the phone.

Maggie missed her mark hanging up the receiver; it swung by its cord and slammed against the wall. Maggie snatched her car keys from the hook by the door and stormed out of the house. She turned her crappy car's ignition and pumped the gas pedal. "Shit!" she yelled. She tried starting the car three more times pounding the top of the steering wheel before the damn thing finally started. She drove through the fog of a mind-numbing hangover as her thoughts raced along the highway. She ran into the police station ripping the seam of her dress in the process. Tiffany jumped off a metal chair and into her mother's outstretched arms. The two of them broke down crying as a female deputy looked on. Moments later, the deputy took the pair aside and into an empty office to explain things to Maggie.

As the events and details of the night before slowly unfolded and came to light and then dawned on her, Maggie began to shake. She realized with sudden horror that the man she had known as Carl Mason was in fact; Sheriff Carl Montgomery. Carl hadn't left her in the room and run off with some two-bit whore after all. Carl was dead. Carl was shot dead. Maggie began to shake even harder. The deputy noticed Maggie's anxious state and asked her quietly, "Are you alright, ma'am?"

Maggie wasn't alright. She didn't know what to think of Carl and his fate and her involvement with him but she was certain of one thing; those things mattered little compared to the fact that her baby girl could have been killed! Maggie's blood boiled when the deputy had mention Jimmy's name.

That son of a bitch! Maggie thought. *I hope he burns in hell!*

Maggie's anger turned suddenly then into fear. She became terrified. *What was to become of her daughter? Would Tiffany have to stand trial? Was her sweet baby girl headed to prison? Dear God in heaven!* she thought and then she began to shake almost uncontrollably.

The deputy repeated her question a little louder; "Ma'am, are you alright?"

"I could use a glass of water," Maggie said abruptly as she broke through the dark fog swirling in her head.

The deputy stood up and walked out of the office leaving Maggie alone with Tiffany.

"Tiffany... did you *know* what Jimmy was up to?"

"No, Momma, I swear. That's why they're lettin' me go. I've been up all night tellin' the deputies and detectives and some lawyer they drug in here in the middle of the night everything I know about Jimmy; everything 'cept the gun that is."

"You *knew* that Jimmy had a gun?" Maggie whispered.

"Yes, Momma, he showed it to me last night before we left but I had no idea he was plannin' on usin' it like that. He said we was just goin' for a ride is all."

"Well you did right, child, just hush up about the gun you hear me?"

"I know, Momma, I'm not stupid."

"I never said you were, sweetheart, I just don't know what I'd do if you got into serious trouble. No... that ain't right, I *do* know what I'd do; I'd go surefire shit crazy I would," Maggie said and then she leaned over and wrapped her arms around her daughter. Maggie imagined her beautiful daughter in handcuffs and leg-irons dressed in one of those hideous orange jumpsuits as she stood for sentencing before a misogynistic judge. The thought terrified Maggie. She began to shake again. The alcohol and pep-pills still coursing through her veins didn't help matters any. When the deputy returned and handed her a bottle of water, Maggie calmed down.

Maggie learned that Carl was married when the deputy mentioned that he'd left a widow. Maggie's fragile state of mind began to crack; the thought of Carl having a wife at home while she was out dining and dancing and fucking him suddenly sickened her.

"We're still waiting on the county prosecutor to sign off on the paperwork. After he does though, you can take your daughter home, Miss Taylor," the deputy explained to Maggie. "Feel free to wait here, or in the hall, or get some fresh air if you'd like. I know that you've *both* been through a great deal as have we *all* here; losing one of our own last night, so please, just try to relax. It shouldn't be much longer."

"Thanks so much, you're a dear," Maggie told the deputy. "If it's okay with you, we'll just sit tight right here."

Maggie drank long sips of water in an attempt to rehydrate herself but the water just seemed to stir things up inside her as she became partially drunk again. She was grateful to almighty God in heaven above that Tiffany would be alright. Nothing else really mattered.

Maggie hadn't told Tiffany that the man she had a date with that night was a cop; the very same cop who'd been shot and killed by her daughter's boyfriend. It was looking as though Maggie's affair with Carl might not come to light. Because Carl had paid for their room in cash and had signed his name Carl Mason, Maggie would be able to keep certain facts a secret from the authorities and more importantly; keep them a secret from her daughter. Not only did Maggie *know* Sheriff Carl Montgomery, a.k.a. Carl Mason, she was on an elicit date with the man the night he was shot and killed. Maggie shuddered at the thought of Tiffany and Carl's widow and the whole wide world knowing what she had done. She began to wonder if she'd become bad-luck to cheating husbands. She thought that maybe that two-timing, son-of-a-bitch Carl had it coming to him but then quickly and regrettably realized what a horrible person she was to even consider it. Maggie felt pity for man's widow but was grateful that she wouldn't have to cause the woman any more pain by confessing that her husband had died an adulterer. At least the poor widow would be set for life with Carl's death-in-the-line-of-duty pension. Maggie wondered just how much that would amount to.

"Is that the woman he was with?" the station commander asked as he watched Maggie and Tiffany walk away down the corridor and then out through the station's glass doors.

"Yes, captain," the female deputy replied.

"Can't say that I blame him. I wouldn't mind taggin' that myself," he said and then he slapped the deputy's ass adding, "Keep up the good work, McCormick. I just might put you in for a promotion."

The narcotics aspect of the case was turned over to the Feds. Thanks to the bloody results of the botched robbery attempt and the subsequent deaths of everyone involved, the county prosecutor's case was open-and-shut. There would be no time-consuming loose ends cutting into anyone's weekend golf game. All parties concerned felt no need to make public the indiscretions of the fallen sheriff. His fine reputation and that of their neighboring county would remain untarnished. As far as the local newspapers were concerned, Sheriff Carl Montgomery had died a hero. Carl's widow would not be suffering the embarrassment of his recent activities and his apparent widespread penchant for loose women throughout the area. After all, "Men have needs and men find ways to fill them," was the prevailing opinion of the officials who'd gathered in the county attorney's office; an opinion that would later be shared by other officers of the law gathered around squad room water coolers.

Maggie had believed for quite some time that she had men all figured out. She felt ashamed when she realized that she hadn't. She'd been played. She had spread her legs for married men before but she had always known that they were married going in. Carl had slipped through the cracks though, and Maggie's dream of a life with the man had ended up; a horrible nightmare. She realized then that she was just as gullible as her daughter was.

Tiffany realized for the first time and finally admitted to herself that her mother had men all figured out. She imagined that when she reached her mother's age that she too, would have them all figured out. Her momma sure was right about Jimmy; he turned out to be a bad seed after all. Tiffany wondered if she would miss him much. She hadn't so far. She had a young deputy on her mind that morning. He looked mighty fine in his starched black uniform and treated her awful nice the night before. She thought that he might be the kind of man she could actually fall in love with someday; if she hadn't done so already. She was sure that he would treat her a hell of lot better than Jimmy had. She planned on calling the deputy later that week to thank him again for his kindness. It excited her to think how nice it would be to show him just how grateful she really was. She realized then that most law men wouldn't be stupid enough to mess around with a high school girl, but what was the harm in trying? He just might surprise her.

Not having slept in over twenty-four hours, Tiffany fell asleep on the long ride home from the police station. Having been mostly drunk for the past twelve hours and having only slept a few hours during that time, Maggie was exhausted as well. She stayed awake at the wheel by trying to remember the name of that room service boy at the Rain Tree Inn.

Tiffany didn't go to Jimmy's funeral. Maggie had left it up to her daughter but in the end, Tiffany had decided against it. They both felt it best to begin forgetting that any of it had happened. Tiffany thanked God that Jimmy hadn't knocked her up again that summer. She couldn't imagine explaining to a child that its father had shot and killed a deputy and two fellow criminals before he himself had been shot dead.

As summer ended, Maggie got real busy at the hair salon with all of the back-to-school haircuts and crazy hi-lights the girls were into. The tips were good so she was able to let Tiffany pick up a few more new outfits for school. That made Maggie real happy; probably happier than it had made her daughter.

Maggie was right about Tiffany's return to school; the boys went wild over her recently developed figure. Boys who'd never even given her a second glance before were tripping over one another to get a better look at her. Tiffany took a shine to one of the few boys who wasn't constantly gawking at her chest. She'd known him casually during her sophomore and junior years but he had, in some subtle way, suddenly grown up over the summer. To Tiffany, he seemed like a man among boys at the school.

"Sorry 'bout what happened, Tiffany. I can't imagine how hard it must have been for you and your family," the young man told her between classes.

"Aw... thank you kindly but I'm okay now, really I am. How was your summer?"

"I spent the whole summer working room service up at the Rain Tree Inn. That might not sound like much fun but at least I was able to save up enough money to buy myself a car. It's not much to look at but it runs real good. Do you... do you think that maybe you'd like to go for a ride sometime?"

"Are you asking me out?" Tiffany asked, deliberately putting the poor boy on the spot in a test of his courage and sincerity.

"Well, I suppose I am. But it's okay if you say, no, because... because I know how popular you are and all. I was just hoping that maybe..."

"I'd *love* to go out with you!" she said, touching his wrist as the tardy bell rang and the hallway all but emptied and suddenly grew quiet.

"Well, I'm hearing bells so that must be a good sign!" the boy announced with a smile.

"Ha-ha! That's funny! You've always been able to make me laugh, Robbie. I like that in a man, especially now. I could really use some cheering up these days. And after what I've put my poor momma through... it sure would make her happy to see me dating a nice boy like *you* for a change."

Tijuana Taxi - el Diablo

On the southern side of the Mexican-American border, in the bustling San Ysidro Land Port of Entry in Tijuana, Mexico, he hailed a Tijuana taxi. The taxi was a dark green, chrome trimmed, 1967 four-door, 289 two-barrel V8, Ford Fairlane 500 with vertical pairs of headlights and a wide, grinning chrome grill. When the taxi driver pulled up to the curb, he too was grinning. His bright white smile stretched from ear to ear. The noonday sun sparkled on his single gold tooth. The passenger opened the taxi's rear door and tossed his suitcase onto the torn, tan-colored, vinyl backseat. He closed the door and then reached for the front door handle but as he did so, the driver pulled away suddenly in a swirling cloud of Tijuana dust. The would-be passenger watched dumbfounded as the taxi's fuzzy dice swung back and forth in the hot dry breeze.

He hailed another Tijuana taxi. It was a cherry-red, 1969 four-door hardtop, 350 Turbo Fire V8, fourth-generation Chevy Impala with horizontal pairs of headlights and a wide, grinning chrome grill. When the taxi driver pulled up to the curb, he too was grinning. His bright white smile stretched from ear to ear. The noonday sun sparkled on his single gold tooth. The passenger opened the taxi's rear door and was about to toss his briefcase onto the shiny, black vinyl backseat when he thought better of it. He closed the door and pulled on the front door handle as the driver leaned over and said, "Buenos dias! Welcome to Tijuana!"

"Buenos dias," the passenger replied as he bent his tall frame forward to sit shotgun in the taxi. He sighed as he leaned back against the brightly colored serape that stretched across the bench seat. He laid his large hands to rest atop the leather briefcase on his lap. The driver noticed a fine gold ring on the man's finger when he asked him, "Where to, señor?"

The passenger replied, "Plaza Monumental Bullring by the Sea, por favor."

"Bueno, señor, I know it well," the driver acknowledged with a smile as he turned blindly into traffic amidst a chorus of angry honking horns. The taxi accelerated and changed lanes abruptly, swerving left and then right and then back again as it weaved its way through the heavy traffic. It passed filled-to-capacity city busses and over-filled rundown delivery trucks that belched choking black clouds of carbon monoxide from their red-hot tailpipes. The driver turned toward his passenger, who was decked out in a black pinstriped Armani suit, and asked him, "Are you a matador, señor?"

Although the passenger did *resemble* a matador, the driver didn't actually believe that the Italian gringo actually was a bullfighter, but he asked the question nevertheless.

"No," the passenger replied with a laugh. "I am not nearly that brave. I am an attorney. I'm visiting your fair city today in order to facilitate a bit of bullfighting arbitration."

"I see," said the driver, not having a clue as to what the man was implying. The driver looked away from the attorney and back toward the road when he yelled, "Aye Carumba!" and slammed on his brakes. The men lurched forward as the car's brakes locked up and squealed the taxi to a stop mere inches away from the rear bumper of an old Datsun sedan that had suddenly stopped in front of them. The traffic ahead of the Datsun had come to a complete standstill. The taxi driver pounded the top of his steering wheel in disgust.

"So sorry, señor, are you okay?" the driver asked humbly.

"I'm fine, no problem," the attorney reassured the driver adding, "It happens to the best of us. It happens to me a lot; while I'm checking my phone or reviewing case files or while I'm sneaking a quick peak at my wife's beautiful cleavage."

"So... you won't be suing me then?" the driver asked with a nervous chuckle.

"Well that depends..." the attorney said, rubbing the back of his neck as if he were a recent victim of whiplash, "how much are you worth?"

The driver became concerned. The two men stared at one another as the taxi sat idle. A tiny dashboard fan blew hot air across their faces. The attorney's stone cold stare slowly surrendered to a subtle smile. The anxious driver relaxed a bit in cautious response. The attorney finally grinned and then laughed out loud. The driver followed suit and clapped his hands in joy. "Bueno, señor! Muy bueno!" he laughed.

The taxi inched its way forward along with the traffic and then slowed down again before coming to yet another dead stop. Suddenly, the passenger told the driver, "I'll be right back," before he jumped out of the taxi leaving his briefcase on the seat. The driver watched as the passenger approached a taxi in the adjacent lane two car lengths ahead of them; it was a dark green Impala. Through the open driver's side window and without warning, the passenger sucker-punched the driver. The assailant's heavy gold ring tore a gash and drew blood. The driver keeled over unconscious across his front seat. The attorney opened the rear door of the taxi and grabbed his suitcase off its backseat. He slammed the door shut and then returned casually to his ride where he tossed his suitcase on the backseat and retook his seat up front.

"Muy bueno, señor!" the taxi driver applauded, having

witnessed the entire scene. He smiled broadly, a sunbeam glimmering on his bright gold tooth. "You are a super-hero, señor!" the driver proclaimed. "Do you have a secret, super-hero cape under that fine attorney suit?" he asked.

"No," the attorney laughed, relieved that he had retrieved his fresh change of clothes and his grey Armani suit. "I did a bit of boxing in the Navy and have refused to put up with any crap ever since."

"Good for you, señor! There is *too much crap* these days. We need *less crap* and more attorneys like *you*, señor. My own attorney weighs two hundred kilos. He couldn't swat a fly if it was stuck in his flan," the driver complained, "and he wears cheap suits, señor, not like yours."

"Do you use him often?" the attorney inquired.

"Only twice so far, señor; both times in our corrupt traffic court. They hit us taxi drivers pretty hard and as often as they can, señor. The judge was after a bribe the first time. I was cited for speeding. I had to pay a three hundred peso fine and a two hundred peso bribe. Five hundred pesos for ten kilometers over the limit, señor. My lawyer claimed it would have been twice that much if he hadn't negotiated on my behalf. Who knows? My lawyer probably shared the bribe with the judge. The second time, I accidentally bumped into a mounted police horse. Or, I should say; a police horse accidentally bumped into *me*. That big clumsy horse knee dented my rear door on the passenger side. Maybe you noticed it when you got in, señor."

"No, I didn't happen to notice," the attorney said.

"I'll show it to you later, señor. Anyway, the judge didn't see things my way, but that was no surprise to me. He didn't believe me when I told him that the mounted officer wasn't paying attention; he was cantering his horse sideways, looking the other way, flirting with chiquitas on the sidewalk. He rode his stupid horse straight into my taxi! *That* court visit cost me a thousand pesos plus two hundred more to my lousy lawyer. I still can't afford to get that dent pounded out; too much crap, señor."

The attorney opened his briefcase and sorted through a stack of business cards. He chose one, added one of his own from another stack and then handed them both to the driver.

"If you ever need representation in the future, mi amigo, call this attorney in town here and tell him that I sent you. He's on the up-and-up and won't screw you around."

"Gracias, Señor... George... Rosetti," the driver said as he read aloud the name on his passenger's business card. "I will definitely call him, heaven forbid I need to."

The attorney looked up to his left past the fuzzy dice hanging from the rearview mirror. He read to himself the driver's name from the photo license that was strapped to the sun visor with rubber bands; "Jorge Rosetta."

"We Georges need to stick together, Jorge," the attorney suggested with a smile.

"And we Rosettis and Rosettas do too!" the driver said, smiling himself as he noticed the similarities of their names.

The two men shook hands and laughed. Suddenly, car horns blared loudly behind them as the traffic ahead began moving again. Slowly but steadily, the taxi inched along the wide, congested avenue.

"Do you happen to know the driver who made off with my suitcase, Jorge?"

"Sí, señor, I do."

"Please, Jorge, call me George."

"Sí, Señor George, unfortunately, I do know *of* him and see his car often. He is an unlicensed gypsy driver and a part time drug runner. He may also be worse but I cannot swear to that."

"Do you think he'll come after me?" George asked.

"No way, Jose," Jorge laughed. "He's a petty freelance criminal and a coward. If you were a little ol' señora he might find the courage."

"That's good to know. My enemy list is long enough."

"You have enemies, Señor George?"

"Most attorneys do, Jorge. It comes with the job. We deal with all sorts and some of them blame *us* for their so-called misfortunes. Too much crap and not enough people willing to take responsibility for their own actions."

"Most people are good at heart though," Jorge observed.

"Yes they are thank God, but those who aren't make it tough on the rest of us."

"And keep you in nice suits?" Jorge asked.

"Ha! Yes they do, amigo, yes indeed they do."

"You told me before but I did not understand, what is it you'll be doing at la corrida?"

"I'll be acting as a bullfight arbitrator. I hope to settle a dispute between my client, a bull known as el Diablo, and a bullfighter named Jesus Moreno who wishes to kill my client."

"Ah yes... Jesus Moreno. I know the name well and have seen him perform but did I hear you correctly, Señor George, you have a *bull* as a client?"

"I do indeed. I've been hired by an organization known as HETA, H.E.T.A., Humans for the Ethical Treatment of Animals. They've taken el Diablo under their wing so to speak. It is a symbolic adoption of sorts. They wish to spare him the usual fate of a fighting bull. They are trying to make a point and have chosen this particular bull with which to make it."

"Don't take this the wrong way, Señor George, but that sounds loco to me," Jorge confessed.

"As loco as it sounds, Jorge, it is nevertheless; true. I have a two thousand pound bull as a client and a client is a client so I will do my best to represent him. In this particular case, I hope to save his life because as you well know, el Diablo is facing a death sentence."

"Good luck with *that,* Señor George. I'd like to see how it turns out."

"Oh, but you *can,* my friend. There will be a public hearing tonight at la corrida before the fights begin. It is the opening act if you will. In fact, I have extra tickets to the festivities if you'd like to come see for yourself."

"I'd love to, señor! I take my family there, when I can afford to that is. I am sorry to say, George, but we Mexicans *love* bullfighting. It is in our blood you see."

"As well I know, my friend. HETA doesn't oppose the ceremonial aspects of bullfighting per se, but they adamantly oppose the killing of bulls for sport. They're trying to transform bullfighting into a more gracious and forgiving sport. More like a rodeo I imagine but to be honest, they oppose rodeos as well."

"Rodeos? What's wrong with rodeos? We have those too."

"The calves they rope are often badly injured, as are the horses they ride. HETA also opposes horse racing for reasons I'm sure you're aware of. Thoroughbreds are often doped and over-worked. They're destroyed when they're injured or when they no longer turn a profit. A few of the better horses are retired to stud but most are sold to dog food companies."

"Aye carumba! This HETA is trying to spoil all of our fun! I would like to attend this evening and cheer against them. But then again... my apologies, Señor George, I would be cheering against *you* I'm afraid."

"Do as you must, Jorge. I am in no position to argue with you. My arguments will be directed against the bullfighter himself. How many are in your family?"

"There is me and my wife Maria and my sons Paco and Pepe and my daughters Alba, Carmella, Lolita and little Elisa and my mother Maribel and my wife's father Señor Ricardo and my wife's mother Señora Paloma and our dear Uncle Adolfo... there are twelve of us all together."

"Wow what a family! I'll bet Christmas is a hoot in the Rosetta household."

"Every day is, George. I just wish I could spend more time with them. I drive this taxi twelve to fourteen hours a day and even longer during festivals. When I'm not driving I'm usually under the hood or under the carriage trying to keep her running. We're riding on her third engine. She has over four hundred thousand miles on her. I'm not sure how many kilometers that is but it must be six hundred thousand or so."

"That's incredible! I'd never imagine that this car had that many miles on it. You keep it in excellent shape, Jorge."

"This car was my father's car, rest his soul. He was a soldier in the Mexican army until he retired. He died three years after that, rest his soul. My great grandfather fought with the victorious Mexican Army at the Alamo. Unfortunately, rest his soul, he was killed a month later when the Texans got their revenge at the Battle of San Jacinto. Or, at least that is the story my Uncle Adolfo likes to tell. He tells it often and always as if *he* himself had fought in those battles. He likes to say,

We stormed the Alamo, or, *We held off the Texans*, meaning *we* the Mexicans but implying himself. Papa never mentioned the Alamo though. To be honest, he never talked about much of anything at all. He was a quiet man, a very good man but a very quiet man, rest his soul. Mi madre Maribel has always been the talker in our family. She forbid me to join the army when I was a young man. She said it was no way for a father to look after his family; being away from home. My father never opposed her. He remained silent on the subject altogether and silent about most other things as well. So here I sit my friend, telling you my life story and driving my father's car for a living."

"And you do both quite well, Jorge, but I do believe that you take after your dear mother, my friend," George said with a light-hearted chuckle.

"Es verdad, mi amigo, it is true, my friend," Jorge said heartedly. "I *do* like to talk, but I also like to listen."

As the taxi pulled up to the ornately sculptured façade of the Plaza Monumental's main gate, George looked through his briefcase and found his stack of tickets. He counted out a dozen and then added a few more. Jorge turned off the taxi's motor to allow it to cool down a bit in the sea breeze that was blowing across the stadium grounds. George handed Jorge the tickets along with a fifty dollar bill.

"Keep the change, mi amigo," he said, "and enjoy the show tonight. I'll be looking for you in the stands."

"Muchas gracias, Señor George! It is very generous of you. My family thanks you and I thank you as well. Let me help you with your suitcase."

"That won't be necessary, Jorge," George said as he got out of the taxi, grabbed his suitcase from the backseat and then closed the rear door. "That *is* one heck of a dent, Jorge," the attorney said, examining the car's damage. "How could you *possibly* hit a horse with the *side* of your car? Were you driving your car sideways, Jorge?"

"Of course not! You *can't* drive a car sideways," Jorge said as he walked around to the passenger side of his taxi.

"Did your attorney mention that in court?" George asked.

"No."

"Did the judge see the actual damage?"

"A tiny photograph as I recall," Jorge thought.

"You need a new attorney, my friend. The one you've been using should be disbarred."

"The one I've been using should be *behind* bars," Jorge said sadly but then the two men began laughing.

"I meant to ask you earlier, George, is there an H.E.T.H.?"

"H.E.T.H.?" George asked.

"Sí señor, H.E.T.H.; Humans for the Ethical Treatment of *Humans*," Jorge explained.

"That's a good question. I don't know of one offhand but there should be if there isn't. Hang on a second... I'll check my phone."

George pulled his cell phone from his shirt pocket and did a quick search. "Here it is, Jorge; H.E.T.H., Humans... for the Ethical Treatment of... Hippies. According to their website, they are a splinter group of HETA."

"*Hippies?*" Are you serious?" Jorge asked.

George turned his phone toward his friend to show him the photo of a police officer beating a hippie with a nightstick. "It's obviously a joke, Jorge... more crap in a crappy world."

"I think it's funny," Jorge said, laughing at the ridiculous photo. "Maybe we shouldn't take everything so seriously."

"You are right, my friend, besides, I have more important things to consider. I have a bull to defend!" George said and then realized for the first time, just how odd that sounded.

"Be careful with the devil, Señor George," Jorge warned.

"The devil?"

"Si, señor, the devil; el Diablo. El Diablo means; the devil."

"You know, Jorge, now that you mention it, you're right. I actually knew that but hadn't made the connection until just now. I am defending the devil."

"Well, maybe not *the* devil, but a devil nevertheless so *do* be careful por favor."

"Oh I *will be,* my friend. I'd be careful regardless of the bull's name. I hear they can be heartless at times."

"They are only heartless *after* the fight, when they're butchered. During the fight, they have the heart of a lion. Do not turn your back on el Diablo or you will kiss the sand and your life goodbye, señor."

"I'll definitely take your advice, Jorge," George promised.

The men shook hands and then hugged. George walked off toward the stadium gate. He showed the gate attendant his credentials and then waited for the man to unlock the gate.

"Good luck tonight, señor!" Jorge called out from his taxi.

George turned around toward Jorge, set his suitcase and briefcase down on the ground and then gave his friend a bullfighter's wave and a deep bow of gratitude.

After Jorge had left the plaza behind, he encountered a caravan of chartered busses approaching him. He counted: uno, dos, tres, quatro... *There must be a dozen of them,* he thought. As the last of the busses passed by, Jorge read aloud the words on the colorful banner plastered on its side; "HETA Olé!" For some reason, Jorge was reminded of the Alamo.

Jorge Rosetta drove his Impala slowly that late afternoon. With eleven passengers inside, the car was riding low to the ground. Jorge had propped the trunk open with a broom stick to prevent it from knocking his two sons and his eldest daughter in the head as they sat riding in the open-air trunk. Jorge's wife and mother sat with little Elisa between them on the front seat. Jorge's mother-in-law, father-in-law and Uncle Adolfo kept their eyes on Carmella and Lolita in the backseat as the two tiny girls stood between the grownups' knees on the floorboards, or jumped up on the adults' laps, or wiggled their way between them on the seat. The tiny girls were excited. They hopped around the car like Mexican jumping beans. Everyone in the car was excited that day. They were even happier than usual because that afternoon, thanks to Jorge's new American friend; Señor George Rosetti, they were all going to la corrida at the Plaza Monumental Bullring by the Sea - Aye Carumba!

Earlier that day, twelve chartered busses from across the U.S. rendezvoused in San Diego. From there, the HETA busses caravanned across the border into Tijuana. The rally and demonstration were eighteen months in the making. George Rosetti Esquire Attorney-in-fact was chosen to represent el Diablo; HETA's beloved, poster-child bull. El Diablo had been scouted in Mexico by a HETA infiltrator. The bull was first spotted in a picturesque, pastoral valley nestled between gently rolling hills and an oil refinery. When the HETA agent first spotted the bull, it was nibbling alfalfa peacefully when a beautiful butterfly landed on the bull's broad snout. Surely that was the sign the agent had been waiting for, and so it was; el Diablo was chosen to represent HETA's cause.

In an orderly yet enthusiastic manner, six hundred or so HETA members disembarked their air-conditioned busses for the stifling hot parking lot of the Plaza Monumental Bullring by the Sea. Their bright red t-shirts appeared even brighter in the blinding glare of the afternoon sun. The name "el Diablo" was splashed across the front of their shirts in bold black letters above a silk-screened portrait of the bull itself gently grazing in a peaceful pasture. On the backs of their shirts, "HETA Olé!" was printed in bright blue letters. The effect of the bright blue lettering on the bright red fabric was quite psychedelic and made some of the members dizzy. Generally speaking though, all of the members liked the shirts despite the fact (and much to their collective dismay) that the shirts had apparently been manufactured in a Chinese child-labor sweatshop. The organization reconciled that disturbing fact however, when it was assured by the manufacturer that no animals were harmed during the production of the shirts. The organization would also come to realize (much to everyone's horror) that the inferior red dye used in the Chinese-made shirts ran profusely when the shirts came into contact with warm, human sweat. As a result, streams of blood-colored dye dripped down the members' arms as they assembled in the hot sun outside the arena. That disturbing phenomenon made more than a few of the members violently ill.

George Rosetti was greeted in the administration office of the Plaza Monumental Bullring by the Sea by Oscar D. Larento; the facility's director and CEO of Bull Corp. which served as the marketing agency responsible for keeping the facility in the black.

"Nice Armani, George," Oscar said as the men shook hands.

"Nice Oscar de la Renta, Oscar," George replied.

"Muchas gracias, amigo. Sit... make yourself comfortable," Oscar suggested with a wave of his hand.

As he took a seat behind his mammoth, highly-polished, antique mahogany desk, Oscar pressed the intercom button on his phone. "Esmeralda my dear, tequila por favor," he requested and then he turned toward his guest. "You know, George," Oscar said as he ran his hand along its rich surface, "this desk was confiscated from the Alamo."

"I know now," George said and then he opened his briefcase and handed his business associate a manila folder made in the Philippines. "It's a beauty," George said of the desk as the stunningly beautiful, mahogany-complexioned, Esmeralda entered the office with a bottle of tequila and three, gold-rimmed shot glasses on a sliver tray.

The trio toasted, "Salud!" as they raised their glasses, at first into the air, and then to their lips. Esmeralda smiled lovingly at her boss and at George as well before she left the office, her shapely hips swaying.

"I was surprised to see a new girl at your front desk, Oscar. What happened to Lucinda?"

"Unfortunately, Lucinda was deported. As it turned out, she was an illegal from the Sates."

"That *is* unfortunate. She was a goddess," George recalled.

"Do not mourn her, my friend. She is gainfully employed in the States as a Las Vegas showgirl while she awaits approval of her Mexican immigration papers. I myself anxiously await her return and entertain Esmeralda in the meantime."

"If Lucinda should happen to require legal advice in the States, do not hesitate to call me," George offered.

"Thank you, my friend," Oscar said as he poured two more shots which the men then gulped down con mucho gusto.

While Oscar thumbed through the file he'd been handed, George reported to him that the Plaza Monumental Bullring by the Sea could expect twelve, full busloads of additional paying customers that afternoon and right on cue, he and Oscar heard the rumble of the busses as they pulled into the arena's grounds. The men rose from their seats and walked to a majestic bank of tall, lead-lined windows to witness the event for themselves. As George and Oscar watched, streams of passengers in bright red t-shirts filed out of the busses. Oscar put his arm around George's shoulder and said, "Muy bueno, mi amigo, muy bueno."

Oscar unlocked his desk drawer and then reached into it. He removed a thick envelope of greenbacks which he handed to George.

"We put word out on the street that the HETA busses were coming, my friend. We expect a sell-out crowd this afternoon and renewed interest and increased revenue in the weeks to come," Oscar reported with a sparkling white smile.

In the packed stands of the Plaza Monumental Bullring by the Sea, amidst a chorus of mariachi musicians, thousands of fans who had been cheering the procession of heroic bullfighters into the arena, suddenly and vehemently began booing the appearance of the HETA contingent. A proud line of matadors and banderilleros on foot and picadors on horseback faced the foreign invaders who had come that day to challenge their age-old traditions.

"There he is...!" Jorge announced excitedly to his wife.

In the center of the wide sweeping circle of blood-stained sand, six hundred and sixteen HETA members gathered around George Rosetti Esquire in a show of solidarity.

"We should invite Señor Rosetti to dinner, Jorge; to show our appreciation," his wife suggested as loudly as she could.

"¡Qué buena idea! Voy a hacer eso, Maria," Jorge shouted, agreeing and promising to do so.

The HETA spokesman and his attorney stepped forward toward the lead matador. The three men faced one another at attention. A young boy ran up and handed the spokesman a wireless-microphone. George Rosetti Esquire handed the lead matador, Jesus Moreno, a cease and desist order and then rejoined the HETA members. The matador read the document to himself in the bright afternoon sun. As the words sunk in, the matador's blood began to boil. A Spanish-language version of the document was projected on the arena's video screen. The crowd in the stands read along with the matador. In English, the document read:

We, respectful members of H.E.T.A. U.S.A., do hereby adopt the bull known as "el Diablo," as our own. In so doing, we compel this facility to show him mercy and spare his life. We request that el Diablo be immediately released into our custody so that we may give him a good and proper home. We further compel this facility and everyone associated with its cruel practices, to treat all of the other bulls in your custody, humanely. Thank you very much, muchas gracias.

The lead matador tore the document to pieces and then threw them into the air. The scraps fluttered on the hot breeze as they fell to the ground. Using the sole of his leather boot, the matador crushed the shredded document into the sand at his feet. The crowd in the stands erupted in wild jubilation. The matador stood at proud attention amidst the roaring applause. He removed the montera from his head, waved it high into the air and then took a deep bow. The crowd went loco. The matador pivoted sharply on one foot and then strode back proudly to rejoin his fellow toreros who filed in behind him as they left the ring in protest. The crowd stomped their feet and cheered wildly. The arena's stands shook and rattled with a deafening roar.

"Ladies and gentlemen..." the HETA spokesmen announced loudly through the crackling public address system, "...bulls are people *too* you know."

The arena's P.A. announcer, situated far above the ring in the reporter's booth, paraphrased the spokesman's English for the crowd in Spanish; "Ladies and gentlemen... I am obviously crazy!" to which the crowd roared.

"And, my friends... just to prove that bulls are not the vicious creatures that so many of you make them out to be..." the HETA spokesman continued, "...we will release el Diablo now to prove our point."

The announcer repeated the spokesman's statement in Spanish and then added, "This gringo obviously has a death-wish, my friends!" to which the crowd roared even louder.

Amidst a loud burst of applause from the stands, el Diablo was released from his pen. With an immediate burst of energy, the bull charged into the center of the ring and then stood there defiantly. Weighing well over two thousand pounds, el Diablo was an impressive specimen. His powerful muscles twitched in anticipation as the sweat on his jet black hide glistened in the white hot sun. The HETA spokesman instructed his fellow members quietly. The entire contingent approached the bull slowly, encircling it. Recalling Jorge's advice, George Rosetti slipped out of the back of the pack and hid safely behind a wooden barricade. El Diablo spun around in his tracks as he contemplated the rolling sea of red shirts surrounding him. The HETA members joined their anxious hands in solidarity.

"Do not be afraid," the spokesman whispered into his microphone as he left his supporters to approach the bull closer. The arena crowd suddenly fell silent as they held their collective breaths.

Up in the stands, little Elisa, who was sitting on her father's lap asked him, "Papa, what is that man doing?"

"He is doing something very dangerous," Jorge explained to his daughter, not quite believing the sheer stupidity he was witnessing.

As the spokesman slowly approached el Diablo, the bull stared into the man's belly and saw red. Much to the horror of everyone present, the spokesman suddenly tripped in the sand. His arms went flailing as he flew through the air toward the agitated bull. El Diablo charged the waving red torso. The bull's horns cradled the spokesman's midsection and then tossed the man like a ragdoll high into the air. The terrified spokesman screamed into the microphone he clutched in his hands. The crowd gasped. Jorge covered little Elisa's eyes. The spokesman's blood-curdling screams rang out as he hit the ground hard. The HETA members scattered in panic. El Diablo charged into the sea of red. One after another, the fleeing members were sent sailing high into the air and then tumbling hard to the ground. El Diablo's hooves broke arms and legs and cracked ribs as the bull continued its rampage.

The lead matador shouted instructions to his fellow toreros. They charged en masse into the ring in an attempt to subdue the bull as it continued tossing and goring a growing number of victims. Scores of brave fans joined in on the rescue. They poured over the gates and into the ring. El Diablo charged through the red shirts surrounding him. He lashed out at the toreros as they came up to confront him. With a sweep of its great horns, the bull tossed a matador aside and then charged toward the far gate. As el Diablo approached the arena's outer wall, he flexed his powerful hind quarters, kicked hard and then sailed over the top of the barrier knocking it to splinters. The spectators in the stands were on their feet. They watched in amazement as el Diablo charged through the rows of parked cars and then disappeared into the dry desert brush beyond.

Later that evening, as George puffed on a fine Cuban cigar in the courtyard of Jorge's modest, yet comfortable and impeccable home, his friend came outside to join him.

"Did you enjoy your pepper-steak?" Jorge asked.

"I did indeed, mi amigo. Gracias," George said as he took an ice-cold bottle of cerveza from his friend's cordial hand.

"I am sorry that you lost your case, Señor Rosetti," Jorge offered in condolence.

"Well, I may have lost *that* case, Jorge, but I've added quite a few clients; hospital patients who'll be suing HETA for reckless endangerment. I might buy another vacation condo with my cut of their pain and suffering. My immediate hope however, is that my clients are resting comfortably in your fair city's hospital. That melee kept the E.R. busy for hours and filled an entire wing of patient beds. It was an absolute miracle that no one was killed," George remarked.

"El Diablo showed mercy this day," Jorge said solemnly.

The men clinked their bottles together.

Later that night, half-empty HETA busses headed back to San Diego. Along a dark stretch of desolate highway, for just a brief instant, el Diablo's eyes glowed hell-fire-red before the lead bus hit him head-on. El Diablo was killed instantly. There were no fatalities in the over-turned bus.

The next day, the English-translation of the Tijuana Time's headline read; "HETA Bus Destroys el Diablo and Vice Versa." The subtitle read; "Defeated Gringos Return Home." Ironically (or deliberately) the advertisement immediately below the newspaper's lead story was sponsored by the Alamo Car Rental Corporation of Guadalajara, Mexico. The ad's banner read in tribute; "Viva el Diablo - Viva la Corrida!

- Fin -

Author's Note:
Bulls are in fact, color blind.
It is the motion of the matador's cape
or a blatant act of foolishness that antagonizes them.

Two Days Before Tomorrow

My little wood framed house shook gingerly on its block foundation with every blast of thunder those July lightning bolts sent our way in a crackling bath of platinum white light that bounced around my tiny kitchen the windows of which were slid wide open to the welcome gusts of cool wind the approaching storm offered as fair warning of the fury to follow. I cranked open the handle of my faithful forty year old refrigerator which had demanded nothing more than an eight dollar relay over the course of the nine months I'd owned her during which time she'd kept my beer three degrees above freezing a bottle of which sat sweating and dripping on the black and white checkered chromed rimmed linoleum kitchen table top before me. I snapped the beer bottle open with a church key and watched the cap sail and then hit and bounce "tic-tic-tic" rolling across the table and then jumping over its edge onto the floor escaping straight out the back door which had been blown open by a huge gust of wind that sent my threadbare kitchen curtains into a brief fluttering horizontal dance. A lightning bolt exploded. The room lit up in a brilliant blue flash before it went totally dark. The kitchen window and walls and every glass, dish and bowl in its cupboards rattled from the aftershock and then; dead calm silence. Even the crickets had stopped chirping their annoyingly soothing chorus. I sat motionless for a moment but then raised the beer bottle to my lips; the bottle's glass mouth knocking lightly against my front teeth as my eyes adjusted to the darkness while a soothing stream of ice cold beer poured down my grateful throat. I would have enjoyed that swig of beer immensely as usual had I not then realized that I was sitting in a darkness so totally enveloping that I couldn't see the bottle in my hand or my hand or even the end of my nose or any reflection or suggestion of light whatsoever. It was with eyes wide open that I witnessed an all-consuming incredibly inky black darkness the likes of which could only be experienced deep in the bowels of a subterranean cave or a thousand feet below the ocean's surface. I didn't feel frightened or disturbed or threatened at all by the darkness but I was however, somewhat vulnerably curious as to where all of the light (and for that matter; the sound) had suddenly gone. I negotiated another lazy sip of beer when suddenly, the sound of the bottle cap came bouncing back in front of me skipping across the tabletop and then onto the floor opposite the door from which it came and from which then came the sounds of slow and heavy, deliberate footsteps crossing my back porch. Someone or something stepped up into my kitchen and then stopped silent and unseen mere feet away from me. I skipped over feelings of fear and confusion while preparing to jump into immediate action but for the life of me, remained undecided as to what exactly, I should do; run blindly toward the intruder, run blindly into a wall, call out, "Who is it, what do you want?" Or should I hurl a half-full or half-empty beer bottle as hard as I can straight between the eyes of the soon-to-be unconscious intruder? Which I did. The sound of a heavy glass beer bottle hitting the skull of a man on the bridge of his nose is unmistakable. The sound of a man so struck, grunting stunned and then slumping to his knees and falling forward flat on his face would be sure to follow. The adrenalin rush of having miraculously hurled the perfect life-saving throw in total darkness would surely be followed by the prolonged sound of a slow, sigh of relief. Unfortunately, the sound that I actually witnessed was that of an air-born bottle whistling inches past its intended target and flying straight out the back door bouncing hard once on the wooden porch planks and then again as it rustled to rest in the thick, un-pruned bushes surrounding my porch. The silence that followed my failed attempt at self-preservation was immediately broken by the bizarre and disturbing laughter of an unseen intruder.

When it comes to the pursuit of the fairer sex, I wouldn't exactly call myself apathetic; lackadaisical would probably be more accurate. I've rarely been the aggressive type whenever an unfamiliar woman sparked familiar feelings in me. During such chance encounters, my approach was most often, in effect; to take no approach at all. I'd simply lounge in standby mode, waiting for something to happen, taking no active role in its potential realization. I'd do so, not out of fear of rejection but because of the aforementioned lethargic nature of my dating skills, or lack thereof. As a result, my advances were rarely rejected because they were so few and far between. And so it was that by default, I spent most of my free time alone.

I'd always worked wherever, whenever and as many hours as possible. During downtime I'd hike foothill paths or along rivers and streams, most of the time solo. I'd always managed to make a few good friends at work; buddies with whom to drink beers with, or watch a game with, or throw back fish with, or gaze upon women with. For the most part though, I went about my life in the company of me. I may have often been alone but I was rarely lonely because over the years I'd become accustomed to entertaining myself. I'd often treat myself to a solo night out; a few drinks at a tavern, a movie and a decent meal (the opposite order of which usually resulted in a full-belly, seven-dollar nap through an un-watched film). After those nights out alone, I'd take myself home without having to deal with those awkward, first-date "goodnight" moments when an actual dating partner was involved; encounters that might occasionally provide temporary satisfaction but would rarely develop into a lasting relationship or a life-long friendship. I often wondered if those who were constantly engaged in the dating scene considered their brief, satisfying encounters as adequate compensation for the numerous disappointments they must endure. To me, "getting lucky" meant meeting an interesting woman with whom I could engage, not merely meeting her reproductive organs. As a result, I rarely got lucky but on one, single, perfectly balmy evening in July, I got lucky twice. The seeds of that luck were planted when, after my solo dining experience had ended, I handed my bill to an adorably cute cashier stationed near the diner's front window.

I had never set foot on that side of town before but I wasn't sure why I hadn't having been a local resident for nearly a year by then. That side of town was separated from the main business district by the deep and muddy Alcorn River from which barges off-loaded goods onto the railroad cars of WAR; the Western American Railroad the tracks of which hugged the far bank of the river. Most of that cargo was rough timber or sawn lumber, some of which I had a personally handled. I had traversed the rusty iron bridge over the Alcorn River many times before but had never bothered to stop on the far bank to look around. I worked enough as it was and all that

that side of the river seemed to offer was more of the same. One night in July however, while driving over the bridge, I happened to notice, through a row of bland and weathered dockside warehouse buildings, the bright red glow of a neon sign. The sign read *"DIN R"* and I thought to myself then that a diner would be the perfect place to fill my empty belly. As it turned out, I was right because it was. Thirty minutes and two pounds of delicious meatloaf, mashed potatoes and sweet corn later, I was handing Lisa Lou Stanton (according to the nametag pinned to her starched white blouse) my check and a ten dollar bill with one hand while I spun a toothpick out of its chrome dispenser with my other.

"Was everything satisfactory?" she asked me with home-town charm and an irresistible, makeup-free smile.

"It was indeed," I replied. "I'll definitely be back."

"I do *hope* so," she offered. "I'd love to, I mean... we would love to see you again real soon," she said, her reddening cheeks failing to conceal her innocent embarrassment.

"Well... I'd love to see *you* again too," I offered quietly, "and I do mean *you*," I said with a wink.

Her eyes darted quickly to her left and then over my right shoulder. She leaned forward slightly and whispered, "So, it's a date then?"

I leaned forward myself and then whispered, "I hope so."

I snatched a "Lou's Diner" business card from its cradle and then handed it to the young woman while asking her for her home phone number. "Wouldn't want you to get in trouble taking personal calls at work," I explained in hushed tones.

She slid a pencil out from behind her ear through her long blonde hair that was braided, coiled and pinned atop her angelic head. She wrote her name and phone number on the back of the business card in delicately rendered script and then handed it back to me with a lingering hand.

"You can reach me any time after midnight," she suggested with cautious optimism.

"Well... it might not be tonight," I told her.

"Of course," she replied, "whenever you get a chance to then, um... sorry, what is your name?"

"Jay, Jay Jackson, at your service, Miss Lisa Lou Stanton," I announced and then bowed slightly to her smiling approval. I turned away from her then and pulled open the heavy glass door; its tinkling bell tickling both our fancies. I winked at the young woman through the window glass as I passed by her adorable gaze. I thought about turning around to wave "goodbye" or "see you later" but thought better of it and then wondered as I walked away if she had done what I had decided not to do.

It was around eight-thirty when I'd left Lisa on guard duty at the diner and nearly eleven o'clock by the time that I'd finally had enough of draft beer and televised baseball at the tavern just down the street from her. I was planning to leave after recycling my beer but as I stood and turned towards the men's room, the black-glass front door swung open and an ivory skinned goddess in a short black dress strolled into the place as the street-side wind blew her long raven-colored hair across her face in a seductively theatrical moment the likes of which I had only experienced second-hand during Super Bowl Sunday commercial breaks. Nevertheless, I proceeded in a feigned, un-phased manner toward my intended destination while attempting to process the visual stimulation to which I'd just been subjected. The tavern had been virtually empty the few hours I'd spent there and unless the woman was attracted to red-nosed, sixty-year-old drunks (from which she had a choice of three) I had to give myself a decent chance of at least striking up a casual conversation with her. At best, I just might finally satisfy one of my long-standing, unfulfilled fantasies involving ivory white skin and raven black hair. I liked my odds as I shook it three times for good luck and then three more times as a wake-up call to potential duty. Despite my usually passive pursuit of the fairer sex, I felt at the time that this particular situation and this particular, incredibly sexy woman were reason enough to temporarily amend my personal constitution. I decided then and there to allow myself the opportunity to masquerade as one of those sex-starved men the likes of which women love to bitch about to their gangs of agreeable girlfriends. After all, should the opportunity arise, those very same women probably wouldn't hesitate at the chance to jump the bones of an Adonis. Surely then, they couldn't fault me for wanting the same chance with a dark-haired Venus.

Ever since I was a kid, I had always preferred wood to metal. Long before I'd ever made that distinction and drawn that conclusion, I remember as a tiny tot, slicing my thumb wide open while playing with my father's double-edged razor that was hidden away from me, high out of reach, in the medicine cabinet over our bathroom sink. At the time, I had to climb up on the toilet seat lid and then up onto the sink to reach the shelf where that sleek and shiny instrument that my father used to shave with every morning before work and before church on Sundays was kept. Dad would normally skip the ritual on Saturday mornings and as a result, his Saturday night goodnight hugs featured scratchy stubble that tickled me and made me laugh. Even though at the time he would pretend otherwise, I realize now, all these years later, that he did it on purpose. My father always loved to make me laugh and as a result of his constant practice, he became an expert at it. At one particular point during those early youthful days of mine, I decided that it was about time that I too, should begin shaving like my father did, after all, I would be six years old soon and surely six years old was old enough to begin shaving. It made perfect sense to me at the time and so it was that I reasoned; I'd better start practicing. After my climb, I grabbed the razor in one hand and a can of foamy shaving cream in my other and then began my slow and deliberate decent back down to earth. I remember standing on the floor in front of the sink holding my plundered goods and gazing into the mirror only to discover that the mirror wasn't there. All that I could see from my vantage point was the cabinet door beneath the sink. *Okay then,* I thought, and then moments later decided to solve my dilemma by climbing back onto the sink. As I was climbing atop the toilet for the second time, my tiny sock feet slipped on the slick seat lid. The can of shaving cream went flying out of my hand and crashing into the sink with loud rattling bangs. Although I had retained my grip on the razor, my free hand fell upon it as I attempted to break my fall. My hand slid across the razor's edge which nearly sliced off the tip of my tiny thumb. I announced the stream of gushing blood to the world with a concert of blood-curdling screams. Having already heard the can of shaving cream bang into the sink, those screams of mine hastened my mother's perturbed walk to the bathroom into a mad dash of maternal rescue. My mother's love and pity overcame her initial disappointment in me as she loaded me and my bandaged thumb onto the backseat of our station wagon and then drove us to our family doctor's office. It was there that I was reintroduced to the cold and unforgiving qualities of sharpened steel. I remember cringing and crying out as a painful steel needle numbed my throbbing thumb. I turned away sobbing as another steel needle pricked the edges of my gash and then sutured my wound. Having survived the horrible trauma of life-saving surgery, I was assaulted yet again when another painful steel needle drove stinging tetanus vaccine into my skinny, five-year-old arm.

Metal can be sharp and unforgiving. It is cold and lifeless and cruel. Wood on the other hand, is much less of a threat. It's true that most people have suffered a wood splinter or two or twenty but splinters are easily home-remedied; they rarely require painful stitches and vaccinations. Unlike metal, wood is living and breathing. It is beautiful and supple and its varieties are many. Wood is not merely some dingy, dark ore that was dug from the dark bowels of the earth and then transformed by fire into cold and heartless steel. Wood lives and breathes among us, and we among it.

I spent a great deal of my childhood playing with wood in the woods. It became an easy ally. My friends and I would use it to fashion spears and clubs and bows and arrows that we'd yield in mock battles against our enemy friends. After the wars my comrades and I would stand watch over our captives as they gathered scattered deadwood with which we'd build glorious campfires lit by wooden matches that I'd snatched from my father's stash. As I grew older I'd cut dead trees and branches with axe and bow saw. We'd build enormous Boy Scout camp fires in which we'd bake Dutch-oven cobbler and around which we'd dry our soaked wet, wool socks after long hikes over snowy hills and across frozen boulders in icy clear water streams from which we'd dip our army surplus canteens full. I'd build wooden birdhouses and boxes, benches and shelves, model motor boats and sail boats and rocket ships (never store-bought kits, who could afford them?). I'd cut, carve, sand and then paint or stain rich, hand-made wood wonders most of which were unplanned and uniquely flawed in some wonderful way.

I would sometimes pine for my vanished childhood; its joys and sorrows, successes and failures, now lost to the adult world of jobs and bosses, bills and taxes, aches and mortality. It was though, in working with wood, that I retained in some small way, a connection to my childhood as I would later cut, saw and hammer lumber for sheds and porches, barns and small buildings, entire houses at times where children could take comfort and enjoy the magic of *their* childhoods.

I traveled to where the work was, chasing not the paycheck but the opportunity to make a living in a way that I chose in a place not necessarily of my choosing. I ended up in more than a few dead-end dumps posing as towns; their vacant boarded storefronts standing post-mortem to the "real world" beyond zipping by. Most often, those dead-end towns were inhabited by living, breathing, human-like zombies prone to drug and alcohol abuse, quick to fight without provocation, their motives lost in drunken desires for random revenge. I did my best to steer clear of those types of towns or leave them as soon as possible to search yet again for a decent place to pass my days. I'd found East Alcorn to be such a decent place. It was generally poor but it sustained a breath of optimism. Its residents held onto enough hope and earned enough income to enjoy their lives with some small sense of satisfaction.

Most of my income those days came by way of the Alcorn Lumber Mill for which I'd labor three, twelve hour workdays when loads of raw timber rolled down from the far away hills and into the outskirts of town on diesel-belching, flatbed rigs. To stay afloat in those tough economic times, the mill only operated three days a week. It conserved utilities and wages by eliminating two workdays. Most of us who worked there spent our four day "weekends" chasing odd jobs to fill our time and pockets.

In my opinion, the elected county officials in the area had done a fine job of environmental land-management by convincing the state and feds to prohibit clear-cutting of the old-growth forests that surrounded East Alcorn. In a rare display of wisdom, the powers-that-be acquiesced to the tree-huggers by requiring licensed, piecework harvesting of any tree greater than twenty-four inches in diameter. As a result, many of the gargantuan trees that had once shaded the pre-colonial frontier still stood in the hills outside of East Alcorn. Neighboring counties on the other hand, had given free rein and authority to coal, gas and metal ore lobbyists the results of which included mountain top removal, strip mining and hydraulic fracturing. Ravaged sites began to replace pristine wilderness. Ground-water was poisoned. Toxic runoff washed downstream to the detriment of ecosystems across tens of thousands of acres. And so it was, with clear conscious, I helped to transform the truckloads of slaughtered trees from timber to lumber with the respect they deserved while their very own offspring saplings stood greening in the forest.

When I first started working at the mill, a co-worker of mine mentioned that a serial killer was active in the area. Because violent crime of any sort was rare in those parts, chances were good that a single individual was responsible for the series of unsolved, gruesome murders. Months later, a local county employee became the prime suspect. According to evidence uncovered during his trial, the county's very own tax collector held a secret obsession to prey upon defenseless women when he found them most vulnerable; alone and isolated. Before his capture, area residents were wary and remained on edge. Hell only knew what horrible fate awaited vulnerable women caught unaware in East Alcorn.

When Calvin Gavin was twelve years old he discovered a box of musty magazines buried under a pile of neglected junk in his family's basement. When he first opened the box, Calvin's eyes widened. His heart pounded in his chest. Two stacks of colorful magazines lay at his fingertips; beautiful women in bright red lipstick wearing sexy blouses that fell from their heaving bosoms gasped in fear as evil-looking men in fedoras and double-breasted suits clutched their trembling arms. Calvin became frightened for the defenseless women. He found himself angry and then aroused. He closed the flaps of the box, struggled to lift it, and then made his way slowly up the basement steps; his chest of treasure in his arms.

Ever since its discovery, Calvin would lock himself in his bedroom at night and delve into the box of magazines that he'd hidden in the back of his closet. One by one, he'd take a beautiful woman in distress to bed with him. He'd lie atop his bed holding the magazine's cover close to his face. "I'll save you," he'd whisper to the woman before he'd kiss her colorful portrait. He'd then wonder if he would be able to save her because many of the women in the stories would be raped and murdered at which point he would promise them, "I will find your killer and bring him to justice." Night after night Calvin would devour the enticing stories he'd find between the covers of *True Crime* and *True Detective* and his favorite magazine; *Spicy Detective.*

By age thirteen, when most other boys his age had begun chasing girls, Calvin began chasing his dream to become an officer of the law. Having read each and every one of his pulp fiction magazines from cover-to-cover, he turned then to crime novels and police manuals that he'd borrow from the library. His obsession with law enforcement began to reflect in his daily speech. As a result, he'd often refer to everyday people as "persons." He'd consider persons with whom he'd disagree as "suspects" and the heated arguments that often ensued as "interrogations." On occasion, Calvin would turn up the heat and conduct "enhanced interrogations" on solitary suspects; persons not inclined to be missed should they suddenly "turn up missing," a contradiction of terms that he found quite amusing.

Unfortunately, because of his piss-poor eyesight and heart condition, Calvin wasn't able to realize his dream of becoming a policeman or a detective. That realization devastated him. He became livid when he was told that he didn't measure up. His obsessive lust for crime and violence in the real world would be condemned forever; to fiction. *Or would it be?* he thought as he thumbed through his titillating magazines.

To his community, Calvin Gavin, step-son of East Alcorn's mayor; Edward James Gavin, was the commission appointed county tax collector. At age twenty-two Calvin had become the youngest ever county tax collector on state record but it came as no surprise to anyone who knew him. Calvin had always been an excellent student, at first, in the local public schools and then later, while away at college. Calvin was a math whiz, a computer geek and despite his young age and lack of real-world work experience, he became a respected county employee and a superb tax collector; a position made easily available to him because of his stepfather's mayoral standing in local government.

Unbeknownst to anyone who knew him however, over the years Calvin had become deeply disturbed. While away at college nearby, after having learned that the police academy had rejected his application, Calvin strangled a prostitute in a roadside motel. She was a pretty young woman; bright red lipstick, long dark hair, big beautiful eyes that bulged when Calvin held her mouth closed and crushed her windpipe.

"I can't save you," he whispered apologetically as she kicked and squirmed frantically beneath him. After the girl had succumbed, Calvin laid his head lovingly on her chest. He closed his eyes. He felt her soft and silent body beneath him. He buried his face in her perfumed blouse and listened for a heartbeat. None came. Tears of joy trickled from Calvin's eyes; it was his very first, true crime.

Calvin stayed in the motel room another night. He enjoyed the good company and found it difficult to leave. Before he left he called the motel's owner to his room. She was a tiny middle-aged woman who lived alone in a modest house behind the motel. Calvin loved her even more.

The body of Calvin's ninth victim lay on a bed over which stood; Sheriff Jack Gavin and Jack's brother, Mayor Edward Gavin. The body remained as it had been found; carefully wrapped in a filthy quilt in an abandoned farm house at the top of a hill overlooking an overgrown meadow. Three young children chasing butterflies had discovered the farmhouse stench. The kids were too frightened to enter the spooky old house and so, luckily for them, they did not discover the corpse. One of the kids told her parents that she'd gotten sick to her stomach up at the old farmhouse. The girl's parents suspected the worst and phoned the police.

As Sheriff Gavin slowly and apprehensively pulled the quilt away from the victim, the stench of death in the room intensified ten-fold. The sheriff gagged as he reported with bated breath, "White female… age twenty to twenty-five… no apparent physical trauma upon initial examination."

A junior officer quickly recorded the information on his clip board and then asked the sheriff if he could leave the room.

While waiting for the county coroner to arrive, the three men on the scene wandered around the hilltop sucking fresh air from the summer breeze. The stench inside the house was too much to bear. They'd opened every window in the farmhouse on their way out but did not linger to search for any evidence of a crime. The victim's death appeared suspicious. All three men rightfully suspected murder. Had they stayed in the house longer to look around, they would have discovered men's socks; Calvin's socks, accidentally kicked under the victim's deathbed and carelessly left there just six hours earlier. Calvin would have returned to the farmhouse that night to spend more time with his victim had she not been driven away by the coroner and identified by dental records twelve hours later.

"Lisa Martin; college-grad, state park ranger, recorded as AWOL from her job and later reported missing by the park's superintendent," Sheriff Gavin reported as he handed a copy of the coroner's report to his brother Ed.

"How'd she die?" Calvin asked his Uncle Jack, as Calvin rose from the porch chair next to his stepfather's.

"The coroner called it; asphyxiation due to strangulation. Fortunately, his team found hair and socks at the scene and a fingernail fragment in the victim's throat. We should have DNA results back by the end of the week. We'll compare that DNA sequence to the evidence the killer left behind when he moved the victim from the state park Jeep she was driving at the time of her abduction. We're looking for a stupid, sloppy individual, Ed."

"Well that narrows it down some. We can eliminate well-groomed college graduates," Mayor Gavin laughed.

"Oh, we'll narrow it down soon enough. State Forensics is sending two teams. One team will comb the farmhouse and the other will put the Jeep under a microscope. They'll start first thing tomorrow, or as soon as they get here."

"I can make a call to expedite them," the mayor offered.

"No need to, Ed. I spoke to your old college buddy Herb Garden at State. He promised to ask the head of forensics to wrap up their in-house work and get here as quick as they can."

"Herb Garden? Is Uncle Jack serious, Dad?" Calvin asked his stepfather.

"He's not joking, Calvin. My college buddy's name is in fact, Herbert Garden, Herb as everyone calls him. And you know what's even funnier? Herb Garden is our state's Director of Agriculture," Ed said laughing before he stood up from his chair and sucked the last drops from his beer bottle.

"Beer, Jack?" Ed asked as he turned toward the door. "Or is that a dumb question?"

"Make it two, Dad," Calvin hollered through the screen door as his stepfather lumbered toward the kitchen.

"Uncle Jack…" Calvin began, "are there any substantial similarities between this case and those other, unsolved homicides in the area?"

"Quite a few, kiddo, quite a few," the sheriff said as he settled himself into a chair. "With any luck, we'll be tying a noose soon."

When I left the tavern's men's room, I was surprised and delighted to discover that the woman who had breezed into the place was sitting at the bar two seats away from my beer. I returned to my barstool, finished my beer, looked over to the woman casually and then asked her, "How do?"

"Not so good really," she replied with a half-hearted attempt at a smile.

"Why's that, if I may be so bold?" I inquired.

"My younger sister has been missing since Monday. She works in the state park outside town here so, I thought I'd come up and have a look around."

"Sorry to hear that but I'm sure she's fine," I offered.

"I'm not so sure," she said. "It's not like Lisa to just take off and disappear. Me on the other hand; that's another story altogether. I promised my mother that I'd get up here as fast as I could. I didn't even take time to change, hence the inappropriate evening wear."

"Yeah, you do seem a little over-dressed for a dump like this," I said a bit too loudly. The bartender gave me what I interpreted to be, a dirty look. "You know what I mean," I offered him apologetically.

"Oh, you're absolutely right and I agree," he said. "We don't get too many women like you in here, miss. I can count 'em on zero fingers."

He and I laughed and then I offered in her direction, "Well then, let's celebrate the first fabulous woman to ever grace this humble dump, shall we? May I buy you a drink?"

"I'd love another," she said, sliding her glass toward the bartender.

I slid over two seats and rubbed elbows with her. I couldn't help but to imagine rubbing her elsewhere and was surprised and delighted that she was so easy to talk to.

Calvin began to worry. In fact, Calvin had suddenly become shit-scared terrified for the first time in his life. He had screwed up and he knew it. He either hadn't been thinking straight or had gotten too cocky and confident for his own good. He began to worry that his career as a successful serial killer might soon be over. If he was lucky, he'd spend the rest of his days in an eight-by-eight concrete tomb with a stainless steel commode and an overly-friendly bunk mate named Bubba. If he *wasn't* lucky, he'd hang for sure after his appeals ran out. Or would he? What if those so-called "other clues" and DNA samples didn't pan out? Was he kidding his goddamn self? He was screwed and he knew it. So now what; run... hide? Fuck all that! If that's the way it's got to be, he decided then and there to go out in a blaze of murderous mayhem. And then, as he sat idling in downtown East Alcorn at a red light that had long since turned green, he puked down the front of his shirt.

"Have you been drinking?" an East Alcorn City Police patrolman asked after Calvin had rolled down his driver's side window. As the cop's flashlight panned the car's interior, the patrolman reconsidered his question as rhetorical noticing at first the smell, and then the chunks of Calvin's dinner dripping down the front of his shirt.

"No, sir, I've got the flu, officer," Calvin lied; about the flu that is, not so much about the drinking as Calvin had drank only one beer with his stepfather and uncle.

"Well, given your present condition, I need to give you a breathalyzer test. Move your car out of traffic and into that loading zone," the officer said, pointing toward a dark, single-lane alley between two buildings.

"Just what I need," Calvin thought, "give a DNA sample that'll be matched to those at the farmhouse. Should I gun it and run? That would bring even more units in pursuit," he assumed. "Should I cooperate and just let the cards fall where they may?" That, he reasoned, was a viable option.

"I said, move your vehicle and do it now!" the patrolman demanded as he placed the palm of his hand on the butt of his service revolver.

"Sorry, officer, like I said... I'm real sick. I can't even think straight. This flu is kicking my ass," Calvin said convincingly and then he pulled forward slowly and turned far up into the alley allowing more than enough room for the squad car behind him.

If the alley had been blind with no means of escape, the patrolman's stop would have been routine. Calvin would have passed the field sobriety test and would have been on his way free-and-clear, at least temporarily. But the alley had an exit on another street and so, while the cop was showing Calvin how to hold the breathalyzer properly, Calvin saw another way out and then took it instinctually and suddenly when he drove his commando knife into the unsuspecting patrolman's belly. The cop gasped as he doubled-over in agony. He sank hard to his knees and fell forward flat on his face. He died while Calvin was wiping his blade clean on the officer's back. Calvin stood up, smiled broadly, got back into his car and then drove away.

"So, is there a decent hotel in town?" she asked me between sips of her gin and tonic.

"There's the Alcorn Inn right across the river. It's famous for its bedbugs and winos," I announced, adding, "the only others are the two motels you probably passed by at the interstate. They're famous for hookers and drug busts."

"That's over an hour away," she said disappointingly. "I've spent the past six hours throwing clothes in a bag, grabbing a taxi, running in heels to catch my flight, hiking down an endless airport concourse to the rental car counter and then driving to, to... I'm totally exhausted, I can't even remember where on earth I am."

"East Alcorn," I reminded her, "it's easy to forget. This isn't exactly what you'd call a tourist mecca," I informed her. "The only thing we have to offer is a perpetual, realistic enactment of lower middle class life. On the upside, admission is free."

She laughed obligingly, smiled and then looked directly into my eyes. She appeared to be somewhat desperate and forlorn. She seemed to be waiting for a suggestion.

"Well, there *is* my place," I offered. "It's ten minutes away, up in the hills."

"Yeah sure... go home with a total stranger in a strange town somewhere up in the hills. Sounds like the beginning of a slasher movie and they *never* end well because there's always a sequel. I really don't think so, but thanks anyway," she said, both cordially and nervously.

"It's your call. I was just trying to be helpful is all. I don't have to work tomorrow so I could help you find your sister or at least show you around town. With all of these hills this isn't exactly the easiest place on the planet to navigate. I've lived here for almost a year now but I still get lost sometimes and have to back-track for miles."

"You'd do that… help me find Lisa?"

"I would."

"You're not a serial killer or a rapist are you?"

"Not yet."

"Yet?" she asked, laughing nervously.

"Lately, I've been turning women down. You know; lonely housewives, single moms on a restraining order rebound. I don't need the drama and I'm definitely not sex starved. My last girlfriend and I went our separate ways a little over a year ago but I still make the occasional booty call when she needs one. She's three counties away though so I keep telling her it's about time she found herself a new man. I'm not a teenager anymore so I don't need to get off five times a day, or even five times a week," I laughed.

"Well, if anything… you're convincing. And I find your twisted sense of humor interesting if not entertaining," she said, sipping her drink slowly while considering my offer.

"Can I leave my rental car parked here do you think?" she asked suddenly. "I really don't want to follow you up in the hills with three drinks in me."

"This town can't afford meter maids. You could probably park on the front lawn of city hall if you wanted to. And you've had four drinks if you don't mind me saying so."

The bartender approached us slowly and considerately

waiting for an opening. "Last call?" he asked.

"Care for a fifth?" I offered her.

"Sure, why not," she agreed. "Looks like I'm not driving tonight and if you turn out to be a serial killer I could use the extra anesthesia."

"Apparently, we *both* have a twisted sense of humor," I teased her and then I asked the envious bartender, "Another for the lady and nothing for me thanks." He gave me one of those "you lucky bastard" grins before he turned away.

"Anesthesia... that's seriously funny," I whispered into her gorgeous ear.

"I suppose so," she said, laughing. "Tell me... does *your* bed have bedbugs?" she asked seriously.

"Absolutely not, and neither does yours," I assured her.

I tossed her suitcase into the bed of my pickup, opened the passenger side door for her and held her hand as she slid up and in. I held my breath as her dress slid higher up the length of her gorgeous legs. "You lucky bastard," I thought, smiling to myself and then to her when she caught me smiling to myself.

"I have to warn you," I warned her, "my place is no palace, after all, I *am* a bachelor, but I'm not a *total* slob like the male roommates I've evicted over the years," I rambled as we rambled out of town and up the first of many hills.

"I know *exactly* what you mean," she agreed. "I've had my share of sloppy female roommates. Not all women are Martha Stewart perfect."

"I think she's sexy," I said spontaneously, thinking out loud and surprising the both of us in the process.

"Really now... Martha Stewart... sexy...?" she asked, as if wondering to herself.

"Yeah, sexy," I began as I searched my memory for evidence with which to support my claim. "For one thing, I admire her calm resolve. You know, having faced prison, serving her time without any overblown drama and all. And she *is,* or is in some ways at least, quite a good looking woman in my opinion. I'll bet I'm not the only man who's fantasized about being her cellmate, or imagined themselves sharing home-made cobbler with her on a cozy bearskin rug in front of a crackling fireplace on a cold winter's night, naked of course."

"Ha-ha! Such an imagination! I suppose you're right though. I never really thought about her in that way before."

"That's because you're not a guy. Men always fantasize about women they can't have."

"Oh, trust me; we women do the same with men. So, which other famous, unattainable women do you fantasize about?"

"Right now... I'd have to say... *you,*" I gambled.

"I don't count," she said quickly.

"And why not, because you're not famous?"

"Well there's that, and the fact that you *can* have me," she said, totally blindsiding me and prompting my next, ridiculous question.

"What sparked the attraction?" I asked her, immediately realizing that it didn't matter at all to me why she wanted me.

"I wanted you from the very first moment I saw you in the bar," she confessed.

"Well then... we have something *else* in common," I too confessed.

We both laughed out loud. She laid her hand on my leg and then squeezed it firmly as she pulled herself closer to me. "In that case," she whispered, "we'll only be needing *one* bed tonight."

"And it's a good thing too," I said, "because I only *have* one bed."

"You dog!" she teased jokingly as she slapped my chest. "You've been playing me all along?"

"Not really," I said in mock self-defense, "I was planning to sleep on the couch tonight."

I didn't sleep on the couch that night. In fact, I didn't sleep much *at all* that night. Three minutes into our first and most intense bout of passion, she startled me when she stopped suddenly and then asked, panting impatiently, "What's... your... name...?"

"Jay, Jay Jackson," I announced calmly and then paused as I awaited her approval of who it was that she was actually sleeping with.

"Maya Martin," she announced abruptly. "Pleased to meet you, Jay!" she said playfully before she resumed pouncing on me passionately.

Thirty minutes after we'd finished, she started right up again, having easily gotten *me* up again.

"Correct me if I'm wrong but, didn't you say earlier that you were exhausted?" I both asked and reminded her.

"The gin must've given me my second wind," she panted as she slammed against me recklessly.

About an hour later, we started up *yet again* but luckily for me, she slowed the pace down considerably to one that was much less frantic and much more romantic. It was four in the morning by the time that we'd finally stopped ravaging each other and had passed out exhausted. When I awoke it was eight o'clock in the morning. She had already started a fresh pot of coffee and was cracking eggs into a bowl when I hobbled into my kitchen.

"Omelet?" she asked cheerfully.

I nodded, "yes," and then asked, "You're up mighty early, considering. Did you get enough sleep last night?"

"I got just what I needed last night... and *four times* no less," she said enthusiastically before she kissed my numb lips.

"Didn't realize we were keeping score," I confessed.

"Well, somebody had to, and you seemed a bit pre-occupied," she laughed. "Let's call it a tie, shall we?"

"Actually, Maya... I know when I've been beaten. You may have humbled me but I am nevertheless; very grateful."

"So *it is* a tie then," she said, kissing me yet again.

The sun began shining brightly as my kitchen curtains fluttered lightly in the late morning breeze. We sat around my kitchen table (upon which was laid; every single plate, cup and glass that I owned) while devouring omelets and bacon and fried onion potatoes and rehydrating ourselves with satisfying gulps of ice-cold orange juice. We cleared the table into the sink and then tossed our clothes onto the bed.

"I didn't really have the chance to bring it up last night... things started happening pretty quickly between us... I really don't want to alarm you, Maya, but..."

"Jay, what is it?" she asked as we toweled each other dry after our communal shower.

"Well, ironically, after what you'd been joking about last night, unfortunately..."

"Unfortunately what, Jay?" she prompted again.

"We may actually have a serial killer on the loose in East Alcorn," I said abruptly.

"Oh my God!" she shrieked and then she immediately sunk heavily onto my bed.

As I sat down beside her, her cell phone rang. We stared at

one another with mutual dread as it rang again. For some unknown reason, I think we both expected the worse. It was her mother calling. I wrapped a dry towel over Maya's shoulders as she listened. The news was bad. The news couldn't have been any worse.

"That fucking son of a bitch!" Maya screamed after she'd calmly explained to me in a dazed, state of confusion that her sister's body had been found under suspicious circumstances that were later deemed a homicide. When Maya's rage had subsided and she'd stopped pacing around the room, she broke down limpidly and began to sob in my arms. Her body shook with grief. Sadness and dread overwhelmed her and pushed her once again toward outrage.

"My Baby Sister!" she screamed.

I can usually handle most drama with relative ease but the situation at hand, given the circumstances, was almost too much to bear. The unabashed joy of our introduction and the sudden horror of recent events sent both of our heads spinning. I did my best to try and comfort the grief-stricken woman with whom I'd been acquainted for less than twenty-four hours. Maya eased her way out of her trauma slowly but then sprang into immediate action. We dressed quickly and hurried out of the house to the coroner's office. On the way, Maya confided that she couldn't accept the fact that her sister was dead until she saw Lisa's body with her own eyes.

If I hadn't been standing next to Maya with my arm around her when the coroner unzipped the body bag, she would have fallen hard to the morgue's bare concrete floor. As it was, her knees sank instantly. I grabbed her quickly with my other arm to hold her upright. The stench of death and the grotesque condition of her once beautiful sister was too much to bear. Maya gasped and began to shake. She buried her face on my chest. I held her firmly and pressed my lips to the top of her head. There were no words.

Given the condition of Lisa's body, the coroner had forewarned Maya as to what she could expect. He tried in vain to talk her out of identifying the body but she had every right to do so. The body had already been positively identified as her sister's, but Maya had to see it with her own eyes. Once the initial shock had waned, Maya regained her composure and said in short, distressed, gasps, "That's definitely her hair. Those teeth look like hers."

Lisa's beautiful white teeth looked terribly out of place. They were surrounded by the horror of blackened, shriveled skin that stretched tightly across the visible underlying shape of a skull with clenched jaws. The woman's beautiful, silky hair framed an otherwise terrifying portrait.

The coroner's calm and concerned voice broke the silence, "As I've said, ma'am, we made positive I.D. by dental record. The state park superintendent herself and Lisa's immediate supervisor were here and were fairly certain that it was in fact; your sister. And I tell you this only because I feel that you have a right to know, ma'am; the superintendent broke down crying. She told me that she knew your sister personally and thought very highly of her. She has a sister of her own around Lisa's age and can't imagine the grief that you must be feeling. She and Lisa's supervisor both want you to know that the full force of their resources will be summoned to help hunt down whoever did this to your sister. As we speak, several of your sister's co-workers are searching the park for additional evidence. The better part of this city's police department and the county's sheriff department are searching the area where your sister's body was found. State forensics experts have arrived. They are scrutinizing the scenes and evidence. We *will* find the man or chase him to hell in the process. This is such a terrible tragedy, ma'am. I am so very sorry for you and your family's loss."

The coroner laid a kind hand on Maya's shoulder. He paused for her unspoken permission before he zipped the body bag closed.

After Calvin had gutted the patrolman in the alley, he went to his sparse apartment one last time where, in the dead of night, he loaded all of his worldly possessions into the trunk of his car and then wiped clean what he could of his fingerprints. He drove down to the far bank of the river where few others went that time of night. He was sitting in his car staring at the slow flow of the dark muddy water when he happened to notice a blonde girl pass by in his rearview mirror. She looked simply delicious to Calvin and as it was, he was starving. He sat up excitedly and pulled his car around to the side of the diner from which the girl had just left. She stood in the diner's parking lot with her hands in her purse as she fumbled through it searching for her car keys.

"How do?" Calvin asked the girl from his car window.

"Get lost," the woman suggested without looking up as she continued to search for her keys.

"If you've locked your keys in your car, I can help you get in," Calvin suggested to the girl. "My dad's a locksmith. He taught me all the tricks," Calvin lied.

"You wouldn't be lying would you?" the girl asked him as she bent over nicely to look inside her car. "I can't see if my keys are in the ignition or not, it's too dark in there."

"Let's find out," Calvin suggested as he continued to plot the best way to take her away.

Calvin parked his car, got out of it, and then joined the girl at her side. "Name's Hank Johnson, I'm at your service, ma'am," he said, tipping his ball cap to prove it.

"Thanks, my name's Lisa," she offered.

"Lisa what?" he asked as he bent down to look in her car through the window.

"Lisa... Lou Stanton," she said hesitantly but then realized that her nametag would provide him that information anyway. She pulled her sweater closed to cover it up nevertheless.

"Lisa Lou Stanton; such a pretty name for such a pretty girl," Calvin said as he stood up. "Looks to me you've locked your keys in your car," he lied. "But I'll fix you up in a jiff. Let me get my tools," Calvin said before he walked back to his car.

Calvin slid into his car and then reached over into the duffle bag on the passenger seat. He removed two silk neckties from the bag and then stuffed them into his pants pocket.

"Lose Something..?" someone shouted from across the parking lot.

Calvin looked up and saw two middle-aged men in restaurant whites walking toward the girl. One of them was holding up a set of car keys. He jingled them teasingly as the men approached the girl's car. Calvin banged on his steering wheel, damned the intruders, turned his car's ignition key and then sped away cursing. As he did so, Lisa memorized his license plate number. She would never forget his face.

Calvin drove up into the hills to an abandoned hunting cabin where, over a year ago, he had thoroughly enjoyed his third, squirming victim. He was surprised to discover that over the interim, the cabin had become completely overgrown with vines and vegetation. It took him until sunup to machete through the brush and open the cabin door. Once inside, he performed an impromptu eviction on a family of raccoons and then finally, settled in. The well pump at the pantry sink belched sour air at first but soon began spitting rusty water. After twenty or more cranks the water eventually ran clear. Calvin splashed cold water on his face and then opened a tin of corned beef hash which he ate cold from the can. Fed and exhausted, he passed out in his clothes on a rotted and broken bunk bed and slept until sundown. An hour before he awoke, Calvin experienced a recurring terrifying nightmare which he thoroughly enjoyed.

To Calvin, she looked like a high school dropout and a skanky one at that. But then again, "Aren't they all?" he thought, laughing. Calvin liked her immediately. She was skinny and dirty and strung out on something another dose of which would render her a limp bag of young and tender bones in his unforgiving hands. As she leaned over into his car window, her rain soaked filthy blonde hair dripped water on his aroused lap.

"Lookin' for a date, mister?" she asked dizzily, apparently oblivious to the torrential rain that was pouring down her back, slipping beneath the waistband of her ragged shorts, funneling along the crack of her flat ass and then wicking its way down her skinny white legs. Her untied tennis shoes squished full of water as she shifted her eighty pounds back and forth anxiously as if she had to pee. "So, you lookin' for a date?" she repeated with a pale catatonic expression that resembled a smile.

"Maybe," Calvin suggested. "What're *you* lookin' for?"

"You got twenty-five for a hit?"

"Hop in."

"Pull across the street around back to twenty-two," she told Calvin and then he did.

Calvin followed the girl into her unlocked motel room. Another girl; dark haired in a grey, long-sleeved t-shirt and dingy panties, was passed out on one of the beds. Her bare legs looked real nice. They had some meat on them, Calvin noticed.

"Don't mind her none," his date suggested as she slipped out of her sopping-wet shoes and then dropped her t-shirt and shorts atop them on the floor. She picked up the room phone, spun its dial once and then announced into the receiver, "Hang on..." she turned to Calvin and asked, "You got twenty-five, right?"

"I got fifty for you and your friend if she's game."

"Make it two," she said and then she hung up the phone.

Ten minutes later a fat man at the door took fifty dollars from the girl while Calvin sat on the toilet filling the bathtub.

Thirty minutes later Calvin was deep inside the blonde girl. Her roommate watched complacently while waiting her turn from across the room. As strung out as she was, the dark haired girl didn't even realize that her friend was dead; drowned in the bathtub, toweled dry and tossed lifeless on the bed. The second girl bit down hard on Calvin's thumb when he pressed his hand over her nose and mouth. He watched her beautiful terrified eyes bulge as she kicked her feet and pounded his fat-covered ribs in vain. He felt the girl twitch and tremble as she serenaded him with a heavenly chorus of muffled screams. He felt her stiffen and then freeze and then fall limp beneath him. Calvin groaned in ecstasy. He spent the next three hours enjoying the corpses. He rearranged them around the room in various poses and positions. He lay between them, atop them, and beneath them. He re-enacted their dramatic deaths to re-establish his dominance over them. He loved them both for allowing him the pleasure and he told them so.

Due to the motel's reputation and the drug paraphernalia found in the room, the deaths of the girls would later be carelessly and mistakenly dismissed as overdoses. Calvin sat up excitedly on his cabin bunk with one of the dead girl's throats still in his hands. The cabin was pitch-black. As he fumbled for and then finally found and lit his lantern, he realized that is was Saturday night. Unless he called in sick Monday morning they would miss him at work. He had thirty-six hours to plan his next move; thirty six hours to find and enjoy his next victim. Calvin had really wanted that blonde girl at the diner. Despite his full belly, he was starving.

Despite what the coroner had told Maya, I assumed that the city police and county sheriff departments didn't have many clues as to who they were actually looking for. As it was, there were no eye witnesses to Lisa's abduction from the park and little physical evidence at either scene that would point the authorities toward any one, specific suspect. Without substantial forensic evidence, if killer didn't surface by other means, he would remain on the loose. When I shared those thoughts with Maya I made it clear to her that I was by no means an expert in such matters. But having been an often bored and lonely bachelor, I'd spent more than my fair share of late nights watching cop shows and crime dramas on TV. And so it was that I spoke with at least fictional authority on the subject at hand. Oddly enough, as it turned out, I was right.

"State Forensics has accumulated substantial evidence in the Lisa Martin case over the past twenty-four hours," the East Alcorn Police watch commander announced to the morning shift. "We have fingerprints, footprints, hair and fiber samples but so far, no match to anyone in the data bases. We suspect that this individual may have also been involved in other unsolved homicides involving local females of various ages over the past eighteen months. As you all know, we lost our youngest squad member; Patrol Officer Kip Daniels, last night. The perpetrator in the Lisa Martin slaying may have also been involved in Kip's death. All I can say now is to remain vigilant and be on the lookout for a suspicious-looking, young white male with a stocky build and light brown or blonde hair wearing cheap sneakers, a flannel shirt and khaki cargo pants."

"That sounds like half of the boys down at the pool hall, captain," a back-of-the-room newspaper reporter chimed-in.

"And you would be correct, Mr. Duncan, but until we obtain a positive I.D. on the suspect, which *will be* forthcoming, that is all we have to go on so; eyes and ears open and side arms at the ready. It goes without saying; we need to apprehend this suspect before he finds another victim. If I were you, I'd advise the females in your life to be extra cautious. Tragically, Officer Daniels made mistakes last night that cost him his life. *Never* assume that a traffic stop is routine. *Nothing* should be considered routine until *after* the fact. When patrolling alone, *always* call in a vehicle's tag number before initiating a breathalyzer test or before apprehending *anyone* outside of their vehicle for *any* reason. Unless the public is in eminent danger, *always* call for and wait for backup before placing yourself in a potentially compromising situation. We can all learn from Kip's mistakes while we do our damndest to bring his killer to justice. You heard it from me, Mr. Duncan, and I trust in your confidence when I remind everyone in this room that deadly force is *always* an option. Do *not* become another statistic, people. If you feel that deadly force is warranted, use it. If you determine that you or *anyone* else is in clear and present danger, use your weapon. Am I clear?"

The entire room agreed with fervor, including Mr. Duncan whose thoughts turned then to his wife and three daughters.

Without a captive or corpse with which to pass the time and make it all worthwhile, Calvin soon realized that he hated hiding out alone. Hiding out in a filthy abandoned cabin without a companion or electricity was nothing short of torture. He needed to either relocate or find his next victim soon. As he recalled from months past, there were isolated homes scattered along the same ridgeline upon which his cabin stood leaning and leaking. Whether or not any of those homes were occupied by solitary females remained to be seen. Calvin couldn't chance that his license plate number had been called-in when he was stopped for vomit-driving the night before, so he had parked his car out of sight in thick brush at the base of the hill. Without electricity, the police scanner in the trunk of his car was worthless. As a result, he'd have to lie low in the cabin and go it on foot from there.

By the light of his lantern, Calvin wiped his filthy eyeglasses clean. He was relieved that he could see clearly again. He tossed his much-preferred sneakers aside and then slipped into and tied his hiking boots. He filled his knapsack with two bottles of water, a can of corn beef hash, a coil of rope, a roll of duct tape, four silk neckties, a small caliber hand gun and his commando knife which had recently proved itself worthy, yet again.

The fresh air and early sunlight outside the dark, dank cabin were invigorating. "A fine day for hunting," Calvin decided. He looked to his right through a thick stand of trees toward the bright, blue and orange sky. He chose north.

After half an hour on foot, Calvin came upon a house. He knelt down in the thickets surrounding it; watching and waiting. A pickup truck parked in the gravel drive suggested that somebody was home. When a woman came out twenty minutes later to hang wet laundry, Calvin's disturbed mind immediately kicked into overdrive. Deep inside the thick layers of his bulk, Calvin's heart rate rose to an unhealthy plateau. He was well aware of his condition and tried to calm himself down by taking slower and deeper breaths. He'd always experienced heightened enthusiasm while evaluating potential victims for their worthiness as subsequent playmates but for some reason, the woman he found himself watching pushed him beyond the levels of excitement that he'd previously experienced. *Was he losing his nerve or was this particular woman just too tantalizing?* Calvin decided that whatever the case it didn't matter because regardless of the risk, he *must* have that woman. In order to limit his risk, Calvin realized that he would need to return to his cabin and wait for darkness to set in. Despite the unlivable conditions there, it was a hell of lot better than waiting for sundown in tick-infested weeds. An hour later, while lying on his decrepit bunk bed, Calvin reveled in violent and filthy thoughts. The woman was absolutely gorgeous. She was a goddess. She was a temptress whom Calvin would soon conquer and then offer as sacrifice to his deepest and darkest desires. The ungodly things that he was going to do to her in that house would make any mortal man jealous. Calvin felt privileged that once and for all he would soon become; the man that all other lesser men envied.

"The laundromat is only five miles away," I reminded her.

"But I need this, Jay. It helps to distract me. It takes my mind off things," Maya claimed as she rinsed out more of her things in my bathroom sink. "After the incredible highs of what we shared last night and the horrible lows this morning, I really need a good dose of the mundane," she explained.

"Well, you picked the right spot for it. This place couldn't be any more boring."

"I could *never* be bored with you around, Jay. If I weren't so exhausted and heartbroken I'd be all over you right now."

"I'm that irresistible?"

"Yes, as a matter of fact you are," she said as she turned away from the sink and then kissed me quickly so as not to rekindle our fire. "And not just because you do me right in the sheets. I *really* appreciate your companionship, Jay. If not for your gentle ways and calm compassion, I'd be in some hospital, suffering a nervous breakdown."

"I think you're stronger than that, Maya. You don't give yourself enough credit."

"Well, then you'd be wrong, Jay. I don't handle tragedy very well at all. I actually *did* have a nervous breakdown, or an anxiety attack, or whatever they call it, when my father was killed. I ended up in the hospital for three days. The only reason they discharged me when they did was so that I could attend his funeral."

"My God, Maya, I'm so sorry. Your father was killed?"

"Nothing like this, Jay. A drunk driver killed him when I was twelve."

"I'm so sorry, Maya, but surely, you're stronger now than when you were twelve."

"I'm not so sure. Kids bounce back. The older I get, the more things tend to affect me. And I'm thinking of my mom. She lost it too when dad died. Lisa had to stay with an aunt while another aunt looked after our mother. When she wasn't sleeping, my mom screamed for two days straight. She almost joined me in the hospital. Can you imagine what was going through my poor little, five year old sister's head; her father suddenly gone and her mother and sister suddenly gone crazy? Our auntie tried to comfort her but Lisa cried day and night. She lost a lot of weight and got physically ill. I've never gotten over the guilt of leaving her alone like that and now... she's gone forever, Jay."

Maya tried to wring out a pair of panties in the sink but she began to sob. I felt the full weight of her sorrow and anguish as I held her from behind in my arms. I ran my hands through her hair and rubbed her head. I pulled her hands out from the sink and dried them with a towel. I led her to my bed where we both sat down. She leaned over to me and laid her head on my lap. She spoke intermittently through her sobs.

"I really need to get back to my mom tomorrow. She never remarried when dad was killed. She never even dated after he was gone. Lisa and I were all that she had and now... I'm all that she has."

"Wow, that is tough. This world is almost unbearable at times."

"Yes it is, Jay," she agreed as she wiped away tears with her shirtsleeve, "but good people like you make it bearable. I need to try and make it bearable for my mom."

"Well, I say... you let *me* hang those things out to dry while you take a nice hot bath after which, you go straight to bed. I'll ride with you to the airport tomorrow, okay?"

"I can't argue with any of that," she said.

Maya was passed out sleeping when distant thunder started rumbling loud echoes through the hills. It was hard to say if the storm was headed our way or not, but I went outside before sunset to take her laundry off the clothesline just in case it was. I hung the clothes that were still damp over the shower curtain rod. I folded the clothes that were dry and placed them in her suitcase.

Having waited impatiently in the cabin for several hours, Calvin was anxious as he made his way back to the temple of his chosen one. He had removed the bottled water and canned food from his backpack but he added a flashlight and kept the tools of his trade in place. Soon, he would be putting them to good use. His only hope was that his tools were worthy of the maiden's perfect flesh.

Calvin welcomed the lightning that had begun crackling and flashing around him. It made for easier walking through the pitch black woods without the need of a flashlight that might draw attention to him. He had expected to get soaked in the rain but by the time that he arrived at the house, rain had not yet fallen. He crouched like a cat in the same spot that he'd chosen earlier to survey the scene one last time. Except for a dim light that shined out from a window onto the back porch, the house was dark. When lightning flashed again Calvin noticed that the pickup truck was still parked where it had been earlier. The clothesline swung empty in a breeze that moments later would kick up into a strong stiff wind. Calvin could wait no longer. He stood tall and strode straight for the door at the back porch. As he stepped up onto the porch a gust of wind blew its screen door open. Inexplicably, a bottle cap came bouncing out of the house and landed at his feet. As he bent down to pick it up, a lightning bolt exploded in the yard. Calvin jumped in his tracks. The house went suddenly dark. Thunder rattled his ear drums as he wondered, *Had she turned out the light or had the storm knocked out the power?* He couldn't decide. He tossed the bottle cap back through the open door and into the house to prompt a response. He waited for a reaction but none came. As he stepped across the porch and then up and into the house, Calvin heard and felt something whistle past his left ear. Whatever it was, it bounced hard and rolled across the wooden porch. It sounded to Calvin like an empty glass bottle. He had no idea whatsoever what was happening. *Was she drunk? Was she a slob who made a habit of tossing her trash in the yard? Did she somehow know that he was coming for her? Was she making a pathetic stand against her inescapable fate?* As odd as it was at the time, Calvin didn't hear a single sound; no wind, no thunder, no voice, no heavy breathing, nothing. He stood motionless in the silent house. It was pitch black dark. His excitement began to swell uncontrollably. Suddenly, he broke the silence himself by laughing loudly and then teasing,

"Here, chickie… Here, chick-chick. You wanna play, chick-chick…? Aw, come out now, chickie, play with me…"

Without a moment's hesitation or thought, I lunged forward in a blind furry pouncing in the direction of the intruder's ridiculous voice. I slammed suddenly into a hulking body that fell backwards fast and hard against the kitchen wall rattling the entire room. I grabbed at the intruder blindly in the darkness and luckily, grabbed ahold of what I thought at the time were his overall suspenders. I pulled him toward me with all of my might, lowered my head in the process and head-butted him as hard as I could. He let out a loud groan. Suddenly, the kitchen light came back on. He swung at me blindly; his eyeglasses lying crushed at his feet. I caught his thick wrist in one hand and twisted his arm down hard. As he doubled over, I cracked the bottom of his jaw with a swift kick of my knee. The blow sent him stumbling backwards. He tumbled over a kitchen chair. As he reached his arms out in an unsuccessful attempt to break his fall, his backpack flipped over his head and flew to floor alongside him.

Maya screamed, "Jay, my God!" as I jumped on top of the intruder's back.

I began pounding each side of his head with my fists; one after another, harder and harder. Maya grabbed the backs of the man's ankles and pressed them to the floor. He stopped struggling at last and then finally stopped moving. He may have stopped breathing. I sat still atop him, breathing hard.

Maya dug her knees into the backs of the man's legs. She leaned forward toward me and pressed her chest against my back. She threw her arms around my waist and then gasped, "Jay, my God, are you alright?"

"I am now," I decided. "Sorry to wake you, my love, but thanks for jumping in."

"Who the hell is he?" she asked as she let go of me and then rose to her feet to inspect the unconscious intruder.

"I have no idea but do me a favor, see what's in his backpack."

As I remained sitting atop the man, Maya reported the contents of his backpack to me as she emptied it out on the kitchen table. "Rope, duct tape, neckties, a knife, a gun, my God, Jay, what the fuck?" she asked.

"Bring me the rope, Maya," I ordered.

I raised the man's arms behind his back and then tied his wrists together with one end of the rope. I slid off him and dug a knee into the side of his ribs. I bent his legs up at the knees toward his fat ass and then coiled the same end of the rope around his ankles. I pulled the rope tight and tied knots. I looped the other end of the rope around his neck twice and then tied it off. As I stood up, our hogtied guest fell over on his side. I kicked him once in the mouth and then again on the bridge of his nose. I spun around and grabbed his pistol off the table. As I extended my arms and pointed the gun at his head Maya shrieked, "Jay, no please, don't!" So I didn't.

East Alcorn city police arrived at my house five minutes after Maya had phoned them. I guzzled two bottles of beer while we waited for them to show up. The county sheriff department joined the party five minutes later.

"We owe you big time, Mr. Jackson," the first officer to arrive said after he'd identified the still-unconscious intruder as Calvin Gavin; county tax collector and suspect serial killer who had most likely and recently killed a cop.

"Have a beer with me and we'll call it even," I suggested.

"I just might do that once the sergeant gets here, if he gives the green light that is. Something tells me he will because this definitely calls for a celebration," the officer said.

"Good enough," I acquiesced and then I opened my third bottle of beer in the past fifteen minutes. I never realized before how much a man's thirst could get worked up while subduing a serial killer, but I knew well and good how alcohol could calm rattled nerves such as mine at such times.

"I'll have one with you," Maya said as she wrapped her arms around my waist.

"I thought you were a gin and tonic girl," I reminded her.

"I'd much rather be *your* girl," she said discretely.

"But you already are," I said and then we kissed.

Calvin, who had finally regained consciousness, was none too gently dragged out of my kitchen, across the back porch and then tossed into the back of a police van by three sheriff's deputies. After four of our city's finest police officers had clocked out with their captain and had helped me empty my fridge of beer, I decided that there was no good reason to stay up any longer. Soon thereafter however, Maya gave me a really good reason to stay up as long as I could.

The next morning, after we had returned her rental car to an agent downtown, Maya and I made the long trip to the airport in my truck. We were running a bit late and I was praying that she'd miss her flight and stay with me longer but unfortunately, she didn't on either account. I held her in my arms as I kissed her at the security gate. I didn't want to let go of her and it seemed to me that she didn't want to let go of me either.

"I need some time with my mom after the funeral," she said

finally, with tears in her eyes. "If your ex-girlfriend happens to need you in the meantime... don't deny yourself on my account, you hear?"

"Actually, Maya, I was planning to fly down tomorrow to pay my respects. I'd go with you right now but the sheriff's office asked me to talk to the feds later today. After the way I roughed up our houseguest, it wasn't so much asking as it was a demand from Calvin's attorney."

"There's just one problem, Jay," Maya said, her eyes suddenly cast down away from mine.

"And what would that be?" I asked as I raised her chin gently and then looked into her eyes.

"Martin is my maiden name. I'm married, Jay."

The world stopped spinning.

"I see."

"It's not what you think though, Jay, whatever it is that you're thinking. I don't love him anymore. I haven't loved him for a long time. It's complicated and screwed up but I'd really love to see you again if you'll have me. It just can't be soon."

"I see," I said again numbly as a crushing feeling twisted my stomach in knots. "Just do your best to sort it all out, Maya. And be good to your mother in the meantime. Call me when you can and I'll see you... whenever."

We kissed forever during those last few moments together.

As the Alcorn River Bridge came into view, I suddenly realized that all I had for breakfast that morning was a glass of orange juice. I had skipped lunch altogether while taking Maya to the airport and dinner time had passed while I was talking to the feds and receiving way too many handshakes and pats on the back. As it was I was starving and for some reason, only one thing came to mind; meatloaf.

I turned the wheel hard before the bridge took me over the river. I walked into the all-but empty diner ten minutes before closing.

"Well, hi there, stranger!" Lisa said enthusiastically as she counted the contents of the cash register drawer.

"Is there any chance that I could buy some quick meat loaf to go?" I begged her.

"Absolutely not!" she said, crushing my most recent dream. "You'll sit right down and I'll bring you whatever you want on the house, Jay. You're a hero around here don't ya know?" she asked me matter-of-factly.

"I guess I know now. News travels fast," I supposed.

"Thanks to the newspaper it does," she said, handing me the latest edition of the East Alcorn Gazette. "You're quite photogenic," she quipped as she walked away to the kitchen.

There I was alright; holding up a bottle of beer in my very own kitchen; Maya on one side of me, two deputies on my other. The headline read; "Local Hero Earns a Cold One!"

"Hey... wait a minute!" I mumbled under my breath, "I *bought* that damn beer myself! And I worked damn hard for the money at the mill." I laughed out loud.

"What's so funny?" Lisa asked as she placed a steaming hot plate of gravy-covered meatloaf and mashed potatoes in front of me.

"Can I tell you later, Lisa? I'm plumb starving right now," I asked her as kindly as I could.

"I've got all night," she said whimsically and then she walked away sweetly; her narrow hips swaying nicely under her starched white skirt.

Ten minutes later, Lisa, the cook and the dish washer came

out from the back clapping their hands, hooting and hollering and embarrassing me terribly. Lisa explained to me how her coworkers had scared Calvin off and saved *her* life the night before. My gut wrenched when I imagined Lisa in Calvin's hands. The cook and dish washer shook my hand. They patted me on the back before they left for the night.

"Guess we don't have to ask if you'll be alright, girl," the cook teased Lisa.

"Be good to our hero now," the dishwasher chimed in with a wink in her direction.

The two men shoved one another playfully and laughed as they made their way out the door.

Lisa sat down across from me. She slid the slice of blueberry pie that she'd brought out with her friends, closer to me; the birthday candle stuck in its center had gone cold by then.

"So... who's the woman?" she asked me casually, her gorgeous eyes sparkling, her long blonde hair undone and down along her shoulders, shimmering in the diner's bright fluorescent light.

I leaned forward closer toward her and then hesitated. I pulled the candle out from the pie and then sat up straight. "She's... a real good friend... and occasional lover," I said, as honestly as I could and then added, "but that was yesterday, tomorrow's another day."

"So... are you alone *tonight?*" she asked me in a whisper, even though I was the only other person in the otherwise empty diner who could have heard her question.

"Not yet," I said and then I reached out for her hand.

"I've been waiting for you since we first met, you know?" she asked, smiling sweetly, taking my hand in hers, and when she did I couldn't help but think of another girl named Lisa;

most likely a sweet girl herself, a girl I never had the good fortune to meet. And then I thought of Maya; staring out into the cold night sky through a tiny airplane window, mourning the loss of her sister, shedding tears, thinking of her mother, and just maybe, missing me. I imagined then; Maya rushing into her husband's arms upon arrival, sobbing on his shoulder as he held her tightly.

"And so have I, Lisa," I realized, "so have I."

Western Sunset

Saddle-sore and parched, I plowed ahead slowly. Truthfully though, it was Rusty who plowed ahead. I just hung on for dear life prayin' that my horse was faster than the life-blood oozin' from the bullet hole in my chest. That blood, soaked the front of my filthy shirt and began drippin' on Rusty's chestnut hide as I held onto his thick neck; my head bouncin' on the coarse hair of his bony mane. Better me than him I reckoned. If he'd been shot we'd both be dead but so far, we were both still alive. The wind-blown dust burnin' our eyes and noses and fillin' our ears reminded us of that fact.

After untold hours on the desert prairie, Rusty let out a loud snort and slowed his gait. I raised my head best I could to find out why. Through the dusty haze a dark shadow loomed. Rusty stopped and swung his head around. He beat my leg with his muzzle urgin' me to wake up and dismount. I lay on his back motionless in response. Rusty strode up to the cabin and kicked its door with his hoof. He waited a spell and then hit it again, harder and louder. A woman inside screamed as a shot rang out. The bullet grazed Rusty's shoulder before it sunk into my leg. The horse flinched and I hollered. I was gettin' damn tired of being shot. I grabbed my leg in pain and slid off my horse in a heap. To this very day, I remember the sound I made when I fell flat on my back. It was the sound a dyin' man makes.

"I tied up your horse under the lean-to," I heard a woman say. "He's watered down. He didn't flinch a bit when I cleaned his wound with alcohol."

"He's had it worse these past sixteen years," I reported groggily as I stared up at the underside of the cabin's roof wonderin' where on earth I was and why was I freezin' cold.

"I cleaned your chest and leg wounds. I didn't want to dig out the slugs until you came to," she told me.

I raised my head off the bunk and realized that I was all but naked. That explained the cold. She approached me with a red-hot blade and slipped a wooden spoon between my jaws.

"I can't tell which will be worse for you so I thought I'd start with your chest. Any objections?" she asked.

I looked straight into her beautiful eyes and figured there were much worse ways to die. She waved her blade in the air to cool it off some and then slipped the tip of it under my skin and into the nasty crack in my breastbone. I grabbed her long thick skirt and pulled her off balance. The blade slipped, causin' me even more pain in the process.

"Just squeeze my leg now and keep as still as you can," she suggested.

She poured alcohol past my lips onto my tongue and a little more on my chest. She put the spoon that I had spat out back between my teeth. Her knife dove in. I squeezed the back of her leg through her skirt with one hand and the bunk frame with my other.

"This here bone saved your life but I need to twist it open a little further. Hold your breath now and bite down hard," she said but I'd already been doin' both of those things long before she told me to.

The spoon cracked and splintered in my teeth cuttin' my lip but that silly little pain almost made me laugh and helped to keep me conscious despite the agony I was feelin' elsewhere. She held up a bloody bullet in her bloody fingers. My body

relaxed and then went totally limp. I let go of her leg but
didn't really want to. It was a really nice leg. She dipped a
wad of grey cotton into a pan of alcohol and pressed it firmly
on my chest wound. That pain was child's play compared to
what I'd just been through. When she lifted my shoulders off
the bunk I winced in pain again. She held me upright with one
hand and slipped a torn strip of white linen behind my back
with her other. She eased me back down and then tied the
bandage around me like a sash. She laid a shirt over my bare
chest. It wasn't my shirt though. It was soft and clean.

"You're doin' fine so far," she announced. "Need another
drink before I dig into your leg?"

"Couldn't hurt," I said, wonderin' if a knife in my leg was
gonna hurt more than the knife in my chest had.

She poured a few sips of the grain alcohol across my tongue
and then dabbed a bit more on my split lip.

"Do you want your spoon back?" she asked.

"Couldn't hurt," I said, wonderin' briefly what her name was
before I asked her, "What's your name?"

"Selma, Selma Lou Campbell. And yours?"

"Some call me Monte. Friends call me Ted. Better friends
call me Teddy."

"What did your parents name you?" she asked me.

"Theodore Montgomery Mason at your mercy, Miss
Campbell."

"It's Mrs.," she announced, returnin' to my bedside with her
red hot blade, "but please, call me Selma seein' how's I'm not
that formal of a woman."

"Can I grab your leg again, Selma? Seein' how's you're
married and all," I asked her.

"Do it quick now before I start diggin'. This one went in a lot deeper," she warned me before she laid the spoon between my teeth again.

She turned her back to me and bent over my cold bare legs. I was enjoyin' the scenery when she asked, "Are you ready?"

I mumbled, "Uh huh," and then wrapped the fingers of my right hand around her leg above her knee. I thought about raisin' my hand further up along her skirt but then I recalled that she had a knife in her hands. I squeezed her leg hard when the blade dove under my skin and into my flesh. I do believe that she hit every nerve on the way in. The pain was unbearable. I bit the splintered spoon in half. The pieces slipped out of my mouth. I watched them as they bounced on the hard dirt floor. She dug in even deeper. I yelled out loud.

"Almost there," I heard her say before my eyes went black.

Aside from a dim orange glow in the hearth, the cabin was all but dark when I finally came to. I felt warm thanks to the wool blanket that covered everythin' 'cept my face.

"You're awake," she said, slammin' the door shut as she entered the cabin. An icy blast of night air turned the orange fire bright red. "Your horse likes my stale biscuits better than my fresh turnips."

"Ha! Can't blame ol' Rusty for that," I said as I cringed from the pain of laughin' and then made it worse when I tried to sit up.

"Lay still, let me help you," she said kindly.

She slipped off the serape she was wearin' and then folded it into a tidy bundle which she worked slowly and gently behind my head and shoulders.

"I imagine you're hungry," she imagined out loud.

"Haven't given it much thought."

"Stew's on the fire," she said, givin' me first notice of its delicious aroma. "Even though I've had to do it for six months or more now, I still hate eatin' alone. I wish you'd join me, Mr. Mason."

"I will if you call me Ted, Selma."

"I prefer Teddy," she suggested, handin' me a hot bowl and a cold spoon.

"Watch that split lip of yours now, that stew is hot," she warned as she pulled a chair up alongside my bunk and then handed me half of her fresh biscuit.

I watched as she dropped her half of the biscuit into her bowl. She raised her spoon to her lips and blew. I imagined those lips touchin' mine. She smiled at me as she slipped her spoon past those sweet lips of hers. I followed her pace at first but then quickly devoured the contents of my bowl. I'd split my lip back open but it was well worth it. She took my empty bowl away and then handed me a cup of hot cider. She pulled her chair closer to me and then slipped her soft, calloused hands under my itchy blanket. Those cool hands felt heavenly on my warm bare skin.

"Your dressings feel dry, Teddy. I do believe you'll live."

"Well if I don't, I'll die a happy man, Selma. Thanks to you that is. Look after Rusty for me, okay?"

"Hush now, I'll do no such thing. If you die on me I'll sell him to the first pack-mule miner that passes by. Your horse will spend its last days haulin' boulders under the whip."

"Somethin' tells me you're not ornery enough to do that, Selma."

"Well, stay alive then and you won't have to wonder," she said, starin' at me coldly until a smile gave her away and we both laughed and sipped cider.

I awoke early the next mornin' to yet another icy cold blast as she slammed the cabin door shut and announced, "Snow on the ground this morn. It's a good thing too, seein' how's the well's nearly dried up."

She set a large bucket of snow down near the fire and then asked me, "You up for some salted pork and biscuits? I have some nice marmalade if you have a sweet tooth."

"I do believe that I've died and gone to heaven, Selma. But I still hear ol' Rusty snortin' out there so I guess you haven't gotten around to sellin' him yet."

"I decided to keep him after all. I need him to drag the boulders out of your grave. Shall I dress you proper for the ceremony or leave you as is; bare naked?"

"I could really use a bath first," I suggested. "I'd hate to meet my maker stinkin' to high-heaven. It's been ten days or more I reckon."

"I'd say closer to twenty, Teddy, maybe more. And I'm glad you mentioned it first. Would you prefer your bath before or after breakfast?"

"Breakfast might be more enjoyable if I stunk a little less but I'm not sure I can stand up right now."

"No need to, I'll take care of that," she said and then she went about heatin' bath water on the fire.

She washed me down head to toe and all places in between with warm soapy water. She rinsed me off with a wet rag and then patted me dry with a cool soft towel as I just lay there enjoyin' my recent death.

"Enjoy this last day on your back, Teddy. Tomorrow you're trousers are goin' back on and I'll be forcin' you up on your feet. Wouldn't want those wounds to fester or pneumonia to set in."

"Fair enough," I agreed, wonderin' where on earth her husband was until I asked her, "So where is your husband these days?"

"He's been off fightin' a war for the past six months," she reported. "Last letter I got three weeks ago said he was goin' plumb stir-crazy in some Texas fort... the Alamo I think he called it. He said they were all just sittin' around waitin' for somethin' to happen. He said he missed me and was thinkin' about runnin' off back home to see me."

"The Army will throw him in the stockade or shoot him dead if he does, Selma. I hate to say it but it's true."

"I know that, Teddy, and Jake knows it all too well. He was just sweet talkin' me is all. You know... a love letter of sorts; his way of pretendin' that he still cares about me."

"He'd be a fool to leave such a fine lookin' woman as you behind, Selma."

"Well, if I may be so bold, Mr. Mason, I'd have to say that you're a fine specimen of man yourself, despite the bullet holes that is. So who shot you anyway?" she asked as she brought me a plate of pork and biscuits and sat beside me with a plate of her own.

"You did, remember?"

"No, silly... not in your leg, who shot you in the chest?"

"Don't know his name. Some outlaw on foot tryin' to make an easy score. He waved his arms from afar so I rode up on him. I imagine he was after my horse and gun and whatever else I was carryin'."

"So he shot you and tried to take your horse?"

"Not exactly. He shot me, I shot him and then I rode off."

"Aren't you afraid he'll come after you?"

"Not exactly. The way I see it, he probably didn't get too far with that bullet in his head."

"So you killed him?"

"If I didn't, the desert has by now. I didn't stick around for the details."

"This is one crazy world, Teddy. I've had my share of those types around here myself and I thought you was one of 'em comin' a callin'. The last drifter come around here tried to bed me down while I was hangin' wash. I swung on him with a shovel and knocked him out cold. His rifle's hangin' on the wall over there," she said, pointin' to a Winchester that had seen better days.

"Aren't you afraid he'll come back after it?" I asked her.

"Not exactly," she said, "he'd have to climb out of his grave to fetch it."

"So you killed him?"

"I'd tell a judge that the shovel killed him. But between you and me, I'd say that his own rifle finished him off. I wanted to make sure I didn't bury him alive. His horse is outside right now. She's probably makin' love as we speak to good ol' Rusty out there just to stay warm."

"You are one hell of *fine* woman, Selma. Hats off to you," I said, raisin' my biscuit in a toast of admiration.

"That's nonsense now. A woman's just got to do what she's got to do to stay alive alone in these parts. I thought you were comin' in after me yesterday. When I hollered, 'Who is it, what do you want?' and you didn't answer, I let you have it. Sorry about shootin' you and all."

"I never did hear you call out and never mind about shootin' me. You've more than made up for it, Selma. You saved my miserable life and I am forever in your debt."

"Good to know, Teddy. I sure could use a nice strong slave

around here, until my husband takes leave from the Army that is. When you're back on your feet and strong again you can build me a barn and dig me a proper well. Come springtime you can plow my fields while I sit in this here cabin paintin' my toenails."

I laughed out loud at that and nearly choked to death on my breakfast. I finally cleared my throat and said, "Somehow I can't imagine you paintin' your toenails, Selma."

"And why not?" she asked me, a bit rattled. "Do you not consider me a proper lady?"

"Actually, Selma… no, I do not. A so called, proper lady isn't good for much of anythin' except spendin' her man's money on fool hardy things. You're much more worthy of a man's affections than any proper, worthless woman, Selma."

"But don't men find proper women desirable?"

"No more so than any barroom hussy in my opinion. They just get paid for it in other ways is all."

"So you'd rather have a woman like me than one of those *fine lookin'* specimens?" she asked playfully as she rose and took away my empty plate.

"Believe me, Selma, you *are* one *fine lookin'* woman, mostly because you don't even know what a fine lookin' woman you are. But to be honest though, if we don't change the subject soon you just might have to take a shovel to *my* head."

"So, are you plannin' on chasin' me around this here cabin with a bum leg and a bruise on your chest the size of a summer squash? Is that it, Teddy?" she teased, handin' me a tin cup of hot black coffee.

"Well, I wouldn't have to chase you too far, now would I?" I said as I gazed at her beautiful face through the steam risin' off my cup.

"I suppose you wouldn't," she agreed, gazin' right back at me. "Then again... maybe I'd just let you catch me," she suggested and then the cabin suddenly grew hotter.

"Selma dear... you're about to drive me wild I'm afraid."

"I know, Teddy. I'm sorry. Maybe I'm doin' it on purpose, I don't know," she said, standin' up and then pacin' around the place. "It's just been so long since I even talked nice with a man let alone felt one close to me. I don't know how much longer I can stand it!" she almost shrieked before she calmed herself down again.

"I wouldn't want to come between you and your man, Selma, especially not while he's out there fightin' for the Republic," I reminded her.

"And that just makes it worse," she said a bit distraught.

"What does?" I asked, not really understandin' what she meant.

"The fact that you're not a scoundrel, the fact that you're a good and decent man makes it all the harder on me to keep my hands off you, Teddy. Jake and I never were too terribly close. Yeah, we're married and all but his *true love* had always been the Army and remained so even after we were wed. When the baby came, things got better for me. I could handle the days and weeks and months without him because I was never lonely with my little angel in my arms."

"So... what happened, Selma?" I asked as gently as I could.

"I buried my baby girl late last winter, Teddy. I was alone when I did. I wanted to die right along with her. I slept on her grave in the snow. I've prayed every night since then that I would die as well but so far the good Lord has decided to keep me alive and torture me here instead."

I wanted to mend her broken heart but didn't know how.

"I'm so very sorry, Selma, truly I am. I can't imagine what you must be goin' through. I do believe though that you still have good reason to live. You're still young, Selma. You have most of your life ahead of you."

"I stopped prayin' for death when I took you in, Teddy," she confessed, catchin' me off-guard.

"You did what?" I asked.

"I stopped askin' the Lord to take me when you showed up on my doorstep. I'm not sure why. I saw somethin' in your eyes, Teddy. I can't explain it. I don't want to die anymore. You saved *my* life can't you see?" she said and then she ran to me and laid her head gently on my chest and began to cry.

I was out splittin' wood two weeks later when I noticed three riders approachin' from the distance. They rode tall in the saddle. Their mounts were finely bread horses. Their pace was quick and deliberate and steady. Long before their uniforms came into view I knew they were Army. I set down my axe as Selma came out through the cabin door. She had sensed somehow that they were comin'. She glanced over at me and then out toward the range. She cast her eyes on the riders. She searched for her husband among the three.

Was that Jake on the left? I wondered.

I walked over to Selma and stood by her side. The riders pulled up. The soldiers dismounted ten paces away. While two of them stood at attention, the captain approached Selma. He asked her if she was Mrs. Selma Louise Campbell; wife of Sergeant James Jacob Campbell. She nodded her head, yes. The captain removed his hat. One of the privates followed suit while the other dug into his saddlebag and then approached the three of us. The captain looked over at the private and then gave him a nod. The soldier handed Selma her husband's tattered Army hat. Inside the hat, a gold pocket watch on a chain lay atop an envelope. The captain returned his hat to his head and saluted Selma as the others did the same. Selma invited the captain and his men inside but he cordially declined her offer. They had other business to attend to; other wives and families to visit. I reached my arm around Selma as we watched the men ride off and then vanish on the horizon.

Later that evenin', after a nearly silent supper, we stepped outside. We held hands as we watched the western sunset.

- The End -

Zeus Shrugged

Recent non-scientific evidence suggests that a perpendicular
universe (that is fifty percent different from ours) may exist.
What follows may shed some light on that possibility.

It was cold, damp and dark on that hot and dry, cloudless
summer day as he stood under the overpass of the beltway;
thumbs in suspenders, waiting for the crossing light that would
signal him to walk yet again. He considered the mission that
awaited him; "Would it prove to be exciting, or mundane, or a
measure of both?" Before he could make a rational prediction,
the pedestrian light beckoned and he crossed the empty street
passing on each side of him; long opposing lines of empty idling
cars waiting impatiently to proceed. As he hurried along the
city's streets in the steady driving rain, he came upon his
intended destination at last; an upscale apartment building. He
discretely chose and then entered the rear service entrance
where he proceeded to climb the five flights of stairs down to
the third floor above. Upon exiting the bleak and barren
concrete stairwell that announced his every footstep with an
echoing echo, he entered a long, straight, winding hallway
elegantly appointed with silk wallpaper and plush patterned
carpet that silenced each of his silent footsteps. Three doors
down on the left he turned right and stood before a door the
brass placard of which read; 330. He double-checked the
address he'd penned on his hand; 303. "This must be the
place," he thought and then he tapped the door briskly three
and a half times. On the third tap, the closed door opened ever
so slowly on its own revealing an exquisite Italian marble tile

floor that stretched gleaming across the wide entrance foyer of an enormous and lavish luxury apartment.

"Please, come in. She's been expecting you," an anonymous voice directed him.

And so he did.

After walking several paces through the foyer, he found his prospective client in an incredibly spacious parlor lying with her back to him, half-reclined on a velvet Parisian sofa.

He asked himself, "Was she sleeping?"

"No, I'm just resting," she replied. "Come join me, will you?"

He walked around the room to face her and then, standing before her, a glass table between them, Hunter cast his gaze down and discovered the most ravishingly beautiful woman he had ever seen in his twenty years on the planet or in his twenty years on others. Her skin was perfect poured cream. Her long raven black hair, wisped with shimmering shades of indigo and violet, bedazzled him. Her moist lips, painted the darkest of rose reds, glistened. Her eyes, sparkling brightly amidst the deepest of blues, the blackest of blacks, and the most brilliant of whites, entranced him. The ivory white, silken gown resting below her bare shoulders did little to disguise the length of her gently curving figure. The bare toes of her left foot playfully wrestled the toes of her right but the match was interrupted when she leaned forward to place her crystal wine goblet on the table which she did without making a sound.

"It's a pleasure to meet you, Jon Ghent," she announced, extending the long slender fingers of her right hand toward his.

"My name is Hunter Gather," he said and then he asked the woman, "You are Miss Catherine Crumb are you not?"

"I am not," she replied, slightly disappointment. "Catherine lives in apartment three-oh-three down the hall."

"I'm so sorry, miss," he offered.

"I am not," she replied.

"Good day then," he said, somewhat embarrassed as her slender fingers finally found the tips of his and then wrapped themselves ever so slowly around his hand.

Unexpectedly, she pulled him gently yet forcefully off of his feet. He tumbled then somewhat less-gently atop her in dramatic slow-motion. Their noses touched, their eyelashes intertwined, her lips found his firmly embracing them for what felt like forever as they exchanged warm breath one to another in heart-pounding silence. As her right leg slid out slowly from under the weight of his left, it discovered the long hard shaft that he had attempted in vain to conceal from her.

"Oh my, Mr. Ghent... is it loaded?" she asked in a delighted whisper.

"It's loaded and ready to discharge," he replied and then he reminded her, "My name is Hunter Gather."

Suddenly, they were both frozen by the sound of a gunshot. Hunter's immediate thought was, "Who *is* this Jon Ghent she speaks of?"

The gunshot was accompanied by the sound of shattering glass and was immediately followed by the loud low moan of a man and the thumping sound of a body hitting the floor all of which came from the direction of the apartment's kitchen.

Hunter drew his gun and a short deep breath. He placed his free hand on the woman's shoulder and whispered, "Stay down."

"Are you a cop?" she asked him.

"Not anymore," he replied.

Hunter crept around the sofa and along the wall toward the open kitchen door; his loaded weapon drawn in its direction.

He crouched low to the floor and peered slowly around the door frame. He discovered a butler in formal wear staring directly at him. The butler was slumped spread-eagle on the floor. He was covered in blood from the waist down.

"Are you going to make it?" Hunter whispered.

"I sure do hope so!" the butler replied loudly, adding, "Why are you whispering?"

"Where is the shooter?" Hunter whispered.

"What shooter?" the butler asked loudly and then explained, "I dropped a jar of spaghetti sauce on my damn foot and it hurts like hell!"

Because he was a highly trained experienced professional, Hunter quickly processed the information, assessed the situation and then concluded that the butler's chance of survival was pretty good.

Their ensuing conversation was suddenly interrupted by the sound of a second gunshot that came from the direction of the parlor. Hunter asked the butler, "Do you store jars of spaghetti sauce in the parlor?"

"Of course not!" the butler retorted.

"Okay then, stay down and keep quiet, I'm in control of the situation," Hunter announced.

"I can see that quite clearly," the butler said sarcastically and then laughed to himself wickedly.

Hunter had had enough of crawling and creeping around for one day, so he charged straight into the living room; gun at the ready.

"Freeze, ex-police!" he shouted.

"There's no one else here, Jonathan, sorry... *Hunter*," the woman replied.

"Are you shot? Who shot you? What do you mean there's no

one else here?" Hunter asked the woman.

"Yes, I am shot," she replied, adding weakly, "and I don't... think... I'll... make it."

"Who did this?" he asked again.

"The butler did it," she answered feebly.

"But, how?" he inquired. "The butler is in the kitchen."

"Apparently, my pillow was rigged with an explosive charge that was triggered by a remote control detonator. Look for yourself..." she suggested.

Hunter lifted the woman's limp shoulders off of her tattered pillow and then leaned in to inspect the back of her head. Alarmingly, he found her head split wide open from ear-to-ear. Wires and electrodes and tiny circuit boards hung in a tangled smoking mess out of the cracked cavity of her fiberglass skull.

"You're a robot?" he asked, both rhetorically and astounded.

"No," she replied, "I'm a wobot."

"A wobot?"

"Yes, a wobot; a woman robot. Or, I should say; I *was* a wobot. My circuits are damaged beyond repair. I'm afraid that I haven't much longer to function."

Hunter was utterly and totally devastated. He had just met the woman of his dreams no more than five minutes ago and now, here she was; fading fast right before his eyes. The fact that she happened to be a robot or a wobot as it were, had no effect whatsoever on his feelings for her.

"I weally, weally, wuv you, wobot!" Hunter cried out loud in anguish like the little boy he once was.

"I wuv you too, Jon Ghent," she struggled to say with her last dying breath or whatever it is that robots or wobots do in place of dying and breathing. As she slipped into unconsciousness, her entire body began to twitch violently in uncontrollable spasms. Her mouth and nose became twisted in a distorted snarling grimace. Tiny puffs of acidic smoke whiffed from her nostrils and earholes. Her frizzed and burning hair crackled and then began dissolving in singing sparks. Her eyelashes fell in tiny flames, one-by-one, from her melting eyelids. Her glass eyes rolled in opposite directions and then sunk further back into her cracked skull where they shattered into jagged shards.

"My God, she is beautiful even in dying!" Hunter thought to himself and then he laid his head down gently atop her soft wobot breasts.

She lay beneath him then, still and silent.

"*Butler!*" Hunter screamed, anguished and angry.

He stood up then suddenly and ran back to the kitchen; gun at the ready.

The butler was nowhere to be found. The only evidence that remained of him in the spaghetti-sauce-stained kitchen was a remote control detonator that Hunter found on the floor in a puddle of marinara.

"This must be the detonator that the butler used to take my wobot wuv from me!" Hunter surmised correctly.

Assuming that the butler would be long-gone from the building by then, Hunter resigned himself to the fact that he might never be found and brought to justice. Hunter walked out of the kitchen, his head held low as he traced the butler's spaghetti sauce footprints through the apartment's foyer and then out into the hallway. As he followed the path of the footprints with his eyes, down the long, straight, winding hallway, he thought out loud, "I wonder which way he went?"

Hunter returned to the sofa one final time to bid fair adieu to his wost wuv. "West in peace, wobot," he whispered as he gentwy pwessed hewr mewlted eyewids cwosed. "West in peace," he wepeated; a sad teawr wowing down his cheek.

When Hunter finally left the apartment, to his surprise he discovered that during his recent absence, the previously empty hallway had suddenly become occupied by dogs of various breeds.

"What on earth are they doing?" Hunter thought to himself but then he quickly realized that the dogs were licking up the spaghetti sauce footprints. "They're destroying evidence!" he proclaimed out loud and then he shouted, "Stop! Ex-police! Stop licking those spaghetti sauce footprints!"

A few of the dogs turned a complacent glance his way but then continued their enthusiastic licking never-the-less. The other dogs however, paid him no attention whatsoever as their tongues waggled rapidly in and out of their hungry mugs.

"You dogs have no respect for ex-authority at all!" he said, feeling ignored and beaten until it suddenly dawned on him to follow the trail of the footprint-licking dogs instead of attempting to trace the trail of the spaghetti sauce footprints themselves which, on the blood-red hallway carpet, would prove difficult at best.

The first two dogs that Hunter approached were a precious pair of adorable Pomeranians the size of fuzzy slippers. Not surprisingly, the dogs also *resembled* fuzzy slippers. They were licking a nearly intact footprint because after all, the dogs were using tiny Pomeranian-size tongues. The third footprint-licking dog that Hunter encountered was an enormous Great Dane. It had already finished licking up the second footprint; not a trace of it remained on the carpet. The Great Dane had since moved down the hallway to the third footprint where it was battling a miniature Dachshund for the licking rights. Surprisingly, the tiny

Wiener Dog was holding its own against the Great Dane as it inflicted vicious bites on the larger dog's toes. The Great Dane became so incensed by the annoyance, that with one swipe of its giant paw, it sent the poor little Dachshund flying through the air and flat up against the wall. That atrocity only served to infuriate the Dachshund even more as it jumped up, charged, and then jumped again repeatedly as it conducted a vicious assault on the Great Dane's vulnerable nut-sack.

"Pooches, pooches," Hunter implored, "don't fight! There are plenty of spaghetti sauce footprints for the both of you. Can't you two share?"

Both dogs suddenly stopped their skirmish, turned toward Hunter, gave him dirty looks and then immediately resumed their battle which he side-stepped cautiously as he continued down the hallway.

The fifth dog along the trail was an amazingly beautiful Bulldog, but then again, aren't they all? Unlike the other dogs, the Bulldog was dining on its spaghetti sauce footprint by candlelight while reading a leather-bound first edition copy of Friedrich Nietzsche's classic; *Beyond Good and Evil.* As Hunter approached the Bulldog closer, it used its paw to point out a passage in the book. Hunter's curiosity compelled him to read the passage which he did so aloud; "Be careful when you fight the monsters, lest you become one."

"That's good advice, my friend," Hunter told the dog and then realized for the first time in his life, that not only are Bulldogs well-bred but apparently, they're also well-read. That sudden realization elevated Hunter's previous favorable opinion of Bulldogs even higher over those of the lesser dog breeds.

As he stepped past the Bulldog (singing his pants leg on the candle flame in the not-carefully-enough process of passing it)

Hunter found himself standing at an apartment door beneath which the spaghetti sauce trail ended abruptly.

"Well, the trail's gone cold. I'll never find the butler now," he thought out loud but as he scratched his head quizzically, Hunter noticed the placard on the apartment door; 303. "This must be Miss Catherine Crumb's apartment," he announced to himself before he knocked on her door; gun at the ready.

As Jonathan Ghent stepped inside the apartment, a petite, adorable maid with neatly-cropped, short black hair, gasped slightly in the presence of such an incredibly handsome man. She greeted and then directed the guest shyly in a charming French accent, "Please, come in, she's been expecting you."

As the maid closed the door behind Jon, she evaluated his hands which she quickly determined to be worthy of spanking her naughty bare buttocks should the opportunity arise.

"Would you care for a beverage?" the maid asked him sweetly as he stood facing her. She imagined then, pulling his long wool trousers and cotton briefs down off his hips and straight to the floor in one swift motion.

"Thanks, but no," he replied politely through lips that she knew would feel heavenly pressed against her aroused nipples while she pounded herself atop him for hours on end and then again at midnight until they both passed out; wet, sticky and sweaty, from their passionate and exhausting love-making. "Ooh, la-la… it was so *very* good for me… merci beaucoup, monsieur!" she sighed to herself.

"Well then," she said, slightly breathless and moderately moist, "if you should change your mind later, please let me know whatever it is you might desire." She winked at the man and felt him shudder and erupt inside her as she screamed his name (which she imagined to be Hunter) and then he himself screamed, "Suzette, Suzette, my love, marry me please I beg you! I cannot bear to be without you another second, another minute, another hour or day as long as I shall live!"

"I will," he promised as she imagined herself rolling off of him and then raising her bare buttocks in the air, confessing to him that she had indeed been a very bad girl and was ready to be punished by the unforgiving slaps of his oh so strong hands.

After walking several paces through the foyer, Jon found his prospective client in an incredibly spacious parlor sitting perfectly postured with her back to him at an exquisite, antique desk. Shimmering sunlight radiating from the open balcony doors reflected and danced across the desk's brilliantly polished surface. As he approached closer, Jon noticed over her shoulder on the desk in front of her, a state-of-the-art laptop computer locked-up and blue-screened across which a warning message scrolled; "...*MELTDOWN! ...MELTDOWN! ...etc.*"

"Allow me," he offered as he reached past the woman and took ownership of the keyboard.

After several quick keystrokes the warning message vanished. After several more keystrokes the screen flashed, went black, and then powered back up blue displaying the message; "Welcome back, Miss Crumb! Please enter your passcode."

"Well, I *am* impressed, Mr. Ghent! You're a life-saver," she said as she stood to face him and as she did so, Jonathan Ghent discovered the most ravishingly beautiful woman he had ever seen in his twenty years on the planet.

Her skin was perfect poured cream. Her long, straight, deep auburn hair hung glowing along each side of her face; a face so angelic that no cosmetic ever concocted could ever hope to improve upon. Her thin sculptured lips rested temptingly below her delicately shaped nose. Her dazzling eyes sparkled amidst a circular pallet of infinite hues that twinkled as they danced against pure white ovals. The beautiful black silken gown that hung below her bare shoulders did little to disguise the length of her gently curving figure. She leaned forward and placed her near-empty crystal wine goblet on the desk without a sound.

"It's a pleasure to meet you, Mr. Ghent," she said, extending the long slender fingers of her right hand toward his.

"And I you," he responded as her slender fingers found the tips of his and then wrapped themselves ever so slowly around his hand.

Unexpectedly, she pulled him gently yet forcefully toward her nearly knocking him off of his feet as he stumbled into her arms and soft bosom in dramatic slow-motion.

Their noses touched, their eyelashes intertwined, her lips found his firmly embracing them for what felt like forever as they exchanged warm breath one to another in heart-pounding silence. As her right leg shifted slowly across his left leg, it discovered there, a long hard shaft that was growing longer and harder with every anxious moment that passed.

"Oh my, Mr. Ghent! Is your hard-drive loaded?" she asked in a sultry whisper.

"It's loaded and about to reboot, ma'am," he announced.

They stood on her terrace balcony watching a new day dawn. Jonathan pressed his hips against Catherine's backside as he caressed her lower belly. He gazed down toward the deck at his feet and noticed there; a crusty red footprint. While he was wondering who could have left the footprint, she asked him, "Will I see you again?"

"Absolutely," he assured her. "I do however; have classes

every day next week. But I'm free on Saturday."

"Then, Saturday it is!" she confirmed delighted.

"Do you think that your neighbors would mind if I offered them my services on my way out?" he asked her.

"Not at all," she said. "All of my neighbors are polite and most of them are quite friendly. Just tap on their doors."

After sharing a breakfast of kiwis and croissants and then leaving Catherine to her own appointments, Jonathan felt an immediate longing for her as he knocked on the door across the hall from her apartment. A middle-aged man opened the door, smiled and then asked, "May I help you?"

Jonathan handed the man his business card and then explained that he was a full-time college student offering part-time computer diagnostic services in order to help him fund his exorbitant tuition. The neighbor took the card from him gladly and then said, "I hope I won't be needing your services, but I'll keep your number handy just in case."

"Thanks so much," Jonathan replied as he turned to continue down the hall upon the floor of which he noticed wet spots; evenly spaced, a pace apart each. At the far end of the hallway, Jon spotted a janitor on his knees scrubbing the carpet. Having apparently finished his task, the janitor rose, gathered up his scrub bucket and rag and then pressed a button aside the service elevator door.

The remainder of the tenants on Catherine's floor were either indisposed or were ignoring his knocks in hopes that he would "just go away" until that is, when he reached apartment 330 where he was suddenly surprised by the man who answered the door. Despite the fact that the man was twenty years older than Jonathan was, the men shared an uncanny resemblance to one another. Jon felt at the time as if he were looking into a mirror two decades into the future. He couldn't tell if the man had noticed as well, but he did appear to act slightly askew during their conversation. Jon offered the man his business card which he accepted cordially before closing his apartment door. After having struck out at the last two unanswered doors and having slid his business card into their jambs, Jon left the building and then began making his way back to his college dorm room on foot. He was looking forward to sleeping in his own bed; something that he hadn't done in the past thirty-six hours. On the other hand, Jon couldn't get Catherine out of his mind; the fragrance of her, the taste of her, her warm soft skin, her sexy voice, all of which lingered vividly in his senses.

Later that evening, while Jon was tapping away at his English Composition paper; *Zeus Shrugged,* a wild science fiction tale involving perpendicular universes, his cell phone vibrated once, twice, three times, and then moments later chimed voice mail. Jon spent the next two and half hours knocking out his story without a break and unfortunately, without barely moving an inch. As a result, Jon's legs froze in instant painful paralysis when he finally did attempt to stand up. After having retaken his seat, Jon decided to give his legs a chance to resurrect themselves by shifting his body back and forth and rocking his backside on the chair. As he did so, he proof-read a passage which he had written earlier that evening; *Three doors down on the left he turned right and stood before a door the brass placard of which read; 330. He double-checked the address he'd penned on his hand; 303. "This must be the place..."*
Before Jon could read any further, his cell phone vibrated. He picked it up immediately and without thinking stood up quickly,

limping unexpectedly on his still-numb legs.

"Hello?" he asked abruptly, cringing in pain.

"Jonathan Ghent; Computer Diagnostician?" a woman's voice inquired.

"Yes, that's me," he said, collecting himself.

"I have a problem with my computer," the woman continued. "My sex partner was called out of town this afternoon and couldn't walk me through a fix over the phone so he suggested that I call you. Can you help me?"

"I'd be glad to, ma'am. Is tomorrow evening good for you?" he offered.

"Actually, it's a bit of an emergency. I was really hoping that you could help out me this evening," she inquired.

"But it's one a.m., ma'am," he somewhat complained. "*This evening* ended an hour ago."

"I'll make it worth your while, Jonathan, let's say... *triple* your going rate?"

"Luckily for you, ma'am, I can really use the funds. What is your address?"

"Eleven-Eleven, West Seventh Avenue, apartment three-thirty. I'll leave the door open."

"I know the building well, ma'am, I was just there earlier today. I'll see you in twenty minutes or so."

"Perfect, I'll be waiting for you," she replied in a soft and sultry whisper.

Before he left his dorm for the service call, Jon checked the voice mail he had received earlier that evening. When he did so, he heard a woman's terrified voice whispering desperately, "Hunter, come quick! There are bloody footprints on the floor! I think someone has broken into the apartment!"

Although the frightened woman's French accent sounded

familiar to him, it was obvious that she had called the wrong number. Jon hit the "Call Back" button on his phone and then waited. No one answered. He left a message to call him back.

"Poor thing!" he thought. "I sure do hope she's alright."

If her number had displayed on his phone, Jonathan would have called the police immediately. As it stood though, there wasn't anything else he could do to help her. Nevertheless, Jon's stomach twisted in uneasy knots as he contemplated the woman's fate. "Wow! Damn!" he said out loud. "I should have answered my phone when she called. I could have tried to help her," he thought, assuming the worst.

Hunter had already been on edge over the phone call he'd received when he rushed out of his building earlier. When the luxurious front entrance of Eleven-Eleven, West Seventh Avenue finally came into view and he saw an ambulance with its lights spinning and flashing parked at the building's curb, he broke into a brisk run. As he approached the ambulance, the building's lobby doors opened on their own. A pair of paramedics came through the doors wheeling a gurney. Hunter was shocked to discover a woman resembling Suzette lying on the stretcher. She was being whisked right past him.

Hunter called out to the paramedics, "Stop! Wait! She may be my lover! Is that Suzette DuBois?" he asked them, at which point the woman, having heard her name called out by a familiar voice, opened her eyes and looked directly into his.

"Hunter," she cried, "you finally made it!"

"Suzette, thank God you're alright!" Hunter replied as he came up alongside her. "When I missed your call I was afraid that I would lose you, my love."

"Don't fret, mon amour, you've found me," she assured him.

"May I ride along?" Hunter asked the paramedics.

"Sure, hop in," the driver replied and then Hunter did so.

"Oh, Hunter…" Suzette cooed as he placed his hands gently atop hers, "it's *so* good to see you but I have a confession to make; I've been a *very* bad girl. I've killed a man."

"But you had to, my love, it was self-defense."

"I suppose so… but it was a bad thing to do nevertheless."

"Would it make you feel any better if I were to spank your naughty bottom?"

"Oh, Hunter!" Suzette cooed.

Hunter leaned over his love and then pressed his lips against hers. Suzette's sweet, French tongue danced inside him.

As the ambulance pulled away from the building, three floors above, a woman asked Jon as she read aloud from the business card that her sex partner (Jon's estranged father) had left for her on the kitchen table earlier that day; "So… Mr. Jonathan Ghent… Computer Diagnostician, do you think you can fix it?"

"Shouldn't be a problem, ma'am. Your firewall failed to block a virus the likes of which I've never seen before. It appears to be quite clever but I should be able to wipe it from your hard drive. By the way ma'am, I happened to notice police officers down the hall when I came in. Do you know what happened?" Jon asked the woman as he continued to try but was failing to block the virus that had infected her computer.

"A man was pushed to his death from a balcony earlier this evening," she said matter-of-factly.

"That's horrible!" Jon said, turning to face her.

"I suppose," she replied, "but so was he; horrible that is. He was a butler in the building. He was accosting the maid of a friend of mine but the maid was able to push him over the railing and save her own life in the process."

Jon found it odd that he had received a phone call from a distressed woman that very same evening. It weighed heavily in the back of his mind as he worked diligently on his client's computer. As he did so, the photovoltaic cells in his client's eyeball cameras reported his every keystroke to her brain-like control center which in turn, telepathically adjusted the laptop's distorted configuration every time that Jon got close to normalizing the computer's operation. After spending nearly two, incredibly frustrating hours trying to defeat the virus, Jon eventually threw his hands up in disgust.

"I'm really sorry, ma'am, but no matter what I try, I can't seem to beat this damn thing."

"Enough about that," she said. "I can see that you've done your best. There is one other thing though, that I'd like you to take a look at," she announced, taking his hand in hers.

As the recently-restored, synthetic musculature controlling her graphite skeleton whirred away softly beneath her recently-regenerated, human-like flesh; flesh that would soon prove life-like to Jon in every imaginable way, the wobot led Jon to her bedroom where he uploaded a substantial DNA sample into her quivering extraterrestrial data bank.

Early the next morning while his client was still sleeping, Jon uploaded a copy of the then, un-named Zeus virus, to his USB. He took the virus back to his dormitory where he shared it with several of his computer science classmates. He asked them one after another to evaluate it and suggest a possible fix but they too failed, just as Jon had.

Perplexed as to what to do next, Jon decided to send a note of explanation and a flash drive containing the virus to the head of the university's computer science department.

Professor Malcolm Middle removed an envelope from his inbox in the faculty lounge. After reading the return address, he asked himself, "Who is Jon Ghent?"

Later that evening, after having failed to unravel or even phase the mysterious virus, the professor threw his hands up in surrender and then asked himself, "Who *is* this Jon Ghent?"

Jon had explained in his note to the professor that he was a student at the university but the professor logged into the university's data base nevertheless to search for Jon's name in the student directory. As he did so, the professor unknowingly spread the virus that Jon had sent him to the university's mainframe. From there, the virus migrated to the mainframes of academic institutions the world over. From those points, the virus further migrated into the global banking system and beyond. Along the way, the virus infected the central nervous system and subconscious of anyone who had merely touched an infected computer or another person associated with one. In a matter of days, virtually everyone in the developed world was infected but since exposure to the virus didn't cause any physical symptoms, it remained undetected and dormant in the bodies of its hosts while it awaited further instructions.

As Zeus gazed down upon planet Earth, he laughed heartedly and shrugged. "Thank you, Jon Ghent! And thank you, Wobot! That was much too easy!" he roared as he clicked his computer mouse and initiated the Resurrection Program.

"My Goddess..." Zeus announced jubilantly, "your subjects have been prepared and await you. Go forth now and welcome them all as members of a new and civilized society free of selfishness, hatred, greed and violence as was so prevalent in their lives as subjects of lesser Gods. In due time, my Goddess, you and I will yet again rule, not only our own galaxy, but the sum of *all* universes; parallel, perpendicular, or otherwise."

Zeus' exquisitely beautiful wife and sister Hera smiled as she contemplated her impending road trip (and the opportunity it presented her for a discreet rendezvous with her lover Jupiter). In response to Zeus' commandment, the Goddess Hera raised her goddess arms above her goddess head. Photons sparked and flashed from the pulsing beams of brilliant blue and white light that radiated from her goddess eyes as she spoke.

"I shall do as you command me, my Lord, God, Brother and Husband, but while I'm away, will you do me the honor of cleaning out that damn garage of yours?"

"Yes, dear," Zeus acquiesced.

"And clean out the gutters... it looks like rain," she added.

"Has she gone yet...?" a sultry woman asked as she stepped out from behind one of the palace's massive marble columns.

"Who goes there...?" Zeus demanded to know as he turned toward the voice. "Lady Catherine Crumb!" he proclaimed, a god-like grin sweeping across the deity's face.

"Shall we retire to your bedchamber, m'Lord?" she tempted.

"Uh... I'd love to, Catherine, but I've chores to do."

Catherine approached Zeus and then stood directly before him. She dropped her gown to palace floor revealing to Zeus; her heavenly birthday suit. "Can they wait?" she asked him.

Zeus shrugged and then decreed god-like; "Heck yeah!"

- The End and a Glorious New Beginning -

Made in the USA
Middletown, DE
30 April 2015